AMERICAN SAVAGES

American Savages

J.J. McAvoy

This is a work of fiction. Names, characters, places, and incidents are either products of the writer's imagination or are used fictitiously and are not to be construed as real. Any resemblance to actual events, locales, organizations, or persons, living or dead, is entirely coincidental.

American Savages
Copyright © 2015 by Judy Onyegbado
Ebook ISBN: 9781625178190

NYLA Publishing
350 7th Avenue, Suite 2003, NY 10001, New York.

DEDICATION

To all my ruthless readers:
I hope this book makes you
Chuckle,
Cringe,
Cheer,
And
Cry.

Because this is goodbye.

PROLOGUE

"I was born lost and take no pleasure in being found."
—*John Steinbeck*

ORLANDO

FOURTEEN YEARS AGO

H is fist collided with her face, sending her to the ground so quickly that her hair whipped around her face before she hit the mat. She stayed there for a moment, frozen on the boxing ring's floor, almost dead, before she tried to push herself up. Her arms wobbled, and her chest rose and fell as she desperately tried to get the air back into her lungs. She managed to get to one knee before crumbling back onto the mat.

Pitiful.

"Get up, Melody," I said to her, as I leaned back against the wall of the old boxing gym outside of the city. It was just as run down as the town itself. No one but our people came over here anymore—sweat of sweat, hot blood of hot blood, we were Italians; one people. And she was disgracing herself in front of the very people who needed to respect her the most.

She didn't move, she just lay there like a dead *thing*. Neither a human nor an animal.

"I said get up, Melody!"

With a small, frustrated cry, she pushed herself to her feet, and threw herself onto the ropes of the ring in order to stand, as Gino held on to her.

"Miss? Miss Giovanni? Are you alright?" Gino asked her, glancing at me, wide-eyed when she did not answer.

"Let her go. And I swear to God Almighty, Melody, if you fall again…"

"I'm fine." She pushed the loose strands of her dark hair behind her ear and stood straighter as she raised her wrapped fists. She shook her head a few times, and tried to maintain her composure.

"See? She's fine. Now start again," I said to him.

"Sir, it's been two hours—"

"I don't care if it's been two days!" I snapped, and it was then that I saw it. All the eyes in the gym looked upon my daughter with pity, and at me with disdain as if I were some kind of monster.

"EVERYONE OUT!" I called suddenly, causing them all to jump and run towards the door.

Gino looked between Melody and me before he exited the ring.

"You and I will be having words later," I said to him, and he nodded before walking out.

The gym was dim. The only source of light came from the center of the ring where she waited without a word. Stepping inside as well, I grabbed the padded mats, circling her as I placed them.

"You are a disappointment, Melody," I whispered. "And not just that but you're embarrassing me and your goddamn self. How old are you now, twelve or four? Do you still need someone to save you? To baby you? Is that what you want?"

"No, sir." She held her head up. "I'm fine, I can keep going."

"Fine? A minute ago you looked like a newborn deer. Is it because we're alone now that you don't want to put on a show?"

She glared at me. "I've been doing this for two hours, Dad. Any normal person—"

"You are not normal! You are Melody Nicci Giovanni, daughter of Iron Hands—my daughter! Normal is never the adjective used to describe you! Exceptional. Notorious. Unstoppable. That is what you should aim for. You're in pain? Your body aches? Guess what? That's your life. You think those idiots outside helped you because they cared? Because you're *so precious*? They stepped in to make you weak, to drag you down to *their* limitations, *their* weaknesses. A helping hand is a selfish one. If you can't save yourself, you have no right to be saved." I met the glower of her dark brown eyes. "Do you understand?"

She didn't answer, she just kept staring me down.

"I asked you a question."

"Yes, sir. I hear you," she barely uttered.

"Good." I raised the pads. "Now, fists up."

"Ti odio," she said under her breath as she beat into them.

"I'm sorry, you hate what—?"

"Nothing."

I thought so.

One day she would thank me for this.

SEDRIC

FOURTEEN YEARS AGO

"Liam, I'm heading to lunch in the next hour with Neal and Declan, would you like to come?" Evelyn asked, more like pleaded with him to come.

Liam sat, surrounded by books, in the corner of my study. His long legs were stretched out across the ground, and his back rested against the bookcase. He paused for a moment and looked to her, my wife, and she withstood his icy gaze.

"Thank you, mother, but I already had lunch," he replied as if he had no emotions to spare her.

"Well then, I will leave you both to do whatever it is you do in this dungeon." She grinned at me and I tried to return the smile, but for some reason I couldn't.

"I will call you later," I said, when she kissed my cheek before leaving.

It was only when the door closed that I walked over to his corner and smacked him over the head.

"Ouch! What in the—"

"Why must you be so much like me?" I sighed, as I took a seat beside him. "You're supposed to take the good traits from me and drop the bad ones. Holding grudges against family—"

"I'm not holding a grudge."

I stared at him, my son. It was almost funny how well he could read other people, but failed to understand himself.

"You're still mad at her..."

"No, I'm not—"

"I'm still mad at her too sometimes," I cut him off and he froze, averting his eyes whilst his grip on John Steinbeck's *In Search of America* tightened. "I try not to think about it. The years she spent pushing all of us away. How you had to—"

"I'm fine," he snapped.

"So fine you can't let me finish a sentence?"

He took a deep breath.

"Be the bigger man, Liam. Let it go. She wasn't there for you as a boy, I know, but let it go and love her more for the fact that she desperately wants to be there for you now. You're never too old for a mother."

"I thought you said I was like you? You always give advice you don't take." The smartass mumbled, and I fought the urge to smack him once more.

"We have dinner as a family, and your mother and I have dessert every night."

"Ugh, dad! Don't say that, it sounds like you're talking about sex." His face scrunched up before he buried it into the book.

Grabbing his head in a lock, I pulled him towards me. "That's not what I meant, you idiot."

He pushed my arms away when I let go and laughed.

"But we do that too."

"Seriously! Eww...stop sharing please," he begged, and I laughed again as he cringed.

"Everything we have, and everything I do, is for family, Liam. The Irish Clans, our personal blood, no matter how badly they hurt us or let us down, family is the only safe haven we have from this life. This all started because no one took care of us...they called us Irish mutts. Left us to rot in the streets...we banded together, survived, and now we stand together so that we do not die alone. That is the job of the Ceann na Conairte. The only way you can do that is to..."

"Let it go," he whispered, and I nodded.

"Go have lunch, because if you don't pass target practice tonight, you won't eat until supper tomorrow."

That got him up and on his feet. When he opened the door, Neal stood right outside of it, towering over his younger brother who either didn't care that he was shorter, or didn't notice. Liam, with more pride than a boy of fifteen ought to have, stared at his brother.

"Mom really wants you at lunch," Neal said.

"I was already going, *big brother*," Liam replied. The edge in his voice was evident as he walked out the room.

Neal. Liam. I wonder what will become of you two.

ONE

"Though this be madness, yet there is method in 't."
—*William Shakespeare*

LIAM

DAY 1

123.
124.
125.
126.

I counted as I pulled myself upwards. The bars running across the ceiling provided an ample structure for my workout. Ignoring the burning ache in my arms, I continued with my routine. If I disregarded the husky, deep, and howling voices around me, I was able to find silence in my new six-by-eight stone and steel cell. For one hundred and twenty-seven days, I'd drifted from one cell to another in different jails all across the state for my "safety." But none of that mattered; I was away from her, from my son, from my family. Drifting and working every muscle to the brink of exhaustion, was the only way to keep the last bit of sanity I had left.

No emotion. No fear. That was the mantra I kept while I waited.

"How are you liking your new palace, Callahan?" one of the officers asked as he beat his hand against the entrance of my cell. Without the shackles and steel, his bravado would be nonexistent. I knew that, and he knew it too.

"It seems like you've never been to a palace," I replied stoically as I pulled myself up once again; one hundred and fifty pull-ups, two hundred crunches, two hundred and fifty push-ups…those were my days here.

"Well, that's what ya get when you murder your wife. The warden wants to personally welcome ya to your new home," he said, and I wanted bash his face in.

With a sigh, I stretched before I grabbed my shirt off of the dog mat they called a bed. Placing my hands through the open slot of the door, the little prick pressed the cuffs around my wrists harder than he needed to. But if he was looking for a reaction, he was looking in the wrong fucking place. Stepping back, I waited for him to slide open the door before I walked out. It took three of them, all heavy set and balding, to escort me.

"Walk," the eldest of them stated, as he nodded towards the corridor with his chest puffed out like a penguin. This was nothing new, this was the third penitentiary, and for some reason they all felt the need to prove themselves and show me who was king of this shithole. As I walked, the insults were the same as other facilities, a barrage of noise and threats always came my way.

"Wooo, look at the pretty white boy."

"Where's your money at now, Callahan?"

"Callahan, you're *my* bitch now."

"You ain't shit, boy!"

Walking towards the silver steel stairs, I simply ignored them. Everyone was looking for a reaction, just to be noticed. For one moment in their miserable excuse of a life, they wanted to be seen and heard. I wasn't going to lower myself to their incompetence...I had people for that.

"You better watch yourself, Callahan," the guard, whose name I wouldn't bother to learn, said as he opened the steel door for me.

She sat sandwiched between an old organized desk and a wall that was covered in awards, certificates, and medals. She had short red, shoulder-length hair, wore dark framed glasses, and a suit jacket. She couldn't have been older than forty, and the golden plaque on her desk read: "Dr. Rachel Alden."

"Have a seat, Mr. Callahan." She pointed to the wooden chair in front of her desk as she spun around and grabbed my file.

As I sat down, the two guards behind me made sure that their presence was known. She eyed me like a hawk. Her hands were folded, and her body leaned forward as though she was about to pounce.

"Your court date is in twenty days."

"I'm aware," I replied.

She frowned. "And your plea has not changed."

"No."

"They found your boot with your wife's blood on it, a call from your house—"

"Am I on trial now? Because if I am, I think you owe me a lawyer." I leaned back into the chair and relaxed my shoulders.

She took a deep breath before she leaned back as well. "Fine. Would you like to explain why you're at my facility? Or better yet, why you've been to three county jails in the last four months?"

"I'd rather not."

"Enough, wise guy, or you're going to the hole!" the man behind me barked, as he gripped onto my shoulder. I glanced down at his hairy hand before turning towards her. "Apparently I'm not very good at making friends...if you want more than that, maybe you should call them up. Or better yet, read my file, after all, it's right there in the center of your desk."

"I'm going to make this very clear, if in the next twenty days, you act out in any way, or say anything to endanger the lives of my staff, I will personally make sure that you're sent to the worst maximum prison in the state after you're found guilty...and believe me, you *will* be found guilty with the amount of evidence that keeps falling out of the sky against you. Do you understand me?"

She almost made me want to laugh. Was she supposed to be intimidating?

"Yes, ma'am," I grinned causing her eyebrow to twitch. "Will that be all?"

She nodded, and once again the two guards put their hands on my shoulders, signaling me to rise.

As I did, I turned back one last time to address her. "I will want a *handwritten* apology after this is over, Warden."

"That cocky attitude of yours may have been charming on the outside. But in here, it will get you in trouble, Mr. Callahan. Enjoy your lunch," she snapped as the door opened.

I could hardly call the shit they forced us to eat lunch, but I didn't say anything as we headed to the lunch pit. This place was nothing much, just steel, brick, and orange jump suits. There was nothing to look at, and nothing worth noting. I'd been the most exciting thing to step inside the building since Al Capone. The officers snickered as they took off my chains once we reached the double red doors.

"I hope it's up to your standards, Callahan. Cause it ain't getting any better for ya," he said as I bit my tongue to keep from speaking.

Without another word, I headed to the empty back table in the corner of the room. However, before I could even make it halfway through the hall, two men, with tattoos up their arms and necks stood in front of me.

"You can't cross this way," the skinhead, covered in tattoos barked in a heavy Chicago accent. The men at his table all crossed their arms, trying their best to intimidate me.

The other man took a step forward. "Or at least *you* can't without paying a toll."

"Really? And why is that?"

Flexing their muscles, they grinned. "Listen you little cunt, this is our house, you best be moving along, or we may have to hurt ya. It only takes three minutes for the riot squad to show up, boy, and we can do a lot of damage in that time."

More of the crew stood up and that was when I noticed the Jell-O just sitting on the table.

"Are you going to eat that?"

They snickered.

"Boy, you fucked in the head? Do you want to fucking die? Get the fuck outta our area before we beat the shit outta you."

"I'm sure you know or have heard my name," I whispered, not backing down from him, "but you don't *know* me, and I'm sure you don't *want* to."

They glanced at each other before laughing like hyenas. "Look, you—"

Before he could get another word out, a melted and sharpened spork was in his neck.

They came in so hard and fast that I could barely see their faces. The group at the table was pulled from their seats into the struggle that had broken out in the middle of the cafeteria. After all, we were called the fighting Irish for a reason. It spread like the plague in a locked room. Infecting everything and everyone. As I glanced over the room, I saw that even those who had nothing to do with this were dragged in, and were fighting for their lives as every last man with even a half a drop of Irish blood beat into them.

"Urh..." The skinhead at my feet coughed, as his hands covered the deep puncture wound in his neck.

"This is going to be a long three minutes. You should have just let me go." I frowned as I took a seat at the table and picked up the cup of red Jell-O.

Counting the seconds until the riot squad finally made it into the hall, I noticed on the top most level stood Warden Alden, arms crossed and glaring. Raising the cup to her, I toasted her with a smile before I dug in.

"Everyone on the floor!" the save-a-bitch yelled, as he began pulling people apart.

I finished off the Jell-O, and took my spot on the ground, without ever breaking eye contact with her. She would learn just like the rest of them. She didn't own this place...I did. All I needed was three days in any jail. The first two days I burned it down, and the third day, I rebuilt it how I saw fit.

If I was going to spend the next twenty days in this hell-hole, I was going to make sure that they all knew who I was and what that meant if they ever crossed me. I was still a bloody Callahan, locked away or not.

Day 2

"You weren't exaggerating when you said you had trouble making friends. That riot was because of you," the warden said from the other side of my door. Stopping mid-crunch, I glowered at her. "Did anyone say it was me?"

"This is my facility, Callahan."

"Those who need to claim something as their own don't really own it. If you did own it, then it goes without saying, Warden."

Her hawk-like eyes narrowed in on me. "Your mother was here to see you. Sadly, your stunt yesterday has us on lockdown. She even brought photos, cute boy you got, but those are not allowed for criminals. Child pornography is contraband."

I leaped to my feet and rushed to the door. "What the fuck are you trying to say?"

"There's that anger. We know you're a murderer, but what other type of monster are you? I see men like you all the time, and the amount of darkness in your eyes is the same. Like I said, this place belongs to me."

Calm Liam. Stay Calm. No Emotion. No Fear.

9

I leaned forward against the door. "You've never met a man like me before, Warden, and I'll gladly prove it to you."

"Enjoy your day, Mr. Callahan, we'll let you out tomorrow," she hissed, as she turned away from me.

The guard pushed my tray of food through the slot as hard as he could when I stepped back, dropping it on to the floor…there wasn't even any Jell-O.

Clenching my fist, I stared out the window as I tried not to think of *her*. I wanted her out of my fucking head!

"Damn you, Mel."

Day 3

Looking over the yard, I watched them walk past me. No one met my gaze, they just kicked the rocks on the ground as they moved past. They all stayed away, and a small group of Irish, those not sent to solitary, stood not that far off from me, leaning against the wall. I was going to get out of here, and when I did, the last thing I needed was the police trying to make connections. They knew that. Or at least I thought they did until one of them approached.

"Mr. Callahan."

"Yes, O'Connor?" I asked the bigger man with orange hair and a mustache.

"We took out four. But lost one yesterday."

"Send the name to my brother. His family will be taken care of as always."

"We know, sir. Thank you. But there's something else you gotta know."

Sighing, I nodded as I glanced at the man. "Then out with it."

"There are few Italians here. Not much, but enough to cause problems."

I didn't speak for a moment. My jaw set. "They believe I killed her."

"Yes, sir, and they want retribution."

Of course they did.

It had taken my family years to work the penitentiary system. It was much more complicated than it seemed. You had to have a leader that was loyal to you enough to hold all the Irish in line behind bars, smart enough to know how to keep a low profile, and strong enough to strike fear into the hearts of every other motherfucker out there. On top of that, they had to be committed to life in prison with no hopes of getting out. If they weren't, they would gladly sell us out in a plea bargain...O'Connor was that man. He'd killed two policemen after they took his wife and son. He would've been in the county prison now had it not been for the overflow.

"Who's the leader on the inside?" I finally asked.

"The Spoon."

Gazing back up at him, he just grinned.

"The Spoon?"

He shrugged. "The man bends spoons, what else can I say?"

Laughing, I shook my head before I ran my hand through my hair. Then I bent my head back to bask in the sun.

"Fine. Get me a meeting with *The Spoon*. I swear Italians and their names."

"You got into bed with them, I don't know how this is all going to work out," he muttered.

Frowning, I stood straighter. "It isn't your place to know. Just get me the meeting. Is there anything else?"

"There are a lot of people in here searching for product—"

"Goodbye, O'Connor," I cut him off.

With a nod, he turned and headed back towards the corner with the rest of the Irish.

I needed to focus on anything but her. But how could I do that when every time I felt my heart beat, I thought of her and Ethan.

A call came over the intercom. "Callahan, you have a visitor. Callahan, you have a visitor."

Pushing off of the fence, I felt their eyes on me as I headed towards the building.

Those left in the group of skinheads kept their eyes on me, but didn't dare to come closer. The Mexicans just parted as I came through, while the blacks pretended as though I didn't exist. As long as they didn't get in my way, they would be fine.

The guards at the door escorted me, in chains, inside. My mother without fail came to visit me every other day no matter what jail I was in, and no matter how far it was. She always came with her hair curled, her dress pressed and even through the glass, I could smell the delicate scent of her rose perfume, and no matter what was going on, she always had the largest smile for me. I hated that I had to see her like this.

"Mornin', Mom," I whispered into the phone.

"Morning, baby. How are you?" She frowned looking me over.

"I'm fine—"

"The warden told me there was a riot yesterday."

"Mom, I'm fine."

"Stop saying that!" she snapped. "You are *not* fine. Being in here is *not* fine. I hate you in here, with these dogs. You did not kill Melody."

"Don't you think I know that, mother?" I snapped back, rising from my seat just slightly. The guards took a step forward and I sat back down. Running my hands through my hair, my hands ended back up on my chin and mouth.

"I'm sorry," she whispered, but she shouldn't have been.

"No, Ma, I'm sorry. How's Ethan?" The knot in my chest pulled tighter at the thought of him.

The grin on her face returned. "He's so...he's amazing. Yesterday, he almost pulled the hair out of your father's head, and the moment Sedric began to yelp, he started to coo at him. It's like he was trying to bribe him with his cuteness."

I snickered at the thought.

"Liam, it's been four months, you need to see him—"

"No, Mother. I will not have my son coming to see me in jail. That is not his life. I refuse for him to ever see the inside of this place." He was a Callahan. I'd never subject him to this unnecessarily.

She sighed. "Fine. I show him pictures and videos of you everyday. He knows you, and I won't let him forget."

"Make sure he sees *her* too." He needed to know her.

"Then she needs to get her ass back home and get you out of here," she hissed through her teeth.

"Mother."

"Fine. I know. But when she does come back, she and I will be having words."

"Of course—"

"Wrap it up. Visiting hours are over!" the guard yelled.

Reaching up, she placed her hand on the glass. "I'll see you during your next visiting session."

"Mom, you don't have to come—"

"I'll see you during your next visiting session, Liam," she said again.

"Okay then." My hand matched hers on the glass before I had to hang up. Placing the phone back on the hook, I took a step back.

Once again, the cuffs came on as they led me away from the scent of fresh roses. I was hoping for a moment alone in my cell, but instead, I was led back to the cafeteria. The entire place was sterile, bleached from top to bottom as if the riot had never even happened. The cuffs were off just as quickly as they came on, and O'Connor nodded me over to the man sitting alone in the middle table. He was big, of course, and olive skinned, with a full head of gray hair.

Waking forward in the same path I had taken in the days prior, not one of the Skinheads dared to look up at me or even move. They were aware of my presence, but didn't react.

Who says you can't teach an old dog new tricks?

I took a seat across from the man that smelled like lunchmeat.

"The Spoon?" I asked, and to answer my question he just bent the *plastic* spoon in the center. Did he want a medal?

"You rang, Callahan?" he asked in disgust, as he picked through his food with his fingers.

"You work for my wife."

"Worked," he corrected, his dark eyes glaring into me. "Past tense."

"No, present. My wife is still alive."

He snickered. "What, you just want me to take your word for it?"

"Yes. Because I am a man of my word and you should think about the consequences of forgetting that. After everything my wife and I have done, do you truly believe I would be stupid enough to get caught for murder? You really think the Chicago PD, not the FBI or CIA, but the fucking Chicago PD was able to finally put a finger on me? Really, you don't look like an idiot to me, and yet here I am, as my wife would say, 'wasting words.'" Taking the pudding off his tray, I opened it and ate a mouthful using the same spoon he'd bent.

His jaw clenched and he looked me over and sized me up for a moment. The wheels of his very small brain looked like they were working overtime, trying to comprehend everything I had said. Finally, he simply froze.

"You're in here because you want to be?" he whispered, so very confused.

"More like I need to be, but you're on the right track," I corrected before taking another bite.

"You're planning something big."

I wanted to roll my eyes at how excited and stupid he sounded. "I am. We are. So get your motherfucking men in line, because you work for my wife and by that definition, you work for me. If I have to remind you of that, you will curse the day you were born, Nicoli. Yes, I do know your name and you should stop calling yourself "The Spoon." They are made of plastic, my four-month-old son could bend them too," I said as I rose from the bench and left behind the empty cup for him.

Seventeen more days. Seventeen fucking more days.

Two

"I am, indeed, a king, because I know how to rule myself."

—*Pietro Aretino*

LIAM

DAY 11

My gaze swept over them, their bodies hunched, trying to block my view of their hands. I hated being in situations such as this.

Throwing another packet of ketchup into the center, the three inmates glanced at me.

"You're bluffing," Chris, a small black man with a scar marring his face, said with a frown.

"I don't bluff, even for five million," I replied before returning my gaze to the cards in my hand.

"Fuck, bro, I'm out," Justin, Chris' lover said, as he threw the cards onto the center. They weren't open about their love affair, but I could tell.

"I was out a while ago," the eldest, Matty, muttered before folding his hand.

One by one, they all folded until it was only the blabbermouth and me.

He stared into my eyes, looking for any signs of weakness, with a frown on his lips before he finally folded as well. A Grinch-like grin spread across my face as I showed them my hand.

"You bastard! You fucking played us!" Chris snapped, rising from his seat.

"I think the correct term is *bluffing*," I said, as I took all the packets of ketchup.

Matty glared, crossing his arms. "What happened to not bluffing, even for five million?"

"Rule eight: Money is money. If you can't make it, then take it," I replied, already shuffling up the deck. "Now, I better have my money by tomorrow."

Chris spat to the side of him. Then he walked to the other side of the cafeteria and spoke with a few of their people, hopefully about getting me my money. Chris was part of a street crew who most likely sold my drugs at a higher price to people in his neighborhood. It was one of the drawbacks of using middlemen. Once they bought the product from us, it was no longer our concern, they could sell it at any price they wanted. I didn't mind that. What pissed me off was when they tried to mix their own shit into it, as if they were bloody scientists. The idiots didn't realize that if a person overdosed, we would lose customers and profit. Anything that took money out of my pockets needed to be dealt with.

"Your money will be wired to you, Callahan," Chris sneered when he came back. He sat back down, but he didn't touch the cards.

Glancing up, I noticed O'Connor waiting at the last table on the left; across from him sat *The Spoon*.

"Good to know men in jail keep their word."

"What, you think you're better than us?" Matty hissed through his blackened teeth.

"You don't want to know what I think," I said before standing up. "I've pressed my luck enough for the day, thanks for the game."

"How the fuck am I going to win my money back?" Chris yelled.

"You don't," I replied.

As I was about to take my leave, he grabbed onto my arm. Looking down at his fingers, my jaw clenched

"Chris," Justin muttered under his breath.

The entire cafeteria froze. No one dared to breathe. O'Connor, along with The Spoon rose, all of them ready for another violent day.

"If you want to keep your arm, you should let go," I told him simply.

His eyes widened as he did what I asked. "Mr. Callahan, I'm—"

"Callahan, you have a visitor. Callahan, you have a visitor," the familiar voice broke over the intercom.

Leaving the fool, I headed to the doors. I noticed O'Connor nod over to two men who simply walked over to the table to take my place. I could spare him, just brush it off, however this was the shark tank. If you couldn't swim, you drowned. If you messed with the alpha, you got eaten.

When I stepped out, Thing One and Thing Two were waiting, cuffs in hand. They chained me up like I was Hannibal fucking Lecter. I was used to the walk to visitor's room. Each time I went, it felt like I was being led to my death. For my mother's sake, I tried to think of one good moment, one bright spot in hell to make her feel better. I could handle confinement, but it was the look in her eyes each time she came to see me that was wearing me down. I almost didn't want to see her.

When I reached the separation glass, it wasn't her sitting on the other side, and I felt myself sigh in relief.

"You look like shit."

"Nice to see you too, Dad," I said into the phone. His eyes roamed over me, his face cool, expressionless, before he shook his head.

"From the moment you were born, I knew, I just knew you would drive me to an early grave. You were always the one who just had to cross the line—"

"Pops, I'm in jail, do I really need a lecture?" I smirked, causing the corner of his mouth to perk up.

His eyes dropped to the cuffs around my wrists. "Even though you look like shit, you still look good according to jail standards."

"I'll take that as a compliment. Is that your way of asking if I'm alright?"

He didn't answer, but I knew it was. He was just as worried as mom was, but at least he tried not to show it.

"You do have a plan, correct." It wasn't a question.

I nodded. "I do."

He waited. "Liam—"

"Rule nine: a secret is only a secret if one person knows it. Trust me, Dad, I'm fine."

"You maybe, but the rest of the family isn't."

"I will fix it."

"And I would trust you if you trusted yourself. It looks like you're just playing it by ear with no plan whatsoever. We're losing business. We look weak. You're in lock up, Liam—"

"Will you stop telling me where the fuck I am?!" I snapped, as I pulled on the cuffs. "I fucking know where the fuck I am damn it. I know we're losing business; I'm working on it. Who gives a rat's ass if we *look* weak? We aren't. And if anyone thinks that now, in a few days they will be kissing my feet again."

"What if she doesn't come back, Liam?" he asked.

Rising, I prepared to hang up, I didn't want to go there.

"Liam, please, sit back down," he said.

But I was done. I turned away from him and looked over towards the guards.

"Ethan has an ear infection."

It was like someone had dropped me in a pool of ice. Facing him, I tried to think of what to say.

"Ethan has an ear infection, which is why your mother isn't here. She was with him all last night in the hopes of getting him to bed," he added.

"Have you called his doctor? Is he okay? What medications is he taking? Did this just happen? Mother was here yesterday and she didn't say—"

"He's fine, Liam, breathe. Babies get ear infections. It's painful to watch, but he will be fine. Between everyone in the family, the poor boy is now probably crying because he can't get a moment of peace."

Breathe, he'd said, as if it were that easy.

Resting my head in my hands, I tried to calm my damn heart. But it was beyond my control. I wanted to see him. There was an urgent, painful need to see his face. There was no bullshit to spew or attempt to save face, it hurt. It hurt knowing that I wasn't there for him. It hurt knowing that he may not know me. And worse of all, it hurt knowing that I'd failed him; by not protecting his mother, I had failed him.

"Liam—"

"I'm fine," I coughed out as I sat up a bit straighter. "As long as he's fine, I'm fine. And he is fine, right?"

He smiled sadly and nodded. "Son, if he wasn't okay, I wouldn't be wasting time with you. He's happy, he's healthy, and he has your eyes. The same exact green."

I was silent for a moment before I nodded.

"Callahan, time's up," the officer behind me said.

Staring at my father, he gave me a look, the one he used to give me as a child. Like he was trying to read a complex book in an unknown language.

"She will come back," I whispered. "Call me crazy, foolish, or just plain delusional. But I know her. Despite my better judgment, I still love her and I have to believe she's coming back."

Thing One and Thing Two came up beside me, and led me out to the familiar stretch of cells. I didn't want to speak with anyone else, I didn't want to do anything. Each time I saw my family, it felt like another chip had fallen away from my soul. Callahans weren't meant to be locked up, bad things happened when you tried to keep a monster in a cage.

"Open cell D2344."

My door opened, and when it did, there on the top bunk laid some no good teen, with brown skin and black eyes. He was tall and thin, no older then eighteen if that, and most of all, he was scared...I could smell it coming off him in waves.

"Meet your new cellmate, Callahan. Avery Barrow," they snickered.

Stepping inside, the door closed. Sticking my hands through the designated hole, they took off the chains as I turned back to them.

Such idiots.

"Hey, I'm not going to get in your way. I was just—"

"Stop talking," I said as I leaned against the bars. "Move out of that bed and it will be the last thing you ever do."

He didn't speak and I didn't close my eyes. The warden had done this and she would pay.

DAY 14

*A**re you fucking kidding me?*
Each inmate laid face down on the ground as the paramedics swarmed the dumbass who was having a seizure in the middle of the cafeteria. I hadn't even gotten lunch yet and this motherfucker was cutting into my time.
He was most likely overdosing on the smack he'd ordered. He wasn't going to make it, so why bother with the fucking dramatics?

"Is he dead?" Avery whispered, eyes wide. For a guy who had supposedly took a shotgun to his stepfather's head, he was greener than all the hills in Ireland.

"Yes," I said as they finally took the body away.

"Whatcha all looking at?" the fat guard yelled. "Sit your asses down and eat."

None of them moved, and a few of them glanced at me.

Moving forward, my footsteps echoed throughout the hall. It was only when I took my seat that everyone reverted to normal. Again, I grinned. Matty and Avery came over as well, sitting around me. Part of me wished that I could at least sit with my people. But for now, I was stuck.

"It's like you're a king here," Avery leaned over as I ate my basically frozen peas.

"That's 'cause he is, kid," Marty snickered. "Your cellmate is *the* Liam Mad Hatter Callahan."

"The Mad Hatter?" he asked as he glanced at me. "What did you do? Are you like Jeffrey Dahmer or Ted Bundy?"

I fought the urge to roll my eyes.

"How the fuck ain't you know who this man is? Ain't you got a TV boy?" Marty threw a roll at his head, but I grabbed it before it hit him and took a bite.

"Thanks," he muttered to me then glanced at Marty. "My step father believed television was a source of sin."

"You ain't ever read a newspaper? Step outside? What the fuck did he do? Keep you in a cage?" Marty joked.

"Something like that, you don't need a chain to be locked up," he replied picking at his food. "But it doesn't matter anymore. I blew his head clean off."

I shook my head. He was trying to hide his fear but instead he came off like a dumbass.

"If you don't want a needle in your arm, don't be saying shit like that," Matty told him, picking through the mashed potatoes.

"If I eva get a trial. The guy they gave me says I could be in waiting in here for a while. You got to trial quick, who's your lawyer?" he asked me.

I felt like he was trying to take notes or some shit. Without a word, I rose from the table and walked away.

Once I left, so did a few others. They didn't say anything, they simply followed me up the stairs. Our cells were just over the cafeteria, it was one of the few places we could move without the cuffs.

"Stop," Thing One snapped, as he stepped in front of me. The rest of the men lingered on the stairs a few paces behind me.

"What are you doing?" I watched as they threw every-thing out my cell.

"Cell search. Since you've been here, there's been an influx of drugs. The warden doesn't like that."

The warden can kiss my fucking ass.

"And you think the drugs are hidden where? In my mat?"

He didn't answer, he kept his arms crossed as the other guard ripped through anything and everything. And with each rip and toss, the urge to bash their skulls in grew to the point that my hands twitched. Seven more days. Seven more—

"Are you pissed, Callahan? You look like you're having a tough time," Thing One remarked.

Fuck it all. I was a goddamn Callahan.

Turning around, I leaned on the rail, and stared down at all of the men who were just itching for an order. O'Connor glanced up at me.

"Callahan, I'm talking to you."

"For the sake of your family, I hope you have a good life insurance policy," I nodded, never breaking eye contact with O'Connor.

The men on the stairs rushed the guards, grabbed onto their necks, and tackled them to the ground. Below us, chaos erupted, which pulled in every guard and staff member in the area. The sirens went off like a symphony orchestra; it was music to my ears.

"It's open season, my friends, let your inner monster out," I stated softly.

Stepping over the fallen guard, I grabbed the sheet, and ripped part of it before I held it to my nose and mouth. I started my countdown from five, and as expected, when I got to one, gas cans exploded, spreading below like fog.

"Everyone down! Everyone down on the ground, now!"

I wonder what the warden will say now.

DAY 17

151.

152.

153.

"How are you doing it?" she screamed, as she slammed her hand against the door.

154.

Ignoring her, I did another push up.

"Callahan, I'm speaking to you!" the dear old Warden snapped.

"I'm sorry, Warden, solitary has messed with my hearing," I said as I stood up to stretch. "How are you today?"

"You've been in here for three days. No visitors. No contacts. No nothing, and yet six of my men's families have been targeted. *Six.* Two every day. How are you doing it? I know it's you!" she howled, as she slammed her hand on my door once again.

"Let me get this straight." I used my shirt to wipe my face. "When I am in jail, it's my fault. When I'm not in jail, it's still somehow my fault? Maybe it's not me. Maybe it's the Chicago Police Department. Maybe it's you, for pissing me off. But then again, this all just hypothetical...."

She swallowed slowly. "So this is the beast you are?"

"I'm just a man in a cage."

"And you expect me to believe that you're an innocent man?"

I didn't answer her, I really didn't give a fuck whether she believed me or not.

"You're insane."

"Oh believe me, Dr. Alden, I haven't even put in work yet," I walked up to the door and almost chuckled as she took a step back. "I told you to read the file, after all, this is your facility."

"Three more days and then you're out of my hair." Her nose flared.

I smirked. "So then by your hypothesis, six more families? By the time I leave here, no guard will ever want to work in this hole. If that isn't the case now. Oh, and how did the drug search go?"

"You sick bastard, I will make you pay for this!" she hissed.

The conversation was already boring me, and by my tone of voice I was sure she could tell.

"I tremble with fear. This cell is the worst you can do to me, even if you let me starve. Imagine what could possible happen if I put my mind to it."

She opened her mouth to speak, but nothing came out.

I was so close to the window, the tip of my nose touched it. "You want this to end? Accept that I'm not your prisoner. You are mine. The sooner you realize that, the fewer funerals you'll have to attend."

Dropping her head, she took another step back before turning away. "Take him to his brother in the visitor's room. Take him there, then to his cell," she said before walking away as fast as her tiny legs could take her.

"W-w-we need y-y-your h-hands Mr. C-C-Callahan," the guard stammered. He looked as pale as a sheet and ready to piss himself.

Turning, I allowed them to cuff me.

"Is that too tight?" he asked.

I shook my head. "No. It's fine."

"Cell 16012," the guard called as the door opened.

Break a few and everyone follows.

As I walked in, no one made eye contact. They cleared a path for me as if I were Moses. After the second riot, they'd thought that all their problems would end if they threw me in a dark cell and never looked back. Sadly, I had planned for that. There was only so much damage that could be done from jail before we were all locked up. However, on the outside…on the outside anything goes. All O'Connor had to do was send out a name every few days.

Walking up to the glass, Declan just shook his head, as a smirk spread across his face.

"How's Ethan?" It was the only thing I had been obsessing about.

"He's fine. The infection is gone and now he's back to leaving toxic bombs in his diaper," he said, and I felt slightly lighter. "Oh, and by the way, I fucking hate you man."

"Nice to see your pale face too," I muttered into the phone.

"Only you could buff up and turn a profit while being in jail. I checked our funds, and for a second I was baffled. So again, I fucking hate you man." He sat up on to edge of his seat grinning. His hair was a little shorter and darker but he still looked like the same old Declan.

"What else am I supposed to do with my time?"

He shrugged. "Well, I'm glad you aren't coming home sickly and depressed. Seems like the world is going crazy without you running it."

"How is the family business going?" With my luck, he and Neal had probably burned everything to the ground.

"Stable-ish."

"What the fuck does that mean?"

"It means we're walking on thin ice. For now, everything is fine. We go day by day. Everyone is a ticking time bomb."

"And you?"

"That includes me." He frowned and I wondered if he was holding back.

"I—"

"Mr. Callahan, you have a few more minutes," the guard behind me said.

Turning to him, I raised an eyebrow causing him to just look away while his hands shook slightly.

"Jesus Christ, it's like high school all over again," Declan snickered, as he stared at the guard wide-eyed before returning his attention to me.

He was right though. "It's exactly like high school. Take out the weak links, break the leader, and the next thing you know, your table is the popular one."

"I'll never forget that slide show you played during class that exposed everyone's dirty little secrets."

"I'm surprised you could see it through your emo hair," I laughed at both him and at my twelve-year-old self. I thought I was so badass, but it was the best revenge I could think of short of actually hurting anyone.

"Ahh, God." His hands went to his face. "I'd forgotten about my two years as a Cyclops. Dark times."

"Mom hated your hair so much, she'd always try to brush it out of your face."

"Yeah, I was half expecting her to sneak into my room and give me a haircut."

I was sure the thought had crossed her mind.

"How's the public reacting to this, or better yet, to me?" I sighed, pinching the bridge of my nose, I needed some real sleep and I needed it soon.

"CNN poll says seventy-three percent of the public think you're guilty. On the other hand, Nancy Grace has you at eighty-eight percent and is calling all your past girls to testify on just how much of a controlling asshole you are. I say fuck them all. No fucking respect. I swear. After all we've done for this goddamn city."

Or at least all the good things we'd done.

"What did you expect? This is Chicago. You can't trust anyone with anything at anytime. This city and its people will eat you alive. If they didn't, it wouldn't really be the same." Even with all the fuckery, it was still my home.

"There is also something going on, Liam. Evidence. Evidence that shouldn't exist keeps finding its way into the police's eager little hands. At first, without a body, I would say that this was a sad attempt, but someone is helping them out."

He looked frustrated but I couldn't tell him. Not yet, I had to be out and off government phones before I pointed a finger at the director of the FBI.

"The case is still weak," was all I could say.

"Yeah, well it doesn't help that Natasha was found dead in a ditch." The smile on his face made me want to punch through the glass and into his nose.

"Even from beyond the grave, she's still pissing me off. She's like a neverending nightmare. Coraline always told me to stay away from her."

Something flashed in his eyes with just mention of her name.

"How is Coraline?" I asked slowly.

He smiled. "She's good. She went through this phase of horrible wigs for a while. But the cancer is gone. She's now the head of the Free Liam Campaign."

"The Free Liam Campaign?" I was almost afraid of what that meant.

"Yes, it comes with cute baby pictures of Liam, along with pictures of you and Mel, all over Twitter, Facebook and Instagram. With stories of how great a person you are. Eighty-eight percent isn't everyone. My wife is an organizer, what can I say?"

For the love of fuck.

"Tell her I said thanks, I guess."

"Liam, about Mel."

"Declan, don't. She will be there." I couldn't have him doubting as well.

"It's been five months. No other calls, no check-ins."

"Declan—"

"Maybe she wants to come home but can't. Or was taken again. You need to prepare yourself for all the possibilities. Your trial is in three days. You cannot count on her being there, especially when I know that there's something you aren't telling me. Give me something, Liam, anything. What are we fighting?"

He searched my eyes, however I hung up the phone, stood, and walked back to guards.

What were we fighting? What did Ivan DeRosa truly want? And how the hell was I going to kill him?

They were all questions I needed answered before I could answer him.

DAY 20

I couldn't sleep. I wouldn't. Not on day like this. I sat up, my shoes loosely tied, hair just as messy as it always was, and waited. Three minutes until two a.m.

"Mr. Callahan."

"Go to sleep, Avery," I said, staring at the wall.

"Can I say something?"

"You already have." In fact, the kid never shut the fuck up. I should have told the Warden to get his ass out of my cell. I wasn't sure why I didn't.

He was silent and I just rolled my eyes before pinching the bridge of my nose.

"What is it?" I asked.

I heard him swallow as he licked his lips.

"You have five seconds, Avery."

"I just…I don't think you killed your wife. You don't seem like a killer to me or a bad man. I know what a bad man looks like. You aren't *nice,* but you aren't a bad man. So good luck I guess."

I laughed. I just laughed. It actually felt good. I hadn't heard something so bloody ridiculous in my whole life.

Pausing for a moment I knew what I could do.

"My people will look after you in here until I get you out. The moment I leave, the race lines will be brought up and you will feel the need to join the other blacks. Don't. This is your one get out of hell card. Once you're out, you're going to work until you become somebody great..."

He laughed. "I can't play basketball or football—"

"Is the only way you can become successful through sports? Stop talking before you piss me off and I change my mind. We. Will. Get. You. Out. You will work your ass off to become someone worth a damn because that is the only way you are going to pay me back for this. Ten or twenty years from now you will pay off your dues. Because believe me, I will come to collect. Do we have a deal, Avery Barrow?" I asked him seriously.

I heard him sit up. "You serious? How the hell are you gonna help me if you got your own shit to fix?"

"Do we have a deal?" I rolled my eyes not quite sure why I was helping this brat.

"Yea. Yes. Imma try my best."

He was going to need to do better than his best.

"Callahan." The officer knocked on the door.

Finally.

Turning my back to him, he placed the cuffs on through the door.

"Open Cell D2344," the guard called.

"Wait, what about your books?" Avery asked.

My mother had brought them for me to stay sane. Sadly, I had finished them all in the first week.

"Take them. Start fixing yourself," I told him as I stepped out into the hall.

All around me people began to pound on their doors, yelling my name with pride. With each step I took, it became louder and louder.

They knew I wasn't coming back…not ever. All I had to do was make it through this trial.

THREE

"Our trials, our sorrows, and our grieves develop us."
—*Orison Swett Marden*

LIAM

"Do you understand, Mr. Callahan?" my lawyer, Dillon DiMarco, asked me.

I pulled my gaze from my son for a moment. He was chewing on his own fist with not a care in the world as he sat in Coraline's lap. However, Olivia held onto one his hands. I tried not to make my blatant disapproval of that known. The family knew how I felt about her, but now was not the time to harp on my preferences. I had him in my sights and that was all that mattered. He was like a magnet to my eyes, I couldn't keep them from him for more than a few seconds. He looked like a mini Mr. Clean in a suit; his bald head even had a glint.

"Mr. Callahan?" DiMarco asked again, and the army of lawyers all paused their shuffling to stare at me. "I know this can be quite daunting. But I will do everything in my power to get you out of here."

Everything in his power. If only he knew how worthless his power was to me.

"Don't smile or laugh because the jury will think I'm not taking the situation seriously. Don't be too serious or cold, because then they will think I'm heartless. Find a balance and set my face to it. Yes, I understand." I didn't know how that was humanly possible, but I understood.

Turning back to Ethan, Coraline took one of his chubby arms and made him wave at me. His green eyes stared directly at me and he smiled so wide I couldn't help but smile back. I'm not sure if he knew who I was or if he was just a happy baby, either way, seeing him made life worth living again. Coraline grinned as well, then turned to face me and I shook my head at the black T-shirt she wore with my face on it. Declan must have loved that one. She looked healthier than the last time I saw her, but she still had a scarf on her head.

Declan rolled his eyes at me before he unzipped his jacket to show me that he was wearing one as well. Oh God. Thankfully my father and Neal had enough sense to wear suits.

But when I took better look at them I noticed the buttons pinned to the lapels of their jacket suits. It seemed as if the only person not wearing 'Free Liam' paraphernalia was Olivia. In fact, she didn't even look as if she wanted to be here. Her blonde hair was pulled back making her face look icier than normal. She shook her head at me before returning her attention to my son. I wanted to snap her ugly neck, but again, it was not the time, nor the place.

My mother pointed to my neck signaling me to fix my tie. She and Coraline had dropped off a brand new suit for me, along with a deep green tie that supposedly highlighted my eyes. It was odd how even with all the clothing I had on, I still felt naked without my ring on. It had been taken when I was arrested, and I wouldn't be able to get my personal effects back until after this sham of a trial was over. I fixed the tie as she directed, and she smiled and gave me a thumbs up. Sometimes we were so *Brady Bunch* it made me sick.

The entire family was here...all but one. Looking towards the door, I noticed for the first time all the cameras directed at me. There had to be at least twelve leading news stations here, covering 'Liam Callahan; The Billionaire Murderer.'

"Show time," DiMarco said, as he buttoned up his suit jacket.

I looked at him with a raised brow.

This was a show to you?

"Please rise, the Honorable Judge Kelly Weston presiding," the bailiff called out, and we all stood.

Fuck.

She was a short woman with simple features and stringy dark hair. People who were short always overcompensated in other ways. Most likely she was a hardass.

"Good morning, please be seated," she said, sounding almost bored. "Okay we're on the record, case number 67F82C5 State of Illinois vs. Liam Callahan. All parties are here and present, is there anything else we need to take up before we call the jury in?"

DiMarco, who was still standing, shook his head. "Not at this time, Your Honor."

"We're ready to begin as well," the prosecutor said.

He looked like a grease ball, with his slicked back hair and alligator shoes. I knew Coraline and my mother were making some sort of face at him, and I wished I could look back at them to see it.

"Okay, bring them in," Judge Weston said.

I wasn't sure who thought these people were a jury of my peers. It looked as if someone had picked them up at last call in some bar...or at a Wal-Mart at three in the morning.

"Good morning ladies and gentlemen, I hope you all have no problems being here. I just need to ask you one question. Did any of you read, listen or hear about anything regarding this case?"

"No." All of them shook their heads and they were all lying...maybe they were my peers after all.

"Okay then." She nodded over to the prosecutor, and DiMarco, along with his lawyers, all sat down.

"Once again, good morning ladies and gentlemen." He pressed a button on his laptop and a photo of Mel in her wedding dress, smiling brightly and looking happy, appeared on the projector screen. It made me want to laugh because at that time in our relationship she'd wanted to kill me. But the photo captured her beautifully beyond the lie.

"I want you to take a good look at Mr. Callahan, that man sitting there, one of the sons to the infamous billionaire Callahan family, and remember that he is not one of you. You see, Mr. Callahan hasn't worked a day in his life. He's never had to worry about bills or food or even safety. Everything has always just been handed...no, *thrown* at him. Women especially.

"Go back only two and half years ago to his life without his wife, Melody Giovanni. Party after party, girl after girl, almighty freedom. Liam Callahan did whatever he wanted, *whomever* he wanted. No woman lasted on his arm for more than a month before he threw her away. Then *poof,* he's married to the beautiful Ms. Melody Giovanni, and you'd think that would be enough. You'd think he would be happy. But a man like him can never be tied down without repercussions. Past girlfriends of his are either dead or their lives have been so altered that they cannot function as they once normally did; he breaks them and then throws them away."

For the love of Christ, someone needed to put one between his eyes.

"Does this sound like a man ready to be married? A man ready to start a family? No. Liam Callahan did what all the Callahan men do; they get married while young, a tradition.

"The evidence today will show that Mr. Callahan wanted to return to his previous life. He wanted the parties, the girls, the fun, and he would do anything to get it. He couldn't live the immoral life he wanted to with the devoutly religious and beloved Melody. When she became pregnant with their first child, Liam panicked and tried to get rid of it because he felt trapped. Melody was hospitalized with a stab wound to the stomach, and she'd claimed that she fell down the stairs with a knife."

FUCK YOU. How dare you? I screamed in my thoughts.

The pain of losing our first child still stung. *We'd lost our child…*

From the corner of my eye I noticed that Olivia stood up, took Ethan out of Coraline's arms and walked over to the exit.

"Sadly for Mr. Callahan, Melody didn't die. The baby was gone, but she did not die. However, that wasn't the last time Melody was hospitalized. In fact, she had taken a gunshot wound to shoulder. She had been in car accident. There was no explanation. How does a car accident equate to a gunshot wound? *Coincidentally,* Melody was pregnant again. This time, Mr. Callahan knew what to do. The way to get his freedom back, was to get rid of her. Only moments after giving birth, Melody disappeared. The only people who could have been there were her doctors and Mr. Callahan himself."

You are going to pay. I was going to make sure you spent your entire life regretting this one long ass fucking opening statement.

"Ladies and gentlemen, her blood was found on his clothing and his boots. Witnesses will testify to his anger, hospital logs will show Melody's suffering. Do not let that man in the fancy suit fool you. Liam Callahan murdered his wife. We don't have body; we wish we did so that her son could at least have that. But money can buy you a lot of twisted things in this world. Liam Callahan wanted to wipe Melody off the face of the earth, and he thought he could get away with it. Don't let him walk away from this. Melody Nicci Giovanni-Callahan needs justice. Baby Ethan Callahan needs justice." He turned and walked to his seat next to his proud peers.

He's using my fucking son?

The blood in my veins felt as though it would boil over at any moment. What made it worse was the fact that the jury actually looked as though they were believing his bullshit. They all looked towards the screen, staring at her picture sadly. He let it hang there for a few seconds before he finally clicked it off.

DiMarco stood, walking forward, his bald head shining as he wiped the corners of his mouth and shook his head. "That opening statement you've just heard is the very essence of this case; no facts, all assumptions, made against my client, Liam Callahan, because of two things: he's rich, and he has a past. That is why the state of Illinois wants to lock him away for life, for something he did not do. Mr. Callahan has never shied away from his past. In fact, he and his wife joked about it openly to the press. The difference with Mel was the fact that he loves her.

"Mr. Callahan told me not to call her Melody because she hates that. The prosecution doesn't know her. If they did, they'd know that Mel was a proud owner of a gun and often went hunting. She enjoyed opera though she couldn't sing to save her life, but did anyway just because Liam Callahan told her he loved her voice. Every last person who is close to Mel stands by my client; they believe he is innocent. All the evidence the prosecution will attempt to present is nothing but circumstantial at best.

"There is no smoking gun. There is no crime scene. This is just another case of the Chicago Police Department failing to protect its citizens and searching for a scapegoat. I ask all of you; do you really trust the police in this city? After everything they've failed to do?" Turning back to the screen he clicked and again a photo of Mel appeared.

"This photo is upsetting, I cannot imagine what my client must be feeling knowing that his wife is still out there, but he cannot search for her. He can't help to find his wife because the Chicago Police Department gave up their search and pointed a finger at him. This isn't justice. This is a *witch hunt,* and I will not let an innocent man be burned at the stake for the prosecution and the state department to give themselves a pat on the back. Tell them to do their jobs. Tell them to find Mel, because Liam Callahan *did not* kill his wife. Liam Callahan is an innocent man. He and his family *need justice.*"

He confidently walked back to our area before taking a seat beside me.

Staring at her photo, the lump in my throat wouldn't disappear. Turning away, I looked at the door. People came in and some left. But none were her.

Where the fuck are you, Mel?

"Please state your name for the record," the prosecutor told the blonde haired woman on the stand.

45

"Dr. Amy Lewis," she leaned into the microphone.

"Dr. Lewis, you were Melody Callahan's doctor, correct?"

"Yes. I was there during her first pregnancy."

"Can you take us through the incident that happened the very first time you met Mr. Callahan two years ago?"

She looked at me and then glanced over at the jury. "That night, his wife came in with the stab wound to the stomach. She was in surgery, and Mr. Callahan was angry. He took me by the neck and slammed me into a wall."

Fuck me.

DiMarco sat up a little straighter in his chair, and flipped through his papers.

"Did Mr. Callahan say anything to you?"

"Objection!" DiMarco stood. "Relevance?"

"Your Honor, Dr. Lewis is here to testify to Mr. Callahan's character, I do believe that is relevant." He glared back.

"I agree," the judge said looking to DiMarco. "Overruled."

"I'm sorry, Dr. Lewis, as you were saying, what did Mr. Callahan say to you?"

Nodding, her hands reached for her throat. "He said something along the lines of 'I will rip your head from your shoulders, you classless, low life, idiotic bitch.' That he owned the hospital and owned this city."

Oh that bitch.

The jury turned to me with shock and distaste coloring their eyes.

The prosecutor looked to the jury. "So he threatened you?"

"Yes."

"Do you believe he meant what he said?"

"Yes."

"Thank you, Dr. Lewis. Your witness," the prosecutor said to DiMarco.

Rising from the chair, he fixed his jacket. "That must have been scary. Did you call the police, Dr. Lewis?"

Leaning back, all I could do was glare into her eyes. She looked trapped as she tried her best to look away from me.

"No, I didn't."

"But you just told these people that he threatened you, that you truly believed what he said, why didn't you call the police?"

"I…I don't know."

"You don't know? Why don't you know you? It seems simple; a man threatens your life, you call the police."

"Objection! Badgering the witness!" The prosecutor all but jumped out of his seat.

"Sustained. Mr. DiMarco please allow the witness to answer your questions," the judge said, and I fought the urge to roll my eyes. If this was "badgering the witness," Dr. Lewis should find religion and fast, because after this was over, I had no doubt we would be meeting again.

"Of course, Your Honor," DiMarco said. "Dr. Lewis, while Mrs. Callahan was losing her baby, fighting for her life, were you or were you not trying to flirt with Mr. Callahan?"

Her mouth dropped open and her eyes almost fell out of her head.

"I…I…No…I…"

"So you did not place your hand on Mr. Callahan's arm and offer to do *'anything'*?" he pushed.

She swallowed as she shook her head. "He may have misunderstood, I was trying to comfort him—"

"Instead of helping his wife," he cut her off.

"There were more than enough people working on her."

"Were you assigned to Mrs. Callahan's case then?"

She sighed loudly. "No, I was in the wing when he came in—"

"So you approached him?"

"Yes."

"Did he seem distraught?"

"Yes, that's why I went to him!" she snapped quickly. "He looked like he was going to break down at any moment."

"Because he loved his wife and was worried?"

She stopped for a second and nodded. "Yes. I guess so."

"Dr. Lewis, did Mr. Callahan threaten anyone else at the hospital?"

Her head dropped as she stared at her hands. "No."

"These are Mrs. Callahan's X-Rays taken after she lost her baby, correct?" DiMarco clicked, and on to the screen x-rays of Mel's chest, hand and legs appeared.

Dr. Lewis looked slightly confused, as she leaned in to see before she nodded. "Yes, those are hers."

"And how do you know?"

"The old breaks in her left radius, right tibia, and long with the healed breaks in her proximal phalanx."

"Proximal phalanx?"

"Those are the bones in her hands."

"Yes, of course. And what about her rib cage?" he asked as he clicked to another picture.

"More of the same, healed breaks along fifth, sixth, and seventh ribs."

"How long ago was this?"

She shrugged. "I'm not a forensic anthropologist, but I would say anywhere between twelve to fourteen years ago for some of them."

"At which time Mr. Callahan could not possibly have—"

"Objection! Beyond the scope!" the prosecutor yelled.

"There is no way Dr. Lewis can testify to that."

Are you fucking kidding me? She can say I scared her but she can't fucking testify using her bloody medical degree?

"Your Honor—"

"Sustained. Please keep it on the facts, Mr. DiMarco," the judge stated, and I was torn between screaming and taking a bat to her little head.

Maybe both.

"Why would someone have those types of breaks, Dr. Lewis? Could it possibly be that she was a fighter?"

"Objection—"

"No further questions, Your Honor," DiMarco said as he walked back over to me. The good doctor quickly got off the stand, trying her best not to look at me.

"Your Honor, the defense would like to call to the stand Fedel Morris," DiMarco said reading from his paper.

I wasn't even aware that any of our men were in the room, but there he was, dressed in his Sunday best. It was odd how everyone seemed to look the same. I'd been away for five months, and the only two people who looked different were Ethan and myself.

DiMarco stepped forward again. "Please state your name for the record."

"Fedel Gino Morris."

"Thank you, Mr. Morris. I'll get right to it, how long have you worked for the Giovanni family?"

"A little over a decade." He looked bored.

"So you would know why she was so badly hurt?"

"Yes, I can testify to being the reason for at least one of her broken hands," he snickered.

49

"You broke her hand?"

"More like she broke it against my jaw once."

She'd probably done it more than once.

"Was she violent? Why did she hit you?" he asked him before looking to the jury.

"We trained together. She spent years learning to defend herself. Her father didn't want her to be a victim for any reason."

"And if Mr. Callahan had put a hand on her…"

"She would be sitting in his place right now."

"You have a lot of confidence in her."

"Objection! Is there a question in there somewhere?"

This motherfucking prosecutor was working my last fucking nerve.

"Excuse me, Your Honor, let me rephrase," DiMarco replied. "Why do you have so much confidence in Mel?"

"She's a fighter, always has been, always will be. She isn't some weak abused Stepford wife that allows her husband to take advantage of her. And if in some twisted reality Mr. Callahan was hurting her, I can say without a doubt that he would not be sitting here today."

Well that's comforting, and here I thought I'd been making progress with her people.

I hear the door open, and the clicking of heels along the ground, and the hope in me built up as I fought with myself to not turn around. It wasn't her. It was never her. There was no point in turning back.

"No further questions. Thank you, Mr. Morris."

As he sat down, the prosecutor stood. "We have no questions for this witness, Your Honor. But we would like to call Officer Anthony Scooter to the stand."

It's like a who's who of everyone hates Liam.

I had no doubt that this would be entertaining.

He sat tall and proud as if he were expecting the city to give him a fucking medal. I wanted chop off his head and stick it on a motherfucking flag pole.

"Officer Scooter, you were one of the arresting officers on scene, correct?"

"Yes, I was. I was also the point man on the case."

Keep talking, asshole, you're burying yourself six feet deep and you don't even know it.

"Why did you suspect Mr. Callahan?"

"Mr. Callahan did his best to avoid talking to us. Then I found a connection between his past girlfriends and it became increasingly clear that Mr. Callahan was hiding something. There was blood belonging to Mrs. Callahan on his boots, along with three guns, in his bedroom alone."

What, they'd only found three? Declan must have locked down everything else.

"Surely you questioned him about your findings, what did he say?"

"He said nothin'. His hotshot lawyer came in and he didn't say a word to anyone. He looked dazed."

"Dazed?"

"Yeah, like he was high or drunk—"

"Objection! Speculation." DiMarco stood.

"No further questions," the prosecutor replied, saving us all the time.

"Officer Scooter, is it true that this isn't the first accusation you've directed towards my client and his family?" DiMarco asked.

"I don't understand the question," he replied.

Really this was the man everyone trusted to tell the whole truth?

"Do you have a vendetta against the Callahans, Officer Scooter?" DiMarco snapped causing the jurors to shift in their seats.

"No. I just believe the rich shouldn't get away with murder. They aren't untouchable, no matter how badly they want to be," he snarled, glaring into my eyes.

"So it's the rich you have a problem with."

"I ain't have a problem with anyone. You do a crime, you have to pay the price. Simple."

"And you've just been waiting to make Mr. Callahan pay. You chose routes close their homes to patrol, you are always one of the first people at the scene when it comes to their family, are you not?"

He nodded. "Yeah, sure."

"In police terms, you're still a rookie, correct?"

"I have almost two years under my belt."

"And in those two years, your department has been suspected of bribery, and the crime rate has risen, correct?"

"Yes." He crossed his arms, not wanting to back down.

"You will do anything to clean up the streets and you believe that all stems from the Callahans?"

"They have this city under their control, and because of that, people look the other way."

"You, a police officer, would look the other way? Your people on the force would look the other way?"

No answer.

DiMarco turned to the jury. "These men are supposed to protect us. But he says they look away? From what? How did *you*, Officer Scooter, manage to accuse and get a prosecution of Mr. Callahan, when so many others, wiser than you, have found no evidence that my client ever did anything wrong?"

"A lot of men have tried. We've lost too many good men, many of them are jaded and just want to get their pay and go home to their families in peace."

If he was smart, he would have done the same thing.

"Ladies and gentlemen, you heard it," he said to the jury. "The police department is tired of doing its job. Which means they were too *tired* to find Mrs. Callahan."

"Objection!"

But he didn't stop. "They were jaded, sick and tired of losing too many men so they pointed to easiest exit—"

"Objection!—"

"They wanted to go back to the donuts and coffee. Who cares if an innocent man rots in prison? They're *tired!*"

"Your Honor!"

"Mr. DiMarco!" The judge banged on the gavel. "Ladies and gentlemen of the jury, please strike the previous statements from the record. Mr. DiMarco, you are walking on very thin ice."

"My apologies, Your Honor, I'm just a little bit *tired*," he said, and if I could've, I would have laughed.

The court stilled.

"Well then, would you like an hour and a half recess for lunch now?" the judge asked the jury, and they all nodded, which meant I was going back to the tombs underneath the court.

"I want to go on the stand," I whispered to DiMarco as the bailiff and another guard came up behind me, hand-cuffs at the ready.

He looked at me like I really was mad.

"Mr. Callahan—"

"Only the guilty and the weak sit back. I'm neither of those things. I was telling you I am going on the stand, I wasn't asking your permission." He worked for me, not the other way around.

"It's your trial," he muttered, shaking his head at me.

Nodding, I glanced back at the door, and once again people came and people went, but the one person I needed was still nowhere to be found. I wanted to see Ethan again but after Olivia left, she never came back in.

Turning, they led me out of the courtroom. The holding cells under the courthouse felt like a tomb; dark, damp, and probably infested with mold. There was one toilet, a bench drilled into stonewall in the corner, and not much else. Luckily, no one else was there.

"Someone will have your lunch brought down," the bailiff said as he locked me inside.

I took a seat on the bench, as there was nothing else to do.

She's not coming. I didn't want to believe it. It hurt to believe it. Part of me wanted her to be hurt, to be captured like Declan had said, at least then she would have a good reason. But this…five months and not a word, how could she abandon us? If she didn't care for me, then at least I thought she would've come back for Ethan.

But then again, she never wanted kids.

Maybe this was her way out. She had money and properties hidden all over the world, and she could hide out for the rest of her life without worry.

"Think any harder and you might pop a vein," Coraline smiled, as she stood outside my cell with a bag of fries and what smelled like a burger.

"How did you get down here?" I asked, checking for the guard.

"Cancer. If it didn't suck so much it would be great. You can get people to do almost anything. Now eat." She stuffed the bag and the drink through the bars.

"Thanks, Coraline." I wasn't hungry, but I doubted that she would let me off.

She glanced behind her. "I really have to go before he comes back. But whatever you're thinking, *stop.*"

"Coraline—"

"Doubting is a sign that you're at the finish line. You've been fighting for months and you're at the end. Stop thinking about it, we will push through this and come out at the other end whole. We always do." She smiled once more before doing her best to sneak out. She, like the rest of my family, was crazy, but you had to love them.

FOUR

"Don't fight a battle if you don't gain anything by winning."
—*Erwin Rommel*

LIAM

"Liam Alec Callahan," I said into the microphone.

"Mr. Callahan, I'm going to get straight to the point," DiMarco said to me. "Did you kill your wife?"

"No. I did not kill my wife." I don't know how many times I had said that bloody sentence, but I was fucking sick of it.

DiMarco turned jury and then back to me. "That's not very convincing, Mr. Callahan. So can you please explain to us what your wife means to you and why you wouldn't kill her?"

"She…she drives me insane." I paused for a moment, trying not to smirk at my next thought. I forced a watered down smile instead. "She's the only woman I want scream at and make love to at the same time. She can make me smile with a single glance or glare. She sings in the shower and it's God-awful. And when she comes out, she pretends as if it didn't even happen. She kicks me in her sleep because she doesn't understand where her side of the bed ends and where mine begins. She is bossy, brilliant, and beautiful. The reason why I couldn't kill her is because I'm hopelessly in love with her. I couldn't imagine not having those moments with her. Actually, that's a lie, I can. Being locked away from her and my son is more horrendous as I could have ever imagined."

"No further questions, Your Honor," DiMarco said, as he nodded to me and allowed the asshole in the alligator shoes to step up.

I had spent the this whole time doing my best to keep a straight face, but watching him size me up made me want to stomp his face in. I bet those pretentious shoes of his could cause a good amount damage too.

"Mr. Callahan, you love your wife even though this was an arranged marriage?"

How the fuck did he know that?

"Excuse me?" My jaw clenched tightly at his question. I heard a few mutters from the peanut gallery, and the fucker grinned.

"Your marriage to Melody, it was arranged, correct? A way to pull the family millions together," he pressed.

"Billions, and no. Mel and I met because of our fathers, but she hated me in the beginning. She wouldn't have married me if she did not want to."

"Really? And why was that?"

The fucker. He was trying to trap me.

"In the beginning, she was misguided in her thinking as to who I was."

"And what was her opinion of you, Mr. Callahan?" The fucker smirked and again I had the urge to make him identifiable only through dental records.

"She thought I was a spoiled party boy who spent way too much time *with* the fairer sex." I'm sure they got my insinuation, but saying it reminded me of a time that felt like decades ago, instead of the few years that actually had been. One of those mistakes was haunting me now and even aiding in this sham of a case.

Fucking Natasha.

"Did she change her mind? How did you *persuade* her to?" Again I tried to ignore his insinuation. But I'm sure a few molars cracked with how hard my jaw was clenched at the gall this idiot seemed to have.

"She didn't need to be persuaded. I pursued her, showed her who I was behind the lies and rumors. She wouldn't have married me if she didn't see something in me that could provide her with what she needed."

"And at the same time you would get what *you* needed." Again, that fucking intonation.

"I'm sorry?" I asked as if I was clueless as to what he trying to say.

"Her money, Mr. Callahan. You gained control over it all after your wedding, did you not?" As he asked that question I locked eyes with him. I'm sure he saw his future. There were two ways this could go. He could try his hardest to get me put away for life, and in order to do so, he needed to pull out all these underhanded tactics, and then he'd gain the fame and glory of being the one who put the infamous Liam Callahan away. But then he'd die. There was no question about that. It was really that simple. But the alternative didn't seem to be any better. If he eased up, did a half-ass job, and I didn't go to prison for the rest of my life, he may live. It was his choice. He would get crucified by the press, probably lose his job or get demoted. But he would live, maybe.

"Objection!" DiMarco yelled standing up, effectively ending our staring contest and stopping the sadistic smile I was sure had started to grace my face.

"Let me rephrase: Did you marry Melody Giovanni to make your family richer? After all, with the Giovanni's controlling interest in stocks of major corporations, your net worth has skyrocketed."

I guess he chose his path.

Sighing, I looked towards the jury. Their faces were expectant and eager, as they prepared to latch onto my every word. The press were all intently gazing at me, waiting for me to respond but I wasn't sure what to say. I looked towards my family, they all sat in the second to last row. Olivia had returned, and was sitting next to Coraline who once more had Ethan in her arms. Olivia didn't look pleased, but Coraline didn't seem to care as she handed her phone to Ethan. Lifting him, she hugged him to her chest as Ethan tried to hand the phone to someone sitting right behind them, in the last row. He was babbling up a storm, and was the only noise that could be heard in the courtroom.

Coraline nodded at me, her eyes wide, urging me to speak, but I just kept watching. By now the woman Ethan was "talking" to was visible to me. She had short blonde hair, and a smile that radiated as she looked at Ethan.

I knew that smile.

She glanced at me and she smiled again. It was sadder, but she smiled and I swallowed. Pulling off her sunglasses, she handed them to the woman next to her, Anna from Interpol. Then she pulled off the wig and the bobby pins that'd been holding it in place as she met my stare head on.

Deep brown eyes.

Black wavy hair.

Devious smile.

Mel.

She looked me dead in the eyes and I wasn't sure if I was dreaming or dead, but I was afraid that she would disappear if I blinked. I could hear ringing in my ears as my palms began to sweat.

"Mr. Callahan!" The prosecutor snapped at me. "Are you pleading the fifth now?"

I spared him a single glance before returning my stare to her, she was still there.

Thank God.

She opened her lips and mouthed, *"Cut him down."*

Anna got up slowly and approached DiMarco. Her steps sounded like stomping in the quiet courtroom. She started whispering to one of his assistant who all but beat DiMarco on the back to get him to listen. No one else paid attention to them, they were too busy staring at me. Even my own family was confused, Declan pinched the bridge of his nose, and shook his head at me. Neal kept mouthing something, but I didn't even bother to try and understand what he was saying. My mother, my poor mother, was on the verge of tears.

"Mr. Callahan, I will repeat the question—"

"Save your bloody questions," I snapped causing his eyes to widen. "You are a snake. Despicable. And not because you try oh-so-hard to make people believe that you are worth more than the hot air you spew out, but because you are an idiot of the highest order."

"Mr. Callahan!" the judge screamed at me, but I held up a finger at her.

"Ma'am, you should let me finish, I'm just getting to the good part," I said as looked at the man in front of me. "You took a case from the Chicago Police Department like a fiend. You didn't need evidence or probable cause. All you wanted was for the world to know your name by connecting it to mine. Well too bad, because I still don't know it and I don't care to. You want to make a name for yourself, don't do it riding on my coattails, because when I throw you off, you will be damaged beyond repair. And before you ask, no, that isn't a threat, it's a promise."

"Mr. Callahan! One more outburst like that and I will hold you in contempt of court," the judge yelled.

"There's that Callahan anger we've all be waiting for," he snickered even though I could see the pulse at his neck quicken.

He licked his lips, took a step back, and turned to judge. She looked as if someone had just slapped the hell out of her.

"I think I've gotten my point across, Your Honor."

"Great," DiMarco smiled, standing up. "Then, Your Honor, the defense is calling for an immediate release of Mr. Callahan and a drop of all the charges."

"Is there something in your people's water? Because you all must be crazy! On what grounds?" the idiot asked.

"On the grounds that I'm still alive," Mel said as she rose up from her seat.

She was dressed in an all-white suit and red shoes. She looked like an avenging angel. Anna and two men followed her action and stood beside her with their badges hanging from their necks. Everyone's heads whipped around when they heard the commotion.

"Oh God!"

"Mrs. Callahan!"

"Mrs. Callahan!"

"Mel!" Coraline gasped, as she stood up. Ethan, who was in her arms, now had her phone in his mouth. Mel leaned forward to kiss his head for what felt like several minutes before she pulled away.

"Order. Order in my courtroom! I want both the defense and the state in my chambers now!" the judge yelled and sputtered, drawing my attention away from *her*.

"Mr. Callahan, as it appears that the premise of this case is obviously compromised and no longer needs to be presided over, it will be dropped, pending investigation. You and your family are not allowed to leave the state until we meet for another hearing. Do you understand me? Bailiffs, please escort the jury and anyone who is not family out of the courtroom."

I turned my attention to the back of the room. They were all trying to talk to her. All of them were screaming her name or shouting out questions. But she ignored them. She just held on to Ethan, and wrapped her arms around our son who seemed completely at ease. It was as if she were just another person holding him. No one significant.

I hadn't even realized that I was walking until I could smell her. She smelled the same, but different at the same time. Her scent had a different effect on me than it used to. She smelled of relief, yet at the same time, the possibility of drowning in the torrential rains that she'd brought with her lingered.

Please do not let this be a dream.

I opened my mouth to speak, but someone else beat me to it.

"Where the hell have you been?" my mother yelled, as she wiped the tears from the corner of her eyes.

She looked up, and once again green met brown. But I couldn't go any closer. I just couldn't. I felt as though I was being torn; part of me wanted to slap her, and the other part just wanted to hold her, to hold her and my son forever.

MELODY

All of them looked at me with some form of confusion and anger in their eyes, even Liam. He seemed to be permanently fixed in his spot between Neal and his father. There was so much I wanted to say, to tell him, but I couldn't, not now anyways.

Ethan fussed as the phone dropped from his chubby fingers and onto the seat, and as I reached down to get it, Olivia immediately reached for Ethan.

"Mel, be careful, he just ate. He should be going down for a nap anyway." Olivia reached for him, but I gave her a look that clearly stated she needed to back the fuck off, now.

I reached over to give Coraline her phone. At the same time Ethan tried to grab it from my hands, but Olivia snatched it from my grasp.

"It needs to be wiped down for germs. Seriously, Mel, give him to me so he can rest. This is madness, you can't just come back and take over—"

"I did and I am. I've got him, Olivia. Today of all days is *not* one to test me," I told her as I pulled Ethan to my chest. I reached into my pocket to get my phone and give it to him. The moment he had it, he clapped his hands against it.

"Oh look, you do have a phone. Care to explain why the fuck you haven't used it?" Evelyn snapped at me again.

She looked as if she needed to be put down for a nap as well.

"I just got it today," I told her, trying to get used to the feeling of him in my arms again. He felt so much heavier, but he still smelled the same.

"Mel, this isn't a game! Where have you been? Neal and I spent millions looking for you. We sent men all over the fucking globe," Declan stepped up.

"Not to mention the damned late nights, the worrying, and the fact that our brother spent five months in jail because you up and disappeared off the face of the earth. And now, out of the blue, you're back," Neal said as he squeezed the bench's backrest so hard I thought it would break.

"Yes, now I'm back," I repeated.

The door swung open and DiMarco, I believe his name was, stepped out with Anna along with the two extra Interpol agents who worked for me. The prosecutor kept his head down as he walked directly to his table that was littered with papers.

DiMarco walked up to Liam and shook his hand. "Mr. Callahan, when this story gets out, I do believe I'm going to be out of a job, and I doubt you all will ever need a lawyer again."

"Never say never, DiMarco," Liam nodded, his voice barely over a whisper.

DiMarco looked at me and reached for a handshake as well. Shifting Ethan over to my hip, just like I'd envisioned doing for months, I reached for his hand.

"And thank you for everything you've done, Mrs. Callahan, I'm sure it couldn't have been easy. I will keep a lookout for the President's press conference," he said to me.

Smiling, I nodded. "Thank you too. I'm so sorry you were not told—"

"No, I completely understand. National security trumps a hotshot Chicago lawyer, I'm just glad I'm on the right side of history. Again, good luck to you all!" he said as he waved once more before he exited the courtroom.

Liam's eyes snapped to me like he was trying to piece together the web of lies I had spent the last few months concocting. The prosecutor came over next, he opened, then shut, and opened his mouth before sighing.

Turning to Liam, his head hung low in defeat.

"The damage has already begun. I'm sure by morning I will be completely broken," he tried to laugh it off.

"Word of advice; move. The damage will linger, but at least there is hope that you may one day be able to show your face again," I told him seriously.

He closed eyes, sighed, and nodded. "I'm truly sorry, I didn't know. I will make a formal apology as well."

When he left, Anna snickered as she looked me dead in the eye. "No more favors. I'm done."

"No you aren't," I told her. She was family, no matter how many times she was removed or added.

"I fucking hate this family," she muttered as she gave Liam a small hug, which he didn't return. "Oh right, you have to fill them in. Well good luck with that, I have a press conference to get ready for."

When everyone else left, they turned to me expectantly.

"How big is this cover up?" Sedric finally spoke. He seemed just as reluctant as Liam.

"When your grandfather is head of the FBI, as big as humanly possible." And judging by their reactions, I guessed that he hadn't told them because all of their eyes, with the exception of Olivia who kept watching Ethan, just about fell out of their heads.

"Liam?" Sedric turned to him.

He nodded, and finally moved closer to me, but he didn't to touch me like I had hoped. Instead, he reached out for Ethan, but I didn't want to release him. It hurt to let him go again, but I gave up. Ethan giggled, as he smacked his father's face a little bit.

"Neal, have Monte and Fedel bring the car around back. Liam and I need to talk," I commanded, resuming my position as if I had not disappeared for almost half a year. The sooner they got back to the way we ran this ship, the better it would be, for them. Because no matter what, we were the heads of this family and I was never giving up that position.

Olivia must have pressed down on her heel too hard because it broke. Without a word, she took off and stomped out with Neal following behind her. Evelyn pulled Liam into a small hug, which he returned.

"I'm so glad this is finally over," she whispered.

But it wasn't. In fact, we were only at the beginning, and looking around at the way things were within this family, I knew that everyone wouldn't be intact at the finish line.

Evelyn turned to me, but she didn't say a word; she kissed Ethan's head before leaving.

"Babe, we should head back as well, I'm going to need a whole lot of booze to handle this shit," Declan muttered as he took Coraline's hand. But she broke away for a moment and came over to me.

"The entire family has to wear one, no exceptions," she smirked, as she pulled her 'Free Liam' campaign button off, and pinned it onto my suit jacket. "Welcome home, Mel."

I nodded not wanting to speak. I wasn't sure if I could put into words what I was feeling.

In a matter of moments, we were alone. Liam, Ethan, and I; our fucked up, beautiful, little family. Liam sat down and placed Ethan on his lap.

"Liam—"

"Four minutes, Melody. Four minutes, that how long it's going to take them to bring the car around, and I just want four minutes with the most important person in my life, and to not deal with what the hell you're about to drag me into," he spat at me causing Ethan to frown and smack his check again until he smiled at him.

What I was dragging him into?

I felt a cold sweat envelope my body at his words. It wasn't what he said, I've heard worse things directed at me. But, it was how he said it. Disdain was the prevalent emotion that I could hear. Although I didn't expect to be welcomed back with open arms, just hearing his voice and being beside him made me wish that that was what greeted me instead of this. Sitting down, I didn't say anything more. He tried to distract himself with Ethan, but my little one couldn't even keep his green eyes open for more than a minute. His head started to nod back and forth, and I reached for him but Liam shook his head and held Ethan to his chest tightly.

"Why start pretending like you care now?" he muttered.

I guess our four minutes were up.

"Is this the game we're going to play?" I whispered, trying not to look at him.

"No one is playing any games but you. Did you find yourself wherever the fuck you went? Was it amazing? Please tell me, was it worth keeping me in jail, and away from my son? Was it worth abandoning him?!" he snapped and

Ethan stirred for a moment before he readjusted himself. "I thought about everything I would say to you when you got back. And all I can think of saying is I'm done. I'm done worrying or caring about you. You are as coldhearted and as manipulative as your fucking mother."

Closing my eyes, I bit the inside of my cheek as I tried to calm down. He wanted to hurt me. He was pissed, and he was trying to hurt me. It was working.

"Either way, I'm done. If I knew marrying you—" he stopped.

"You would of what?" I asked him seriously. "Married Natasha? I'm brewing with jealousy."

"Really? When did the wizard give you your heart back? When did you develop emotions or care about anyone other than your fucking self? Not even your own fucking child..."

"Enough!" I hissed rising from the chair.

I was trying to fight off the stinging in my eyes. I had to turn away. I refused to be weak. Weakness got you killed, it was what had been the end of Aviela. It had turned her into a sniveling, pathetic maniac, and I refused to be compared to her. Especially by the one person I loved more than anything in this world, with the exception of the little person he was holding onto.

There were so many things I needed to say to him. I didn't know if he would even care. They weren't excuses, they were reasons. I had to make him see that what I did was for him and Ethan. He had to understand that only they mattered, and I refused to put them in danger without a way to eradicate it myself. I wasn't physically or mentally capable of doing those things after I'd gotten free from Aviela, and I doubted that I would've been able to. Not with the road-blocks I'd encountered at every turn.

I tried not to think about it…about what had happened. I didn't want to fight with him. I wanted to talk, to explain everything to him. How each time I tried to get closer to him, things only got worse. But most of all, I needed him on my side, not against me. I could take on everyone in the world, but I needed a reason to. He and Ethan were that reason. But if he gave up…

"Ma'am."

I turned around and there was Monte.

"Welcome back."

"Thank you, Monte, I hope you all have enjoyed your vacation. From now on, everyone will be working overtime."

"Wouldn't have it any other way," he said.

"Good. Is a car-seat installed?" I glanced at Ethan again. His thumb was in his mouth. I used to do it as well…until my father cut my thumb and placed a bandage on it so I could break the habit.

"Yes, ma'am, your mother-in-law had it put in."

Liam stood without saying a word. He was focused on his son in his arms. I wasn't sure what he wanted from me. I couldn't regret my choice. There was so much that I had to tell him, and I didn't want to do it screaming. In the back of my mind, he had always been there. Every day, I thought of him and Ethan. But Avian hadn't only made me suffer. If I were the forgiving type, I could overlook that. But he'd made Liam suffer…he'd left our son without his parents, and for that, I was going to get my revenge, even if it killed me.

FIVE

"We have the best government that money can buy."

—*Mark Twain*

LIAM

"*Good evening, I'm Stan Mercy.*"
"*And I'm Toni Blake.*"

"*This is KW4 Evening news. Tonight, we will be running live coverage on the story that has captivated the nation. The Callahan name has been heavily gossiped, and in national news for years, but no more than in the past few months. In a surprising turn of events, the Callahan name is now synonymous with national security. For the past few months, federal agents have been conducting an investigation that has resulted in the deaths of Joseph Williams and two other homegrown terrorists responsible for bombings across the Mexican border and Europe.*

"*Five months ago, government agents uncovered information, through the help of a witness, which led to this discovery. The world knows her as Mrs. Melody Callahan. After an attempt on her life, she was placed into witness protection. The only people knowing of her whereabouts were her husband and those of the highest clearance. This operation required a great deal of sacrifice from a great deal of people. At the latest report, the total casualty count has reached six. These were all government agents that unfortunately lost their lives protecting their country. Roger Kane, Kimberly Green, Beatrice Sinclair, Adam…*"

"Holy shit," Neal whispered as he stared at the six agents on the screen. "Did she really kill them for the cover up?"

All of us, with the exception of Mel, Evelyn, and Coraline who were in Ethan's room, were watching the news coverage. We watched as the President, the one I had spent a fortune creating, covered for Mel...covered for us all.

"I wouldn't put anything past her," Declan came around, and handed me a glass of brandy on the rocks. Taking in the scent, I almost moaned as I took a large gulp.

"How did I live without this?" I asked him. "I should have had it smuggled in instead of the rocks. I could have made a whole lot more money."

"You shouldn't have needed anything to be smuggle in," Olivia snapped, crossing her legs in the chair as she glared at the President on the screen.

"Thank you for your concern. Five months without a visit, I wouldn't have thought you cared." Downing all of the brandy, I walked across the room to the mahogany bar in the corner.

"This cover-up...it's deep. Why did she choose terrorism?" Neal asked, looking at the television as the President went on.

"Because there are only two wars in this country that people care about," I muttered, "the war on drugs and the war on terror; she'd rather them focus on the latter, for obvious reasons."

What a smart wife I had, she'd planned it all out perfectly.

"We're going to have to do press conferences, and a lot of them, this isn't just going to go away. We'll be in the news for weeks, if not years," Declan moaned, and I was there with him. The last thing I wanted do was sit in front of the same sharks who were calling for my blood only a few hours ago.

"Did Melody speak about any of this with you?" my father asked.

"Talk to me about something? What do I look like, her husband?" I laughed bitterly as I drank.

"Liam?" he questioned me again.

"Why the hell did you let me get married?" I sighed, as I pinched the bridge of my nose. "She didn't say anything about it, and I didn't give her the chance."

"What are you going to do?" Neal asked.

"Right now I'm going to try to wash the stench of jail off of me. Then I'm going to drink...actually I'm going to do both at the same time, and only after that I *may* speak with her." *Or strangle her...*Walking out the room, a few maids curtsied as I passed them, which reminded me that I needed to do another background check and establish some sort of leverage on all of them.

"Liam," Olivia called out from behind me.

I stopped in the middle of the marble staircase.

"Liam, I'm sorry I didn't come to visit you," she whispered. "I spent most of my time with Ethan."

"I noticed, you seem *attached*," I replied, as I turned back to face her. *Which was why I hadn't wanted her near him to begin with.*

She squeezed her hands, and bit her bottom lip. "I am, and that's not my fault. I've been here for five months and I've watched him become more amazing with each passing day. I care about him, and I'm worried that whatever you all are getting into is going to affect him. I'm sorry to say it, but neither of you have been great parents. In fact, neither of you have been parents. But what do you expect when the both of you are so wrapped up in this *family*. I don't want him to get hurt."

"He is *not* your son, Olivia."

She looked as if I'd just slapped her. "I...I know that."

"Do you really?"

I stared at her for a moment, but apparently she couldn't find the words to say anything else, so I turned around and walked away.

"Goodnight, Olivia, I hope for your sake you never bring this up again, ever."

"Threaten me all you want, Liam, but that doesn't mean I'm wrong!"

Rolling my eyes, I tried to ignore the headache that seemed to have been building all day. I'd literally just gotten out of jail for the love of Christ. There should be a waiting period before dealing with all this shit.

But I knew I wouldn't get one.

I knew we would have to face off with Ivan—Avian—whatever the hell he called himself. But we couldn't just jump back into everything like nothing had happened.

Step one was to fix my family.

It was going to take some time to get to our revenge.

But it would be worth it.

MELODY

"Mel, I'm sure this can wait," Coraline said to me as I moved the furniture in Ethan's room around. But it couldn't wait. It wasn't safe.

"I'd rather not," I said to her.

Ethan was fast asleep under his custom-initialed, teal, cashmere blanket. They had kept the theme I had chosen for him—the rainforest, though they'd done what they always did and made it over the top, but it was still beautiful. However, his crib needed to be further away from the door and the window. Surprisingly, as I moved it, he didn't wake up.

Evelyn sat in the rocking chair, glaring at me as I ignored her. She wanted to scream, but she couldn't do it here. So instead, she threw out small jabs at me.

"He'll wake up at three a.m. No matter when we let him down for his nap, he'll sleep until three a.m. and then wake up again," Coraline snickered, as she picked a pair of tiny socks up off the ground and moved it to his dresser.

"Yes, if you plan on being in his life longer than a day this time, you should get used to it."

That had been Evelyn's fourth underhanded comment since we had stepped into the room.

Turning to her, it took all the strength I had to not strangle the life out her.

"Okay, that's our cue to leave," Coraline wrapped her arm around her mother-in-law and lifted her out of the chair as if she were some old woman.

"And we're supposed to just leave her in here? She has no idea how to raise him...or what he likes..."

"When he wakes up, I need to play the ambient sounds of the ocean." I pointed to the mp3 in the corner. "When you change him, you only give him a bit of powder because it makes him sneeze. He likes applesauce instead of milk when he wakes up, and if it's quiet for long enough, he will fall back to sleep before finishing the cup."

Her mouth dropped open, as did Coraline's. Her eyes squinted together for a moment.

"Mel, how did you—"

"Just because I haven't been here doesn't mean I haven't seen what I need to," I whispered, as I took off my suit jacket and placed it onto the changing table.

"But Declan said you haven't checked into any of the cameras," Coraline replied.

"That he knows of. Next time, tell him to make his virtual footprint smaller."

Her face went blank and she clearly didn't understand the term, but I knew that Declan would. Evelyn didn't say anything and simply left. But I had a feeling she would be back.

Coraline kissed Ethan before walking to the door. "Goodnight to you both."

I just nodded. When the door closed, I pulled both of my guns from my bag next to the changing table. I placed one behind the dresser and walked back over to Ethan. For the first time in months, we were both alone and I felt like I could breathe again. He was alive and happy and beautiful. "I'm so sorry, sweetheart," I whispered down to him as I kissed his head. "I'm so sorry. I won't leave ever again, I promise."

Not wanting to wake him, I wiped my eyes before I sat down next to the window. I glanced outside, but all I could see were trees.

We're going to need sensor lights back there, and I was going to need body heat indicators around the whole house. There had already been one attack on our house and it could never happen again. Part of me was worried that I had triggered something even worse by coming back, but I didn't have a choice.

Pulling off my heels, I tucked them to the side of me before I crawled into a small ball by the window. The safety was on my gun as I held it against my side. Through the gaps of wooden crib, I could see his chest rise and fall...proof that he was alive and well. It felt like I had only closed my eyes to blink, however the moment I heard the floorboard creek, I was on my feet with my finger on the trigger.

Liam's green eyes were wide as he stared down the barrel of my gun before he relaxed. Glaring at me, he stepped forward.

"You can't be fucking serious, Melody."

It took me a moment to adjust. Backing away from him, my hand shaking slightly, I sat back near the window.

Breathe, Mel.

Placing the gun beside me, I took a deep breath, and glanced once again at Ethan.

He's okay. You're okay. Everything is okay.

It felt like ages before I relaxed again. Resting against the wall, Liam looked down at me, with anger, worry, and confusion written in his eyes.

"What was that?" he asked me, and for the first time, I took a good look at him. He must have just taken a shower because his hair was still wet. He wore nothing but black silk pajama bottoms. I swear he must have worked out every second in jail. Every one of his muscles, from the six-pack of his abs to the muscle of his arms, were tightened up and flawless. He looked like a gladiator, and I was the lion he was trying to slay.

Stop staring.

"I'm no psychologist, but I'd have say that that would be a side effect from the last five months," I replied as I pulled my knee to my chest.

He looked over at Ethan. "Should I take him out of the room?"

"I don't know. Would you like to keep your arms?" Because if he tried to take my son away from me, he may just lose all his limbs.

"If I have to lose them to keep him safe, I would do it," he said as he brushed Ethan's hair back.

"Safe from me?"

"Yes, you. You hurt people. The only person you care about is yourself."

He was starting to piss me off.

"You know, I was in this room when you called," he whispered. "He was so small, I swear he only took up the space between my wrist and palm. He was so calm...so sleepy. I wanted him to have the world, but most of all, I wanted him to have his mother. I thought it was my fault— that Aviela had gotten to you because of me. Then you had to fucking call and tell me you needed *time*. The rational part of me knew that something must have happened. But, Melody, for the life of me I cannot understand what in the hell it was that you couldn't come to me with? Am I that incompetent that you couldn't trust me? Couldn't tell me the truth?"

"I was strung out on enough coke to kill a parade of elephants," I answered, cutting him off before he could insult himself and me any further. I refused to be his emotional punching bag.

His entire body turned to me. "Wh...What?"

With a sigh, I closed my eyes. I was only going to tell this story once, he needed to know, no one else.

"I was doped up with coke three times day and it wasn't the low quality stuff, it was the best of the best...ours, courtesy of Aviela and Nelson, the flight attendant on my jet. You know, what I remember the most was the feeling. My heart felt like it was constantly trying to pound a hole through my chest. Escaping, killing Aviela, it was all a blur. But I also remember the phone call, I had walked five miles in the snow covered hills of Friuli to make that call. Every word of it was the clearest moment in my mind. Listening to Ethan breathe through the phone, I swore that I would not allow my son to see me like that. I couldn't come home because I physically Could. Not. Come. Home. Somehow I ended up in an abandoned cabin. And the moment I thought I was safe, I passed out for two straight days. But that was the easy part." I sighed, keeping my eyes closed. I didn't want to see him.

"I won't go into the effects of my withdrawals, I'm sure you can imagine. It took me four weeks, two days, and nine hours to reign myself in. No contact. No news. Just cold baths, training, potatoes and water.

"I didn't even know you were in jail. In fact, it was only when Avian sent his first agent, Roger Kane, after me that I realized what was going on. He caught me by surprise while I was in the bath. One moment I was thinking of how to get home, and the next, his hands were holding me under. There was no way I was going to fight him and win. When he thought I was dead, I came up for air and returned the favor with a cord around his neck. When he woke up, I *made* him talk.

"Avian wanted you in jail and he needed me dead. We have our men, he has his agents. They all think that they're serving their country. They belong to the White List...a group of FBI and CIA agents hidden in plain view. They are willing to do anything and everything it takes. Our tax dollars at work. After Roger, Kim, Beatrice, Adam, Dillon, and then Tom followed. They hunted me across Europe. But Beatrice, she came prepared. She had somehow gotten one of Ethan's pacifiers." My head felt like it was on fire thinking though it all. Remembering how I'd bashed her face in during our encounter in Belgium. I'd waited until she gained consciousness before forcing gasoline down her throat. Then I set her on fire. My son was off limits.

"I couldn't come back until I knew it was safe. I had reasonable explanations on where I was. I checked only when I could, knowing full well that Avian was waiting to find out where I was.

"My life went from *The Godfather* to *Jason Bourne*, from the hunter to the hunted. I wish I could have been in jail. So if you're looking for an apology, pull it out of your ass, you son of bitch. I will not let you, or *your* fucking family, try to tear me down when I myself am barely holding on."

He was sitting on the opposite side of the room, and hadn't said a word. Finally he spoke. "So I was right. You did think that I was incompetent. You truly believed you couldn't trust me. Thank you for your answer," he replied softly as if everything I said didn't even touch him.

Was he fucking kidding me right now?

"Did you hear me? I didn't just run—"

"I heard you, Melody. I always hear you," he said, still calm and it was driving insane. "When the shit hit the fan, you did it all on your own."

"Because I was on my own!" I hissed.

"Because you chose to be, Melody. I get what you're saying. You were left out alone, and instead of working with me, your husband, you decided that you were going to do it on your own. You've once again proved that you need no one. You are the strongest. You are a survivor."

"And I'm damn proud of it."

He smirked sadly, but it was half-assed. "I've never thought otherwise. You've been trying to prove how strong you are since the first day I met you. But what you did to me wasn't strong. Relying on me, on us, that would have been strong. Instead you left an ocean between us, all because you didn't want me to see you weak. Instead, you let Avian get into your head and you faced his people alone, you *suffered* alone. That is what he wanted, and you gave it to him. You didn't trust me enough to believe I would have your back. So, Melody what do you want me to say to you? Thank you? I love you and I'm glad you're alive, but other than that, it's taking every ounce of restraint I have to not rip into you."

"I did what I thought was best."

"You did what *you* thought was best and it wasn't. We were a team and you went rouge."

Even with how calm he was, I felt like he was gutting me.

"The contract says—"

"The contract? We're going back to the *contract?* "In it, did it not say we made plans together? I think you even added that part. First, your mother, now, your grandfather. Orlando sure made the fine print extra small," he replied, as he pinched the bridge of his nose.

"Be thankful. As if your family could have made it with me as an enemy. You were all dying slowly and you know it—"

"But we're bleeding out all over again, and right now it seems like we were better off," he sighed. "I'm done with this, Melody. Right now I just want peace."

I took a deep breath, but didn't say anything. My chest felt too heavy to speak about this anymore.

LIAM

She had kicked my world off its axis. I didn't know where to start or how to even begin to process everything she had just told me. It was like one blow after another with her. Her phone call replayed over and over in my head. And not once did I realize how much trouble she was in. Why hadn't she said anything? She always had this wall up, and I was tired of trying to break through it.

I tried not to look at her but it was hard. She was comfortable in the corner, her gun tucked behind her back, as strong as ever.

It was selfish of me. I know. But I wanted…I needed her to need me as much as I needed her. I was fucking confused.

Would she have come back if it weren't for Ethan?

It seemed that after two years, we were back to square one. Was this how all marriages were? A neverending roller coaster of emotions trying its best to beat the shit out of you?

Six

*"If you cannot get rid of the family skeleton,
you may as well make it dance."*

—*George Bernard Shaw*

CORALINE

I paced slowly, from the door to the window of our bedroom, waiting to see what my husband had discovered.

"Well? Do you see the footprint thing she's talking about?" I asked Declan as he worked.

He shook his head. "Baby, I would have known if someone was...holy shit."

Rushing to his side, I almost pushed him out of the way to stare at the screen. It was a map of Europe, and it was littered with tiny red dots.

"What am I looking at?" There was no conceivable order, just dots.

"It's hard to think when you're so close to me," he whispered before kissing my cheek and pulling me into his lap. Trying to get a more comfortable position on his lap, I felt him harden underneath me.

"Declan, concentrate," I muttered, as I bit my lip.

"I am," he mumbled as he kissed my shoulder.

A shiver went down my spine as he kept trailing kisses along my body. I had to clench my eyes shut in order to get out my next sentence, though it pained me to say it. "Declan, the computer...footprint thing...this is important." At least it sounded like a complete sentence in my mind.

"Fine," he sighed, kissing my neck once more before stopping. "But this isn't over."

Turning to him, I kissed his lips quickly. "I wouldn't dream of it. Now what is this?"

"All the spots Mel checked in from."

"Holy shit." There had be at least a hundred dots all over Europe. France, Poland, Romania...the list went on. *How did she move around so much?*

"From what I can tell, she's been keeping tabs on Ethan and was able to access the video feed, but not audio. Thank God for that, I think I might have told Ethan a few of his parents' secrets," he snickered and I could only imagine what those were.

Between him and Neal, Ethan was going to be a hellraiser and a heartbreaker. Females of the future, you've been warned.

Wait.

"She said she knew that Ethan liked to listen to the sounds of the ocean. How could she have known that if she couldn't hear?"

He pulled up the live video feed of Ethan's room, Liam and Mel could both be seen sleeping in opposite corners of the room. Declan zoomed in on the iPod dock.

"It's labeled *Ocean,*" he chuckled at me.

Well duh. Now I felt stupid.

"You said she was rearranging the room?" he questioned as he swept the entire room over with the camera. "She put Ethan's crib in the best defense position for her. With her sitting near the window like that, she can see through the back and have a clear shot at the door before anyone can make it further in."

It's not safe yet. That's what she was talking about.

"I think there's another mole in the house." There were at least a dozen people that came into Ethan's room to take out the trash, clean, sweep for bugs...

"Great, I'm sure Liam and Mel will love hearing that," he muttered, as he rested his head on my shoulder.

"I'm not going to tell them right now, not yet, at least not until I figure out who it is."

"*You?*"

"Yes, me. And don't say it in that tone. I'm kickass, remember?" He grinned and I glared, which only made him grin even more. Ugh! I hated him sometimes.

"Okay. Am I a suspect?"

"Keep looking at me like that and you will be. And I was right about Mel. I knew that she couldn't just drop of the face of the planet without a care." The way she looked at Ethan after just giving birth, that was the look of a mother in love. She couldn't just forget him.

"Let's not get ahead of ourselves. This proves she cares about Ethan. But it does not absolve her of all her sins. If only she cared about Liam that much," Declan muttered, as he continued to click through the data stream.

Getting off of him, I bit my bottom lip as I began to pace again.

"Babe, what's wrong?" he asked, spinning to look at me.

I wanted to tell him, but I wasn't sure if I should. Mel would be pissed.

"Coraline." The smile on his face dropped as he looked me over carefully. "Are you feeling sic…"

"No!" I said quickly. "I just know something, but I don't know if I should tell you. I want to because…you know I'm going to end up blabbing later, but Mel would—"

"Just tell me before you pass out." He smirked, crossing his arms. That smug look on his face was so annoying.

"I'm not going to pass out."

"Now you're trying to change the subject."

"Now you're being a butthead."

"A butthead? What are we, five?" He laughed and I loved seeing him so carefree, even if it was at my expense.

"I'm trying not to curse. Ethan's going to grow up thinking normal people use 'fuck' in every sentence."

"Fine, I'm a *butthead*. So just tell me, you know I can keep a secret, after all, I still haven't bragged about that thing you do with your—"

"Oh my God, shut up, I'll tell you."

And the asshole winked at me.

"So after we left Ethan's room, I was coming to see you but I forgot my watch. I went back and I found Olivia standing outside the door, when she saw me, she asked about Ethan and I told her he was fine then she left."

"Okay, we all know Olivia can't let Ethan out of her sight for more than an hour," he frowned, leaning back.

"Yeah, I know. That wasn't shocking to me, but it was what Mel said to Liam."

"So you were eavesdropping?"

I didn't like that word. "I was outside the door when they started arguing in hush tones. How was it my fault if I overheard what happened to her? You know I have good hearing."

"Her, as in Mel?" he asked.

I nodded.

"And what happened to her?"

It wasn't my place to tell.

"Coraline." He leaned forward and his eyes felt as if they were piercing my soul. I hated when he looked at me like that, I always melted.

"This stays between you and me, Declan Callahan. I'm serious, if you speak about it to anyone, I will personally hurt you, and you know I can—"

"Coraline, now you have to tell me," he said, rising slowly.

Declan

"For the love of God," was all I could manage to say before I sat on the bed. "This whole time I had thought she had just...I don't even know!"

"I can still hardly believe it," she whispered crawling onto the bed with me. Pulling off her scarf, she rested her head on my chest.

"Yeah, well it explains a lot...actually, it explains everything. I'm going to do some more research on these agents Avian sent after her. Maybe Liam will have some information."

"You can't tell him I told you." She sat up quickly.

"I won't. But we need to get more information. Plus, all their names were in the news broadcast. Even the President released a statement about them. They are already taking precautions, the guards said we already have cameras lining the gates." Once again, Liam and Mel were ahead of the curve, they could have the President make up anything in their favor and pass it on as a "leak."

"Great. Now they can focus on fixing their relationship," she muttered, as she sat up against the headboard.

This was not good.

"Coraline..." I said slowly. She was up to something, I could see it in her beautiful, deep brown eyes.

"Look, Liam is pissed at her for not coming to him—"

"As he should be," I cut her off quickly.

"What? You're on his side? Didn't you just say everything makes sense?"

Oh shit. Here we go.

"Yes, I did. It makes sense, but it would have made more sense to work together as a family. She went rogue."

Her eyes widened and I knew I was in for it. Why did I even open my fucking mouth?

"She didn't go *rogue*, she was *kidnapped* by her psychotic mother, who, need I remind you, she did not even know was alive."

"And I understand that. But if she managed to spy on Ethan, then she could have at least sent out an S.O.S to me. Liam spent five months in jail."

"Oh boo hoo," she frowned, crossing her arms under her ample chest and I couldn't stop my eyes from looking at her breasts. "Weren't you the one who told me he was basically running the joint anyways?"

The joint?

"Yes, but that doesn't change the fact that he was locked up, strip searched, verbally abused, and worst of all, kept away from his son. Mel at least saw Ethan. Liam was denied photos."

"He could have seen Ethan if he asked, but no—"

"He didn't want his son to have to visit his him in jail, and if the tables were reversed, I wouldn't either. That is no place for a child, let alone a Callahan."

"Some might argue that this house is no place for a child," she muttered, grabbing her book off the bedside table.

Gritting my teeth together, I got up from the bed and pulled my tie off. "I'm going to pretend you didn't say that.

I'm not saying Mel is completely right, because she's not, but neither is Liam. Everything happened so fast, and they did what they both do best, they relied on themselves. It's like default mode to them."

Throwing my shirt to the side, I stretched out only to find her staring at me once again, I winked at her, causing her to snap out of it.

"It's okay, just say it: I'm sexy and you know it."

Rolling her eyes she nodded. "Fine. I am sexy, and you do know it. I called this look 'long day chic.'"

"That's not what I meant," I pouted and she laughed.

"Have you ever not been on Liam's side?"

"I have. It was dark and terrifying and I'm not going back there," I tried to say seriously to which she only laughed at me more.

"I will never understand this undying loyalty you have to him. Don't get me wrong, Liam's great when he's not being an ass, but still..." She leaned into her pillows a bit more.

I thought about the best way I could explain it. "He's just 'the one.' Not in a religious, demi-god sort of way, even though I wouldn't put it past him to think of himself like that. Since we were kids he always had a plan, and even if things didn't work out the way he had planned, he still managed to come out on top. Like this whole jail thing, everyone who spoke badly about him, not only owe him an apology but they've also tarnished their reputations. He always comes out on top. You have to respect a man like that."

"Yeah," she sighed and I watched her chest rise and fall. She would've looked miraculous if it weren't for that damn shirt.

"As much as I respect Liam, I would prefer his face not being on your chest anymore," I motioned to her shirt.

The free Liam Campaign could now finally be put to rest. She glanced down and shrugged before pulling it off and throwing it at me, revealing the yellow bra she had on underneath. I almost moaned at the sight of her. Bright colors always looked amazing against her skin.

"Is it later yet?" I wanted to rip everything off her body right now.

She smirked and signaled for me to come over with her finger. Crawling back on the bed, I kissed up her stomach as her legs wrapped around me.

"Not yet," she whispered once I got to her lips.

"For the love of God, Coraline." I wanted to hear her scream and feel her writhe underneath me as I slammed into her. I wanted my fucking wife, and I wanted her now. Why did she have to torture me?

Kissing my nose, she ran her hand up my back. "You're going to talk to Liam—"

"Coraline..."

She silenced my protests with a kiss. "And I'm going to talk to Mel. You're right, they are both hardheaded and they need to vent, just not at each other. You help him see it from her perseverative, and I'll help her see it from his. He listens to you."

"Can't Sedric do it?" I muttered, as I cupped her breast.

"You want me to seduce your uncle into talking to Liam?" The grin on her face was so large I might have actually smiled in return.

"You're not seducing me," I whispered only inches from her face.

"Oh really?"

"*I'm* seducing *you.*" My lips came closer to hers, and just as she was preparing to kiss me, I kissed the side of her neck as I slid my hand between her thighs. She moaned. "You see, I'm going to have you tonight, baby, but my question to you is: do you want one orgasm, or do you want lose track?"

I slid another finger inside of her as she rocked against my hand.

"Fuck, Declan," she hissed and moaned.

There was my hell raiser. "Oh, what about no more cursing?"

Pulling her bra down, I took her nipple into my mouth and bit and sucked hard and fast before letting go.

"But if it's a fuck you want, it's a fuck you'll get." I'd planned to do so much more than that. She was already so wet, and her pussy was dying for more. However, I stopped before she came and pulled my hand away causing her to whimper.

"Do you feel seduced yet, baby? Because you sure look like you do."

Taking a deep breath she licked her lips. "What do you want, Declan?"

"A lot of things. I want to make you scream. I want fuck you so hard this bed breaks, and then I want to make love to you so thoroughly, so passionately, that my scent is imprinted on you for days."

"That's not what I meant," she gasped, as her eyes glazed over...her payback would be as sinful as it was beautiful.

But now, I wanted our previous conversation completely over.

"I'll talk to Liam, but you have to promise me even though you're on her side, you'll make her see it from Liam's perspective. Melody doesn't need a cheerleader, she needs a reality check. Got it?"

She frowned and nodded. "Fine. But do you need a cheerleader? It would be a shame to let such a good costume go to waste."

God bless her.

SEVEN

*"You'll tell yourself anything you have to,
to pretend that you're still the one in control."*

—Jodi Picoult

MELODY

This morning, true to form, Ethan woke up at three, screaming as if his head was on fire...and it was the greatest sound in the world. Liam and I jumped up off the floor and ran to him, but he didn't want us, he wanted his music. Liam was confused when I told him, but pressed play anyway. With seconds, Ethan began to calm down and I fed him his applesauce until he fell back to sleep.

Liam and I didn't speak other than that. Once Ethan went down, he looked like he wanted to go to bed but thought better of it and sat back against the opposite wall. He looked tired, but because he was an egotistical asshole, he wouldn't close his eyes until he thought I was asleep. And because I was stupid, I allowed him to think so. I hated him and I hated that he made me feel so vulnerable.

I needed a moment to clear my head and to shower. Evelyn had kept our room untouched like a time capsule. My shoes, makeup, clothing, everything was in the same place, including a note left to me by Adriana. I knew if our room hadn't been touched then neither had hers and I'd been correct. I thought I would feel better after being in her room, but all I wanted to do was to get back to Ethan. Her glasses were still on the bedside table, her bed was still unmade, and the bat Antonio had given her after they'd gone to see the Chicago Cubs, rested by the dresser. Antonio had come to me privately and asked for the weekend off. Adriana was pissed, hating the fact that he'd spoken to me behind her back. However, I told her to go. I didn't know how it turned out, I really didn't care to ask. She looked happy enough. Now Antonio was dead, and so was she. But at least he'd died with honor and loyalty. At least he hadn't betrayed me.

Walking over to the dresser, I grabbed the bat, and the first thing I swung at was her mirror. Swinging it with as much force as possible, I watched it shattered before I moved on to the lamp. I swung at it so hard it flew off the table before it splintered into a million pieces. It sparked once before going dark.

I unleashed my anger at Adriana on her belongings. After that, I didn't care what it was, I just wanted it in pieces; the chairs, glass table. I swung at it all. Everything in this room was Adriana, it was all a lie…the Adrianna I'd known was a lie.

"Ma'am?" I heard someone call out.

I glanced back to see Fedel standing in the doorway. Stopping mid-swing, I threw the bat onto the ground before fully turning to the door. Fedel, Monte, and Liam all stood there, staring at me and the destruction that I'd caused.

Maybe they thought I'd lost it…Maybe I had.

"I want to talk to everyone close to the family in the basement," I spoke directly to Liam. This wasn't up for debate.

He said nothing to me, but he addressed Fedel and Monte. "You heard her," he said to them, and within seconds, they were gone. Calling over a maid, he pointed into the room. "Have everything in here cleared out. I don't want to see any of it ever again."

"Yes, sir." She nodded before turning.

"My father is with Ethan."

"He came in as I left and told me to wash up," I told him.

"And you listened?"

"I'd planned on taking a shower anyway."

With a nod, he turned away and part of me wanted to reach out and punch him square across the face...or kiss him. I felt as if he was continually pulling at parts of me.

"I'll meet you down there."

"Fine."

We went our separate ways and I was fine with that. I was fine. I had to be fine.

The walk back to Ethan's room felt too long, I wanted to run to him. The fact that he had been away from me for so long had left me nervous. It was like I needed him near me all the time.

"Olivia, maybe..." Sedric stopped whatever he was about to say once I came in.

She turned to me with Ethan in her arms. He was holding on to her hair, laughing in her arms, babbling away completely oblivious as to what was going on around him.

"He likes his back rubbed in the mornings," she told me before returning her attention to him.

"I'll go check in on Liam. But I hope you and I can speak later, Mel," Sedric said to me, but I wasn't paying attention to him. All I could do was nod in response to whatever he'd said. When Olivia kissed Ethan's forehead, I tried not to snatch him from her. Instead I reached out for him and she backed away.

"Mel, it's fine. You can't smother him," she snapped at me.

"Olivia, give me my son or I swear to God I will torch you alive." Holding on to Ethan, I lifted him from her. He cried, trying to reach for her again.

"You're so fucking selfish! You can't just take him. He doesn't know you!"

"That's the thing, he's *mine to take*, Olivia, he is *my son*! My blood! Not yours. So I won't tell you again, Olivia. Leave. Get out of my face before I bash yours in."

Ethan was still reaching for her. However, I walked him to the window out of her reach. I knew that if she reached for him again, I'd have to repaint the nursery after I got through with her.

She sighed deeply as I rocked Ethan in my arms. He calmed down but still didn't look pleased.

"Look, Mel, I'm not trying to replace you. I know I can't. I'm just trying to appeal to your better nature—"

"That's just it…my nature doesn't get any better. So why are you still in front of me?"

The door opened and Coraline walked in holding on to a pair of small earmuffs. "Am I interrupting something?"

"No," Olivia sneered before she stomped out of the room.

How could she even dream of taking care of a child if she was still behaving like one?

"What was that about?" Coraline asked, eyes wide.

"What is it, Coraline?" I ignored her question opting instead to kiss the side of Ethan's head.

"I wanted to talk to you."

Of course she did.

Everyone wanted to talk or yell at me, but I was done listening.

"Mel, you know you can trust me right? I would never do anything to hurt you…"

"Coraline, please just spit it out."

She sighed, walked up to Ethan and placed the earmuffs over his ears before looking me straight in the eyes.

"You are a bitch."

"Excuse me?" I stood straighter, my body tensing while I glared at her.

She crossed arms and held her head high. "Liam is an ass, and you are a bitch. But you're both still human and under the armor you both wear every fucking day, you love each other."

"Coraline—"

"No. No. I'm still speaking and you're going to listen. If you want to kick the recent cancer survivor's ass afterward, that's your choice." She held her finger up at me and I fought the urge to break it. Who the fuck did she think she was?

"Mel, just tell him you're sorry," she added and I turned away, and pressed my nose against Ethan and inhaled. "I know you love him and he loves you. You have both gone through hell together and apart, but at least when you're both together, you can find comfort in each other. When you love someone, you just have to let them win sometimes. It doesn't mean you're weak. It doesn't mean that you are any less of the woman he fell in love with. He would walk through fire for you…while you were gone, he told Evelyn to show Ethan pictures of you. He wouldn't let any of us doubt you. If you truly love him give him this and move on, Mel, or you will lose him permanently. I'm sure you all will still have plenty of fights in the future."

Handing Ethan to her, I straightened my jacket. "Bring him down to the basement. I have work to do and I don't want him too far from me."

Kissing his head once more, I took off the earmuffs and threw it into the corner of the room as I left. It was only when I exited the room that I took a deep breath. Placing my hand over my chest, I tried to calm down, but my heart kept pounding against my rib cage.

What was wrong with me?

LIAM

What was wrong with her?
What the fuck was wrong with me?

"Liam, have you heard a word I just said?" Declan questioned me, as he leaned against the wooden door.

"No," I sighed as I pulled my shirt on. Five months of seeing their faces on a limited basis suddenly didn't seem so bad anymore.

"Speaking as your cousin, you are an idiot."

Tell me something I didn't know.

"Declan—"

"I know what happened to her," he cut me off and I froze, only for a moment before turning to him.

"What?"

Pushing himself off the wall, he stood before me with purpose. "Mel. I know what happened to her. Coraline overheard you both arguing. No, she did not mean to spy on you, and yes, she did tell me everything. No one else knows, and you are still an idiot."

"Coraline needs to mind her own fucking business. Her loyalty should be to Melody and I, not you. Husband or not."

"When the parents fight, children find people to talk to. So, pin your anger on Coraline, we will have problems, but it's your prerogative. You can add it to your list of fuck ups."

My list of fuck ups?

"Declan, leave. I am not in the mood."

He didn't look worried. "I won't until you admit it."

"Admit what? What the bloody fuck do you and your goddamn nosy wife want? For the love of Jesus, say it and be gone." My brain felt as though it was boiling over. I didn't want to do this now. This wasn't what I thought it would be like…I just…fuck it all.

"Admit you want her to suffer," he whispered.

"You're damn right I want her to suffer. Are you happy now, dear cousin? I said it. I admit it. I want her to feel the pain because I want her to think before she does something like this again." Which made me a horrible husband, but it was true.

He didn't look surprised or even bothered. He just nodded. "The only problem is she has already suffered. She's suffered more than enough. And you're not the one who should be aiding in her torment. She can never match your pain, Liam because it is impossible to match. You need her; she needs you, and the rest of us need you both together. Walk in her shoes for a moment—she's spent her entire life with a dying father, who only ever taught her to depend on herself. You can't change that in just two years. And if you love her as much as I think you do, then you should know that. You've always been good at patiently working towards what you want. I'm not sure why it's so hard for you to be that way with her."

I pulled back on the safety of the gun and looked him in the eyes. He sighed before turning to leave. My father who stood outside the doorway glanced at us then shook his head before retreating. I heard the door close and I had a feeling that Declan would never bring this up again. This wasn't the first time he had ever tried to advise me, and it wasn't the first time I'd held a gun to him.

Which was odd since it was Mel's gun.

I placed the gun down on the dresser and started at my reflection. I looked like shit and felt ten times worse.

Don't think about it. Don't think about her.

I'd said that I was done and I was. Right now, I needed to focus on getting our...my...the men back in line.

Leaving my room, I hoped no one else would care to share their *wisdom* with me. I figured Mel was going to give some sort of speech, which meant I was going to have to add something. Riding the elevator to the basement, I heard nothing. It was completely silent, the air was still and no one moved.

Stepping out, I saw Coraline sitting in the corner with Ethan who stood on her lap. The rest of the men, including my father, Olivia, Neal, and Declan all stood around my boxing ring. Mel was inside, walking in a square, slowly wrapping her fists. Her dark hair was in a tight ponytail and her face was void of anything but stewing raging. When her brown eyes fell on me, she seemed stuck in place, as if I had pressed pause. Moments later, she regained her stride and composure.

"As you all can see, I am not dead. For those of you who doubted me, I will find you and I will weed out your sorry asses. You all were supposed to be rock solid, made of iron, and instead you all look weaker than a newborn calf. Fedel, get in," she commanded. And like the Red Sea, the men parted and allowed Fedel to enter the ring. "Hit me."

He positioned himself and within a second his fist went flying towards her face, fast. I took a step forward without even thinking about it before I stepped back. He was fast, but she was faster. She blocked his fist, and punched him in the neck and chest before dropping low and kicking him off his feet. She pressed her foot into his neck, and held him down.

"Get out of my ring," she sneered, as she lifted her foot. Coughing, Fedel rolled over and picked his sorry ass up off the ground.

"Next!" she called. One of my men, Kain Fionn, slicked back his dark hair and held his fists up, bouncing on the balls of his feet. He had at least a hundred pounds, if not more on her, but that didn't seem to faze her a bit.

The second his arm came towards her, she dodged it. He kept punching and she just kept moving. She was letting the idiot overexert himself, and like a fool, he was letting her. He was pissing me off and making the Irish look bad. His fist slowed as he drew in a breath, and in that second, her arm curled back and her fist collided with his nose. We all heard the sickening pop as his head snapped backwards. His blood dripped from both his nose and her fist as he went down.

Moron.

"You're an idiot, get the fuck out of my ring," she sighed. "Next."

Monte went up and Monte's ass came right back down. None of them could even land a finger on her. She was ten times better than I remembered her being.

But then again, she had spent five months training. God only knows what these fuckers had been doing in those five months...most likely blowing my...our...the family's money away. It would've been funny if I wasn't so pissed off and turned on by her all at the same time. The way she breathed, how her hair whipped back and forth, the amount of damage she did. She was beautiful, even covered in blood and sweat. It reminded me of when I first saw her.

Damn it, calm down. Calm down.

I could not face her with a hard on.

When Declan got into the ring, I grinned. I grinned so wide I must have looked like the Cheshire cat. Declan met my gaze and glared.

This is what your bitch ass gets.

But, she didn't fight him. Instead she began to unwrap her fists.

"How many of our people have betrayed me, Declan?"

This isn't fucking jeopardy. Kick his ass.

"Two?" he asked eyeing her carefully. "Patrick and Adriana."

She smiled. "Wrong."

With that she jumped up and kicked him square in the fucking jaw. The child in me wanted to fist pump. In my peripheral, I saw Coraline stand and glare into Mel's back.

"Three. Patrick, Nelson, and Adriana," she said as she resumed taking off her wraps. "After Patrick had been set on fire, I assumed none of you would want to follow in his footsteps. But I was mistaken. Loyalty is the price you pay to us. Every moment of every second, your life's goal is to please us. And yet I know one you cocksuckers is still stupid enough to try and one up us. Patrick, Nelson, and Adriana are all dead. I will *find* you. I will *break* you. And when I do, you will have to crawl into hell to find relief. No one has the benefit of the doubt. I do not trust any of you. It saddens me that it has to be this way, but it is what you all chose. If I think you are betraying us, I will torture and kill you, slowly. Blood…" She looked at Declan, Neal, Olivia, Sedric, and Coraline. "Or not. I have my own to protect, and if you think that in any way makes me weak, you are sorely mistaken."

Glancing outwards, she waited for me to add something as if I had anything else to add to her display of power. "Things are going to change," I said to them all as I walked towards the ring. "From now on, we will personally call on you at random, even if it's to tie my fucking shoe. If you fail, you will die. If you disappoint me, you will die. If we have to remind you of something twice, you will die. I hope your vacation was well spent. You have streets to run, correct? If I were you, and I'm glad I'm not, I would start double checking them. I feel like I'm losing the money. How about you, dear?"

Mel raised an eyebrow and frowned. "My pockets do feel lighter."

"So why are you all still here?" I snapped at them. "Do your jobs and make us fucking giddy!"

They left quickly, trying to hold on to any sliver of pride they had left.

"Liam, can we talk?" Neal asked me.

"Is it about our personal lives?" I questioned, as I entered the ring with Mel. I knew he had to take over much of the family business while I was away, and I was going to make sure he knew that that had only been temporary. Power was far more addicting than any drug. He had tasted it and my instincts told me to trust him least of all.

"It can wait." He frowned, taking a step back.

"Mel, I've scheduled interviews..." Coraline started to say but my wife cut her off.

"Why?"

"We need the image boost, it must be done," I interrupted. Mel and I locked eyes. "We're going to need a moment."

She looked so beautiful.

"Why get me alone, so you can keep calling me an idiot for not running to you?" Mel questioned once they left.

"Why waste my breath, Melody, you don't give a fuck anyway," I snapped at her.

"Don't speak for me, Liam Callahan, especially when you do not know what you're talking about—"

"Don't I? You are—"

Before I could get the words out, her fist came flying towards my face so quickly I didn't even have time to think. I just reacted. I kicked into her side and she flew back. It was an automatic response, not something that was deliberately done. I thought I'd enjoy watching her hurt, but looking at her as she crumbled to the ring's floor just made my heart lurch. I couldn't look at her anymore.

"I'm not in the mood to play anymore of your games."

I didn't want to do this.

"Good fucking thing this isn't about you!" she hissed, and once she was up again, and her fist flew.

I grabbed onto it and she headed butted me square in the jaw, causing me to squeeze tightly, and pull down on her arm. She elbowed me in the face and I grabbed her by the neck and pinned her to the ground. Her fingers pressed into my eyes, and her legs snaked around my waist as she tried to blind me.

"I will hurt you," I sneered through clenched teeth, as I squeezed her neck even harder.

"Tell me something I don't know," she sneered through a wheeze.

What the fuck did that mean?

Letting go of her, I saw the marks on her neck from my hand and tried to back away slowly, but she held me in place. My eyes went to her breasts as they rose with each passing breath. With one hand, she grabbed my hair and pulled me down to her lips.

It felt like home and I couldn't resist biting into her bottom lip. Using my tongue, I begged for entrance and couldn't stop the groan from escaping as I felt her tongue collide with my own. I cupped her breast and groaned even louder as she pressed into me.

God, I fucking missed—no!

Forcing her legs to release me, I freed myself and moved as far away from her as possible.

"I can't."

I turned away and tried to leave.

"I want a divorce," she called out behind me.

What?

I couldn't even think enough to form words. How dare she? Turning back to her, I stared into her eyes, she didn't move. Instead, she lay on the floor where I'd left her, staring up at me.

"You want a divorce?"

MELODY

I knew him, his blood was boiling. This cold block of ice he was fronting...like he wasn't mine. He was like this to outsiders and I was his wife. So I took his options off the table. He wasn't going to be able to just glaze over this. He was going to have to assert his dominance another way. It was who he was.

Come on, Liam.

"You want one and so do I. It's better this way, then we won't continue to hurt each other," I replied, as I got up off the floor.

His nose flared as he walked forward and grabbed onto my arm. He pulled me towards him taking my lips with his, they were hard and hot. I felt his hands grabbing at my body before finding purchase on my top, both of his hands pulled, ripping it off of me.

"Liam—" I moaned into his mouth as I pull at his belt.

"Don't talk," he muttered as he kissed my neck. We fell towards the hollow floor of the ring together. His hands once again roughly finding a place on my body, he pulled so hard on my leggings that they ripped. His breathing matched mine; short and fast. My own hands found themselves in his hair, tugging and caressing him. I could feel him tugging on his trousers and before I could register him at my entrance, he slammed himself into me, over and over again with a relentless and punishing pace.

"Ah..." I moaned in both pain and pleasure. I missed feeling him inside of me. I wrapped myself around him as he pounded into me. Biting my lip, I fought the urge to scream out...*fuck* as my legs shook uncontrollably. I understood that he needed this, we both did. It was everything we couldn't put into words, it was how we worked out our issues, and even this remnant of the recent past caused my heart to ache, but not the way I was growing accustomed to. I was desperate for this, I needed it, I needed him to remember and yearn for what was, the same way that I did.

"Divorce is..." he paused, thrusting into me with a delicious harshness I enjoyed. He pushed me back onto my back and held both my hands in one of his while he gripped my thigh with the other. "Never on..." Again he paused after a punctuating thrust. "The table." It seemed as if this was a reminder, and I wondered briefly who really needed the admonition.

He didn't stop after those minute pauses. Biting my ear and kissing my lips, his mouth was everywhere. I tried to keep my eyes open, however I couldn't even breathe and think at the same time, much less control my body.

"Liam!" The sweat from his nose dripped onto me as he held me tighter. My toes curled in my shoes as I rode an almost painful orgasm to its end. His cinnamon and honey scent filled all of my senses. He was all I could see, smell, taste and hear. He surrounded me from every angle, and I missed him, I missed everything about him...about us.

"Ugh," he grunted as he came.

He swallowed slowly above me, breathing me in as I was doing to him.

"You're stuck with me. Until the day we both die. The contract says it. I fucking say it. So if you bring it up again… so help me God, Melody, I will you show you the very definition of a madman."

Pulling out of me, he fixed himself and didn't look back as he walked out. He must have felt proud of himself… manly even. He'd fucked me like a caveman. But I had won here. I knew what was running through his mind since I had shown up, I had seen it in his eyes—the conflict, the indecision. I had to remind him of who we were, where we came from, and how we handled our conflicts. Divorce was never on the table for us, not being together was never an option, and he needed to remember that. I'm not sure how he'd ever lost sight of who we were, or that this was how we dealt with things—we simply fucked it out of our system. But I'd made him remember because he had somehow forgotten.

I'd won, not him.

EIGHT

"I have nothing to offer but blood, toil, tears and sweat."

—*Winston Churchill*

OLIVIA

Ring. Ring. Ring.
ARHG! Answer the damn phone! I paced furiously in the bathroom, brushing the tears from the side of my face.

"Olivia," the old voice, smoother than snake oil, finally answered.

"I want out. You told me she wouldn't be back and here she is. I only did this because you promised—"

"Olivia, I'm going to hang up now and you are *not* going to call me again…do you understand? Some of us have work to do. Stand your ground and wait. It's your life on the line, so I suggest that you do not fail and be found out." He hung up and I wanted to smash the phone and scream.

I couldn't breathe. I couldn't fucking breathe. I had told him everything about the family, in exchange for Neal and Ethan. Neal was going to take over, I was going to have Ethan, and everything was supposed to be alright. Everything was going to be the way it should have been.

Falling against the wall, I slid to the ground. I wasn't sure what to do. Mel was going to find out and she was going to kill me.

"Oh, God," I gasped out.

"Olivia? Sweetheart, are you okay in there?" Neal called from the other side of the door.

My hands went to my mouth trying to stop the building panic as my whole body shook.

"Olivia?" The handle rattled.

"I'm fine, Neal," I finally managed to say.

"Okay."

There was silence for a moment and I thought he had left. Standing, I roughly washed my face and opened the door only to find him standing there, arms crossed, waiting for me.

"I hate when you lie to me."

"I don't know what you're talking about," I said bypassing him as I walked to my vanity.

He sighed loudly. "Olivia, look, I'm sorry. I'm sorry I've been so hard on you. I was worried about Liam, and now that he's back, I remember how much of an ass he is. But I don't have to worry anymore. He's going to take over..."

"Do you want him to take over?" I whispered, as I rubbed my moisturizer over my face.

"Are we going to have this fight again?"

"And what fight is that?"

"The one where you tell me to step up. Be a man—"

"You said you didn't want to 'walk on the dark side,' that you hated it. The last thing I want to be is a snake in your garden. So—"

"Olivia." He grabbed my shoulder. "You aren't a snake in a garden. You're a snake in pit full of snakes. And while it lasted, it was nice not worrying about Liam breathing down my neck."

"What are you saying?" I whispered.

He kissed my head as he met my gaze in the mirror. "I have no idea. I just don't want you to ever think I'm letting you down."

"You could never." I was the one letting him down...he was going to hate me. But I couldn't let Bloody Mel win. She had everything, got everything. She couldn't have it all. I was stuck, there was no turning back, and it was either die by Avian's hands or by Mel's. At least with Avian there was a chance that I wouldn't suffer.

He didn't want to control the drug trade or get rid of it.

He had said the junkies weren't the problem, it was the dealers. The junkies didn't care where they got there next fix. As the head of the FBI, he didn't want drug wars breaking out across the country for control. If Mel and Liam were brought down, there would be a vacuum of power left that would be perfect for Neal and me to snatch up. I knew Neal wanted it, he just didn't know how to get it.

Feeling confident, I leaned into him. "I love you, Neal."

"Well, I am good looking." He kissed the side of my head before answering his phone.

They all thought I was obsessed with Ethan and a part of me was; he and I had bonded. He would stare at me with those bright green eyes of his and it would just pull at my soul.

Mel was just jealous. She was to blame for this situation, not me.

She was just a Prada wearing thug. I was the first daughter. I was Olivia Colemen-Callahan. While they worried about me with Ethan, I was going to do everything in my power to bring them down.

They were snakes and so was I. And I was going to do whatever was needed to get everything I was entitled to.

It was all going to work out. It was only fair. They'd had their chance, now it was my turn.

"Olivia!" Neal grabbed my hand and pulled my fist open. I saw the blood that I had drawn myself. I hadn't felt a thing.

The first drawn blood of war.

"Olivia, you're really starting to worry me."

"My nails are sharp, babe. Seriously, don't worry about it." I brushed my uninjured hand over his cheek. "I'm fine. I'm going to clean this up and then we can head out."

"Should I hide the razors?" he half joked, testing me.

"Ass," I muttered, smacking his arm.

"There's my good girl," he mockingly called me what my father usually did.

I *was* the good girl. Now, I was damaged goods, yet that still had to be better than being Mel.

Right?

NINE

"And above all these put on love, which binds everything together in perfect harmony."

—*Colossians 3:14*

LIAM

She'd played me.
She didn't want a divorce, I knew she didn't.

I wanted to be pissed at her. I wasn't over the last five months, and yet as hard as I tried, I couldn't muster the energy to keep fighting. I'd fucked it out of my system... and that was what she'd wanted. It had been two days and I couldn't be around her without wanting to bury myself inside of her. We didn't speak to each other; all we did was look over every last sale in the five months that we'd been away. Neither of us was surprised that we were bleeding money, but that didn't mean we were going to accept it. There was so much work to do, and on top of that, Avian was the anvil hanging over our heads waiting to crush us.

Walking into our room, I stopped. To my knowledge she had only ever come in here to bathe and change before leaving. She spent her nights barely sleeping in the corner of Ethan's room. There were more than a few times that I wanted to pick her up and take her to bed. But instead, I settled for sitting across from her. Now she sat in the center of our bed, with Ethan in the space between her legs. She looked so relaxed in her shorts and silk top while reading through what looked to be work related files.

Hearing me enter, she glanced up and stared at me. Taking off my jacket, tie, and shoes, I walked over to my side of the bed and leaned over to kiss Ethan on the head. He smacked my face with his little hands as if to say, *"Leave me alone so I can concentrate."* He was trying to put the square peg into the circular slot. Moving his hand, I tried to help him place the square into the square slot. He stared at it for a moment and then at me. Frowning, he took the square and once again tried to fit it in the circle.

"He's a hardhead. I wonder where it comes from?" Mel muttered softly.

I smirked, as I glanced up at her. "Both of us? Which means we're screwed when he gets older."

"I'm never letting him grow up then," she replied as a small smile played on her lips.

I think my father used to say that about me.

We fell into silence for a moment, and I fought the urge to pull them both to me and just sleep. It had been a long day.

Should I say something? I didn't want to fight. Not in front of Ethan at least.

"Coraline gave me a very long list of interviews for tomorrow," she said to me as she handed me a piece of paper.

"Dear God." Who *weren't* we talking to? "Did they send a list of questions?"

She nodded. "They did, but it's bullsh—"

Pausing, she stared down at Ethan who looked up at her. "They did, but it's just a front. They're not going to stick to it."

Grinning, I bit back my comment as she glared at me. *No cursing. Got it.*

"What's our story then?" I asked her as I ran my hand over Ethan's feather-soft hair. I wasn't sure if we would've been able to have this conversation if he wasn't here. He kept us both calm and highly entertained.

"You knew the entire time where I was and stayed in jail to protect our family. I can't talk about the *investigation* in any great detail for national security reasons, but I'll go on about how terrible I felt and how scared I was…something along those lines. I've also called *President* Colemen to make sure our story is backed up."

I waited for the anger. Surprisingly, it didn't come. "Okay."

"Okay?" she asked, as she me wearily.

"It's your story, Mel. You planned it, and I trust that it will work." Because nine times out of ten, it did.

"We also have business to discuss," I said as I lay back, and reached for the file at my bedside table.

"Go on."

"Before I do, I need you to be a hundred percent honest with me, Melody," I replied sitting up. Her jaw tightened and she stared at me like she knew what I was going to ask. "The demand for cocaine is rising again, and so far…" I hesitated, unsure of how to approach this topic. I hated how tentative things were between us lately.

"Just say it, Liam."

"What happened to you…will it affect this, our work? If so, I can take over."

"I'm glad you asked, so I can say this once and for all," she frowned, "I'm not an addict. I'm not impaired. I went through a rough withdrawal. It hurt, and I have no interest in going through it again."

"Most people don't have that choice," I whispered.

"Well, I'm not like most people," she snapped at me. "If they cared about anyone or anything, I mean if they truly cared as much as I do, they would stop. It's not yours, mine, or anyone else's fault that they don't. I don't feel any sympathy towards them. We supply, and whatever happens after it leaves our facility is not on our hands. Have I answered your question?"

Ethan burped loudly and I was never more thankful for it because it was like ice water being poured over me...calming my desire to jump her. There was something about her that just turned me on.

"Fine," I replied, trying to keep my cool as I handed her the file I'd just been looking over. "Roy, I believe his name is, has been cutting the product to make a small profit. Nothing major, but it bothers me."

"Declan and I will speak to him. Apparently we were not clear enough last time we saw him."

"No, *we* will."

Her eyes cut into me. "Why ask me to be honest if you don't believe me?"

"I believe you. I've just spent five months away from you, I don't want any unnecessary distance until—"

"Until you're sure I won't disappear again."

Why must she always cut me off? "Your disappearance was my fault, you staying away is all on you. I don't want distance until I'm comfortable that we both won't make the same mistake again."

"You blame my disappearance on yourself?" she asked me slowly.

I really didn't want to talk about this. "433K, our company in Colorado, is going to bring in at least four hundred million this year. We had lines going three hours long. I say

132

we lobby for more states to legalize marijuana. But for now, I want to set up at least four 433K shops in every time zone selling medical marijuana so when it is legalized, we already have a foothold in the area." If we played our cards right, we could control both the legal and illegal markets. It would also help with publicity.

"We can't," she said.

What the fuck? "Why the fucking hell not?"

Her hands snapped to Ethan's ears as he yawned widely and his head bobbed back and forth as he started to drift. It was only 9:00 p.m., but I guessed that that was well past his bedtime.

"The public is going to be paying close attention to us for the next few weeks. Plus, the moment we start moving into that territory, many others will follow. So I say *yes* to your plan, but do it completely under the radar." She lifted Ethan up and he hugged him onto her and he laid his head on her shoulder as his eyes began to close.

Moving the puzzle he'd been playing with, I expected her to take him back to the nursery, but instead she laid him on his stomach in the center of our bed. Resting her hand on his back as she lay beside him, I realized that she didn't have her wedding ring on. How long hadn't she had it on? It had to be since she came back, I couldn't remember seeing her wearing it.

"What happened to your ring?" I whispered from the edge of the bed, watching them both.

She didn't look up at me, instead she stared at Ethan as she answered. "My mother took it. I'm not sure what happened after that."

Mother?

Since when did she start calling that psychotic bitch *mother*? Reaching into my pocket, I pulled out my phone and sent a quick text to Coraline. I knew what ring I wanted to her to have.

"They may not have it," Coraline texted back.

"Offer double…triple, I don't care. Money talks, Coraline."

Placing the phone on the bedside table, I crawled onto the bed, to the other side of Ethan. He sighed as I did, and his fist moved, as it tried to find a way into his mouth.

God, it felt good to rest in our bed again.

"Why do you believe my disappearance was your fault?" she asked as her eyes met mine over Ethan's head.

"Melody—"

"Stop," she whispered. And because she had some sick supernatural control over me, I stopped. I couldn't face her, so instead, I chose instead to stare at Ethan.

"I hate it when you call me, Melody," she said softly. "It hurts. It hurts when you pull away from me. Everything you said before, it hurt me. I hate you for saying them, and I hate myself for caring. I hate more than anything that I… that it's so hard for me to say how much I love you."

Damn it, woman.

Looking up, I was transfixed. I didn't know what to say.

"Why are you saying all of this?" This wasn't like her at all.

She shrugged. "I don't know. I feel comfortable. I finally have you both; this is all I really need. Plus I may have had three or four glasses of red wine."

"You've always had us, Mel. I can't fathom why you don't know that." It's like she didn't get that she wasn't alone anymore.

"I had a dog once," she said, as she shifted onto her back. "His name was Rufus, which was ridiculous seeing as though he was all white and Rufus means red in Latin—"

Was she rambling? Did *the* Melody Giovanni-Callahan ever ramble?

"My father never let me out much. I didn't have friends, and Rufus was all I had. I told him everything and he was always there. One morning around Christmas time, I wanted to go ice skating and ran outside. Rufus ran ahead of me and just pounced on the ice." She paused, and her lips pressed together before they opened again. "He fell through and it was only because he was ahead of me that I didn't make it on to the ice. Orlando wasn't going to risk anyone's life for a mutt. Rufus finally made it out on his own after what felt like hours. He was shaking, and no matter how many blankets I put on him, or how much I tried to warm him up, he didn't get any better. Orlando wasn't going to pass up this moment to teach me another *lesson*. He brought us both outside and handed me a gun.

"*'There are two types of pain, Melody,'* he'd said. *'The first makes us grow, and the second gives no hope and carries us to death. Which one is he in? Why draw out his pain?'* he'd asked me and I couldn't speak. He told me to fire and I did. I missed. I hit Rufus in the leg and he weakly cried out. I just wanted it to be over, so I kept shooting until he was silent. I cried the entire time, I told him he was my best friend, and that I was sorry. If there was anything Orlando hated, it was for me to cry. *'Wipe your face and don't be a disgrace. You don't need any friends. Friends bring you down, Melody. The only person you should ever rely on is yourself. Everyone else will die and leave you. Stop wasting tears because anyone who would care can't see them.'* I was nine."

What could I say to that? Right now I wished I had pushed that needle in slower when I put him to sleep…the bastard deserved a painful death.

"Part of the reason I didn't come back was because I was afraid." Finally she tilted her head to the side and I saw her eyes. Both of them were glazed over. "I was afraid that I was Rufus."

"You thought I was going to put you down?" I whispered. *How in the hell could she think that?* Scratch that, I knew how.

"That's what we're supposed to do, Liam. If someone is a danger to the family, we put them down. No matter how hard it is. It's what we were taught to do. I saw you in the back of my mind pushing me to get better, always worried, doubting; not sure if I could actually make it. So yes, you were right. I checked out. I did what was easier for me and I'm sorry."

She didn't say anything more.

"You trusted me," I said pinching the bridge of my nose. "You trusted me completely when you were giving birth to him. I had never felt more…proud? Happy? I don't know. But the way you looked at me with so much faith and joy. You're good at protecting yourself, and the one time I was supposed to protect you, I failed. Yes, you stayed away, but if I had done my job, you never would have been gone to begin with. You were defenseless and I failed."

"You're not going to listen to me, but I don't blame you. I never thought of it in that way." With a sigh, she reached over, took my hand, and kissed the back of it.

"You're right, I'm not."

There it was, everything was out in the open.

"I love you too, Mel," I whispered, as I closed my eyes. "Always and forever until the day I die."

136

MELODY

We all slept into the late morning, which was odd considering how early we went to bed. But we were so relaxed and Ethan worked perfectly as an alarm. However, he'd missed his three a.m. applesauce and he was not happy about it.

I wasn't sure why I'd shared so much with Liam last night. It'd just spilled out of me…it was just that his presence reminded me of how we were before this nightmare began, and Coraline's damn voice kept echoing in my mind like a fucking mockingbird. Whatever the reason, I guess it worked, because Liam couldn't keep his hands off of me after we woke up. As he fed Ethan on our small couch, his eyes looked me over hungrily. It caused me to shiver, he knew exactly what he was doing to me. I felt so…I felt like teenaged girl.

Stop fucking looking at me like that damn it.

"Our interview isn't for another hour, he's going to need a bath. You should take one with him," he replied, as he put the bottle down and rubbed Ethan's back. For not being around him for five months, he sure knew what he was doing.

Nodding, I stripped off my top and he gasped before he swallowed loudly. He was eye fucking me with our son in his arms. But then again, isn't that what I'd wanted? At least being parents didn't make us any less sexual.

"Please, just go, Mel, I can't look at you like that...I'm dealing with five months of pent-up frustration." He all but moaned.

"Pervert," I snickered.

"You make me so." He winked.

Rolling my eyes, I went to the bathroom, and for what felt like the tenth time since waking up, my toes curled. I felt so typical, like a regular wife doing her spousal duties. I stripped down completely after I'd filled the tub with luke-warm water and added a small amount of the baby wash. I slid in and relaxed for a few minutes before I called Liam in.

"I'm ready whenever," I called out.

It took him only a moment to bring in Ethan who was now buck naked and wiggling in his arms. I looked up at Liam who was obviously trying not to stare at me.

"Are you sure we don't need like a floater or something—" He stopped talking, apparently giving up the fight with himself and leered openly at me.

"Come here, you," I said, as I reached up for Ethan. Placing him on my chest, I gently poured water onto his back.

Liam seemed to fall onto the tiles watching us both. He placed a hand into the tub, and on my knee. I moved Ethan onto my lap and smiled when Liam shifted, moving in just in case...it was cute.

When did I start using the word cute? Who the hell was I?

"I don't want him to be involved in any of the interviews," I told him.

He nodded. "Me neither. The last thing I want is him on display."

Ethan slapped his hands over the water.

"I guess we're agreed then." I laughed, as I gently rinsed off his head, whilst trying to keep the water out of his eyes.

"God, he's beautiful," Liam whispered, glancing up at me. "Like his mother."

"We only have an hour, Liam," I warned. "But thank you."

Pouting, he leaned over to kiss my head before he stood.

It took us more than an hour to finish the bath and get ready. But Liam and I didn't care. We were in a bubble, a very happy bubble. Ethan had been bathed, fed, and dressed, and was now resting in the middle of our bed.

I felt Liam come up behind me. He brushed my hair to the side and kissed the base of my neck before he zipped up my black and white dress.

"I want him baptized," I muttered as I leaned into him.

"On one condition."

What?

I turned to him, and saw him smirk at me before he took a knee and pulled out a small box from his coat pocket.

"Liam—"

"No. You aren't going to stop me from doing this, Mrs. Callahan. You are not going on national television without a ring. So let me finish."

I rolled my eyes at him. "Fine."

"Melody Nicci Giovanni-Callahan, will you marry me again? No contract. Not for money or power, just for me. Just for love." He opened the ring box to reveal a large uncut diamond ring in the middle of an infinity looped platinum band. It was so much better than the first giant ring he'd given me.

"Any day now, Mrs. Callahan." He frowned at me.

Grinning, I shrugged. "This a big commitment, Liam, I'm not —"

"I should have just put the fucking thing on you." He sighed, standing up. He took my hand into his and placed the ring onto my finger. "Such a damn hardheaded."

"His first word is going to be 'fuck' thanks to you." I frowned, as I realized that I had just said it as well. This whole no cursing thing was bloody hard.

"Like father, like son. Right, boy?" Liam grinned crawling over to Ethan and pulling him into his arms. "Just don't do it in front of grandma, okay? Or in church, or in public, or to us. In fact, we will go over the rules when you can speak."

I laughed at his list. "I accepted your ring, now what do you think about the baptism?"

"The ring wasn't the condition. You were going accept that whether you liked it or not." He said seriously, as he licked his lips. "I was actually hoping you would put up a fight."

"Noted. Then what is your condition?"

He grinned widely, as he whispered to Ethan. I didn't like where this was going.

"Liam—"

"Date nights."

"Okay, I will fight you on that. No date nights."

"No baptism," he countered.

He couldn't be serious. I wanted to take off my heel and bash his face in.

"You are holding our son's soul as ransom for a date?"

"Dates...the 's' means more than one."

"Liam Alec Callahan, I will..."

"Remember this look, son, she'll be giving it to you one day." He ignored me, as he bounced Ethan in his arms.

"Liam, no dates. I do not date."

He pouted, which in turn made Ethan pout, and I swear my eyebrows were twitching so badly it was as if they were trying to escape my face.

"Please, Mommy, think of my soul. It's just a few dates with Daddy," Liam said in an adorably childish voice. "Pretty please?"

"Fine! But I'm not going to like it. I'm going to be bitchy the whole time, and you are—"

"Your soul is saved little guy!" Liam grinned, lifting Ethan into the air, which caused him to giggle loudly, as he clapped his hands and swung his feet.

"Come on, Mr. Callahan. The faster we go see these… leeches the faster we can do our job," I muttered

"A not so quickie later to celebrate?"

Shaking my head at him, I turned around and opened the door to find Evelyn standing there with her fist poised in the air, ready to knock. She glared at me.

"You're both late…"

"Mother, we'll be down in a second."

She frowned at me before turning around. "She's really pissed at me."

"Don't dwell on it," he muttered, as he stepped out into the hall.

I wasn't going to…I didn't give a flying fuck. Liam and I were on the right path, and if she tried to screw with that, I would put her in a fucking nursing home quicker than she could blink.

With our blissful bubble obviously popped, it was now time to go face the village idiots. Our family— Ethan, Liam, and I would be fine. Now we need to fix our image and business.

TEN

*"Some soap opera, you know, real people pretending
to be fake people with made-up problems being watched
by real people to forget their real problems. "*

—*Chuck Palahniuk*

MELODY

I watched as the technical personnel adjusted their cameras once again, anxious to get this "interview" started. To my left, I could feel Liam's eyes glaring at the man whose name and title I'd already forgotten, as he tweaked the wireless microphone on my chest. I could practically see the countdown ticking away in Liam's mind. If this guy didn't get it right soon, he was guaranteed to lose his head.

"It's quite alright, I've got it," I said to him, as I took matters into my own hands by pinning it to my dress myself.

"Okay, great." He smiled, completely oblivious to the fact that I only interrupted his grabby hands because I happened to like this outfit, and because Liam would've undoubtedly made a scene if the guy remained had that close to me any longer.

"You can breathe now," I whispered over to Liam, covering the microphone as I spoke.

Fixing his tie, he pretending not to notice. "I have no idea what you're referring to."

Yeah, okay.

The reporter from CNN, Mary Sue, as I referred to her, looked more nervous than anyone else in our backyard. We wanted the interview done at home but we kept the servants around to make sure that no wandered off. She was checking over everything, from lighting to her note cards one last time.

"Are you both ready?"

Are you?

"Do your worst," Liam smiled, giving her a small wink. He was laying it on so thick that the girl seemed unable to speak.

"Take that as an invitation to question him about this dirty secrets...including his addiction to Jell-O." I smiled, trying to get her to relax. If she wasn't calm, then this entire thing would go to shit, and I refused to be subjected to another round of a million and five fucking questions. We needed the public to love, if not worship, us.

"I am not addicted to Jell-O." He turned to me, looking confused as to why I would bring it up, though the smile on his face was real. He turned to Mary who grinned at us. "I am not addicted to Jell-O."

"It's horrible. Poor Ethan has to hide some under his pillow."

"Ethan can't hide anything. Plus, he only eats applesauce."

"That's because there's no Jell-O left."

"And we're on in 3, 2..." the producer pointed to Mary as the camera moved in closer.

"We'll talk about this later," Liam whispered to me.

Rolling my eyes, I focused on Mary who had managed to remain calm and steady as she spoke while looking into the camera.

"Good evening ladies and gentlemen. Today I will be sitting with Mr. and Mrs. Callahan for the first time since her disappearance and his arrest." The camera focused on us and so did she as Liam took my hand into his. "Mr. and Mrs. Callahan, I just have to start off with 'wow.'"

"We know," I said with a smile before glancing at Liam. "Believe me, we know."

"Mrs. Callahan, from what we have gathered so far, all of this started with you getting a simple text message?"

"Yes." The simplest lie worked the best. "I cannot speak too much on it due to the ongoing investigation, which is so odd for me to say. But what I can say is that I got a text message from a suspected terrorist organization that seemed to be corresponding with a colleague. Our numbers were only one digit off."

"I'm not sure if that is the luckiest or unluckiest thing I have ever heard," she replied.

Obviously she didn't get out much.

"The jury is still out on that," Liam added…which was more than a little ironic.

"And you, Mr. Callahan, knew of this?"

He nodded. "Yes I did. At first I thought it was a joke and thought maybe we should ignore the cryptic yet frightening message, but since we are public figures, we called a friend in D.C. Before we could even understand the gravity of the situation, the world under our feet began to shift."

"So you knew your wife was alive and you still offered a hundred million dollars for her return after word that she had been kidnapped leaked?" she asked.

I was starting to dislike her. She did her job well, but those are the ones we had to be weary of.

"Actually, I didn't know everything at the time," Liam adjusted. "She had just given birth and I was still in awe. Before I knew it, my mother was telling me that Mel was not in her room and that no one could find her. The panic…the fear that crippled me in that moment is hard to explain. The hospital shut down, and I hadn't even thought to look at my phone. I just acted...I needed her back, our son needed her. It was only afterwards that an agent came and informed me of the covert happenings. By that point, I couldn't withdraw my statement."

She looked so immersed as she turned to me. "Mrs. Callahan, were you scared? Why did they move you so quickly?"

"In all honesty, I was coming down off of my epidural, I couldn't even move myself. But I believe the CIA intercepted an attack on my life. It was only after I was placed in the safe house did the fear really start to set in," I whispered, as I wiped the corner of my eye.

In a flash Mary had a tissue ready to hand to me.

Really?

Taking it from her, I felt Liam grasp my other hand and kiss it.

"I think what was worse," I said softly, "was watching my husband get torn to pieces by the media night after night. Listening to people who knew nothing about him accuse him of all these horrid things, they painted him as a monster. Liam is just not capable of the things they accused him of."

He squeezed my hand and I knew he was struggling to hold in his laughter.

"I must admit, Mrs. Callahan that I was part of that majority, and I know that no one feels as badly as we do. I apologize Mr. Callahan, but you do understand why we thought you were guilty."

"No," he snapped.

Oh, here we go...

"I do not want people to think that we are okay. That this was just a horrid time in our lives and now everything is perfect again. Our lives were drastically uprooted. The media, *you*, have a responsibility, a duty, to find truth, not to entertain. I was, and am, pissed at you, the media, and the American people. I was found guilty, not because there was evidence, but because of who I am. I accepted your apology but I do not understand it. Give me longer than a week."

So we were playing good mafia boss, bad mafia boss now. I wanted to be the bad one.

She looked startled and glanced at her producer before looking to her cards and then finally back at Liam.

"Well, Mr. Callahan, what of the law and judicial systems? They were so sure—"

"The Chicago PD has had a target locked on this family for years," I hissed.

I wanted to be the bad one.

"Are you saying that the Chicago Police Department was willing to put an innocent man in prison just because they dislike his family? That seems unfathomable."

"More unbelievable than getting a text message from a suspected terrorist organization?" Liam asked calmly.

"Okay, point taken. But why do you think that is?"

I was my turn now. "Many reasons; crime is at an all-time high all across the state, while public trust is at an all-time low, and they wanted to prove themselves. What better way to do it than take aim at this family. But above that, it's perfectly acceptable to be rich in this country, but not too rich. The officer who testified, Officer Scooter, came to me with pointed questions of this family's wealth. Then, after losing a bodyguard, he accused my husband of setting it up. Thankfully the truth came out before their cuffs did. This was the same officer who led the charges against Liam."

J.J. McAvoy

"The Chicago PD has a systematic problem with competence," Liam added. "We were told that the Police Commissioner was called by someone in the state office to drop the charges against me, but he refused to because he thought I was paying them off. While I was in jail repeating over and over again that I did not kill my wife; knowing the truth but not able to say anything. I now wonder how many other people have been incarcerated for crimes that they did not commit. I saw firsthand how broken the system really is."

"Are you going to file a civil suit against the state?"

I fought the urge to roll my eyes. "We are tired. The only reason we're doing interviews is because we want all of this to be put to rest without additional speculation. Right now, we just want to focus on our family."

"Plus, we don't want to cripple the state. We just want justice," Liam added.

And justice we shall have.

"Thank you so much for agreeing to do this interview, Mr. and Mrs. Callahan. And for your work in aiding this country in foiling one of the biggest terrorist plots since 9/11. The world needs more people like you both."

We smiled and nodded...some people were such idiots, they deserved to be lied to.

"And we're off!" the producer called. "You all were brilliant, just brilliant, all we need is a few shots. This segment should air this evening."

"Please send a finished copy to our lawyers as well."

Liam added a 'please,' but there were no ifs, ands, or buts about it. Regardless of what many believed, there was a limit to the freedom of the press.

LIAM

Handing Ethan to my mother, I brushed through the small wisps of his hair. It felt as if years had gone by while dealing with the press. I just wanted a strong brandy and even more time with him and Mel.

"You both seem better," my mother muttered with a frown while she bounced Ethan on her hip. The little bugger would not let go of my finger.

"And you still seem angry," I replied, glancing over at Mel as she spoke to—more like commanded—Monte.

"She was gone for five months without a single word. Ethan—"

"And you were gone for twelve years, *mother*," I reminded her. "Twelve very long years. You were right down the hall, only seventy-six steps away from me, yes, I counted back then, yet we barely saw each other. Five months is a not even of grain of sand compared the beach you have collected. Ethan will not remember. I love you so much, Ma, but this is not the fight you want to have because believe me, you will lose and you will lose badly. And I don't want to ever hurt you like that, so please just let it go."

Her eyes became wide as though I had just slapped her across the face. Her mouth dropped open, and she nodded with a sad smile on her lips.

"I'm sorry," she whispered, as she reached up to touch my cheek, "I know how much you suffered, and I couldn't help you. But you're right. You're so right."

Kissing her forehead, I stepped back when I heard heels clicking behind me. Mel said nothing, only moving to Ethan so she could hold him.

"Mommy has to go teach a few people a lesson, but I will be back," she cooed. It was eerie how good she was with him, even when talking about potentially killing someone. "Evelyn, Olivia is getting more than attached, I trust that you can be civil enough to do as I ask and keep Ethan out of her reach?"

"Of course. Don't worry, the little guy has an entire day of painting with grandma ahead of him." She smiled before giving Mel a small hug.

Mel froze, glancing at me in confusion and annoyance.

Was it odd that I found it comforting that she still disliked being touched with the exception of Ethan and I?

"Thank you, Evelyn, now please release me."

"Is the death machine out yet?" I asked her, referring to our "drug car." It was nothing special, just a beat-up, old, black Chevy on its last leg of life. However, there was no chance for anyone to use global positioning system to track our locations when we used it, nor could they point out the fact that we'd even left the house. All the phones signals would be jammed the moment we got to our destination.

"Yes, we need to be going," she said, but she didn't look ready to leave either. Nodding over to my mother I watched as she walked away.

"What did you say to her?" Mel demanded as soon as she was out of sight.

"About what?" I muttered, looking down at my phone.

"An hour ago she looked at me as if I were the anti-Christ, and now she's giving me hugs."

"Hot flashes? Hormones? All you women change your mind too often for me to keep track of," I muttered, pretending to not feel her glare at me.

"I'm going to tell her about that hot flash comment," she replied, as she walked towards the back door. Small forms of the press were still outside which meant that we had to go through the back.

"Since when did you become a snitch?"

"Around the same time I became a mother. One day Ethan will say something about me and I'll want to know," she said, as she opened the large mahogany door that led down to the marble steps and into the kitchen.

The kitchen staff pretended that we weren't there as they moved around to get lunch prepared for the rest of the family. "So you're joining the sisterhood of meddling moms now?"

"I drive." She rolled her eyes, and oddly enough, Kain Fionn held the door open for us instead of Fedel. His face was still black and blue from her "lesson."

"Nope." I held my hand out for the keys and without a second thought, Kain handed them to me.

"Kain," Mel sneered. "You're new to our private detail and may very well end up back on the streets if you ever act without waiting for us to come to agreement. Are we understood?"

Poor bastard.

"Aye, ma'am."

"Follow behind us," I told him before getting in and putting the car into gear. Neither Mel nor I spoke as we drove. But in the corner of my eye I watched her as she watched me. The old Chevy trembled and it felt as though we were an old couple on the way back to the farm.

"What?" she asked.

"Nothing."

Flipping the radio on, I fiddled with the dial until I found the opera station, satisfied that I'd found what I was looking for, I listened to a woman weep mournfully. Sadly my Italian was still not as good as I had hoped it would be. Mel listened for a mere moment before shaking her head and turning it off.

"Excuse you?"

"You were enjoying *The Duke of Milan?*"

I didn't even know it had a title. "Yes, it's a classic," I bluffed.

"Yes, it is, but it's not opera, it's a play being sung horribly. Besides, I'd rather not listen to another dysfunctional family."

"We are not a dysfunctional family." I mean every family had issues.

"Your brother's wife wants to raise our son. The only reason I haven't killed her is because her father is the President and we don't need any more bad press. Seeing as you just got out of jail, and I just came out of—"

"I see your fucking point, jeez," I muttered as I pulled in at a hotel that was no doubt at the pinnacle of opulence in the 1920s before it was abandoned. "But in our defense, it's been an off year."

"And last year?" she asked grabbing hold of her guns before stepping out.

"It's been an off two years, but we're making up for it now, aren't we?" I replied, as I held the door open.

The hotel looked like something out of Stephen King's dreams. Almost all of the windows were boarded up, leaving only a limited amount of natural light. There were dull lights illuminating the space, and the base of the hotel seemed to glow in a soft, yellow and orange hue. The men at the door nodded to us, and placed their guns down as we walked up what used to be a grand marble double staircase. Now almost all of its tiles were missing, and rats littered the area.

Peeling back the plastic curtain, ten people—five women and five men—all stood naked as they cut up the white powder. Coke was on one side and was meth on the other. Everyone wore surgical masks to cover their faces... after all, we couldn't have them getting high on the job.

"Well isn't this a surpr—" Sadly before he could even get finish his sentence, Mel shot him right in the kneecap, causing all of the idiots to scream and jump back.

"Surprise? Yes, I know," Mel smiled.

Sighing, I turned to our staff.

I guess one us had to be the mature one.

"If you would like to live, I suggest you get back to work. This part does not concern you, and please remember, we chose you all because we know you. We know where you work, where you live, how many goddamn times you take a piss," I called out, as I waited for them to get under control. "Thank you all so much for your cooperation as we deal with a transition in personnel."

And on cue Mel shot him through the wrist.

Damn she was good shot.

"Roy. Roy. Roy. You stupid little man. I really thought you understood me the first time we met." She sighed, walking closer to him as I looked over the product and pull out the prepared test tube from my jacket.

"I didn't do anything!"

"Lying to a woman with gun? I thought you said he was smart, wife," I called out to her, not bothering to turn around from what I was doing at the table in front of me.

"See what you did? Now my husband thinks I can't judge a person's character—"

"Okay! Okay! Okay! Please don't shoot. My daughter got sick. I didn't have any choice, neither of you were around—"

"So you're saying it's *our* fault you stole from us?"

Oh he was surely an idiot.

"It was only a couple hundred. Swear I will pay you back double...no triple. Anything you want..."

Staring at the tube, I waited for the liquid to turn blue. That's how we tested if was pure or not...It turn yellow instead. The weakest form. Someone had added shit to our fucking product goddamn it. The moron.

I turned back, I held up the test tube, telling her to kill him with my eyes. I stared as she put her gun away shaking her head at me.

What do you mean no?

"Fine. We need to discuss certain things, and by the time we come back, you'd better have an explanation. A bloody good one," she stated.

Walking past the blood soaked floor, we stepped beyond the plastic curtains. She didn't pause to explain, instead she kept walking until we reached another door.

"My father used to say 'an apology isn't an apology until you get a gift,'" she said as she opened it for me.

There sat our favorite police officer with two women; all of them were strapped down to their chairs, covered in their own urine, and coughing against the duct tape that covered their mouths.

"Oh, you are too kind," I whispered to her, as I resisted the urge to thank her more thoroughly.

As she handed me my brass knuckles, all our favorite officer could do was stare at us helplessly.

It was my turn to be a little immature.

ELEVEN

"If someone puts their hands on you, make sure they never put their hands on anybody else again."

—*Malcolm X*

LIAM

Pulling up a seat in front of my old friend Scoot, I leaned back before I turned to my darling wife who stood against the brick wall to my right. I noticed a red gallon tank of what I hoped was gasoline sitting beside her. She grinned and it was as though she could see into my mind.

"I know who this fucker is," I said, as I rested my foot on his hand, which was taped to his thigh. One of the greatest gifts given to man had to be duct tape. "But I am not acquainted with these *lovely* women."

"Meet Lacey, Scooter's wife." My own wife pointed to the woman on the left with dusty blonde hair. "And to the right is Shelby, Scooter's prostitute. How he had so much time on his hands is beyond me."

"Which one do you think he loves more?" I asked as I tilted my head to the right to stare at the brunette. They both seemed simple enough to me.

"I couldn't figure it out," Mel sighed dramatically, as she pushed off the wall and walked behind the blonde. The woman's tears rolled past her taped mouth and dripped off her chin. "His wife has the house and he always comes home to her. She was his high school sweetheart. Right Scooter?"

Mel pulled his head back roughly before letting go, and he didn't struggle or speak. Instead he sat there with his head hanging so low that he tipped forward. Had it not been for the tape, he would've fallen to the floor.

He was broken on the inside.

If only he hadn't pissed the hell out of me, that would've almost been enough. But it wasn't. I wanted him broken on the inside and destroyed on the out.

"Yet, he's put up the prostitute in his old childhood apartment, she also has a stake in his will."

Scoot's wife's head snapped over to him as her eyes went wide.

"So, it's hard for me to say who's number one, I thought I'd let you figure it out," Mel whispered as she moved over to me.

With a sigh, I look to them both. "What did King Solomon do when he wished to find who was the true mother of the baby?"

"You want to cut them in half." She gasped in mock horror. "So messy."

"You're right, but the suspense is killing me." I dropped the brass knuckles as I pulled a razor tooth knife from my boot. Cutting the tape from his mouth, I held the blade to his nose and said, "You're going to tell me who you love more, or I will start cutting off their fingers."

He didn't speak, he didn't even look as though he were breathing.

Sighing once more, I moved over to his mistress and ran the blade over her thumb. Her breathing became rapid and her tears fell faster.

"You know what separates man from beast?" I asked her as she closed her eyes. "Our thumbs."

I slammed the blade down and started sawing off her thumb. She wailed so loudly that her body began to shake. Scooter watched the entire time, as tears fell from his face.

"Who do you love more?" I asked him again, as I wiped the blood on his jeans and walked towards his wife.

"I...I..."

"Too slow."

Holding the hilt of the blade, I drove it into her ring finger. She screamed as loud as her reluctant competitor, but the truth of the matter was that those kinds of wails no longer fazed me. Grabbing her dismembered finger, I held it in front of his face and tilted it ring-side down, he watched as the ring he'd given her dropped to the ground and nestled itself into the pool of her blood.

How poetic.

"Eighteen fingers left between them both. I've got nothing but time, and this is a very sharp blade, Scooter. Just pick one. I promise I won't kill her."

He swallowed and his head turned to his wife, then to me, and then back to his wife again. It seemed that he'd lost the ability to speak.

With a sigh, I moved to another one of Lacey's fingers. "I'm so sorry, Lacey."

Moving to her thumb, I paused, and looked at Scooter who only stared back at me. This time I didn't look away from his eyes as I once more pressed the knife into her other thumb. She screamed over and over again.

I didn't even ask before turning to Shelby.

"St—Stop. Please stop," he finally said, as he looked to his mistress. "I love her. I love her."

"Your mistress?" I asked calmly.

"Yes!" he cried.

Before I could blink, a bullet struck his mistress between her eyes. Turning to Mel, I watched as she placed her gun down.

"Well that was a plot twist," I said to her.

"I hate home wreckers." She shrugged as she glanced at Scoot's wife who sat in shock. "You're welcome," she added.

"AH!" Scooter screamed as he fought against the chair. "You no good fucking liar! Damn you to hell! You sick fucking bastards!"

"Wow, he really loved her," I said, wishing that I'd tortured her more.

"He's disgusting," Mel muttered. "I don't have to tell you what will happen if you ever think—"

"I know," I snickered, as I dropped the knife to ground.

I pulled out my own gun and shot his wife in the heart, finishing the heartbreak that he had caused. That woke him up and he began to fight against his restraints, trying in vain to reach her as she bled out beside him. Her blood gushed out, sending a hot spray of it into his face. Fortunately for me, I remained a safe enough distance away to avoid any splash back, and I simply watched as she died.

"You know, I always saw this ending," I told him calmly as he wept. Picking up my brass knuckles, I pulled my fist back before I slammed it into his face.

"In fact, I warned you," I sighed when I heard the sickening pop of his nose.

"You came after my family." The brass of my knuckles connected with his teeth and he coughed as they undoubtedly lodged themselves into his throat.

I held his blood-soaked face, looking to see if there were any bones that I hadn't yet broken...there was.

"You had me sent to jail," I sighed again, as I wiped his blood off my hands and onto his shirt. Pulling back once more, I struck and felt his jaw crack from the sheer force of my blow. "But it's alright, because I'm over it...now."

Looking him over as though he was a fine painting, Mel walked forward before she poured gasoline over the bodies. He coughed up a few teeth as he choked for breath. "Any last words, Officer?" I asked him. All he could do was struggle to breathe. "I guess not. Funny since you had so much to say on the stand." It didn't matter, he was done. He was just the first of many who had to pay the price.

I exited the room because I hated the smell of gasoline. Neither Mel nor I said anything as we walked back to visit Roy and the idiots who were still cutting useless product. Monte, Fedel, and now Kain, stood at the exits with their guns clearly visible.

"It seems as though our business is done here," I stated as I walked back towards the exit that led down to the grand staircase.

"I swear on my life, Callahan, I will repay everything," Roy called out, as he used the arm of a naked woman to stand.

It was clear that he had indulged in a little too much of our product in the time we were gone.

"Oh no," Mel smirked, as she pointed between the two of us. "*We* are done *here*. You...well you're just done."

"Kill them and burn this place to the ground." I commanded. And before they could blink or even run, Monte, Fedel and Kain emptied their clips into them, making sure to double tap the heads.

MELODY

We sat at a beautiful diner, about a mile out from the old hotel and we watched as it burned. The fire department had been called, but they apparently thought it best to allow the building to burn out safely. No one else was in the diner but us, however, it wasn't supposed to be open for another hour anyway.

"Do you think we're pyromaniacs?" I snickered, as I gazed at the rising smoke that tainted the sky in varying shades of grey.

"Not at all. The fires we set have purposes," he replied as he cut into the sausage links before him.

"True," I said, as I reached for my phone. I wanted to check up on Ethan.

"No phones." Liam glanced at the device in my hands.

"You're funny." I chuckled as I signed in and saw that Ethan was sitting with Sedric and Evelyn, the latter was reading something between them…I fought the urge to smile, and as I glanced up, I noticed that Liam was peeking over my shoulder to see them.

"Yeah, no phones," I mocked. "I see what you're doing, Callahan."

"And what is it that I'm doing?" he asked from behind his coffee cup.

I waved my hand over the spread of toast, waffles, sausage and eggs in front us, and his eyebrow raised as *my* grin spread across his face.

"Oh come on, this is you trying to get me on a date."

"No. This is brunch. I was hungry." To prove his point, he grabbed a slice of French toast and took a bite.

"Callahan—"

"When I take you on a date, Melody, there will be dancing, the best wine in the country, and food that is ridiculously overpriced," he replied.

"I don't understand your obsession with romance. It's like you're a love child of War and Peace," I muttered before I bit into my apple.

"What do you have against romance?"

"Nothing. It's fine when it's not being directed at me. I'm understanding of love, but this need to buy flowers, and chocolates—"

"You do know love and romance are synonymous, right?"

"No, they're not—"

"And you are aware that what you did for me today was romantic, right?"

I swallow slowly, unsure of how to reply, and he knew that he'd bested me. Leaning back, he pensively crossed his arms.

"Why *did* you do it?"

"I don't know, I thought you needed it or at least wanted..." I muttered as I reached for my tea. I didn't like where this was going.

"And it made you happy to do it?"

Oh God, must he drag this out? "Yes, fine. I was happy that you were happy. Can you just say what you mean now?"

"You, as my wife, anticipated my needs without having to ask or be asked. I, as your husband, wish to do the same."

"But I have no need for restaurant wine, I have my own. Nor do I care for dancing, and if you want overpriced steak, then I'll let the cook know."

He rolled his eyes at me. "How do you know what you like if you've never done it before?"

His smugness was slowly killing me.

"Because I know myself."

"I know you too, and you've already agreed so we're going on a date and you're going to enjoy it without being a bitch."

"Now you're trying to change my personality, Callahan? So controlling. I think this is an early sign of an abusive relationship."

"You can bring your sarcasm and wit, I find it entertaining."

Oh how he annoyed me.

"Can we talk business now?"

"Of course. It's not like this is a date or anything," he winked.

"It isn't. Now how would you like to handle all those who testified you against you? And I meant that as a completely unromantic and platonic question."

I watched as his eyes glistened. "I do wish to *handle* them. But sadly I can't deal with them in the same manner we handled Scooter," he said seriously.

He was right. If all the people who testified against him suddenly went missing or turned up dead, suspicion would surely follow…it would've sent a clear message though.

"Oh what a shame." I sighed. "Because here comes Dr. Lewis now." I pointed to the woman with short blonde hair. On her arm was an attractive looking man…who possessed the same hair and eye color as Liam. He kept her distracted by making out with her and grabbing onto her ass. He covered her eyes with a laugh as he led her into a back booth.

"Did you know she would be here? You picked the diner?" Liam grinned at me.

"Who me? Really now Liam, I can't control everything."

He looked as though he didn't believe me. However, when the mystery man stood up to join her, so did I.

"I'll be right back."

"Mel…"

I raised my hand and placed it over my heart. "I'll be good, I promise."

"Fine. But you sure as hell don't get the warden too," he muttered, as he rose and followed me.

"What do you think she values more than her life?" I asked Liam as we walked through the maze of white tables and chairs that led to the bathroom in the back.

"Her career," he grinned, as he listened to the sounds that seemed to echo in the empty space.

"Exactly."

We silently entered the bathroom and watched as she sucked on his small, naked mole rat dick while her breasts hung out of her tight blue dress. The sight made me want to bleach my eyes; it was like a bad amateur porno.

"Hello, Doc," Liam snickered.

Her eyes went wide as she pulled away. "Oh my God!" she screamed, and as her eyes began to water, she looked up at us as though we were some ghosts of mafia past.

"*Oh my God* already?" I sneered in disgust as I sat on the white and yellow couch in the bathroom.

"What the fuck are you doing here?!" she yelled as she tried her best to stuff her breasts back into her bra. "Daniel! You told me you were closed!"

"I'm going to take a wild guess and say he lied," Liam said, unable to keep the grin off his face as he leaned back against the wall.

"Daniel," I said to him and he nodded as he walked out and left her in fear.

"Daniel? Daniel!"

"You just have the worst luck with men, don't you?" I said to her.

"Wait," Dr. Lewis whispered her brain slowly catching on. "He's been working for you this whole time? No. I can't be. We've been dating for—"

"Two and a half months, I know. While Liam was in jail, and right after you gave your first testimony to the police. Just so you know, he was paid handsomely for your time together. He didn't have a penny to his name...but then again, you didn't know that. You thought he was a rich doctor who happened to own a few restaurants on the side. Wouldn't that have been amazing? Shame," I laughed. It was pathetic how easy it was to predict some people's actions.

She was shaking badly and we could tell that she was going into shock as reality crept in.

"Wow, you must have truly believed that you were falling in love," Liam gasped mockingly. "This must be embarrassing."

"What do you want?" She spat, not realizing how kind we were truly being.

"You know all those rumors you spread about me? About my family? How we take out anyone who crosses us. How we control this city to the point where you could run into the police department right now and still not be safe? What if I told you they were true, Doc? What if I told you half of the people you treat were sent to you by us?" Liam replied stalking up to her.

"You're lying," she stuttered. "You're the Callahans—you feed the inner city kids and..."

"And cut off fingers and bash in heads...which makes me wonder what will happen to you," Liam finished for her.

"Please—"

"Oh no, we are well past begging." He walked closer to her and stared into her scared mouse-like face that was now streaked with tears. "Now you're going to go to the media and you're going to tell them that you were forced to testify against me. Are we clear?"

"I..."

He took her by the neck forcing her to stand on the tiptoes. "Don't be stupid here. I wanted to crack your skull open. But it's been a busy morning for us. So take this gift and know that if you ever speak about us other than what we tell you to do, your sweet boyfriend knows all about you by now, and believe me, Daniel won't be so gentle with you this time around."

He said nothing else to her before he turned towards the door. However, before we left I glanced at her and tilted my head to the side as I took in her shaking frame.

"Have a nice day, Dr. Lewis. Daniel will stick around for a while just in case you have any doubts."

We walked towards the cars and I noticed that both Monte and Fedel were drinking coffees and eating muffins whilst Kain stood there glaring at them. I smiled; Monte and Fedel didn't take kindly to new people.

Liam opened the door on the passenger side of the truck for me and I entered without argument. However, I moved across until I was in the driver's seat.

"I'm driving," I said.

"Only because you were so good," he mocked before he slid in beside me and handed me the keys.

"All that's left is Dr. Alden and the prosecutor. I'm sure we can think of something. They won't be too much trouble.

And we still have Avian to deal with," I whispered, as I pulled out onto the road.

I wanted Avian dead. I didn't want him to suffer, and I didn't want some fancy, elaborate plan. I just wanted his head separated from his neck. The end.

"The mess our 'scandal' has created must be keeping him busy. But I doubt that will last any longer than another week," Liam said, as he clenched his jaw and leaned back into the truck's seat. "You'd think he would just stop."

"Would we?" I wouldn't. "Before this was just business, but now we've fought back. We've embarrassed him and taken out his daughter, all while looking as clean as ever. He's Italian. Questo è l'orgoglio."

"Pride? Well that's comforting," he said as understanding dawned. "I don't want to be taken by surprise from that mother-fucker ever again. We've been two steps behind up until now."

"Yes, and I'm positive that we have at least one more rat in the house." I had no clue who it was, but I would peel the skin from their flesh with salt filled nails the moment I found out.

He sighed as he pinched the bridge of his nose. "Of course we do. I'll have Declan go through the phone logs—"

"I did it while I was away. I couldn't find anything suspicious, but I know there's still a mole. I think it's someone as close to us as Adriana was. If my mother could get to her, then I can only imagine who Avian could get to." Thinking about Adriana only pissed me off.

He tensed as he looked at me. "On three, we say who we think it is."

"One..." He began.

"Two..." I countered, and on three, we both spoke.

"Neal."

"Olivia."

We both paused.

"Why Olivia?" he asked me, and all I could do was look at him with my eyebrow raised. However, he shook his head. "She's jealous and spoiled, but I doubt she has the skills to pull anything this elaborate off."

That was true, but... "Maybe if it was just Olivia alone. But Avian could be protecting her."

"But Olivia is adamantly against our lifestyle. We're 'evil,' remember? Sadistic even, according to her," he mocked as we stopped at the light.

"You know what I think is sadistic? People know who we are and what we do. But yet they still lie, cheat, and steal from us, thinking that there will be no repercussions. Somehow we're the depraved ones in their fucked logic. Don't cross the mob and you get to live. How many more mafia movies does Robert De Niro have to be in before people get that?"

He looked at me before he broke out into a fit of laughter.

"Look, I'm not a hundred percent sure about Olivia, but my instincts tell me to not trust her. Why do you believe it's Neal?" I asked him.

"He's my older brother," Liam replied as if that was reason enough. But then again that *was* enough. I wasn't sure if anything could have ever cleansed the bad blood between them, but at the end of the day, Neal was still his brother.

"Do you think they're in it together?" Though I wondered how either of them could possibly keep such a thing from each other.

Liam thought for a moment and then sighed as his phone went off. Reaching for it, he quickly read through the text and smirked.

"What is it?"

"The White House chief of staff is wondering if we had time to come to pay a visit late next week for an award ceremony and dinner dedicated to our service. It's perfect. Let's leave tomorrow."

What?

"Tomorrow? Why in the hell would we do that?" I'd just gotten back.

"We're at war, Mel. We've taken things slow to repair as much as possible." He smiled before sitting up. "But it's time we stopped fighting in our own backyard and go into Avian's. He's been separating his criminal life from his professional, so now we're going to collide them both and watch it burn."

"I'm not a pyromaniac, but you just might be," I said, as I turned into the city. "Fine. But I do want the whole family to come along as well. If only to keep an eye on them."

"Coraline and Declan will have to stay behind. There's a void in dealers with Roy gone. Someone else will try to push their luck and step up, I'd rather keep them all on a very short leash," he reminded me.

"Short leashes easily lead to the master," I paused, thinking for a moment. "Have you ever thought that maybe Declan and Coraline could be the mole?"

The moment I said it, his face fell and he shook his head. "Not Declan. Never Declan."

He said it with such conviction that I didn't push him any further on the matter. However, I had to get the thought out there.

I wasn't sure about Declan, but I knew Coraline...*But then again, I'd thought I knew Adriana as well.*

"*Wife.* Not Declan," Liam said to me again as if he could read my mind.

"Okay." For everyone's sake, I hoped it wasn't anyone in the family.

Twelve

"Everything in the world is about sex except sex. Sex is about power."

—Oscar Wilde

MELODY

B y the time we'd gotten back, it was almost time for the family dinner. Liam had taken a shower while I visited Ethan, so now I was running behind. The last thing I need-ed was for Evelyn to hate me even more for messing up her family time. I had just put in my earring when I turned to find Liam leaning against the frame of our bedroom door. He stood there, arms folded over his chest, with his green eyes focused on me as they traveled down the length of my body, from my heels, to my back, to my eyes.

"What is it, Liam?" I said as I placed my hands on my hips. Something felt off. "Do you not like the dress—?"

"No, so take it off," he demanded as he closed our door and locked it.

"Liam, later. Dinner is—"

"Dinner has been canceled. Ethan has eaten and is now resting in Cora and Declan's room, where he will stay for the rest of the night. Why isn't that dress off yet?" he asked as he took his suit jacket off.

What the fuck was this?

"It wasn't a request, Melody." He turned to me and I couldn't deny that I was just a little turned on. Slowly, I reached behind me and pulled down the zipper, and when it slipped from my body to the ground, he glanced up at me briefly before he returned his attention to removing his cuff links.

"Your bra and panties, I want them gone." His voice even sounded deeper...no, colder. He had given me no room to argue, but I didn't want to. So I did as he said and undid my bra, allowing it, and my panties, to join my dress on the floor.

I stood there completely naked, with the exception of my heels, and once again he spared me one glance.

"Necklace, and earrings."

Taking them both off, I dropped them onto the growing pile on the bedroom floor.

"What about my heels—?"

"Keep them on," he cut me off as he took a seat. He had taken off his shoes, belt and coat jacket, but other than that, he was still fully dressed.

"Liam, this isn't fair, you're—"

"I could give a damn about being fair, *wife*. Keep your hands at your sides," he replied leaning back in the chair as his eyes followed every single line on my body.

That was the second time he had bloody interrupted me.

"You're pushing it, hus—"

"Did you really think I would be satisfied with one quick screw in the boxing ring?" He finally stood up, loosened his tie, and walked over to me. He reached up and stroked the side of my face, then he smeared the lipstick off my lips with his thumb. "I'm hungry, Mel. I was starved for five months. I need more than one quick fuck."

His hands wandered down my neck, and I felt like it was getting harder to breathe. His presence, his dominance, everything about him made my whole body feel like liquid fire.

"You won't bow down to me outside of this room, but I swear that tonight I will watch you tremble underneath me," he whispered as he placed his hands on my shoulders and walked behind me. Soon I felt his hands travel down my spine as he circled back around me and stared into my eyes.

"That way we won't be separated again, because when I'm done, you'll need it every day for the rest of your life. I'm going to make sure you are only addicted to me in both *pleasure* and *pain*. Any questions?"

I swallowed and nodded my head, I wasn't even sure if I still knew how to speak.

"Take my tie off, Mel."

Reaching up I pulled it from his neck.

"Now tie it around your eyes."

As I did, my world went dark and I felt his thumb once more as it brushed over my lips.

"These lips of yours, if you only know how sinful they make me. What I want to do to them…and to you."

He lifted me up. Two steps. That was all it took before he dropped me on my back in the center of our bed. I could feel him above of me. His fingertips spread down the length of my arms until his hands were in mine.

"Mmm…" I moaned against his mouth when he kissed me so hard, so passionately, as his tongue explored my mouth. I couldn't help but clench my legs together.

"Liam," I whispered as he broke away from his embrace. It was sudden, and before I could react, he lifted my hands above my head and pressed them against the headboard. Kissing the insides of my wrists, he quickly tied and fastened them to the frame of the bed. Repeating the process with my other arm, I was soon restrained, though I longed to touch him…to kiss him again.

"How strong are these knots?" I grinned as I pulled against them to see if they would hold.

In return for speaking, he pinched my nipples, and my already sensitive body jerked in response.

"Didn't you know, wife? I was a Boy Scout."

If I could have seen him, I was sure he was smirking at me.

Do your worst, my mind begged.

But he left me there, and all I could feel were his light touches. He was teasing me and torturing me all at the same time. He knew how badly I wanted him. I bit my lip, and with each of his soft and gentle touches, I grew more and more excited to the point where I, Melody Giovanni-Callahan, was ready to for him to end this and just take me.

"You're so wet, baby."

I expected his hands, but it was his tongue that found its way between my legs, and as I felt it, I ached against it.

"Fuck, Liam!" I gasped when his tongue entered me, I tried to reach for him, forgetting for a moment that my wrists were bounded. I wanted to hold onto him, to feel him against my fingertips, and yet I was forced to endure his torture.

"Not yet." He stopped and I cried out.

How could I be this weak already?

He kissed my inner thigh as I took a deep breath and tried to not think about how close I just was.

"You're shaking, but baby I said *tremble.*"

"Liam!" I gasped in both pleasure and pain as something hot dropped onto my nipple. The pain was quick, but the sensuality of it lingered. Slowly the drops fell onto my skin, each one driving me more and more insane.

"Liam." I moaned again when he finished with my breast and worked his way downwards. I could feel my body tremble, and when that drop fell right between my legs, I couldn't hold back anymore.

"Ahh...Liam!" I shuddered as I came.

"Much better," he replied.

"Fuck you." *Fuck you for torturing me so easily like this.*

"Oh, love, I plan to," he muttered, and I still trembled as he ran what felt like the cold blade of a knife, against my skin and slowly peeled off the wax. I again I bit my lip. I was used to knives in one way and this was not it. Finally he stopped, but that relief died down quickly as he placed an ice cube against my skin.

Where the fucking Christ did he get this from?

I didn't dwell on it. Instead, I concentrated on the freezing drops of water at they dripped down my breasts. I could feel his hands on either side of me. Meaning that the ice cube was between his lips as he ran it across my body, he worked from my neck until he was hovering over my lips. The water dripped onto my tongue, and I moaned as he kissed me and allowed the ice to melt between our lips. I felt like I was melting just as fast as it was. He knew my body too well. He knew where I was sensitive, and how to keep amping me up.

Even though I hadn't been able to break out of his ties, he freed one of my hands. But I didn't even have time to get use to the freedom before he flipped me over onto my stomach.

"For my last trick," he whispered, as his hands traveled down my spine and cupped my ass. "I'm going to see just how loudly you can scream my name."

"I scream only when you earn it, baby."

SMACK!

"Ah..." My mouth dropped open and I tried not to moan any louder, as I gripped onto the ties around my hands. I felt the sting of his slap on my ass, and the ripple effect it had through my body.

He rubbed his hand gently on the round of my ass, and just as I relaxed...

SMACK!

Fuck!

"Does it hurt, baby?" He kissed what I knew had to be his hand print.

"Not at all. It's like feather touches," I lied to both him and myself. It felt exotic and sexual, and I wanted more.

"Even now you must test me," he snickered. "No more games then, right?"

"Liam—"

SMACK!

I can't...

SMACK!

Take much...

SMACK!

More of...

SMACK!

This...

SMACK!

So...

SMACK!

Fucking...

SMACK!

Fuck...me

SMACK!

"Liam!" I finally cried out.

"Yes?"

"Fuck me…please"

Never in all of our time together had I felt like he had claimed me more than I did in that moment.

LIAM

My hand was as red as her ass....and it was beautiful. Her body was coated in sweat, and her mouth parted as she tried to control her breathing. Her hair clung to her, but the best thing about the sight in front of me was the way her body shook from both past and present excitement. She was there, her body was begging for me, and I couldn't take it anymore, my cock just twitched at the mere thought of being inside her.

"Liam...please." she pleaded...no begged. My Mel was begging me for more.

God if she only knew how sexy she looked right now.

I needed her.

As I rubbed my hard shaft against her hot, glowing ass, she moaned and pressed back against me.

"Fuck me, baby...please."

Since you're so polite.

"Yes!" she screamed, and threw her head back as I held her waist and slammed into her.

"Uha!" I grunted. She was so tight. I grabbed her breasts and held onto them as I thrust forward.

"J..es...u..s fu...ck..in.g Ch..ri...st, Liam!"

The bed slammed against the wall, moving with us. Every time she spoke, I went faster and harder to the point where

I couldn't even see straight. I held onto her as she held onto the bounds around her hands as tightly as she could.

"Liam, I …I can't! LIAM!"

I didn't stop. I couldn't. Not until…

"Mel…" I moaned as I came inside of her.

She collapsed face first onto the bed, and I collapsed on top of her.

We both laid there, exhausted and breathing in the scent of each other. It took me a while before I could actually remember how to untie her bounds and free her hands. It took all my energy to do that simple task.

Now free, she rolled over to face me as she pulled off the tie around her eyes. Sitting up, she kissed me without saying a word.

This woman was trying to kill me. I thought as her tongue slipped into my mouth. Moaning into her, she broke away and rolled on top of me.

"You fucked me good, Mr. Callahan," she smirked. "How am I going to explain not being able to sit?"

"Tell them the same thing you told me; that your husband fucked you. And the moment I catch my breath, I plan on doing it a few more times," I told her as I ran my hand through her hair.

Her eyebrow raised. "A few more times?"

"I told you I wanted you addicted, did I not?" I said to her.

"And if I already am?"

"I'll be the one to decide that. Right now, call for food. You're going to need your energy for round two."

I kissed her and she grinned as she reached over to the bedside table and innocently arched her back and flexed her body against me.

I lightly bit her nipple.

"Mr. Callahan!"

"You put it in my face, so I have to show it love."

Yes. This was just the beginning. We would deal with all the other fucking things tomorrow.

THIRTEEN

*"I have struck a city - a real city - and they call
it Chicago. . . It is inhabited by savages."*
—Rudyard Kipling

LIAM

As I poured the brandy into his glass, he looked me over carefully, and I was certain that he was confused as to why we were sitting at a private table that overlooked the restaurant.

"Will that be all, Mr. Callahan?" the waiter asked me.

"Yes, it's perfect. Thank you," I told him before he turned and walked away.

Declan reached for the glass and stared at the liquor. "I vaguely remember being witness to a meal similar to this with an old business associate before he lost his life."

"Yes, so do I. We dubbed it his last supper," I replied, as I cut into the nearly red meat before me; I've always preferred my meat just a little bloody. "He never saw it coming. One moment we were laughing over brandy, and the next he was gasping for air. It was quite tragic."

He frowned and placed the glass down before he met my gaze. "Do you believe I've betrayed you, Liam?"

"Have you?" I asked before chewing.

"I'm insulted by the question. We're so close that I think of you as a brother, not my cousin." He picked up the glass once more and drank its contents. "But then again, I know you, and if you truly believe that, you would've had me

187

tied to a chair. We wouldn't be settling anything over filet mignon at the Plaza."

"If you know me as well as you think you do, then why are you sweating?" I grinned, as the beads of sweat rolled down the side of his cheek.

He gasped as he reached for his neck, and felt his own pulse. He had to have known by now...

"Liam, have you lost your damned mind?" he hissed as he took a deep breath and undid his tic. "I would never—"

"I know. It's not poison. You're going to be fine, Declan."

"What the fuck did you give me then?" he snapped, as he pressed his thumbs to his temple.

"Clonidine."

"Isn't that—?"

"Mother's menopause pills? Yes, it is," I snickered, taking another bite as he glared at me. "You see, I know you wouldn't betray me. My wife on the other hand wasn't one hundred percent certain. I can't have doubts about you Declan. Not even a little bit. So, take it as a compliment."

"I'll get right on that when I can feel my tongue again, asshole." He licked his lips before he reached for my glass. "Am I still being tested? Or can I wash this down."

"You should probably ask for a new bottle," I said, as I nonchalantly took another bite.

He sighed, and released his glass to signal the waiter for another bottle. As he did, I smiled and took a drink from my snifter. Again his eyes narrowed as he sat back.

"Do I get an explanation? Or are you going keep fucking with me?"

"I'm just enjoying myself," I replied.

"Yeah, I can see that."

Wiping the corners of my mouth, I addressed the issue that had been plaguing me. "We have a mole."

"You can cross me off the list."

"I know. But I think it's Neal," I replied and he froze.

The waiter came over with a new bottle, and reached for a glass, but Declan took the bottle, waved him off and began drinking directly from it.

"Classy, *brother*," I said, as I dismissed the waiter who stared at him in disbelief.

"Fuck you, my ears are still ringing. But I thought you said *Neal.*"

"I did."

"Liam." He shook his head as if I were crazy. "I know you and Neal have had your issues, but this is insane. Neal loves this family and even though you don't believe it, he loves you too. He's our brother in blood and in arms. He's a fucking Callahan!"

"You think I don't know that? You think I want my older brother to be the person betraying me? But there is something—"

"What did Mel say? Because obviously she thinks it's me and not Neal." He seemed a little bitter about that.

"She thinks it's Olivia."

"Of course." He sighed, as he drank from the bottle again. "I know you both have been to hell and back, but who's next? Mom? Dad? Coraline?"

"As we speak Mel is having a meeting with your wife," I said and once again he froze, before he took another swig.

"If you or Mel hurt my wife in any way, I will make it my life's mission to destroy you both."

"Are you threatening me, *brother*?"

He leaned forward. "I love you, Liam, but I love Coraline more. So yes, it's a fucking treat. Though I'm confused as to how you would think she managed to battle cancer and stab you in the back at the same time."

"Relax, I know that and so does Mel, we're just covering all the bases," I replied. We had to be sure.

"Fine, let's say it is Neal or Olivia. What are you going to do?" he asked me, and I drank along with him.

"What would you do?"

He sighed. "Fuck man. Is this why you want to go to D.C.?"

"There are many reasons. But will you and Coraline be okay here?"

"Yes. I'm more worried about what's going to happen at the capital. You all don't know how to get around Avian. Nor do you know where he lives. Plus he has the FBI on his payroll."

"Thank you, Declan. We know we have to be smarter, but he's also aware of that. He's tried to destroy us, but he failed, and now he knows he needs a new game plan."

"What's yours?"

I grinned. "Political chaos. He's fucked with my work, now we're going to fuck with his. The FBI will soon be receiving a lot of bad press. He's going to have to focus on that for now."

"Is that why you're accepting the key to the city tomorrow?"

Yes, and Mel was pissed.

"We were supposed to go to D.C. yesterday. Every day we waste here, she's more on edge."

"This could look bad on the President."

"Do I look like I give a fuck? As long as the President isn't involved, then he still has three years."

"Let's hope this ends quickly," he muttered just as my favorite lawyer came over.

"DiMarco. Long time no see," I laughed, toasting him.

"Not that long. I'm glad you're enjoying your freedom."

He nodded to Declan who looked fucked up beyond speech as he held on tightly to his bottle. Who would have thought that a few little pills would be the catalyst to this?

"How's the case?" I asked him in reference to my former cellmate, Avery Barrow.

"He's out on bail. I've reminded him of the terms of accepting your help. Also, the Warden wanted me to pass this along to you." He handed me a letter and I smirked as I read her note on the top.

"Your handwritten apology."

"Thank you, DiMarco," I replied as I placed it in my coat.

"Good evening, Mr. Callahan, Mr. Callahan," he said to the both of us before walking off.

"Should I be seeing spots in my vision?" Declan asked me.

With a laugh, I waved for the check.

MELODY

Her fists came straight for my face. However I blocked them and headbutted her whilst I landed a kick into her chest.

"Ah, fuck," Coraline gasped from her spot on the ground, as she held her chest.

"And here I thought you were better than this," I said as I looked down at her.

Frustrated, she charged forward as fast as her legs could. Her fists came at me like bullets. She was tiring herself out, but she was also wearing me down in the process, since I was forced to block her fists. The moment I saw an opening, I took it. I pulled her wrist to me before I managed to flip her over onto her back.

"Okay, fine! You win...ugh!" she called out, as she pulled her arm away from me and rolled onto her side.

"Of course I win. I just wanted more of a fight," I said to her as I unwrapped my hands.

"I—"

"Coraline, if you say anything referring to cancer, I will kick your ass....again." I said, as I leaned against the ropes of the ring.

"Okay, *bitch*, I was going say that I haven't had practice in months!" she snapped, without bothering to get up from the ring floor. It was kind of funny.

She looked like a snow angel, or maybe a dead starfish, just lying on the floor, lazily spread out.

"Bitch? You do know—"

"Yes, you are the boss blah, blah, blah. But I'm also your friend and your sister."

"I'm sorry, my friend?"

She pounded the floor beside her, signaling me to lie next to her, but I didn't move.

"Oh come on, you did not summon me for a fight, you wanted to talk. We're family, so let's talk."

Aren't we observant?

"I didn't want to talk, I wanted to see if all the training you received went to your head."

"Excuse me?" She sat up.

"There is a mole in our house, and now I know it cannot possibly be you."

"And how do you know that?" she snapped as she rose from her seated position and wiped the sweat that rolled down the side of her dark-skinned face.

With a grin, I straighten my stance. "First of all, the fact that you're annoyed that I don't think you are a mole is proof enough. Secondly, you gave up and accepted that I'm better. The person who is plotting to take us down believes that they are just as capable as I am. Therefore it's not you. Good talk."

"Mel, you need someone."

"What?" I asked, as I turned back to face her. "I have Liam."

"I mean you need a friend. Adriana—"

"Don't." I never wanted to hear her name again. "She wasn't a friend. She was an employee because I don't do friends, Coraline. I have a husband. I have a son. *They* are the only people I need. I like you, but we are family, not friends."

"Whatever you say, boss. But I'm going to wiggle my way into your heart," she smirked, as she stepped out of the ring. On her way out, she passed Fedel who came in holding the papers I requested.

"Ma'am," he said, as he handed me the folder. "This is all the information we can find on an Avian Doers or De Rosa."

"This is a very thin folder," I muttered, as I quickly flipped through it.

"He must have buried most of his past after gaining citizenship. As Deputy Attorney General, he was the second-highest ranking official in the United States Department of Justice. He was the U.S. Attorney for D.C. prior to becoming Deputy Attorney General, and he helped prosecute the Mancini crime family, which put him on the map. He has been selling out small organization bosses and families for decades."

"So he's a rat with a fancy title." A very smart rat, but a rat nonetheless.

"Make sure Jinx has the jet fueled. After Liam gets the key tomorrow, we're leaving. I want you to stay behind with Coraline and Declan. Kain and Monte are coming with us."

His eyes flashed and his jaw clenched.

"Is there a problem?"

"No, ma'am."

"You're lying."

"Why is Kain here? What purpose does he serve? He has no skills other than punching his fist through a wall," he confessed.

"He will come in handy." I wasn't a hundred percent sure how, but I somehow knew he would. Stepping out of the ring, I walked towards the elevator bank.

As the elevator opened, one of the last people I wanted to talk to stepped out.

"Evelyn."

"Mel."

"Do you need something in the basement?" I asked, as I brushed past her to enter the elevator.

"I wanted to apologize." She stepped back into the metal box with me.

This was unexpected. "What did Liam say to you?"

She crossed her arms as the doors shut. "Why do you believe Liam spoke to me?"

This family was working my last damn nerve.

"Why must you all question why, or how, I know something? It's a waste of time. You aren't fooling me. So either you let me know the truth or walk away...now." I stepped out as the doors opened, she followed.

"You're right, Liam has spoken to me, but that's beside the point. Goddamn it, Mel, I really want to slap the hell out of you sometimes. If someone purposely broke Ethan's heart and then left him in jail for months, how would you feel as his mother? No matter who I was before, he's still my son and he was in pain."

If it were Ethan, I would have—I saw her point.

"Liam and I are heading to D.C. tomorrow. You and Sedric should be ready to accompany us. I want you to be with Ethan whenever we can't be. We've already bought a house." I wanted to turn and leave. However, I didn't. "And Evelyn, I understand. And as long as we don't have this issue again, I'm sure we will be fine. You are my son's only grandmother, he needs you."

These people were making me soft.

LIAM

When I got back to our room, I heard her horrid singing and I couldn't help but smile. She really had no idea that she was doing it or how bad she really was. She always started off with a hum, and then next thing you know, she was wailing like a suffering banshee. Stripping down, I entered the bathroom and watched as the water trailed down her body.

"Are you going to stand there all day, Jinx, or are you coming in?" she asked and I could hear the laughter in her voice.

Stepping in behind her, I grabbed her waist and pulled her against me. I bit her ear, and cupped her pussy with one hand while I grabbed her breast with the other.

"Joke like that again and I will make you regret it." I squeezed her nipple tightly.

"That's what you get, pervert." I could feel her struggling to restrain the moan that was building in her chest. She was pushing me and I knew it, but I couldn't control myself whenever she was in my arms, especially when she was naked and wet.

Turning her around, I pressed her back against the tile wall.

"If you wanted me to fuck you hard, wife, all you had to do was ask. You didn't have to piss me off." Though I knew how much she enjoyed doing that.

"I'm sorry, Liam. Will you please fuck me…hard?" she asked sweetly as the water poured over us.

Grabbing her thighs, I lifted her upwards before taking her lips with my own, I thrust into her until she covered me to the hilt. My tongue brushed against hers, and I felt her rock against me, as her hardened nipples pressed into my chest.

"Oh…" she moaned into my mouth as her hands snaked around my neck and gripped onto my hair.

"How hard are we talking, wife?" I asked, as I slammed deeper and deeper into her.

Her mouth dropped open, and her body shivered in pleasure. As she closed her eyes, as I and thrust inside of her. Pulling me closer to her, she bit my ear.

"Harder," she whispered, as she moved to lick the water that fell from my jaw. I thrust myself into her, and, like always, she anchored herself with my hair. A smile spread over her lips as I kissed her chest and pinched her nipple tightly.

"Harder."

Dear God.

"You're so fucking tight, baby." I bit my lip. It was taking all my strength to not come right then and there. The way she clung on to me, the sounds that slipped out of her mouth…it was all driving me insane.

"Harder!" she gasped out again.

She loved it rough, it was something that I loved about her. Reaching into her hair, I pull her head back and exposed her neck as I nipped and kissed the length of it.

Her legs snaked around my waist, allowing her to maximize each thrust until we both came.

She laughed as the water continued to cascade around us.

"What?" I asked.

"Nothing."

"No. What?" Why was she looking at me like that?

"Nothing." She paused before she started laughing again, knowing full well that I wouldn't drop it until she answered. "I'm happy. Okay, dammit? And I will be happier once we're through with Avian," she muttered and I kissed her cheek and pulled out of her.

After we washed ourselves off, we walked into the bedroom where I handed her the letter from the Warden.

"What's this?" she asked as she unfolded it.

"Read it," I said while drying my hair.

"Dear Mr. Callahan, as per your request I have handwritten this letter. I wish to express my great sadness at your wrongful imprisonment....basically bullshit, bullshit, bullshit. Why am I reading this?"

"Because tomorrow after we get the key to the city, I will ruin both her and that fucked up correctional system she has going."

She didn't look amused. "Really? You're going to tell the city she was *mean*? Seems a little low on the revenge scale."

"Turn on the news," I told her, as I walked towards my dresser and pulled out a pair of boxers. I checked the live feed on the desk, and watched as Ethan slept in his crib, while he quietly sucked on his thumb.

I heard the television power on and turned just in time to see a woman addressing exactly what I wanted Mel to see. Out of all the wardens I had seen in the last five months Dr.

Rachel Alden was by far the one who had angered me the most. Her consistent need to try and tame me like I was her pet monkey had been infuriating to say the least.

"Sources are confirming that the Chicago Police did in fact know of Liam Callahan's innocence. Although details are still pending, it is being speculated that this was a politically charged move against the Callahan Family who have spoken out about their disappointment with the police department. Among the suspected internal players that are being named are; Officer Scooter, who is currently on the run, Captain Joseph Kent, Superintendent Kash, and Dr. Rachel Alden, who is the Warden of the prison where Liam Callahan was held. Dr. Alden has been accused of abuse of power by people other than the Callahan camp. Correction officers who have worked, and are still working at the institution have even admitted that she was particularly interested in Mr. Callahan and often taunted him in his cell. Can you believe it Chris?"

"No. This is ridiculous! It is absolutely ridiculous what this city has done to the Callahans. It's horrendous. These people abuse the power given to them by the citizens of Chicago to bully good, decent people. If I were the Callahans, I would sue the state blind..."

"She's going to go to prison," Mel remarked.

"Do you know what happens to former policemen and officers in prison?"

"But, that's all?" She pouted from her place on the bed.

My wife was *pouting*. With a laugh, I walked over to her and pulled her into my arms. "We can't kill everyone, love. We have bigger fish to fry."

"Yeah, I know. But I still hate them all." She leaned into me as I kissed her neck. "Can you go get Ethan?"

A small part of me wanted to groan, since we've been back and were able to sort out everything between us, Ethan had been sleeping in our bed at night. And as much as I loved my son, I was really hoping to spend a little more alone time with his mother.

"Liam?"

"Yeah, I'll get him," I replied.

Walking out into the hall, I watched as Neal spoke with my father outside of Ethan's room.

"Is everything alright?" I asked, walking up to them both.

"Neal here believes that you're cutting him out of the family," my father answered before stepping inside the room.

Neal rolled his eyes at him before turning to me.

"Is that so?" I hadn't yet, but I was preparing to.

"Private meetings with Declan, I have no idea what's going on, and I'm finding out from the help that you want us to pack for D.C. I'm starting to feel as though you don't trust me with information, brother."

"I don't. But it's not just you, it's everyone. Father had no idea—"

"Father doesn't care to know. He's pulling out of this life and working on his fucking golf swing," he snapped.

I could've told him the truth...but that would have just set him off, and right now we needed fewer cracks in this family's foundation.

Placing my hand on his shoulder, I made him look me in the eyes. "Neal, we have issues, there is no denying that. Declan had some problems and we talked privately. Right now, I'm repairing my inner family. They come first. If it feels like I'm cutting you out, know that I'm not. I'm just dealing with the fall out of Mel's madness. You sound paranoid and I don't like it. People tend to do stupid things when they're paranoid."

He looked at me and sighed, before nodding. "I'm sorry."

"Nothing to be sorry about. I need us all together while we go up against Avian."

He nodded once more. "Of course."

Watching him leave, I once again wondered if he really could betray me. He just didn't have the balls. Or maybe he was a better actor than I thought.

"Dad, you can go to bed," I told him as he leaned down and stared at Ethan.

"I used to enjoy watching you all sleep, you all were a lot less troublesome when you were children."

As I gently lifted Ethan, I smiled at how warm he was; a little bundle of life.

"Be careful, Liam."

"I know how to hold him."

"Not Ethan. But with Neal. Before you and Mel do or say anything reckless, remember he is still your brother and therefore my son. I love him as dearly as I love you. My dream is for you all to depend on each other, not destroy one another," he replied.

"Only time can tell then."

MELODY

The next morning I found myself dressed like a political Barbie doll as I stood on the steps of the capitol, holding onto our son as *Liam* was given the key to the fucking city on behalf of our family. Chicago had no doors, why the fuck did it have a key? But if it had been me, I would've done my part and smiled. It was a pointless show of gratitude, but I would always play my part no matter how badly it irked me. Even Ethan seemed annoyed with his suit. I wasn't even aware that they made suits for infants.

"Words cannot express how much this means to me," Liam said to the crowd. "I have loved this city all my life and that will never change. No matter what has happened in the past, Chicago is my home...our home."

He turned and reached for Ethan and me. I wanted roll my eyes, but I smiled instead as I moved forward. I did not like to be used as a prop.

"Mel and I have thought long and hard about this and we truly want to do more to make this city a great one. While in prison, I was forced to see, hear, and experience things at that no one, not even a prisoner should. Together, let's work to make our community and our political system a better one. Let's treat humans as such. Let's respect life and celebrate it. I thank you for this honor and I hope that in return I can honor you all." He smiled and we posed for photos as the flashbulbs rained upon us.

"Did you forget to tell me you're running for office?" I muttered through a smile.

"I'm just rolling with the punches and I do like getting the key," he whispered as Ethan reached for it. I knew it would only end up in his mouth. It was like he had to lick everything new he encountered.

"Now that this is over, let's get out of here."

"What am I supposed to do? Cut the Governor short so we can escape?" he asked, as he placed his hand on my back and I could feel it starting its downward movement.

"Are you feeling me up in front of the entire city?"

He looked to me and winked. "It's my city. I have a key to prove it."

I couldn't even begin to wrap my head around his ego right now. Holding Ethan to my chest, I walked off the stage as the last of the clapping rang through the air.

Finally.

FOURTEEN

"Presidents are selected, not elected."

—*Franklin D. Roosevelt*

MELODY

We were in Washington.

Not just Washington, but the goddamn White House.

If you could see me now, Orlando. I looked through the windows. I stared at the green garden, fresh cut and perfectly in place; a picture perfect photo, waiting to be taken. Liam leaned into the chair, and placed his feet up on the desk. Neither of us spoke. This was the beginning; once we went down this road, we couldn't turn back.

We waited though we knew it would not be for long.

Within seconds, the door to the Oval Office opened and the President, dressed in a dark suit, blue tie, and an American flag pin on his jacket, walked in. His aids surrounded him, speaking quickly about a Supreme Court nominee before they froze at the sight of us sitting at the Presidential desk.

"Mr. President," Liam stated, his foot still on the desk, completely relaxed.

"Jane, Chris, please give us a moment, and tell Judy to hold all of my calls," Colemen said as he forced a smile at them.

They nodded before running off like the little, dull mice they were.

"Have you lost your minds?" he almost shouted once the door clicked shut.

"Would that make you feel better?" I asked him. I moved from the window and sat at the edge of the desk.

He glared at my ass and then at Liam's feet. "That is the Resolute desk...a gift from Queen Victoria to President Rutherford B. Hayes in 1880. Every President from Jimmy Carter to now has sat at that desk. Will you both please remove your ass and feet from it?"

I looked at Liam who took his feet down and grabbed the knife from his jacket pocket. Without hesitating, he ran the blade across the surface where his feet had been. It was the only thing that cut through the silence, and Liam never once broke eye contact with the leader of the free world. When he was done, he put the knife away.

"Sorry," he said, as he crossed his arms over the top of the desk.

"I am the President!—"

"Oh no, no, no," I cut him off with a finger. "You, are a puppet; our puppet, bought and paid for in full. Made in Chicago for one purpose and one purpose alone—to work for us. That was the deal. You signed your name in blood, and we made you President. Now you need to pay."

He crossed his arms. "I helped you with you cover up. I have the whole nation believing that you're national heroes."

"You think we spent eighty-nine million dollars for *one* favor?" Liam snickered. "We built you, and if you think we didn't install a self-destruct button, you are sorely mistaken. Now that you have tasted power, are you willing to give it up? You can spend the next four, and if we're pleased, eight years as the 'most powerful' man in the world."

Colemen frowned and clenched his jaw. This was the man with his finger on the button? May God help us all.

"What do you want, *Callahan?*" he asked through clenched teeth.

"That's a good puppet," I smiled and Liam snickered once more.

"We want a list of the FBI's biggest pending cases. The ones that make careers and are made into movies," Liam said before rising.

"What for?"

"Bad puppet," I sighed. "Don't ask questions you truly do not want the answer to."

"You are asking me to breach protocol and expose top secret information. But you will not tell me why? These are people's—"

"Stop," Liam said, as he walked to him and held his face. "We know what we're asking. We also know that you're going to come under fire. But you will stand strong and you will put pressure on Avian Doers, your director of FBI, to fix the issues."

"Tell him to fix the issues that you yourself will cause?"

"See, now you know and now you're upset. You should have listened, puppet," I replied, as I moved in front of the desk.

"I'll have the files tomorrow," he said.

I smiled at Liam, and watched as he moved away from Colemen and walked back to the Presidential chair where he once more placed his feet back on top of the desk.

"We have time. I'm sure if you ask nicely, someone will have it to you within the hour. You should really put a computer on this desk, I'm sure Queen Victoria wouldn't mind," Liam added, and this time I chuckled.

I watched as Colemen walked up next to me and lifted the receiver end of the telephone. "Judy, patch me over to the FBI White House Correspondent."

"Best eighty-nine million I've ever spent." I grinned at Liam.

LIAM

We weren't wasting time, simply because we didn't have any more time to waste. I was sure that Avian knew we were here, and I was beyond ready for payback. This was what we needed. So I sat in the booth, and watched as the hooker in the tight, blue dress and fish net stockings, flirted with the undercover agent who was currently ingesting copious amounts of drugs. I should've be insulted by the fact that he didn't notice my beautiful wife, who was pretending to be a bartender. Normally we had people to do this type of work, but this was personal. It needed to done correctly, and the only people who could make sure that would happen was us.

Mel didn't look bad in her red wig and tight-vested shirt, in fact, I would've taken her into the back and have my way with her right that second if I could've, and I briefly wondered how my blond wig and glasses affected her. She glanced at me and winked as though she could read my mind.

The crowded bar smelled like old smokes, stale peanuts, and booze. I watched as Mel mixed drinks with skills I didn't even know she possessed, and the idiot who was supposed to be a federal agent drank them down as he spoke with the hooker.

When Mel was finished, she took a tray of drinks and walked away from the "couple."

"You look like you need a drink," a woman said, as she stepped into my line of sight and blocked my view of Mel. Her breasts were all but falling out of her shirt, and the skirt she wore was so tight it looked as if she needed to piss when she walked.

"I'm fine." I lifted my glass to show her.

"Yes you are, sugar." She licked her lips.

However, her flirtations only last for a moment before Mel was standing before her.

"Leg it babe, he's not on the market, and I'm the last woman you want to piss off," she said, a lot nicer than I'd hoped. But I knew she was just trying to keep from causing a scene. Luckily the woman didn't bother fighting, and she left quickly and smartly.

"I leave you for a few minutes and you're already picking up strays," Mel said, as she took a seat in front of me.

"Next time, don't leave me and we won't have a problem." I winked at her.

She rolled her eyes at me before she looked back at Agent Wilson and his new friend. "How long will this take?" she asked knowing that the faster we got out of here, the better.

"Soon. He's about ready to jump her."

"And you know this how? Because he's leaning in?"

"Because I know the feeling."

She paused and looked to me. "Not in that wig."

"What? I think I look dashing as a blond!"

"You look like the man that mothers warn their children about. I'll keep mine on, but you'd better take yours off if you plan on coming near me later."

I felt a tightening in my pants and I wished that later meant now. "Noted, wife."

She held my gaze for a moment before it once more shifted to the Agent who was had just left with the woman. We waited for a few seconds before we rose and walked out to the back alley where Monte had been waiting. He handed Mel a large bag before he walked down the quiet alleyway to an awaiting car. We both put on our gloves.

As the cold air kissed our faces, I watched as the happy couple skipped across the street to the motel...after all, what good was a seedy bar if there wasn't a trashy motel close by for a quick drunken fuck?

I took out a smoke only to find Mel glaring at me. "What?"

"You've been smoking a lot lately."

Seriously? "It's cold."

"I'm in a vest and a skirt, but you're cold?" she said slowly.

"Since when do you have a problem with me smoking?"

"Since we have a child. I don't want him getting sick. Secondhand smoke kills. But hey, you're cold." She shrugged, and her lips pulled together as she looked towards the motel.

Sighing, I flicked it over to the corner. "You happy now?"

"Ethan's lungs are," she countered, proving once again how easily my emotions could flip with her.

Rolling my eyes, I began to walk towards the motel. "They should be out by now."

"Lead the way," she said.

I was tempted to look both ways before crossing the street just in case. Whenever my wife tells me to "lead the way," I have to make sure I'm not about to get kicked in the face for her amusement.

Pulling the rusted doors open for her, I watched as she raised an eyebrow at me but said nothing before she stepped in.

"Room thirteen," the manager said.

Reaching into my jacket, I pulled out a thick envelope and threw it at him.

"Take it and walk away from this place tomorrow. This motel is going to be closed for a while," she told him, and he nodded greedily.

Obviously the motel business was not going well for him, the flickering lights and water stained ceiling was proof enough. We both walked down the hall until we reached the wooden door with the number three that was hung upside down on a single nail.

"Let the games begin," I said to her as I opened the door, which creaked as we stepped in.

The room glowed in cheap, dull, golden light, and across the room, the couple's clothing lay spread about the floor.

"How much time?"

The woman, who was still awake, lay on the musty bed next to the naked, tattooed man with a horrible farmers' tan. He was so out of it, that no matter how much noise we made, he didn't even stir.

"Five, four, three…" Mel counted down, "…two, one."

Just like that, the hooker fell asleep. Without a word, Mel opened the bag, pulled out Agent Wilson's badge and credentials, and placed them on the floor next to his clothes. Then she took his gun and threw it against the wall before we proceeded to trash the room. Satisfied with our destruction, we planted the cash, cocaine, and heroin all over the room.

She handed me the knife with a smile, as I walked over to the bed and placed it in the agent's left hand. As I suspended his hand above to the woman's chest, I drove the blade into her, stabbing her multiple times until Agent Wilson's body was covered in her blood. The drugs in their system were untraceable, and luckily for the hooker, she never felt a thing. I took her hand and dragged her nails against his arm. That, plus the evidence of their sexual activities provided more than enough physical evidence.

Releasing his hand, it dropped almost lifelessly with the knife still clenched within it. Turning back to Mel, I watched as she looked through the edited files once more before she left them strewn on the ground.

Avian had declared war, and like any war, there would be casualties.

Mel walked out into lobby knowing that there were no cameras on this block, or anywhere else in the hotel for that matter. Then she dialed from the burner phone.

I listened in as the 911 operator answered.

"Hello? Me at the Nomad Inn at 1325 New York Ave, there was much screaming and yell! No sé lo que está pasando!" she said with a thick Spanish accent that was almost flawless.

The operator questioned for more, but Mel hung up without another word.

MELODY

When we both stepped in, newly dressed and wigless. The one person I needed to see was dressed in a darling little onesie, waiting for me.

"You both are spoiling him. He can't sleep without you." Sedric smiled as we walked into the living room of our D.C. home. Walking over to him, I took Ethan into my arms. He sucked on his pacifier before he rested his head against my chest.

"My father said you came to see him today?" Olivia said as she stepped into the living with Neal.

"Yes we did. Did he tell you why?" Liam asked, as he took off his jacket and placed it on the couch.

Olivia shook her head as Evelyn came into the living room with a tray of drinks.

"Why didn't you say you were going to see him? I would've liked to have seen my father and not be stuck here waiting for your orders," Olivia snapped.

"Olivia," Neal whispered, as he pulled her arm.

"No. We were dragged across the country, kept completely in the dark, watching *your* child as you both—"

"Olivia, enough, now," Neal snapped. But she didn't listen. Instead she pulled her hand from his and stomped back to what I could only guess was her room. Neal looked

215

hurt and tired. He was on the edge...but why? Was Liam right? Was he the mole or was he just losing it?

"What's wrong with her?" Sedric asked.

Neal didn't answer him, instead he looked to Liam. "Do you need anything?"

"Yes, you and I will be going for a run in the morning," Liam answered.

I wasn't sure what he was thinking.

Neal nodded, wished us all a good night, and then turned to follow his wife.

"Well, do we get to know what you both have been doing all day? We just got here and you disappeared," Evelyn said as she sipped on her margarita.

Taking Ethan away from the alcohol, I walked around the teal and white couch and turned on the flat screen. Sitting with Ethan, I rocked him in my arms as the breaking news came on.

"Good evening, I'm Andrea Salvia. At this hour, district police have ascended on the Nomad Inn here at 1325 New York Ave just miles away from the capitol. WPLA is coming to you first with this breaking news. Our sources tell us that senior Agent Timothy Wilson of the FBI has been taken into custody for the murder of an unknown woman who was stabbed several times. Also found in the room; over five hundred thousand dollars worth of cocaine and heroin. Our sources also tell us that Agent Timothy Wilson has been undercover for the last six years, trying to cut off the supply of drugs from Mexico. However, it looks like he, as so many other undercover agents, got lost in the life. This is a developing story and we will continue to keep you updated as we get more information."

"I take that back, I don't want to know what you've been up to. Good night," Evelyn said with half a smile before she stood up and turned in.

"I'll be right up." Sedric kissed her cheek before he took a seat in the armchair opposite me.

Ethan's eyes closed while he lay in my arms. He looked so peaceful.

"You're poking a hornet's nest," Sedric said.

"What else can we do when a stick is placed in our hands and a hornet's nest is kicked into our face?" Liam asked him, as he took a seat beside me.

"Just make sure you're—"

"Sedric, we just need you to look after our son while we're gone and show up for photos. That's it. We're not speaking about what we are going to do. Just keep an eye on the news if you're interested." I told him, not caring if it was rude or not.

"I'm getting too old for this shit," he sighed. "When you're both ready to share your plans, know that I will be here."

Liam nodded, as he watched Ethan sleeping in my arms. Sedric got up and walked up the stairs leaving us alone.

"I knew retiring was never going to work for him," Liam sighed, as he sat in the chair and relaxed.

"If the Pope can do it, so can your father. We just have to give him a bone to chew," I replied.

"Our son isn't a big enough job?"

Rolling my eyes at him, I shifted Ethan in my arms as I rose and headed towards our new room. Tomorrow we had another agent to take down. We intended to keep picking them off until the FBI crumbled from the inside out.

FIFTEEN

"Insanity is relative. It depends on who has who locked in what cage."

—Ray Bradbury

NEAL

Stepping out of the closet, I watched while she gazed at the rising sun. She held herself tightly as if she were trying to hold herself together. She hadn't even bothered to get dressed or fix her hair. She just stood there, staring. It was like we were mourning and I didn't even know why.

"Olivia," I called out to her.

She turned around, and looked me over with no emotion on her face.

"Where are you going?" she asked.

"Liam wants to go for a run."

She shook her head before she turned back to face the window. "He calls and you go running like his dog."

"Olivia—"

"You make me sick sometimes, bending over for your little brother, hoping that he'll finally bring you into the fold. When will you get it? He *hates* you. He will never love you. He only puts up with you, with us, because we are 'family.' Sometimes I wish you would be a man. Why is that so hard for you to even attempt?"

My first instinct was to wrap my hands around her neck and twist it off. Instead, I took a deep breath. "Why is it so hard for you to understand that you are not important?" I calmly asked her as I put on my watch.

"Excuse me?" She turned back to me.

"You. Are. Not. Important," I said slowly. "You want me to be a man? From the very moment Mel came into this family, you've been jealous. No, this is beyond jealousy. This is insanity. No matter what you do, you will never be on that level. When will you understand? Why is that so hard for you to get?"

"Screw you and Mel!" she snapped before she stormed off into the bathroom.

Without a word, I walked out the door to find Liam waiting. He looked at me, but said nothing and I wasn't sure whether or not he'd heard us. If he did, he didn't make it obvious. Setting the timer on his watch, we began our silent run outside the door with Monte following close behind.

I had no idea where we were going, but for some reason I wasn't worried. If he was going to kill me, he would've thought of something much more fucked up and intricate than going for a run. Ten minutes later I finally understood; he wanted to race.

"I don't even fucking know where we're going!" I yelled as he sped up.

"Not my fucking problem," he shouted in reply, running faster.

Just as I was about to pass him, the son of a bitch turned the fucking corner and ran on towards the bridge. Unless he planned on jumping off, I knew I could pass him and I did, but he easily came up next me and matched my speed.

From somewhere behind us, Monte passed us both, which caused us to pause for a moment, though we keep jogging in place to keep our legs from tensing up.

"Isn't he your bodyguard?" I asked him.

"Bloody Italians. All of them are out to piss me off," he replied before he sprinted forward, and caught up to Monte. As he passed by, he looked back and glared at Monte, causing the dark haired man to smirk.

Finally we reached the Arlington National Cemetery and Monte fell back. We ran on until Liam stopped at the base of two of the white graves.

'Eli and O'Neal Callahan' the gravestones read and I felt a chill run up my spine.

"Brothers," Liam said. "They were United States military aviators who commanded the "Flying Spades" during World War II."

"Wow." Where had he found this? How had he found this?

"O'Neal killed Eli, he shot his own brother right out of the sky without realizing it. He was later captured and tortured by the enemy, and he died on a rescue mission back home."

"You think I'm going to shoot you out of the sky?" I asked him, as I stared at the graves and he snickered.

"No. This time I'm in the position to clip your wings, brother." He turned to face me and his face was dripping with as much sweat as mine. "I took Declan out for dinner and poisoned him right at the table. I knew without a doubt that he would never betray me, but I still wanted to get my point across. I don't hold that same confidence with you."

Shaking my head, I tried to figure out what to say.

"Liam—"

"No." He cut me off. "You are my brother, despite everything we've been through no matter how much I've threatened or fought with you, my blood is your blood. And no matter what, I would like to say that killing you would bring me dissatisfaction."

"I do not know what I can do to ease—"

"We think that Olivia is a mole," he said, and he might as well have cut me off at the knees.

"Liam…" I couldn't believe what I was hearing. "You think Olivia is feeding information to…that is…that's insane."

"It is either you, or her, or the both of you. So tell me, brother, are you the mole?" he asked and I felt Monte step up behind me.

I stared into his eyes. My little brother, and yet there is nothing small about him. He was like a giant, and for the first time I saw what my father did. How can one person hold so much pride and confidence?

"Are you the mole, brother? Are you the reason why I spent five months away from my son? Why my wife was ripped away from us? Why she spent months running? Tell me right now and it will be clean. One bullet and I will personally bury you."

My mouth dropped open and before I knew it, I answered with more confidence than I knew I had.

He nodded. "Then it's your wife."

"She's my wife," I repeated. Slower, to myself, as I ran my hand through my hair. "You have to give me more proof than that, Liam."

"Think about it, Neal. Think of everything…can you say with a hundred percent certainty that your wife is not a mole?"

I wanted to confidently deny his accusations. I want to tell him that he was insane, that this whole thing was just madness and he and Mel were just paranoid. But I couldn't, and I saw my life with Olivia flash before my eyes. From the moment she first smiled at me to our moment in the bedroom. It was like a silent movie.

"I love her," I whispered to him.

He placed his hand on my shoulder. "I know. Which is why I wanted to tell you. We aren't going to do anything about it right now. Once we confirm it for your sake, we will use her and then we will—I need you not to break under this, brother. We need you. *I* need you. I understand your pain, and I don't say that lightly. Five months in the dark, not knowing whether or not my wife was safe, being away from my family, from my newborn son…believe me, I understand. But we are blood before anything else. This family, our name, is what we fight for. Olivia went against that. She didn't betray just Mel and me. She betrayed Mother, Father, Declan, Coraline and *you*. She betrayed our way of life. I don't want to shoot you out of the sky, not for anything. Not for her."

With that, he and Monte continued their run back, leaving me behind. I stood there for a moment, staring down at the graves. I stayed still for an hour before I walked my sorry ass home. I knew the way, and with each step I remembered how happy Olivia had been when Liam and Mel were gone. She glowed with a radiance that I hadn't seen in years.

She wanted to be important. The final nail that pierced through me came when I finally made it back to our room. I entered to find her sitting on the bed, dressed in black, with her hair curled. And donning her feet were whites shoes. Mel's white shoes…

"I'm so sorry, Neal," she whispered as she came closer to me. "I was just in a bad mood and I just had so much on my mind."

When she reached for me, I backed away.

"I'm all sweaty. We'll talk after I clean up." I kissed her cheek before I retreated into the bathroom.

When had the world changed so much? Had I been asleep the entire time?

Sixteen

"Older men declare war. But it is youth that must fight and die."

—*Herbert Hoover*

MELODY

Sitting on the bed, I brushed Ethan's hair as he lay in between my legs. He was getting so big. Every day he seemed to grow, and so did that grin of his. Every time I looked at him, all I could see was Liam. They looked so much alike, it was as if he'd gotten no physical characteristics from me.

"If you're going to look like him, you're gonna act like me," I whispered down at him, as I gently tapped his little nose. He giggled and tried to grab onto my finger as if it was something he'd never seen before.

"I'm going to teach you how to shoot, and if he ever tells you that he's a better shot than I am, tell me, and I'll show you all the bullet wounds he got from me." I tapped his nose again and this time he laughed loudly.

"When you're old enough to understand, he's going to tell you all these rules that he claims were passed down through his family, but I swear he makes them up as he goes."

He frowned and I would've liked to think that it was because he dreaded having to hear those rules, but I was pretty sure that he only wanted me to push his nose again.

The door to our bedroom opened and Liam leaned against the frame grinning like a loon. I glared at him and picked Ethan up before sitting him on my lap.

"How long were you eavesdropping?"

"Long enough to hear you trying to turn our son against me," he smirked as he walked to us.

"I wasn't turning him against you, I was just making sure that his love was spilt fifty-one—forty-nine."

"Won't work. I'm the cool parent," he replied. And as he bent down to kiss Ethan's forehead, Ethan started to cry.

"I can feel the good times coming," I laughed, as I pulled him back. Liam looked so confused that it was almost sad, but he should have known better, Ethan loved Liam, if only to pull on his hair. "You stink, babe, try again after a shower."

He sniffs his shirt. "Ah, no wonder he's in tears."

"Yeah, that's the reason," I replied sarcastically. And as he took off his shirt, I found myself fighting the urge to look at his chest...but I lost and caught myself gawking like a teenager.

"See something you like?" Liam asked, as he gazed down at himself before meeting my eyes.

"I'm free to look at what I own."

"Remember that when I repeat the sentiment." He dropped his pants and boxers.

Biting my tongue, I walked to the door with Ethan. "We need to be ready in an hour. How was the run?"

He grabbed another towel from the closet. "It went as well as it could have gone."

"Neal returned an hour ago."

"Yeah. I chose to keep running with Monte."

I nodded but I didn't press him for more. Neal knew he had a choice to make. Hopefully the gravestones would haunt him, they were fake, no one knew that but Liam and myself, but the point remained the same. No matter how Liam felt about Neal, I knew he didn't want to kill him.

I walked into the room we'd been using as a nursery here in D.C., and I saw Sedric and Evelyn standing by the window speaking quietly to each other. They looked like teenagers sneaking around.

"Am I interrupting?" I asked them.

"Yes, but since you brought Ethan, we shall forgive you." Evelyn grinned as she came towards us with open arms.

Kissing Ethan's head, I placed him in her arms.

"Do you want a bath?" she asked, as she bounced him up and down while they walked off towards the bathroom.

"He's already been changed," I said to her.

"But you want a bath. Don't you, Ethan?" She grinned and I rolled my eyes and watched as they disappeared.

"She's been waiting for a grandchild forever. Let her have her fun," Sedric said and smiled, as he leaned against the window.

"Well as long as she's having fun," I replied, moving towards him. "How are you enjoying the role of babysitter?"

"I was enjoying it a lot more before you labeled it. I've taken up a few new hobbies, why does the Great Melody wish to know?"

"Idle hands are the devil's play tool."

He perked up slightly, as if he were waiting for the bone I was throwing his way. I gazed out the window and stared at the Washington Monument that stood in the distance.

"Do you plan to keep me in suspense for long?"

Giving him my attention, I sighed. "I need you to create different identities for us."

"Don't you have those already?" He frowned.

"We do, but I need them to cover every angle. Birth records, passports, taxes, education, yearbooks, I need you to build us eight brand new lives."

"You mean nine, including Ethan."

"No, eight, including Ethan. Maybe even seven, but for now eight."

He stared into my eyes and I didn't flinch.

"Olivia and Neal—"

"Have a choice."

"Do you really believe new IDs will be needed?"

"I don't know. But I'd rather be safe than ignorant to the facts. Avian is different. If anything happens, I want to have my bases covered."

"Fine. I'll get working on it, but it will take time."

"That's why I'm telling you now. And Sedric, don't allow anyone to find out you're doing this, not even Evelyn. Not even Liam knows what I'm asking of you. I don't want him thinking that I doubt us."

He nodded as the door opened and Liam walked in dressed in jeans and a button down shirt with a bag over his shoulder.

"You both look suspicious," he said tentatively.

"They do, don't they," Evelyn stated, as she stepped in with a sleepy looking Ethan in her arms. Liam kissed his head and this time he didn't cry but yawned instead.

"We have a meeting to get to," I said, and Liam nodded.

LIAM

"**N**ame?" a blond-haired bodyguard asked as he blocked our path into the mansion with his hands.

For it being so early in the day, you would think there wouldn't be so many people already here, but that didn't seem to be the case. Nothing got people going more than a millionaire throwing a pool party.

Pushing the glasses up my fake nose, I looked to Mel as she clenched her hand in annoyance, the short hair of her wig blew slightly to the side. She wore a short, red beach dress that had already caught the attention of a few men lingering around the property. The music was so loud it seemed to make the closed doors vibrate from outside.

"We're the tax collectors," I said, and the big man looked to the second guard in confusion.

"We've already paid the tax. I know this because I personally paid it myself," he sneered as he eyed us both.

"You're nothing but a doorman."

"Fuck you. You got ten seconds to get out of here before I put a bullet in the two of yah."

"I think you should let us talk to someone a little higher up on the food chain," Mel replied and he sucked his teeth in response.

"Let them through, Bell," the second guard said as he subtly moved his blazer to make us fully aware of the gun at his waistline.

"Bell? Like Tinker Bell? Isn't that cute," I mocked, brushing past his shoulders as we moved up the stairs.

"You better pray you are who you say you are, or I will personally kill you slowly," he snapped as he led the way. None of the guests paid us any mind as we entered. They were all too busy drinking and groping each other to care. The only ones who focused on us were the guards; they stuck out like the secret service in a kindergarten classroom. The man we wanted to speak with sat under a beach canopy with three women, all of whom were preoccupied with kissing and touching his body.

I hated meeting dealers.

They were a necessary evil that I found myself getting rid of more often than not. He didn't pay any attention to us and instead chose to slobber all over the women around him. Mel took the chilled bottle of champagne and poured it over the girls

"You bitch!" they screamed, as two of the guards came forward.

"Move another inch and you will be face down in that pool," I stated and he froze as a red dot appeared in the center of his chest.

"We don't want to make a scene, Gus. This is an amazing party. But we can and will if we have to," Mel said as she took a seat on the lawn chair and crossed her legs.

He clenched his jaw, making the scar on it quite prominent. "Go, now."

The women glared at us as they staggered away.

"We paid the bosses our fucking share already." He spat off to the side. "And you two ain't the normal collectors."

"About that, we aren't really collectors," I said eying Gus as he sat up.

His guards circled in behind us while Bell began to smile like an idiot. This was why I hated wasting my time with the footmen, they were always a bunch of trigger-happy morons. "What are you going to do? Shoot us? Make a scene and have the cops show up, because we both know they've been gunning for you for months now."

"You gotta be a special type of stupid to crash my fucking party like this." His jaw clenched as he poured himself a glass of champagne.

"It was either we crash it now or the FBI crash it later." Mel smiled and I knew that smile well. We're going to have to find ourselves another dealer in the district.

"What the fuck is that supposed to mean?"

Mel leaned forward. "I'll use small words since you're incapable of comprehending; you have a rat, and not just any rat, but a fed."

He sat still, staring at us for a moment before he put his glass down on the table beside him.

"Who is it?"

"Would you like the honor Tinker Bell? Or should I?" I said as I looked to him.

He froze for a moment before snapping. "They're out of their fucking minds, sir! We don't even know who these motherfuckers are—!"

"Dear God, stop yelling," Mel held her fingers to her ears. "This can be proven quite easily, just check your email Gus."

He took his phone out and scrolled through his emails, reading the files that the FBI had tried to hide, even that of Tinker Bell's family. The family no one knew of; two little girls and a pregnant wife.

Three.

Two.

One.

"You bastard!" Gus screeched as he lunged for him.

Before he could reach him, Tinker Bell tried to make a run for it. It was pathetic attempt. I thought he would have gone down with more honor than that. Holding on to his arms, the guards pulled him back to Gus. He struggled but it didn't matter.

"You're going to wish you were dead by the time I'm through with you."

"Actually," Mel said as she rose from her chair, "we would like the pleasure of getting rid of him."

"Why? What the fuck do you want with him?"

"Let's just say our bosses want to make an example out of him. But don't worry, you will have proof that he's gone," I stated.

Mel clapped as she turned to look at his men. "Now which one of you gentlemen would like to escort our prize to the car?"

"What makes you think I'm just going to hand him over so quickly?" Gus was thinking a bit too much.

"Because if you don't, every one of your consumers will think that you've been working with the FBI and so will your bosses. So tell me, does Tinker Bell really mean that much to you?" I asked him.

He swallowed and shook his head. "Just bring me the proof."

"We said you were going to get it and you will. Word of advice though; start looking for a new city. I'm sure Agent Tyson has already told them more than enough to put you away for life." I stood in front of the man who held his head high as if he had not just tried to run like the little bitch he was.

"We were going to kill you quickly, but then you threatened us."

"Bye, Gus."

Mel and I walk away as his men dragged out the agent. The great thing about Gus' parties was the fact that drugs were so rampant that almost everyone there was high on something. None of them cared that we're dragging a reluctant man through the house. They were in their own personal high.

People were selfish and self-serving. They were ruthless and didn't even know it.

MELODY

"Liam, he's dead, you can stop now," I said as I leaned against the rails of the Theodore Roosevelt Bridge. The bridge had been shut down so there was no chance of anyone driving across it. All we needed were police officers at both ends to let the motorists know that the bridge was closed. The D.C. police were harder to pay off than the Chicago police, but not by much.

Liam had beaten into Tinker Bell's face so badly that both his eyes were swollen shut. We knew he hadn't known much, but we didn't expect him to be so clueless. He had been undercover for eight months, most likely waiting for Gus to refer to the Callahan family. But our name was never openly mentioned. We referred to ourselves as the bosses, and all those who communicated directly with the dealers were simply referred to as "tax collectors."

"Kill joy," Liam muttered, as I pulled out the man's badge along with a note that read "Rat." I placed both items over Agent Tyson's head.

Taking the rope, Liam wrapped it around Tyson's neck before he tied the other end to the rails. Then we picked him up and threw him over and watched as his body-weight pulled the rope taut. He bounced and jerked like a marionette before going still. His body swung and turned as the winds blew.

"Someone's going to make the evening news," Liam whispered.

"All in a day's work, the second agent to fuck up in as many days. Avian will have his confirmation." I smiled. There was no way he could stop us without knowing who we were going to go after next. Colemen had given us a list of names that spanned across the country. The next person was going to be taken care of by Coraline and Declan in Chicago.

Walking to the car, Liam opened the door for me and we both took a seat. We drove across the bridge and the police left without another word. I waited until we were a few miles from the bridge before I turned to him.

"Do you trust them?"

"Not even the slightest." He smirked and slowed down as the cop in front of us sped forward.

I sighed. "Neither do I."

Taking out the burner phone, I dialed, and as people began to honk at us, the police car went up in flames.

"None of them are in any rush now," Liam muttered as he looked into the rearview mirror. A few who stepped out were rapidly speaking on their cell phones.

"Well, I am, let's go home."

"We have dinner reservations," he replied as he pulled off his fake nose and edged the car forward.

I turned so fast that my head snapped. "You're joking," I glared at him.

"You agreed."

"Now is hardly the time."

"Is there any better time?"

Crossing my arms, I leaned back and refused to speak to him. It felt kind of childish, but I didn't care. Liam, much to my annoyance, placed his hand on my thigh, forcing me to look back at him.

"I enjoy going on the dates with you, Mel. They make me feel like we met normally and I swept you off your feet."

"Swept me off my feet? Is there a reason why I can't walk?" I asked him smiling.

He rolled his eyes. "I've never met a woman so opposed to romance in my whole life." He shook his head, and looked out the windshield.

"You have to admit, I'm getting better. One day I may even ask for flowers." The moment I said it I laughed, causing him to frown. This time I placed my hand on his thigh. "Liam, my definition of romance isn't chocolate, flowers and dates...but if you're dying to get me to some restaurant, fine. Go crazy."

He snickered. "Oh I have, baby, I have. You might want to take that wig off."

I eyed him carefully before I took off my wig and pulled the pins out of my hair.

"What are you planning, Callahan?"

He said nothing, as we pulled up to a designer boutique and an older man came to the door, and held it open for me.

"Welcome to the Louvre, Mrs. Callahan," the man said to me, as he helped me out of the car.

I remained silent as Liam exited the car and came around to meet me. One of the valets made a move to park the car, however Monte, who I had not seen until that moment, came around and stepped into the driver's seat.

Liam led me into a store filled with luxury dresses, marble white floors, and antique furniture. Three women, dressed in black, stood waiting. One of them had a make-up belt and a curling iron.

"A make over? If you had told me, I would have gotten dress—"

"Ladies, do not pay any mind to her. She's in your hands."

Liam ignored me before he excused himself and stepped into another room, which was presumably the men's section of the boutique.

"Right this way, Mrs. Callahan. Would you like some champagne?" the smiley woman in black asked, as she placed her bony hand on my arm.

I felt my eyebrow twitch at her touch. "I prefer red wine."

"Mr. Callahan said you would," another woman added, as she handed me a glass. I glared at the section Liam had disappeared into as the women led me into the dressing room and offered me a seat.

Do not make a scene. Do not kill.

"We're going to pull out some dresses, just let us know if anything catches your eye; nothing is off limits," bony hands said with a grin so wide that her face looked as though it was about to crack.

I wonder how much she's making on commission.

"How can I pick a dress if I have no idea where I'm wearing it to?" I asked them as I sipped my drink. The moment I did, I paused; it was my favorite wine.

How the hell did he plan all of this?

We had ten billion things to do, and he had me shopping.

"Don't worry, Mrs. Callahan, your husband told us everything and all the choices will work perfectly for the night."

"He told you everything? Good. Where are we going?"

She giggled, not at all realizing how serious I was. "We can't tell you and you might as well stop asking because you won't get anything from us."

So you think.

Off the top of my head, I could think of at least six different ways to get her talking, four of which involved dismemberment of some sort.

My phone buzzed and I grabbed it to find a text from Liam.

"Be nice. Or have you lost your touch? The woman I married could fool angels into believing she was one of them."

He was taunting me, knowing full well that I would prove to him that nothing had changed. He'd been able to play me like a violin. Since when did he get to know me so well?

With a sigh I sat back and gave them a brilliant smile. "Fine. You win. Dazzle me."

"Great!" They clapped. "The first dress I have for you is a black and gold Dolce and Gabbana piece."

I look it over and frowned; "It's pretty, but I don't have the figure for it."

"Oh, Mrs. Callahan, you're beautiful!" They gushed as I rolled my eyes.

There was nothing a woman liked more than making another woman feel better after she'd put herself down.

LIAM

I stepped out, and pulled on my sleeves as Mel came in wearing a tight, black dress. Her hair was down and curled, her make-up was done naturally, and her eyes shone. She was stunningly beautiful.

"You clean up nicely," she said to me as she walked forward.

I pulled her to me, and kissed her as hard as possible. In response, she wrapped her arms around my neck, and moaned.

"We have to go or you're going to make us late," I whispered, as I broke away from her hold.

"It's hard for me to keep track of time if I don't know where we're going."

"Patience is a virtue."

She leaned into me and kissed my lips. "Who ever said I was virtuous?"

With a groan, I once more forced myself to pull away before I took her hand and walked out of the store. There, both Kain and Monte stood, dressed in suits before the new black car.

Mel turned to me, mouth slightly open before she turned to address them.

"Tell her nothing," I said quickly before they caved under her orders.

She stayed quiet, and entered the car. I knew she was getting frustrated and it amused me. She hated this type of attention, simply because she wasn't in control. God forbid anyone ever surprised her. But thankfully, it was a short ride to the where we were going.

For the last few days, we had been getting our hands dirty, it was only right that today of all days we enjoyed the brief time we had together.

I pulled out the box and waited as she all but pressed her face against the window and stared at the building ahead.

"The John F. Kennedy Center for the Performing Arts? Liam, what—" she turned to me, then stopped short as she stared at the box in my hand. With a sigh, she stared into my eyes. "When I said go crazy, I did not truly mean to go insane, Liam," she whispered.

"You can't take it back, now open it."

She didn't, so I opened it for her.

She stared at the diamond bracelet for a moment before turning her furious gaze to me.

"You cheated on me, didn't you?"

I coughed while the men up front both snickered. Glaring at them both, they caught my furious gaze in the rearview mirror and immediately silenced themselves. Turning back to her I smirked. "Really, that's the best you can think of?"

She frowned. "Thank you for the bracelet, the dress, the shoes, the wine, and I'm guessing that this is an opera?"

"Yes. Bianca e Falliero by Felice Romani. But before that, the symphony will play a piece written solely for you." I smiled as her eyes widen slightly.

"You had a symphony composed for me? As in symphony orchestra?" she asked slowly. "I may not be used to this dating thing, but don't most guys just write a song?"

I wonder where she got that idea from.

"Would you have married me if I were most guys?"

The look on her face right now...

"Liam, for a simple date, you're going above and beyond. How did you even know that Bianca e Falliero was my favorite?"

"Jinx." I frowned at the thought. "And it's not a simple date."

"I knew it. What's going on, is there someone in there that we need to get rid of? I don't remember any—"

Taking her hand in my own, I pulled her to me, and pressed my lips against hers hard and fast. I could taste her, and at this point she wouldn't have any lipstick left before we started our date.

"This isn't a hit, it's a date, our date. After all, it is *our anniversary*," I whispered only inches from her lips.

Her mouth dropped open and it looked as though she was going over every moment we had ever shared together. She glanced at the dress and then at the bracelet that still lay nestled in the velvet box in her hand.

"Now I feel like a bitch."

"You are, but it's a part of your charm." I smiled as I took the box out of her hands and snapped the heavy jewelry around her wrist.

She brushed her hand through my hair. "I forgot, I've been so worried about Avian."

"I know," I whispered. "We *will* get him. I swear. But he can't take over our entire life. All work and no play is not healthy for us Irish, and it's considered a sin for you Italians."

Kain opened the door for us and stood waiting as we climbed out. Stepping past me, Mel turned and shot me a wicked grin. "The faster we get through this, the quicker I can give you my gift," she said before she disappeared into the crowd that stood in front of the center.

Playing with her was my favorite pasttime.

SEVENTEEN

*"I thought we were celebrating being richer
and cleverer than everyone else!"*

—*Scott Lynch*

LIAM

Before the opera started I took my beautiful wife to listen to her symphony, simply titled *A Symphony for Melody*. We sat alone in our private box, since the opera house had been closed off to everyone else. The piece started off strong, then it melted into a soft, almost broken tune, and returned with an even stronger closing...just like stages of our life together.

She'd said nothing throughout the piece, but she openly held my hand as we walked out into the gallery. There was to be a pre-opera celebration that was being held for everyone who had their opera tickets, and it soon seemed like it was a who's who of Washington's most powerful in attendance. The entire top level of the building was just one grand ballroom, and it seemed as though Mel and I were the main attraction.

Had I known this would be the case, I would've made sure that our entrance was inconspicuous. I didn't even truly want be here; I'd only wanted some alone time with her. Instead, we had to spend our time faking it all night for these people.

"Mr. Callahan, it's about time you made it to Washington," Senator Andrew Kelly, of Texas stated. He worked with big oil and some other shit he kept mouthing off about.

"I never knew I was wanted here."

"Mr. Callahan, we all know that if it weren't for your generous donations to President Colemen, he wouldn't be in the big office," Senator Jeffrey Boxer, of North Carolina, replied, and I fought the urge the roll my eyes.

"Generous donations? I have no idea what you mean. After all, isn't that the purpose of super PACs?" I winked, and they all laughed as they ate out of the palm of my hand even though I was feeding them shit.

"Well, you should know, if you ever need anything, we can work something out. We know your marijuana businesses are making significant progress, but there's still some red tape to cross to get your ventures off the ground," Senator Kelly stated as his fat chest puffed out.

I raised an eyebrow at him. "I'm not sure if your constituents are in favor of my new business ventures."

Boxer snorted, as he rolled his eyes and looked around the grand ballroom. "You and I both know that the kingmakers are all here. We can pretend that democracy truly means what the people want it to, but it's about survival, about triumph. And no man embodies that as much as you do."

Politicians were a different breed of ruthless, a dirtier kind.

"You're quite correct, Senator, but before I sign my soul away, I should speak with my beautiful wife," I replied and they all laughed once more before turning to the women who were socializing with my wife.

It was petrifying how well she was able to fit in with the Stepford wives of these men; drinking champagne and probably talking about nothing more than how much of their husband's money they could spend.

"May I say, you have an impeccable wife, Mr. Callahan," Senator Kelly added, brownnosing like the scum he was.

No, you may not.

"I am truly lucky."

"The President is awarding you both with honors this Friday, isn't he?" Senator Boxer asked.

"Apparently getting arrested gets you a medal," I joked, and once again they all laughed. No wonder these people had big egos, they all laughed with each other no matter what was being said.

"Oh, do not be so humble, Mr. Callahan," a smooth and older voice spoke out, as the man I hated more than the devil himself stepped forward.

From his salt and pepper hair, to his wrinkled face and proud stance, all of which were wrapped up in a black and white designer suit…I hated everything about him.

"Avian, you've come down from Mount Olympus? How is life among us mere mortals?" Senator Kelly asked and as he gave him a short bow. I had forgotten that to the rest of the world, he was simply known as Avian Doers and not Ivan DeRosa. The web of lies surrounding this man were deeply rooted.

"Amusing as always, Andrew." He smiled and looked to me, as he extended his hand for me to shake. "Mr. Callahan, it is a pleasure to finally meet you."

I shook his hand tightly. "Of course, Mr. Doers. Who would have guessed you would be a fan of the opera."

"It is a great passion of mine," he stated with a glint in his eyes.

"Gentleman, I do hope I'm not interrupting." Mel walked up behind the snake. Even with the smile on her face I could see the fire burning in her eyes as she stared at him.

He turned and allowed her into the circle. "Gentlemen? Mrs. Callahan, you must be mistaken; we do not have a gentle bone within our bodies."

"Ouch, Avian, we're right here. No need to scare the lady," Senator Boxer said as he laughed, not at all understanding the battle that was being played here.

Mel just smiled. "I do not scare easily, Senator. Do you mind if I steal my husband?"

"Actually, Mrs. Callahan, I've been dying to have a dance. May I?" Avian asked.

Mel's eyes shot to my own before she offered her hand. I didn't like this, but she would kill me if I denied her this moment. As if the fiend could read my mind, he turned to me.

"You do not mind, do you, Mr. Callahan? I am aware that this is your anniversary."

Bastard.

"Of course not, I have a lifetime with her. I'm sure I can spare three minutes. But I would watch your feet if I were you, those heels of hers are a killer." I pretended to joke, and I managed to gather a few more laughs from the peanut gallery around me.

"I'm not as bad as he makes me out to be," she responded, as she held his hand. I'm not sure if it made me feel better or worse to know that he was actually her grandfather.

"It's a good thing I have lead feet then," Avian stated as he led her out onto the dance floor and I instinctively scanned the room. Of course there were secret service agents everywhere. I wanted to snap his neck right off his body, but there was nothing I could do but watch from the sidelines. If he made one wrong move, I would kill him. I didn't mind going back to jail if it meant that he would be six feet under. But I was sure Mel would kick my ass.

"It seems you have competition," Senator Kelly tried to joke, elbowing me in the arm.

"Not even a little bit," I told them. "I always win gentlemen. Even if it looks like I'm losing, I'm winning."

"And that works how?" They laughed.

If you have to ask, then you don't have the ability to comprehend.

MELODY

I shivered at his touch, and not in a good way.

"What do you prefer—Avian, Ivan, or Grandfather?" I sneered, as I tried to keep as much space between as possible without looking odd.

He frowned with absolute disgust. "Anything but *grandfather*. I'm hardly old enough."

"You can dye your hair as much as you please, but you can't hide the wrinkles," I said with a smile so fake it was pitiful.

He laughed. "You're funnier than I thought you'd be. I'm sure that's a trait you got from that imprudent father of yours."

I wanted to drive my heel into his shin, but I knew that it was what he wanted; to rile me up.

"I'm sure your daughter was more humorous than you gave her credit for. But then again, you twisted her mind until she was so unstable, she resorted to kidnapping me for my own protection."

"She was always a little loose in the head. I'm sure your father locking her away for years to care for you didn't help the situation any," he said with no regard.

"My father is already dead, Avian, you can stop trying to kill him," I snapped, wanting more than anything to end him now.

254

He spun me and when he brought me back, he shook his head. "As long as you're alive, your father's only, beloved child, then he still lives."

"I am as much of his blood as I am yours. You're just too arrogant and cold blooded to get it. I have the mind to kill you where you stand."

"We both know why you won't; because you or I will need to walk away. And when I kill you, there will be nothing that ties it to me, so that I can return to a time when you weren't such a pain in my ass," he said.

He was correct, but he didn't know a fucking thing about me.

"Let's say you do win, and that you do beat Liam and me, which you won't, what becomes of you then? You'll have no family, nothing. You'll just die."

He laughed and that grin of his drove me mad. "Who needs family when you have the world? You're so weak, so reckless. Aviela spoke of you as if you were a force to be reckoned with, but I know now she was as foolish as she was insane. Family means nothing. Look around this room, all of them, each and every last one of them holds me in the highest regard. When I die, it will not be at your tiny hands. The world will mourn my passing. People will come from all over to speak of me in ways no family ever could. Unlike you and your mutt of a husband, I rule without getting my hands dirty."

This time I laughed. "Without getting your hands dirty? Really? These people don't know you. You say I'm reckless? The moment we killed Aro, you could have walked away."

"There's a balance little girl," he snapped as his dull, brown eyes sharpened. "We will never get drugs off the streets, but there will not be one family controlling it all.

Icarus flew too close to sun and perished, don't make that same mistake. Take your precious family and disappear. I'll even let you keep all your wealth."

"I am a liar, Avian, which means I can spot another liar a mile away. You can take your half-assed deal and shove it up your ass, because even if I were blind, dumb, deaf, and gasping for breath on my deathbed, I'd still tell you to go fuck yourself."

"May I cut in?" Liam asked coming up from behind me. I let go of Avian as if he had shocked me.

"Please," I said to Liam, without taking my eyes off Avian. "Oh and by the way, Icarus burned because he flew during the day. He wanted the world to see. We fly in the darkness, where people are afraid to look."

Liam took my hand and we walked away, leaving him standing there.

"Do you want to leave?" he whispered as he led us away from the doors, I shook my head.

"Not even a little bit, you planned this night and we are going to enjoy it, even with that bastard here. We aren't running, not now, not fucking ever," I muttered.

He nodded and drew in a deep breath. "So much for a happy anniversary."

Squeezing his hand, I said nothing more. I wasn't sure what to say, he'd gone through so much just to make this night special, and it had been nice. In fact, until we saw Avian, I was having a decent time. Not with the women I'd been talking to of course, but with playing cat and mouse with Liam. Every once in a while, he would look at me and I could feel it. I had to fight the urge to look back at him.

Finding our private box, we sat in a room across the opera house, and from Avian, allowing us to see into his booth.

"You both looked as if you were having a heated conversation," Liam whispered to me as the lights went down.

"It was nothing useful, he was just trying to fuck with my head."

"Did it work?"

I bit my tongue and leaned into the chair. "He took jabs at my father, and despite our issues, I loved Orlando. He made me into what I needed to be and never once held back. Avian is just as responsible for his death as Aviela was."

"So it worked."

"No. He simply pissed me off."

"You and me both. I don't think it's a coincidence that he knew we were going to this opera tonight."

"Olivia?" I asked, as I turned to him but he simply shrugged.

"I'm not sure, I told no one, but it still doesn't sit well with me," he replied as he leaned into his chair as well.

"Did they find Tinker Bell's body?" I'd almost forgotten all about our last agent. Avian may have finally gotten the message.

He nodded. "They found him. My father emailed me. I'm sure Avian knows."

"He looked completely at ease." And that pissed me off even more. He was just sitting there, enjoying my favorite opera as though he had no care in the world.

"I guess we need to turn up the heat," Liam muttered, as he pulled out his phone. He discreetly snapped a picture before he began typing. "We need to take care of another agent by morning and have someone question why the director of the FBI is watching an opera with Washington's finest when his agents are dropping like flies."

"If there was anything I learned from our talk it's that he cares about his name, his legacy." It was what he lived for. He wanted crowds to speak in his honor. I was going to make sure that there wasn't enough of him to be buried.

We both stilled and Liam shot me a glance without moving his head as we heard the ever so slight click of the door.

Someone was coming.

"I'm not sure why you enjoy this opera so much," Liam said in a higher whisper than before, to make it seem as though we had not heard them.

"Of course you don't, you wouldn't know good taste if it smacked you across the face," I replied, as I felt and heard the shift in the pressure of the floor underneath us.

Before either of us could speak, two people dressed in black had rags over our mouth.

Ether.

I held my breath and relaxed.

"Subjects secure," the man said before releasing my face. I felt them drag me out of the room. I couldn't hear Liam and I didn't dare to look until I felt a change in the lighting.

Four.

Three.

Two.

One.

My eyes snapped open the moment I heard the door click. I scratched my assailant's arm as I ripped myself away from him. Liam did the same and once he was free, he took the man into his arms and snapped his neck with ease. The man before me threw a punch much slower than what I would have expected from a trained agent. I punched him square in the jaw not once, but twice, in succession. Kicking him in the knee, I watched him fall as I pulled my gloves off and wrapped it around his neck, pulling as tightly as possible until his body went limp.

"Where the fuck are Monte and Kain?" Liam snapped, as he wiped the blood from his lip.

I patted the man down and found nothing but a gun.

"They were his men. So much for getting away clean," I muttered.

We both froze when we heard the police sirens outside.

"The motherfucking bastard!" Liam yelled.

"Liam, we need to get rid of them now," I snapped. "Avian knew we weren't going to be taken down so easily, he set us up. We need to get rid of them and fast."

To prove my point, the police started pouring in from below like a swarm of bees. I watched as his nose flared and he grabbed an agent by the legs as I did the same.

"Do you know the layout of the opera house?"

"Yes, Mel, I know where every hidden door is to a random opera house in Washington," he barked sarcastically.

I said nothing, there was no point. He was pissed off, and so was I, but one of us needed to be level-headed. I felt my pulse quicken as I pulled the man over the red and gold accented carpet.

"Clear the building, keep everyone calm!" an officer yelled.

We couldn't see them but we knew they were close by.

"Check everywhere for the gunmen!" another yelled behind us.

"Shit!" *Gunmen? What gunmen?*

"Mel," Liam nodded over to door.

"It's a closet," I told him.

"We don't have choice," he said as he opened the door and dragged the man in. I followed him in and Liam closed the door as I pushed their bodies into the corner. Grabbing a few of the coats, I threw them over the bodies.

"Are you armed?" Liam asked quickly.

Lifting up the skirts of my dress, I showed him the guns strapped to my upper thighs. "When am I not?"

He shook his head and snickered as he pressed his ears against the door. Coming up next to him, I listened as well.

"Your grandfather is a son of a fucking bitch," he whispered.

"Yes, I know, thank you."

"Just saying what we're both thinking—"

I placed my finger on his when I heard the police behind the door.

"They're coming," Liam said as he reached for his gun but I stopped him, we were not doing this. We were not going to blow all of our hard work in a single moment.

Pushing down the front of my dress, I gave him a better view of my cleavage before lifting up my dress.

"What the hell are you doing?"

"Kiss me."

"What—?" I pulled him to me, and hopped up until my legs were wrapped around his waist. He held onto me, and as he ran his hands through my hair just as the door opened.

"Get out, now!" an officer yelled as I unwrapped myself from him, and tried to fix my dress before we exited.

"What's going on?" I gasped, pretending to be frightened.

"Mr. and Mrs. Callahan?" one of the cops asked. "Have you been in this closet long?"

"Yes, Officer, is everything alright? What's going on?" Liam answered, as he fixed his bow tie. He spoke with an authority that they were familiar with.

The officer stood straighter. "Mr. Callahan, we got reports of shots being fired on the grounds, we will have an officer escort you out."

"Thank you!" I said quickly, as they led us from the hall. I looked back, watching as the closet door closed and the police ran past it.

I shivered at the cold when we made it out into the streets that were crawling with cops and fire trucks.

"Liam," I whispered, drawing his attention to Avian as he entered his private car. I took pleasure in the slight annoyance on his face before it returned to the cool and collected facade he usually portrayed.

Monte and Kain were both standing beside the car, and I could feel Liam stiffening in anger. *Where the fuck had they been?*

"Boss, two men came towards the room with guns. We didn't fire, but they did," Monte said quickly.

"But it was as if they weren't even trying to hit us, they were just firing," Kain added just as quickly.

"That's because they wanted to draw you away!" Liam snapped, and I pulled him back. "Why didn't you contact us?"

"We tried calling, but the phones had been jammed."

Liam turned to me. "Son of a bitch."

"Have the clean-up crew here take care of the bodies in the closet upstairs. They're under some coats. I want it done fast," I commanded before we entered the car.

LIAM

I lay on the bed with Ethan on my chest. I had my hand on his back and I watched as he breathed in and out slowly as his thumb slid into his mouth. He was the only thing that was keeping me calm right now.

Mel came over and sat on her side of the bed while flipping through the list of agents Colemen had given to us.

"This one, Agent Autumn Smith, she's based in Chicago, she has similar physical attributes as Coraline."

"Do you think Declan and Coraline can do it? I want no mistakes." The truth was that I didn't trust either of them to get it done without problems.

"They don't have a choice," she replied already dialing.

Declan answered on the first ring.

"And here I thought you'd forgotten about us."

"We have a job for you," Mel stated softly getting off the bed so as to not wake Ethan.

"This sounds serious."

"We have an agent we need you and Coraline to get rid of. I'll have the info sent to you." Mel replied, already sending it through our email.

"You want *Coraline* and me—"

"To kill the agent, and we don't want any mistakes."

"Mel, whatever it is, I can do it with Fedel. I don't want to put this type of pressure of Coraline."

"We're under attack, Declan, everyone has to step up, including your wife," Mel reminded him.

"How—"

Mel hung up before he could speak again.

"That was rude."

"He'll live."

"If he doesn't fuck up." And he'd better not.

Eighteen

"Sex and violence: the greatest duo since the Three Stooges."
—*Jarod Kintz*

CORALINE

"Hello, Neal?" I answered my phone at the top of the stairs.

"Coraline..." he said with a drawn out sigh.

"Neal, what's wrong?"

"Everything, Cora," he snorted just before laughing.

Walking into the nearest sitting room, I moved as far from the door as possible and found myself standing near Evelyn's Piet Mondrian painting over the fireplace.

"Neal, are you drunk?"

"I'm Irish love, I don't get drunk."

Rolling my eyes, I sighed. "What happened, Neal?"

"You know, when Declan told us he was going to marry you, I was shit faced. I couldn't believe it. You were so different from all the other girls he'd dated before. I gave you both a year."

"Well, I didn't like your ass either and I'm tempted to hang up now."

"No! Please don't," he sighed, and I heard him take another swig of whatever it was that he was drowning himself in. "You're the only person in this family that...that treats me normally. Declan is Liam's guy. Dad's favorite is Liam. Mom loves me, but she would never pick. I just need someone for a goddamn second to be in my bloody corner! Just one person."

"Neal, we're family. I'm always in your corner. And Declan, he cares about you, and you know it."

"Declan killed our uncle for Liam. Rule fifteen, Coraline, if family ever betrays family, show no mercy, no forgiveness and put them in the earth. I'm next; I knew it since the day I was born. One of them is going to kill me."

"Neal, my husband is sitting in the dining room waiting for me to join him for dinner. But you called me and you sound like you need my help. So instead of eating with him, I am huddled in a corner of one of your mother's drawings rooms. Now, tell me what is wrong."

"Olivia is the mole," he said.

I waited for the shock to hit me. I wanted to feel surprised, but I only felt stupid for not realizing it earlier.

"She played me like a fool and I just let her. I overlooked things she said and did because I loved her. I still love her. I'm fucked. She's fucked. Both of us—"

"Do Mel and Liam know?"

"Liam told me and I didn't believe him. I didn't want to believe him. But I had to know the truth."

"Neal, what did you do?"

"I slipped information to Olivia. I told her that Liam was taking Mel to the opera. They'd called my phone number instead of his to confirm his reservation. I gave them his number and Olivia was just there…so I thought I would slip it to her and see what would happen."

"And Avian tried to kill them. That's what happened," I finished for him.

He sighed. "They are going to kill us both. Liam is still fuming. I wasn't even thinking, I just needed to make sure. But I need to tell—"

"Neal, you will not tell them."

"Coraline—"

"Shut up, Neal. We didn't have this conversation and you will not tell them that you slipped up. None of us can afford to slip up, not you, not me, not even Declan. We're at war. Have you chosen your side?"

He was silent and I held my breath in panic.

"Neal, we're family through and through. This is your moment. You will rise from this, but you gotta be smart."

"Family through and through," he repeated.

Nodding, I released the air in my lungs. "Olivia fucked us all over. Now it's time you pay her back tenfold. You're going to be a motherfucking Callahan. You're going to be ruthless. Do you understand me?"

"If I hurt her, Liam and Mel will know."

"There is more than one way to hurt a woman, Neal. Go on like nothing is wrong. Make her fall in love with you all over again and start sucking information from her. When you have the information, take it to them. Drop it on the table and do as they ask. If Olivia loved you, she would not have done this. She put your life, and everyone in this family up for her own greed. That's not love. You will come back from this a stronger member of this family."

He was silent again and I heard the bottle on the other line touch the table, as though he'd set it down.

"Thank you, Coraline."

"For what? This conversation never happened."

He snickered.

"Oh, and Neal? I will be watching you. I trust you, but just in case, I will be watching you," I said before hanging up.

Deleting his call, I straightened myself up before walking out of the room. I walked into the dining room to find Declan slouched over the head of the table, completely lost in thought. He didn't even notice as the butler placed food on the table that had been set only for the two of us. It was odd being in the house with so many people missing.

"Thank you, Raymond," I told him as he left.

"Of course, ma'am," he said before he headed back towards the kitchen. Declan was still not moving.

"Your eyes used to fall out of your head when I walked into the room," I teased, sitting next to him.

He blinked rapidly, and picked his head up to look at me. Forcing a small smile, he took my hand and kissed the back of it. "Sorry, darling, I've just got a lot of things going through my mind. But you're stunning as always."

Taking my hand back, I reached for the peas and placed some on his plate, along with the salmon and rice. I hadn't seen him eat since last night.

"Thank you," he said, as he took a bite.

"Of course. Are you thinking about what Mel and Liam asked us to do?"

He froze for a moment before he looked up at me.

"What? They called me a few moments after they spoke with you."

"Why didn't you tell me you knew?" he asked.

"Why didn't you tell me at all?"

"Coraline…" he sighed.

I hated when he said my name like that.

"You don't think I can do it." We were back at square one all over again.

He sat up. "Coraline, this isn't game. We're talking about breaking into the Canadian Embassy, kidnapping a fed—"

"I know, Declan, I read the file," I snapped as I cut into the pink fish in front of me.

"Then you know that this is too risky. We're not dealing with thugs. I'm going to figure out a plan with Fedel—"

"If you try it, Declan Callahan, I will divorce you so quickly you won't even be able to finish your damn peas," I told him, as I took a bite.

His mouth dropped open before it turned to a smirk. "You're bluffing."

"Guess who got invited to, and played nice with, every top law firm in the state?" I asked, sipping slowing as he watched me. "While you were getting your hands dirty with the low lives, I've been shaking hands and smiling with a lot of fancy people. I'm not as sweet and innocent as you keep trying to make me out to be. I have a plan to get in, but I need your tech genius to do it. So we're going to do it whether you like it or not."

He stared and said nothing.

"You should eat, babe, this salmon is amazing."

"I'm no longer hungry for food," he said slowly, as he pulled at his tie and rose from his chair.

"Really? Should I call for some wine?" I smirked, as I tried to keep my eyes fixed on my food.

His fingers caressed my shoulder and trailed up my neck, until he gripped it slightly and slid his thumb along the side of my jaw.

"No wine," he whispered into my ear.

"Then what?"

"I want you," he stated.

I smiled, as I pushed my chair back and stood up to face him. "All you had to do was ask." Backing away from him, I stepped out of my shoes and began to unzip my dress. He watched every movement I made, and just as I'd exposed the lace of my bra, I stopped. "On the other hand, you should have to work for me." I grinned before I bolted out of the room, ran up the stairs, twisted around the corner, and just kept running.

I turned back to see how far behind me he was, but he wasn't there. I paused just as the elevator doors opened and he stepped out right in front of me with a grin so wide, it was almost inhuman. He pulled me into his arms and threw me over his shoulder like a caveman.

"You cheater! Put me down!"

"Work smarter, not harder, baby." He laughed as I kicked and tried to wiggle free of him.

I'd just walked right into that!

When we reached our room, he carried me and dropped me in the center of the bed.

"Now that I've earned you, why don't I help you out of that pretty dress?" he said, as he crawled on top of me.

I didn't fight him. I didn't want to.

DECLAN

A ll night I had tried to think of a way to get her out of this. But nothing came to mind. I watched her lace up her boots as I placed my watch on my wrist. I didn't want to do this with her. She wasn't ready for this. This wasn't a game. Neither of us were spies. If she got caught, she'd be done for. Our lives would be on surveillance, gone would be our cover lives. It just didn't seem worth it to me. I had almost everything figured out with Fedel; all we needed was someone who looked like the agent, and sadly, that person was Coraline.

They could have been twins, with the exception of their hair. What's worse was the fact that I'd had no chance to prep her. I felt like we were playing hot potato with a live grenade. It didn't matter who caught it, someone was going to get blown the fuck up.

"I can feel your stare boring its way into my back," she said, as she placed her phone into the back pocket of her jeans.

"Are you sure—"

"If you ask me that one more time, Declan, I swear to God."

Annoyed, I grabbed her cell phone out of her back pocket and threw it on the bed.

"Hey—"

"If you're going to ignore my advice as your husband, you're going to listen to me as your boss. You want to do this? Fine. But rookie mistake 101 is carrying a cell phone," I snapped angrily. Moving to my dresser, I pulled out an earbud, and placed it in her ear. I looked over her outfit once more.

"You're going to the Embassy, Coraline. You're going to need a skirt, some stockings and heels, along with a blazer."

"Wait, we're going now?"

"Yes, now." I frowned. "If we were doing it my way, then we could go tomorrow or maybe the next day. She's married with two children, both of whom are homeschooled. Grabbing her at home is virtually impossible. We could have taken her on her daily ride but Mel and Liam, being the self-serving sons of bitches they are, want to prove that they can take what they want from behind enemy lines. So yes, you're going today. Because today is the only day the agent really leaves her office. She spends the night there, mostly because she's having an affair with her boss. The guards haven't seen her enter today so you can go in using the false credentials."

She took my face into her hands. "Breathe. Fedel is going to be with me, and you're going to be in my ear. I'll be fine, and if you believe that, I *will* be fine."

Resting my head on hers, I nodded.

"Good. Now, what color suit should I wear?"

"A dull color, and something you've never worn before and don't mind burning after."

"Great, I have just the outfit," she said with a touch of sarcasm.

I was tempted to smile, but now was not the time.

As she walked to her closet I moved over to my table and placed the second plug in my ear.

"Coraline, can you hear me?"

"God? Is that you?" Her voice came alive on the microphone.

"Very funny."

There was a knock on the door and I already knew it was Fedel. "Come in," I told him.

When he stepped in with his freshly pressed suit, I threw him the third plug. He caught it with ease.

"Is everything in place?"

"Yes, we have two hours before we need to be on the road. Did you find a woman we can trust to go in?" Fedel asked, as he fitted the plug into his ear.

"At your service." Coraline stepped out looking rather plain, in a gray pant suit.

"You're serious?" Fedel asked, looking to me.

My thoughts exactly.

"The next person to say shit will be walking around toothless. Are we clear?" she snapped at the both of us, as she crossed her arms.

"Yes, boss." Fedel snickered while shaking his head.

"Good. Now, is this enough for me to pass as her?" She motioned to her outfit.

"One last thing." Fedel pulled out a pair of thick, black-rimmed glasses. When she placed them on, I checked to see if the camera was working.

"Let's get this clusterfuck on the road," I muttered as I rose from my chair.

May God help us all.

Nineteen

"Not feeling is no replacement for reality. Your problems today are still your problems tomorrow."

—*Larry Michael Dredla*

LIAM

As I entered our bedroom, I immediately tripped over Mel's shoe. Catching myself, I picked up the red heel, and threw it into the corner.

"Your shoe almost killed me," I called out to the closed bathroom door while tendrils of steam snaked out at its base.

Turning on the television, I pulled off my tie and removed my shoes.

"Good evening, I'm Andrea Salvia, and tonight we bring you more in the ongoing investigation regarding the recent FBI debacle. In only a month, five federal agents have either been murdered or charged with felonies. Meanwhile, the head of the FBI, Avian Doers, was spotted rubbing elbows with D.C.'s one percent at the Opera."

"It looks as if the public has finally caught on," I yelled, as I stood up to take off my shirt.

I listened to the silence and paused when she didn't yell back in reply. She always yelled back, and nine out of ten times it was with an invitation to join her.

"Mel?" I moved to the door.

She still didn't answer.

"Mel." I opened the door and froze the moment I stepped in. She stood in the shower, fully clothed, as the water poured upon her. Rushing towards her, I turned the shower off, thanking God that it wasn't scalding hot, yet she remained standing there, not moving.

"Mel!" I yelled directly in her face, as I shook her.

She blinked a few times and wiped the water from her face before she looked at me confused.

"What are you doing?" she asked me.

"What am I doing?" I tried not to yell. "What the hell are you doing? You're fully dressed and standing in the shower."

She looked herself over with no expression, then moved to take off her black dress and underwear before she stepped around me. Grabbing one of the white towels for her body and a smaller one for her hair, she wordlessly left the bathroom.

"I'm fine Liam," she said as I followed her.

"Bullshit. What happened to you?"

She said nothing as she continued to dry her hair.

"Melody."

"Will you stop saying my name as though I'm a child?!"

"I will the moment you stop acting like one."

"I said I was fine!" she screamed at me.

"And I call bullshit!" I yelled as I reached for her but she pulled away. "Someone who is *fine* does not stand in the shower, spaced out and fully dressed."

"Keep yelling, Liam, the whole damn city hasn't heard you yet!" she snapped, as she stormed off towards her closet and slammed the door behind her.

With a sigh, I moved to the door and rested beside it. I jiggled the handle, trying to open it, but she must have been leaning against the door.

"Wife, open the door and let me in. This is not the type of fighting I like to do with you," I whispered.

"Liam, I'm fine."

"Every time you say you're fine, I get more pissed off because I know you're lying to me. I thought we were over with this? I thought we were partners; that you would—"

She opened the door and glared at me. "Don't try to guilt me into anything."

"I'm trying to be honest with you."

"Liam." she sighed deeply as she turned away from me and grabbed a clean set of underwear. "I had a moment."

"A moment?" I asked slowly, waiting for her continue.

"Yes, Liam, a moment! A lot has happened and I couldn't breathe, okay. Sometimes I feel like I'm—" she stopped before turning to me. Dressed in only her underwear, she propped her hands on her hips but didn't look at me. Instead she looked up at the light fixture, as she chewed on her bottom lip.

"Sometimes you feel like what?" I whispered, taking a step forward.

"Like I'm still running across Europe, still fighting for my life. I wake up sometimes and I have to sit and hold myself together. There are other times that I remember things and my skin burns, my veins feel as though they've been lit on fire, and I have to cool down," she confessed. I found myself speechless.

How in the hell had I missed that? She was still fucking suffering? Jesus Christ.

"Mel—"

"Do not look at me like that, I'm handling it. I just need time, okay? You haven't caught me before and they're becoming less frequent. It's only when I'm stressed—"

Wrapping my arms around her, I held her close.

"I don't need a hug."

"Mel, shut up and just stand here with me."

"Liam—"

"You're still talking."

With a sigh, she stood in my embrace, tense and annoyed, but soon her body relaxed and she laid her head against my chest. A few moments later, she wrapped her arms around me.

"You should have told me, Mel."

"There's nothing you could have done," she whispered.

"I can be there. Why is it so hard for you to let anyone be there for you?" It always came back to the same issue.

"I'm trying, Liam. You have no idea how hard this is for me. It's always been me, it's going to take me time, but you can't treat me differently or pity me." She pulled away from me. "I can still do my job, and that includes seeing our son before we go."

I let go of her as she grabbed a pair of pants and one of my dark t-shirts.

"What are we planning?"

"Tonight, we're going to stalk Avian." She donned her boots before she pulled out not one, but two guns, and threw them to me.

"Stalk him or kill him?" I was fine with either option.

"For now, stalk. We're going to the White House tomorrow and I'm sure he's going to try to kill us again. Change your shoes, we might be running," she demanded.

"Don't we have men for this?"

"Wouldn't you rather make sure it's done properly? Or are you above all this now, Mr. Callahan?"

Rolling my eyes, I checked the chamber of the gun. "Remember when all we used to do was handle drugs? I miss that."

"We can get back to that the moment we kill my dear grandfather. But until then, we do whatever we need to, even if that means jumping across buildings."

"Why the hell would we be jumping across buildings?"

She grinned. "Just think of it as my version of a date."

"You're enjoying this?" *What the fucking hell?*

"I used to do this for my father. How did you think I stole that red diamond when I was eighteen?"

My brain worked overtime to follow her logic.

"So what you're saying is, if our dates were more Mission Impossible, and less candlelight, you wouldn't bitch so much at me?"

Her eyebrow twitched. "I'm going to see Ethan now, get ready."

"Yes, ma'am, would like to me to roll over too?" I was starting to enjoy pushing her buttons.

"Perché non basta giocare morti, ass." she snapped at me.

"Why don't I play dead? Ora che non è cosa piacevole dolce."

She looked at me in complete surprise as I grinned. "Five months in the joint, I had more than enough time to learn your language."

"Firstly," she said a little too seductively, "never say joint. Secondly, you said 'Now that is not nice *thing sweet*' but good try."

She winked before she turned and walked out.

Damn I loved her.

It was moments like these that make up for everything else.

MELODY

I took a deep breath as I stepped out of our bedroom. I was torn between smiling at the effort he'd shown, and slapping myself for allowing him to worry. I'd never wanted him to see me like that. I don't know what happened, one moment everything was fine, I was checking over my plans for tonight, and the next moment, I was standing in the shower. I hadn't lied to him, over the last few weeks moments like that had all but faded away. I just needed to be with him and Ethan. When I was, the rest of the world seemed to drift away...I'd been feeling so unlike myself, and truthfully, I liked it.

I headed down the hall towards the back door, Evelyn had taken Ethan out to sit under the stars. The whole back yard was surrounded by high hedges to block any line of sight in.

They'd thought that we were insane for blocking the view of the city when we'd had the hedges planted. But my gut told me to be mindful of snipers. All of Ethan's clothes, including his beanie hats, were custom made with Kevlar. If I could, I would've placed Ethan in a safe room until this was all over.

When this was over, I needed to spend more time with him.

Reaching the back of the house, I stopped at the glass doors where Olivia stood. Her arms were crossed and her face displayed no expression as she stared at Ethan in Evelyn's arms. She wore a floor-length red gown that had a slit that ran up to her thigh, and white heels. From where I stood, she didn't even look like she was breathing. It was haunting, in an odd way.

"Can I help you with something?" I asked, as I walked up beside her.

She said nothing for a moment before she wiped away a single tear.

How sad.

"I was good to him," she whispered, without looking at me. "While you were gone, I made sure he wanted for nothing. I sat by his side, I read him to sleep, I cried with him when he had his ear infection. I was there and then you came back and you do what you always do. You treat me like shit. Why?" Finally, she turned to me. "Why do you hate me so much?"

"Because you are a liar, Olivia." I took a step towards her. "You want things that are not yours. You are a spoiled child. At first I thought the problem was your morality. You go on and on about how horrible Liam and I are. How horrible this family is. You almost had me believing that you didn't want this life. If that were the case, I think I could have almost come to respect you in time. But sadly, it isn't."

Again, I stepped towards her and she flinched, but didn't move back.

"Instead, Olivia, every time you told me how horrid I was, you were trying to convince yourself that you did not want to be me. For some reason, you can handle men being in control, but you have to outdo all the women in your life. It's why you tried to keep Coraline below you, and why you cozied up to Evelyn. I'm guessing it's the rape, they broke you and you chose not to fix yourself. Instead, you married into a big, powerful family and hid behind Neal.

"You thought that was strength. But I entered your life and I shattered your pathetic little world. I tried to make you stronger, I helped you get your revenge, but you resent me, not because you disliked it, but because *I* gave you that power. I have the child, I have the family, and I have the power. My hatred for you is a direct consequence of your lust for what is mine, even those shoes," I said and pointed to the white shoes that she wore upon her feet. "You started a war. So don't cry because you're losing."

"You're insane." She shook her head as her pink lips quivered.

"Olivia. Sweet, Olivia," I said as I placed my hand on her cheek. "You haven't seen anything yet."

Moving away from her, I stepped onto the porch. Ethan giggled and reached for me the second he saw me. I him from Evelyn's arms and spun him around.

"Ethan!" I laughed. And we both giggled as I pulled him to my chest. I kissed his face as he smacked my own.

"I vaguely remember a woman once telling me she doesn't know how to be a mother," Evelyn snickered as she studied me.

I looked to Ethan, who happily sucked on his pacifier while watching my face. "I have no idea *what* she's talking about," I told him.

"Of course not," Evelyn said for him, as her eyes softened at the sight of us. "You remind me of myself when I first had Neal."

"Is that a good thing?" Knowing Neal, that could have been taken both ways.

"Yes, it is. Are you going out?"

I nodded, not wanting to release Ethan. "This will be over soon and I'll be back to tuck you in," I whispered into his ear. Liam came out as I spoke, dressed semi-casually with better shoes. He came over to us and Ethan rolled in my arms, trying to grab his daddy.

"Well, I can see who your favorite is," I said as I frowned and handed him over to Liam. Not a second later, Ethan was pulling on Liam's hair.

"Nice to see you too." Liam winced, as he reached up to separate Ethan's little hands from his hair.

"Are you both heading out with Neal and Olivia?" Sedric asked as he came out to join us.

"I wasn't aware that they were leaving," I said, as I looked towards Liam who nodded, as Ethan smacked his lips.

"Apparently they're having a date night," Liam informed me.

"A date night?"

"Can't be blood and gore all the time. The moment this is all over, Sedric and I will be going back to Ireland for a while," Evelyn said with a grin while Sedric kissed her cheek.

"A long while," he added.

"Before we take any victory laps, let's win the war," Liam responded, as he placed Ethan into their arms. He reached for us again and I kissed his little hands goodbye.

"Be safe," Evelyn said.

Nodding, we both left them and walked towards the garage where Liam had an old Ford 1963 Mustang waiting for us. It looked so misplaced parked behind the mansion.

"This is new," I said, as I ran my hands over the dark blue paint.

"It is," he replied, taking the driver's seat. He drove off the second I got in without even giving me the chance to buckle myself in.

"What's wrong?" I asked, leaning back.

He pulled out his phone. "Play it."

Taking it, I listened.

"Hello, Neal?"

"Coraline..."

"Neal, what's wrong?"

"Everything, Coraline."

I wasn't sure if I want to laugh or throw the phone out the damn window after I'd finished listening to their whole conversation. Looking to Liam, his jaw was tense and he gripped the steering wheel so tightly his knuckles whitened.

"Is é mo dheartháir amadán." (My brother is a fool.) He snapped in a rage.

"He's chosen to be loyal," I said and he snorted.

"What good is loyalty when he's weak, thoughtless, and a motherfucking pain in my ass? I've been trying to wrap my head around why he thought it was a good idea to use our anniversary as a test for Olivia. His stupidity once again almost cost us our fucking lives. And Coraline, who gave her the right to keep this from us? Since when did they have to right to even fucking think for themselves? They wait for *our* directions and then acted on *our* accord, not their own. It's as if they were children!"

He stopped at the light and pinched the bridge of his nose before he took a deep breath.

"Are you pissed that they acted on their own, or pissed because they ruined our anniversary?" I asked.

He looked to me and frowned. "Do you know how long it took me to plan everything?"

"So it's the anniversary."

"Why aren't you more pissed about this?"

"Because if you'd stop barking at me for a moment, you'd see that this works in our favor. Neal, stupid as he may be, still chose this family over Olivia. We know now for a fact that Olivia is against us, though it was hard to deny it before. If we allow Neal to give us more, we now have the ability to fuck with Avian."

"Do you really think he can accomplish that?" he muttered. "Olivia has been holding his balls for years."

"Only time will tell, but right now we have our proof. As for Coraline, she's shocked me."

He snickered, as he shook his head at me. "Someone's managed to shock Bloody Mel?"

Rolling my eyes, I placed my feet on the dashboard. "Yes, I might have a plan for her later."

"Care to share?"

"No. Now, do you know where we're going?" I asked him as I looked out the window. It was as though he was just driving around for the sake of driving.

He a glared at me and I waited a moment before I pulled out my phone and opened the GPS.

LIAM

Three hours passed and I'd only been able to calm down a little bit. We were now in view of Avian's penthouse. But I couldn't stop thinking about Neal. I wanted to take him by the neck and knock his motherfucking face in. I was eighteen when my father told me that I, not Neal, was going to take over for him. When I asked him why, he said that one day I would understand. I'd always thought it was because I was his favorite, but I now understood. Neal was literally incompetent. I could already see myself spending the rest of my life cleaning up after his utter stupidity. Part of me almost wished he had betrayed me so that I could just kill him and be done with it...only a small part of me did though.

But he chose family. He's loyal.

That made up for a lot. Almost everything.

"I'm counting six agents," Mel whispered, as she looked through the scope of her sniper rifle.

Looking through the binoculars, Avian's penthouse apartment was in perfect view from the skyscraper we'd broken into. We could see right into his Italian styled home. The entire penthouse was surrounded by large, open windows. It was as though he was daring us to try.

"The glass is a quarter inch thick, and I have no doubt in my mind that it's bulletproof." she added, as she remained hunched over. As far as I knew, we weren't going to kill anyone tonight, but she insisted on wasting our time by doing this.

When I didn't speak, she looked to me, eyeing me carefully. "You think this is a waste of time," she stated.

"If we aren't going to kill him, I see no point in watching him solve crossword puzzles all night." That was all the man did; he sat in his silk robe and finished crosswords in old newspapers. Every few hours he walked to the window to smoke a cigar, and then he moved on to the next fucking crossword. If he was trying to drive me insane, it was fucking working.

She released the rifle, and it looked as though she was trying to think of nice way to bitch at me.

"Liam," she said gently, and I wanted to laugh, but instead I smirked at her, as I sat against the wall next to the window.

"Don't go all 'sweet wife' on me now. Go on, I can take it," I said.

Her eyebrow twitched. "I'm working on trying to be kinder to you, but you're a pain in my motherfucking ass sometimes, Callahan. Why in the goddamn hell is it so hard for you to sit down, shut up and just—"

"There's my Mel. I thought you had drowned in a vat of rainbows and pixie dust."

The look on her face as well as the fact that her hand was now twitching towards her gun made me smile. As if I didn't already have enough bullet scars from her.

"Do you enjoy pissing me off?"

"In the beginning, your mood swings drove me crazy, now I find them kind of hot."

That did it; she drew her gun and pointed it at my head.

I grinned. "Put that away before you hurt yourself, love."

Her hands clenched into fists and I waited for it, but she stopped, pulled her gun back, and shook her head at me.

"You son of a bitch. You're trying to entertain yourself because you're bored. If we fight, you'll end up fucking me on the floor."

"I'm definitely not that desperate," I lied and she knew it.

She sighed loudly. "He's been watching us for years Liam. He knows when we sleep, when we eat, he's watched us fight and only God knows what else. The man has basically been living with us and we were blind to it. Yes, I know this is not your forte, and if you want, I can do this part alone. But when I said I was done with this motherfucker, I meant it. I'm going to be better at his game. He got into my head, but I'm going to get into his very soul. I want to know what he does and when he does it, even if that means I'm out here every night. I'm going to be his fucking shadow. He doesn't get the right to sleep soundly at night. He fucked with our family and I'm going to fuck with his legacy, with his life."

She looked back into the scope and watched him again. Rising, I looked out the window, staring at the man who was once again smoking a cigar. The smoke came out of his mouth in rings. He looked deep in thought, and perhaps this was how he came up with all his fucked up ideas of how to kill us. An agent stood right in front of Avian on the balcony, watching the surroundings from all angles while sporting a bulletproof vest.

I wonder if they know what type of man they're protecting.

At least with our men, they knew who we are and what we did. Avian was a different type of monster.

"Kill the agent," I demanded.

"He'll know—"

"I *want* him to know. I want him to feel us closing in on him. Kill the agent."

She pulled the trigger, and hit the agent between the eyes; the man fell back against the glass before sliding down it. Avian, still safely inside, let out one more puff of smoke. He tapped the bullet in window before he looked around, scanning the buildings. He didn't seem fazed by his agent's death; however, the other agents around him scrambled.

Mel broke down her rifle in seconds. "That's our cue to leave. I give it an hour before they start checking all of these building."

"The shot heard around the world," I said, as I looked into Avian's home. "I want to know where he's going next."

"Look who's joined the party," Mel said as she stood at the door and waited for me to follow.

I couldn't wait to shake Avian's hand tomorrow when we got back to the White House.

Twenty

"A liar knows that he is a liar, but one who speaks mere portions of truth in order to deceive is a craftsman of destruction."

—Criss Jami

CORALINE

A s I walked towards the front desk, I held my head high and tried to deny the fact that my heart was beating erratically. So much so that I could feel it pulsing within my eardrums. But I couldn't break now. I was going to have to hold in the panic that was threatening to surface. Pulling out the forged badge, I held it over the scanner, and released a small sigh of relief when I wasn't tackled by some three-hundred-pound security officer.

"Thumb," the guard demanded, without even bothering to look at me, which was a shame really, since I'd put in a lot of effort into getting ready for this.

"It's fine, Coraline," Declan said in my ear.

I pressed my thumb onto the green pad, feeling better because of Declan's reassurance.

"Thank you. Have a good day," the guard muttered as I walked through the rest of the security measures they had set.

"They're going to do a body search. Do not make eye contact, just walk through as if this is a normal routine," Declan told me.

I didn't answer, instead, I tried to follow his instructions as I placed my bag onto the conveyor belt. It reminded me of the security checks at an airport—an x-ray machine, a metal detector, and a line of stoic faces waiting for their turn. Once on the other side of the metal detector, I took my purse and walked towards the elevator bank. I entered without a word and held my bag tightly as the other occupants moved aside and allowed the janitor to enter. I slid my bag off of my shoulder and opened it without drawing attention to myself. From my peripheral, I watched as the janitor slipped a gun in and quietly took his exit on the next floor.

"Fedel will meet you on the top floor," Declan's voice called through the indiscernible earpiece.

Again, I didn't reply. Instead, I examined the number pad in front of me; there were sixteen floors accessible by the elevator and I was only on the fourth.

At the tenth, he spoke again.

"Coraline, get off the elevator on the next floor. I'm looking at the security feed and there are guards everywhere. We're going to have to abort this."

I looked around me and saw that there was only one man left, a man who kept looking at me strangely. He caught my gaze and held it.

"What level?"

"Do not answer," Declan told me.

"What level?" he asked with a little more force, as he reached behind him.

Shit.

"Coraline, get out when the doors open."

"This is federal property. It's off limits to civilians. You are not allowed beyond the ninth floor," the man stated.

"Coraline!" Declan screamed.

I pulled out my earbud and faced him. "I'm sorry, were you speaking to me?"

"Who are you?"

"Excuse me," I snapped. "It's not your business as to who I am, Agent Morgan. Nor do I answer to you, are we clear?"

He froze as he stared at me with an expression akin to shock. "I—I—"

"This is your floor," I told him as the doors opened.

He looked confused as he walked out.

"Agent Morgan," I called out, "if you wish to advance in this career, you'd do well to remember your station and those of higher rank."

I flashed the forged badge as the doors close. When they did, I took a deep breath before I leaned against the wall.

"How in the hell did you know what to say?" Declan asked when I placed the earpiece back in.

"I saw his phone when he was checking his email, it had information that gave me an idea of his rank and status. And as Mel always says, 'if you demand respect, you will get it.'"

I was sure that Mel wouldn't have frozen for even a second.

Declan said nothing, and when the doors opened, I walked out onto the sixteenth floor.

"Fedel should be there by now," he said just as Fedel came out of another elevator, dressed in a suit. Apparently he'd decided to forgo the janitor's disguise for this stage of the plan.

"You ready?" he asked me.

"Are you?" I responded before pulling the gun from my bag.

Nodding, we both walked through the double glass doors. The entire level was filled with computer drives and other electronic devices that littered the area. The single office in the back stood out and marked our destination.

"Do not kill her," Declan stated.

Fedel stood to my side as I slid the badge through the electronic keyhole. The room smelled of sex and stale perfume. As we walked forward, the agent's attention, the very agent I was copying, snapped from the man she was fucking, to us.

NEAL

"I'm really glad we did this," Olivia said, as she placed her hand over my own.

Forcing a smile, I nodded. "We needed a good night out."

"Where did you find this restaurant?" She looked out the window where she was able to see the capital.

"Liam and Mel just bought it. I think they're planning on making this their new headquarters or some shit. They're meeting here after their night at the White House," I lied, as I sipped on my brandy.

She frowned for a quick moment, then smiled. "I should have known from the décor; it's very *Mel.*"

"You two are never going to get along are you?" I fought hard to not roll my eyes.

She snorted before she drank her red wine. "How can anyone get along with *Bitchy Mel?* She is the most conceited and rude person I have ever met. She only cares about herself. I feel bad for Liam."

"Liam is an ass, he deserves her. One day—" I stopped.

She grinned. "One day what?"

"Nothing. He just pisses me off. Karma's a bitch, and everyone gets what's coming to them someday."

"Better him than you."

"You could say that," I snickered. "But I honestly think Avian might beat them—us. He's been fucking over people like us for God knows how long. He sees all their plans from a mile away."

"Their vanity and pride is going to be the end of them, Neal," she whispered as she squeezed my hand. "We can save ourselves, we should just go. After this is all over, we can come back and pick up where we left off."

"Olivia, don't be ridiculous, Avian is coming after all of us. We don't abandon family."

"So they send us all to our deaths and we're just supposed to accept it?" she snapped.

"What would you have me do, Olivia?" I frowned.

She glared at me as she got up. "Sometimes I don't even know why I bother. I'll be right back."

I waved to the waiter for the check as I pulled out my phone. Olivia wasn't aware of the fact that I knew about both phones, nor was she aware that I had bugged her phones while she slept. Putting my phone to my ear, I listened to her ongoing conversation.

"I want to hear the deal again."

"I am not in the mood for games, Olivia," an older man replied.

"This isn't a fucking game, Avian, this is my life. You wanted information and I have it, but I need to know I'm not putting the nails in my own fucking coffin."

"I am a man of my word. I swore that you, your husband, and the little one will make it out unscathed. I do not take kindly to having to repeat myself. So speak if you still wish to stay alive, because right now I am your only friend."

"Mel and Liam own a new restaurant called the Blue Garden, they plan on meeting here after their night at the White House. I think it's something big."

"You *think?*"

"I don't want to push Neal, everyone's a little jumpy. Mel and Liam still think there's a mole."

"Do they know it's you?"

"No. I'm just the annoying, jealous airhead. They don't give me enough credit."

"For your sake, you should be grateful."

I waited for them to hang up before doing so as well. Downing my drink, I enjoyed the burn as it went down. She was going to save Ethan and me? What were we supposed to say, thank you? Thank you for wiping out our entire family, our legacy? If she knew me, she would have known that I was as good as dead without my family. My father? My mother? She didn't give a fuck.

"Babe?" Olivia placed her hand on my shoulder and I flinched. "Are you okay?"

"No, sorry. King Liam needs us back home."

"I can't wait for this shit to be over." She drank the rest of her wine.

"Me too," I muttered as I took her arm.

You are a bitch, Olivia, a motherfucking bitch.

Twenty-One

"For there to be betrayal, there would have to have been trust first."
—*Suzanne Collins*

LIAM

"Look at Mommy go," I whispered to Ethan, bouncing him on my knee as Mel swam through the pool. I could barely keep up with her, she was like a motherfucking mermaid.

"Gagba," Ethan babbled, as he reached out for her.

"No swimming until you at least learn how to walk," I snickered, not that he paid much attention to me. He was just as mesmerized by her as I was.

She said she swam to clear her mind. I just wished I knew *what* she was trying to focus on. In a few short hours, we'd be at the White House for this afternoon's award ceremony where Avian would undoubtedly be in attendance.

There was a small part of me that thought it best to simply kill him and be done with it. Who cared if he got the glory or a bloody parade in his honor as long as he was dead. Somehow I knew that wasn't going to happen. Avian had spent decades planning and plotting, and I wouldn't have been surprised if there was some sort of contingency plan should he die. We needed to not only end him, but make sure our lives, our businesses, were safe.

"Penny for your thoughts?"

I blinked a few times to find Mel out of the water, drying her face off with a white towel. My gaze followed the residual water beads as they rolled down her chest before I looked up to meet her brown eyes.

"Only a penny? You can do better than that, baby," I winked at her. She rolled her eyes at me, but I could see the smirk that was slowly spreading across her face.

"The chlorine is starting to get to you," she said as she bent over slightly and squeezed the water from her hair while she cooed at Ethan.

My eyes followed the lines of her body and I swallowed. "Believe me, it's not the chlorine."

She wrapped the towel around herself, causing me to pout. "Can you take him inside? If it's not getting to you, it may be irritating him. I don't want him getting high or something."

"High off chlorine?" I laughed as I rose from my chair and pulled Ethan to my chest. "Seriously, love, have you ever known anyone who has gotten high off chlorine?"

She smacked my arm.

"Hey, baby on board." And to prove my point, Ethan immediately grew fussy.

"I have no clue what babies can and cannot get high off of. They are usually not in my company, and I don't want to take the chance, so go."

I looked to Ethan, as I bounced him around. "Mommy is bossy, you'll get used to it."

She rolled her eyes and stepped towards the outside shower to rinse herself off.

I was somewhat taken aback by Neal who was leaning against the couch with a glass of bourbon and a file in his hand.

"A little early, don't you think?" I asked him.

"Says the man who used to say 'A bottle a day, keeps the doctor at bay,'" he replied as he took another sip from his snifter. Walking towards Ethan's playpen, I laid him inside before I handed him his favorite teething toy.

"What is it, Neal?"

"Olivia's out shopping with Mom, so I think now would be the best time to give you the information I've gathered." He waved the file at me.

Walking to him, I took the file and the bourbon, downing it all in one shot before I handed him back the empty snifter.

"I'm guessing that this is about Olivia?" Mel asked as she stepped inside.

She was now dressed in a pair of shorts and a basic t-shirt. It was weird to see her dressed so casually. She, like myself, rarely ever wore anything basic.

I nodded, and flipped through the files, before I showed her the document with the one thing we both suspected had been a part of her little 'deal' with Avain. I couldn't believe she'd gone that far.

"She will die," Mel stated stoically as her hands gripped tightly onto the folder. Her tone alone seemed to freeze the room over.

"I know," he replied.

She took a step forward. "She wanted *my son*, Neal. No one can save her from me."

He nodded. "I know."

"You better not crumble on us, Neal Callahan, or I will *put you down*. I don't want to; I can see an end to this. All you have to do is stay strong."

Once again he shocked me by leaning in towards her.

"I'm not a child, boss. I will never be put in this situation again. She'll be back in an half an hour, have at it," he uttered before walking away.

I watched him take his leave, but before he could leave the room I called out to him.

"Neal."

He paused before turning to me.

"Take Declan's Aston Martin."

When he left, Mel gave me a look.

"Don't look at me like that," I told her. "You have to give a dog a bone every once in a while, or it loses its sanity." Declan would be pissed since he personally worked on it himself, but he would get over it.

"Fine. He's your brother. What else does the file say?"

"Apparently that we own a restaurant downtown as a cover for cocaine distribution." I wanted to laugh at the thought and I could see that she wanted to as well.

"A restaurant as a cover? Sure, maybe if we were in *The Godfather*. Avian is going to see right through that. Rule eleven; don't shit where you eat, both figuratively and literally."

"Thanks for the mental picture," I cringed. "However, it seems that my brother has put the deed in our name—"

"He did what??"

"It's not real." Damned woman, never let me finish. "They're fakes, but proof enough for Avian. I think we should sit on this. We'll be seeing him in a few hours, and I'm sure he already has his people doing surveillance. Why not fuck with him a little?"

She chewed it over before she nodded. "In the meantime, I think I should have a little *chat* with Olivia."

"Mel—"

"I'm not going to kill her yet."

Why didn't I believe her?

"Melody, I want her alive for now since she is our key to Avian."

"I know. I'm calm."

She was anything but calm. Then she walked to the kitchen, and oddly enough, started doing the dishes.

"Mel, what are you doing?"

"The dishes."

Never in all of the time we'd been together had I seen her wash a fucking dish.

"Mel—"

"I need to keep my motherfucking hands busy, Liam. Now will you please stop looking at me like I shit unicorns and leprechauns? God damn!"

This was supposed to be calm?

MELODY

It was wrong to be this excited. It was sick. But I couldn't help who I was. I watched the doorknob turn and I heard their laughter. There's a moment right before you cause someone great bodily harm when adrenaline rushes through your veins, your hand twitches, and your mind seems to focus in on one thing and one thing alone: pain. My father used to tell me that there were different types of pain, and once you mastered them all, nothing hurts. I never believed him though; physical pain never seemed to get old. Just ask any of the people I've hurt.

She walked in, seemingly on cloud nine, holding three Michael Kors, a Marc Fedels, and a Christian Louboutin shopping bag. Her red lips were wide and large as she laughed her blonde head off.

Evelyn was right on her heels. "Mel, I have the most wonderful dress for you to wear this afternoon." Evelyn smiled as she moved straight for Ethan. "And I have something for you too, Mister."

"Let me guess, a bow tie," Liam said to her, but I paid them both little attention as Olivia moved into the kitchen to get a bottle of sparkling water. She called for Neal but got no reply.

"Where's Neal?"

The moment she asked, I snapped. Releasing all the rage I'd been holding within, I took one of the plates I had just washed and smashed it onto the side her head. It shattered on impact. When she screamed and stumbled forward, I took a fistful of her hair, pulled her to the sink, and dunked her head into the dirty dishwater.

"Mel! Oh my God, Mel, what the hell are you doing?" Evelyn shouted at me.

"Go mom, and take Ethan with you," Liam said to her. I didn't know if she listened or not, because I was far too busy pinning Olivia's flailing arms behind her back.

Pulling her head up, she gasped and wheezed for air as I tightly gripped her hair.

"You have no idea how long I've waited to kick your motherfucking skinny ass. You stupid, stupid little bitch, did you really think you could outsmart us? Outsmart me?" Before she could reply, I dunked her head into the soapy water once more. She screamed, and tried to fight me off, but I could feel her strength slowly sapping away.

"Everything in me tells me to kill you, to take a knife and skin you alive, Olivia, and I want to! I want to so damn badly," I told her as I brought her up again. "You betrayed us, but in all honesty, I never trusted you to even hold my shoes."

"Please—"

"You're pleading to the wrong person, bitch!" I sneered as I dunked her head back into the sink. She screamed, and as she did, I pulled her out and allowed her to cough up the water.

"I'm really trying not to enjoy this, but I can't help it."

"NO! PLEASE!" she pleaded as her head met the water again. I could tell that she was beginning to lose consciousness. Her struggles slowly dwindled to nothing, and the air bubbles all but ceased.

Pulling her out, I threw her on the ground kicked her once in the stomach as I turned and grabbed the largest knife from the stand. I mounted her and pressed the sharp blade into her neck.

"Hi, Olivia," I whispered pressing the knife into her white skin even harder. Her eyes rolled back and I slapped her hard across the face keep her awake. Her blood dripped from the side of her head from where I'd smashed it with a dish.

"Melody, whatever it is you—"

I pulled onto her hair tighter, her head lifting up. "You helped Avian, and caused my husband to be sent to jail all in the hopes of stealing our lives and our son. That was your deal, right? You stupid, incompetent, naïve, little bitch."

"Mel—"

"That was the deal, wasn't it?!" Taking the knife, I stabbed her in the thigh.

"MELODY!" she screamed as her hands rushed to her thigh when I pulled the knife out.

"Say the truth for once, Olivia. I already know it, but I need to hear it from you," I said, as I pressed the bloody knife into her neck once more. "SAY IT!"

The tears fell from her face as she began to sob.

"I don't have time for this shit," I muttered as I pulled the knife back

"I—I...did it," her voice broke. "I made the deal. He contacted me after my father won the election. He promised me that Neal and I would take over. He wanted you gone, but he still needed the drug trade going and that—"

"And what?" I hissed.

"Ethan. He promised me that I would get Ethan."

"You—"

"Melody," Liam stopped me from craving her face up.

"Get up," he said to her when I let go

She didn't move.

"You have five seconds starting now. Five...four... three...two—" Before he got to one, she got to her feet, and the moment she did, I punched her square in the jaw. She stumbled backwards, but I didn't stop. I couldn't stop. I punched her repeatedly, and her body fell to the ground, I would have gone further, but I felt Liam's arms as they wrapped around me and pulled me back.

"Take her away for now, and make sure she doesn't do anything *foolish*," he said to both Monte and Kain.

I hadn't even noticed when they'd entered.

She was out cold, with blood dripping from her face as I took a deep breath.

"What happened to calm?" Liam questioned me from behind.

Turning to him, I glared. "I was calm! She's alive, isn't she? For five months, I couldn't hold him. For five months, I ran around watching from computer cafes and cell phones while she hold him. While she read to him and tucked him in! While she was his mother, not me! I can handle everything, but not Ethan. Don't fuck with my child."

"I'll handle her," he stated as he put his hand on the sides of my face and forced me to look at him and breathe.

I nodded. "Have Monte patch up her fucking face, and give her a damn Xanax. She'll bloody well need it to make it through the rest of the day. After all, we wouldn't want Avian to miss his puppet. I'm going to sit with Ethan."

Goddamn I hated her.

LIAM

R eaching up, I cracked the smelling salts open under her nose, causing her to wake up. She sat up quickly, and for a moment I saw relief in her eyes until she noticed the zip ties around her wrists. She pulled against them as if they would simply break.

"You're going to leave marks if you keep at it," I said, as I rolled up my sleeves and took a seat in front of her.

"I want to speak to Neal."

"Your wants are no longer any concern of mine."

"You can't do this!" she shrieked at me. "I'm the President's daughter! I'm your brother's wife! You can't do this to me."

"And yet, here I am. Funnily enough, it's because of those two things that you're not dead. Yet."

Her eyes glazed over with tears. "I want to talk to Neal."

"Neal knows where you are, if he wanted to talk to you, he would've been here," I replied as Monte came in with a bag, a rag, and a bowl of water.

"Neal—Neal knows I'm here?" she whispered.

"Neal's the reason you're here, he was the one who got us the proof that you are nothing but a lying, manipulative bitch. Though Melody and I have known that fact for a while."

She began to shake and I wanted to roll my damn eyes at the dramatics of it all.

"I—I…No. I…But I…I don't understand. No! None of this makes sense, this is not how it was supposed to happen. No, I don't understand, everything was fine."

"Just because you have deluded yourself into believing that, does not make it true. Welcome to reality, Olivia, and it's going to hurt like a bitch."

"Liam—"

"No. No. No. It's Mr. Callahan to you, Ms. Colemen. Only family calls me Liam, and that no longer applies to you."

"I'm still your brother's wife."

"Is that so? Where's your ring?" Her head dropped to the empty spot on her finger. Her entire body hunched over as she let loose a dry sob.

I held the ring up for her to see. "This is a family heirloom, and once again, you are not family. Instead, you will be given another ring to wear while out in public. As you said, you are the President's daughter, and you are also our connection to Avian, we cannot kill you outright. Though I'm sure Mel is just itching to rip your head off."

She didn't seem to be listening to any of the words coming out of my mouth, so I gave her the bottle of water at my feet, along with two pills. She looked down at them and then back at me.

"I just said I wasn't going to kill you. Be smart, Olivia, you're going to need your strength for this afternoon's award ceremony. I heard there is going to be strawberry shortcake, your *favorite*." I smiled at her, as I waited for her to take them.

"I'm not going to be paraded around like—"

"Again, Olivia, it's not up to you. Maybe you do not understand, so I will explain it just this once. You went against this family. I always knew that in some way you would come after us, but I, for some reason, thought it was your morality that would be your motivator. But no, you were reaching for the crown and you failed. You fucking failed, Olivia, and in the worst way possible.

"You may have been able to get away with it while Mel and I were both gone, but you should have known better. You were sloppy, prideful, and just plain ignorant. *You are not good enough.* You failed. And failure comes with consequences. It means you have no rights, no dreams, and no hopes. You're nobody. You're nothing but a pawn on my chessboard. So when I say you are going to fix yourself up; wear that pretty dress, come to the White House, and smile with your daddy, the President, that means you have no choice in the matter. Now take the fucking pills."

I pulled out a knife, and cut the zip ties around her wrists, allowing her to take the pills and drink them down.

"Avian is going to know something is wrong."

I laughed. "You think he's your friend? For the sake of your life, you better make sure he doesn't. You're a loose end. The man drove his own daughter to the brink of insanity. One of us is going to kill you, the only difference is that I can promise you that you won't be dumped in some river or buried in a shallow grave only to be eaten by rats. You can still be buried on the Callahan cemetery plot. So start thinking about what you want your headstone to say."

She broke out into a fit of laughter. She laughed as though she had finally lost it, so I calmly waited, which only seemed to add to her amusement.

"Look at the big, bad Liam. You've come a long way from being shoved into lockers. Neal used to tell me the shit people used to do to his 'crippled little brother' and I always thought it was funny. You've worked so hard to be a badass just because you were bullied and they made your life difficult. Oh *boo hoo,* poor Liam, poor baby, you lost your twin sister and your mommy didn't want you either? Oh dear God, how did you handle it?" She laughed some more. "You know what's even funnier? The fact that you went from being everyone's little bitch to being just Mel's. You're pitiful, motherfucker."

I took a deep breath and leaned forward as I stared at her. I have to admit that it was something I'd learned from Mel, and it tended to scare the shit out of people.

"What are you expecting me to do? Puff out my chest and tell you how manly I am? Maybe if I was a weaker, less confident man, I would get myself worked up, but unfortunately for you, I am not."

"I—"

"Here's your second lesson of the day, and pay attention because the third one might kill you. You can throw as many jabs at me as you want, *Olivia Colemen,* but I am not Mel, I will not go into a fit of rage and kill you. It's cute that you tried, and I know that you'd rather just die now and get it over with. But for your sins, there is a penance. That also means that you will not be taking your own life. One, because you love yourself too much, and two, because we will have eyes on you at all times. There are no pants in Mel's and my relationship, we both prefer to be naked. Now fix yourself. Monte will be in here to make sure everything goes well, if you need something, ask him. He might not give it to you, but it doesn't hurt to ask, right?"

Rising to my feet, I rolled my sleeves down as I headed towards the door of the basement bedroom.

"Can you please send for Neal?"

Opening the door, I turn back to her. "What did my wife tell you about that word, Ms. Colemen? Please, is what you say to people who give a damn. And if you haven't noticed, I do not."

"Was I that obvious?" she whispered.

I didn't answer her. Monte walked in, and I stepped out allowing the door to close as I made my way upstairs.

When I did, I found my father reading through the file. He glanced up at me with an ice-cold stare.

"I'm handling it," I told him, as I set the damn thing on fire and dropped it into the nearby sink.

"Have you spoken to Neal?"

"Neal was the one who brought me the file."

"He did?" He sounded shocked.

Facing him, I nodded. "He did. Tonight you're going to take him out. He's accepted it, but he hasn't dealt with it, and I don't want him losing his mind once she's gone. After all, he still loves her."

"How long do you plan on keeping her alive?"

I shrugged as I took her ring out of my pocket and placed it on the counter in front of him. "Until she's no longer useful. Mel and I have had our suspicions for a while, and it all happened quickly. I'm sure Olivia was just as shocked. One moment she's shopping, and the next she's a prisoner."

"Reality is a bitch," he said with a grin.

That's where I learned it from.

I wondered if Ethan and I would ever have a conversation like this.

"Get your tuxedo ready, Dad. Your son's getting an award."
He snickered as I patted him on the shoulder before I
headed to my room to get ready.

Upon walking in, I froze, Mel sat at the foot the bed rubbing lotion onto her legs. All she was wearing was another
damn towel. Locking the door, I watched her.

"How did it go—?"

I couldn't allow her to finish. Instead, I pulled her up
and I kissed her hard as I unwrapped the towel and allowed
it to drop to the ground. I cupped her ass, as I pressed myself
against her, and soon our tongues were battling each other.

"On all fours," I demanded once we broke apart.

Her eyes glazed over and a grin crossed her face as she
obeyed. I stared at her as ass for a moment, my hands twitching. I could see her muscles tensing up; she knew what was
coming.

SMACK.

Her ass jiggled, as I left behind a red handprint. She
shivered as I landed four more slaps on her plump ass.

"Ahh!" she moaned loudly, as her body began to shake.
I could see how badly she wanted me, and I wanted her to
know that the feeling was mutual. I was so hard it felt as
though I was going to burst through my pants. I couldn't
take it any longer, I pulled them off quickly, not caring that
I'd broken the zipper.

I kissed her ass as I traveled up her spine. Then, I pressed
myself behind her, and took her breasts into my hands as I
pulled us both to our knees on the bed.

"Liam—" She moaned once again as I pulled on her
nipple with one hand, whilst allowing my other to travel
down her stomach.

"When was the last time we did this?" I whispered into
her ear as I gently bit it.

Her hands worked their way into my hair. "Two days ago."

"Two days? You're slacking, wife." I pulled her hair back, while I cupped her pussy at the same time.

Her lips parted as she moved with my hand. "I've been busy, husband."

I grinned and she bit her lip as one of my fingers entered her.

"You should never be too busy for this."

"Fuck." she moaned. And as I quickened my pace, she rocked herself against my hand while I pulled on her hair to keep her steady. She was at my mercy, and her eyes rolled back as she came on my fingers. Pulling them out, I held them to her lips.

"Taste yourself."

She did and I moaned as her soft, pink tongue licked my fingers clean. When she took them into her mouth and began to gently suck and swirl her tongue along the length of them, I moaned once more as I released her.

"You're playing with me, wife," I whispered.

She grinned and grabbed a hold of me as she began to jerk me off. "*Now* I'm playing with you."

Grabbing her wrist I stopped her. It took all the strength within me, but I stopped her.

"No," I moaned again as I took her lips with my own. Damn she tasted so sweet.

Leaning back, she rested on her back as I trailed kisses from her lips to her neck.

She wrapped her legs around my waist. I could feel her nails running down my back, and as I took her nipple into my mouth, I watched her. Her back was arched, and her eyes were closed. I rubbed against her entrance.

"Liam—damn it, Liam, I need you."

"Then you shall have me," I whispered into her ear before I slammed into her.

"Fuck!"

Grabbing both of her arms, I pinned them over her head with one hand, while I lifted her thigh with the other.

"Liam."

Watching her beg with each thrust gave me the will to hold out instead of just slamming myself repeatedly into her.

"Open your eyes."

She did and I stared into them, watching as pleasure consumed her. She could only take so much more of this.

Right on cue, she broke free of my hand and pulled me to her lips.

"Mel," I moaned into her mouth.

Using that to her advantage, she flipped us both over, straddled my waist, and pressed her hands against my chest. Then she pushed herself up before slamming back down.

"Jesus fuck, baby," I gasped out.

She grinned, but didn't stop as my hands went to her waist and held her in place. She rode me hard and fast, and there was no way I would've been able to last much longer. My hands traveled up her body until I was cupping her breasts. Sitting up, I kissed and bit them both.

When she slowed, I flipped us over once more, and I took her thighs into my hands before fucking her harder.

"Liam. Fuck. Ahh!" Her voice shook.

I kissed her neck as she came; and moments later I followed her in my own sweet release.

"Fuck, I love you." I drew in a deep breath, and pulled out as I fell beside her.

She ran her hands through her hair, and took a few deep breaths before she sat up. Leaning over, she kissed me deeply and we stared at each other. I smiled into the kiss before she broke away.

"I love you too."

I never got tired of hearing that.

TWENTY-TWO

"In order to become the master, the politician poses as the servant."
—*Charles de Gaulle*

MELODY

"Ladies and gentlemen, today I stand before you humbled, astonished, and proud," the President spoke from the podium, as he raised his hand and gestured towards Liam and me. "And it is because of this man and this woman. Over the years, I have been asked by both nationals and foreigners alike, '*What does it mean to be American?' What do you stand for? How far are you willing to go?'* The answer to those questions is in this very room."

"He's laying it on thick," Liam whispered to me.

I kept a straight face for the cameras and leaned into him as Ethan grabbed my pearls. "I know, I wrote it."

I heard him chuckle, but paid no mind.

President Colemen stood straighter as he read the next lines. "When Melody Callahan saw a threat, not only to our country, but to our way of life, she didn't just report it. She went above and beyond all expectations, asking only one simply question: *What can I do?*

"With no regard to her own wellbeing and only *hours* after giving birth to her son, Ethan, she gave the United States government an opportunity to not only gather information, but to strike swiftly. As a parent myself, I cannot imagine the pain she must have felt not knowing when she would be reunited with her family. I asked her not once, but twice, if she understood the consequences of her actions, and she told me she never wanted to turn on the television and see another building burn, or parents weeping, or our great nation mourn, ever again. If she can sacrifice what she thought was a little, for a greater good, to help fight the war on terror, she can handle her heartache."

Liam turned to me with a grin, and clapped along with all those in attendance. I took Ethan's little hand and waved along with him, smiling at the crowd.

"The injustice did not stop there; her husband sat through criticism, mockery, hate and cruelty, because he too believed in the power of this nation. He willingly and wholeheartedly gave up us his freedom and dignity, spending five months in one the most notorious jails in Illinois, during which time, he was made to endure numerous riots. But Liam Callahan did not waver. He never once asked for anything. He was prepared to go the distance, and despite it all, he held on to his morality; never once did he lie. He told everyone he was innocent, and he was. He declared his unwavering love for his wife, which we can all see is true."

At that, Liam kissed my cheek as they all clapped.

"America, when I say that I am humbled, I truly mean it. Never in my wildest dreams would I have expected two everyday citizens to stand up and say 'yes I shall protect and serve my country at all costs.' And it is for this very reason that I must bestow the Presidential Medal of Freedom, given to those who have admirably contributed to the security and national interests of the United States, and the world, to Mr. and Mrs. Liam Callahan."

The room erupted as Liam took my hand, and holding onto Ethan tightly, we walked to the side of the stage and allowed President Colemen to place the first medal around my neck before moving to do the same to Liam.

"And just so the little guy doesn't feel left out, we have a Presidential pin for him as well," the President spoke to the press, laughing along with them as he placed a pin onto Ethan's collar. He stepped back before posing to take photos with us. He wasn't the only one that joined us. Olivia's mother stood on the other side of Liam.

Through the camera flashes, I met Olivia's gaze, daring her to step onto the stage. She didn't. Instead, she stayed at her table, next to Sedric, who wouldn't let her out of his sight. Looking away from her, I gazed over the room until my eyes reached the son of a bitch in the back. He stood stock still like a statue, and he seemed to be the only person in the room who wasn't clapping or smiling. Instead, he glared at the both of us with undisguised revulsion.

I, on the other hand, did smile. I smiled so wide I wouldn't have been surprised if he was able to count all my fucking teeth. Nothing pissed your enemy off more than seeing you smile.

Finally, Liam walked to the podium to *thank* our President for his kind words.

"Note to self, fire the presidential speechwriter," he said, causing everyone to laugh. Taking a deep breath he sighed before he began his speech. "I wish I could say that everything President Colemen said was true. He made it seem as if we'd thought long and hard about this, but in all honesty, everything happened so quickly that there was barely any time to think. We simply reacted to a problem presented to us. There were many times when we were scared, tired, and just fed up. And while it feels like a lifetime ago, it is not something I ever want to go through again. It was hell.

Being separated from my wife, my newborn son, my entire life; it was hell.

"Which puts into perspective the millions of Americans; firefighters, police officers, government agents, all who wake up every day knowing that they might have to go through hell, but they still get up and do their jobs. Walking five months in their shoes, I can say that those are the people I am humbled, astonished, and proud to share a nation with. There should be medals of freedom for them all to show the gratitude we feel."

When we hugged again, I whispered, "St. Liam, the people's hero."

At that point, Ethan grew fussy, which luckily for us gave us an excuse to escape the press. Liam whispered something into Colemen's ear and he nodded and gave the signal to his advisors that we were through here. Surrounded by the secret service, we walked behind the President through the halls, which were lined with portraits of all past Presidents, until we reached the Oval Office. I should've been shocked to find Olivia standing there, but I wasn't.

"Sweetheart, you look horrible, what's the matter?" her mother asked, as she walked over to give her daughter a hug.

Olivia didn't return it, she just stood there, frozen as she stared at me. I knew she must have thought of running. But with the tracker around her ankle, where could she really go?

"You still have a press conference to do," she whispered.

"They can wait a moment. After all, it's not like they have anything better to do," Colemen replied to their daughter's dismay.

"She was hoping for a private moment to speak with you," I told them, as I took a seat on the couch and placed Ethan on my knee.

"Sweetheart?" her mother whispered, as she brushed the strands of her blonde hair.

"I'm fine. I should head back."

"I don't understand," President Colemen said as he looked between us.

Before he had a chance to say another word, the door opened and Neal came in, dressed quite sharply in black suit and red tie.

He looked straight at Olivia for a moment, and as she took a timid a step forward, he all but cut her down with a look of disgust and anger in his eyes, causing her to take a much larger step back.

"Right on time, big brother, your wife here has a lot of press to do today, isn't that right? I'm sure you both can come off as a loving couple for the camera," Liam said as he waved him inside.

"Yes, I can. Is there anything else you need?" he asked, and I glanced at Liam who smirked.

We'd broken him, which meant that we had to fix him… but that part would come later.

"Wife," Neal called for Olivia with an unfamiliar harshness that caused her to shudder.

She took his arm, and turned to leave.

We were still going to need to watch out for both of them. Neal had proven his loyalty for now, but as easily as he'd turned against his wife, he could've turned against us, if Olivia played on his emotions. He may have been trying to hide his affection for her, but it was still there.

"Who are you texting?" Liam asked me, and for a moment, the old me wanted to tell him to mind his own damn business.

"Sedric. I think it would be best he stayed on their tail as well." If I knew Sedric as well as I thought I did, he was livid about the situation. He didn't take kindly to betrayal.

The stupid First Lady stood in front of me with her hands propped on her hips as if I was supposed to be intimidated by that. "Whatever you're doing to my daughter, I'm asking you to stop. She's a good person and I know *good* isn't something you people are familiar with, but—"

"Should I take this, or would you like the honors?" I asked Liam as I stood holding Ethan to my chest.

"Knock yourself out," Liam replied, as he took Ethan from my arms and allowed me to face the wannabe Jackie-O.

Clasping my hands together, I rolled my shoulders and smiled. "Your daughter is not a *good person*. You are not a *good person*. None of us in this room are *good people*. That's why we're able to stand here today. We've all made deals, we've all signed our names in blood, and we've all looked the other way at some point. I believe in *good people*. I know they're out there, feeding the poor, clothing orphans and all that shit. But they do not cross over into our world; they are not in *our story*, because once again, they are *good people*. If Olivia was good, she would have walked away when she could. If you were good, you would have never allowed her to marry into this family. You would have never gone back to your husband, and you wouldn't be the First Lady. You. Are. Not. A. Good. Person. So let us all be clear on who we are. The good people are the voters, the middle class, the poor, is that something you want to be?"

She didn't answer; she just shook her head.

"I thought so." I took a step closer to her. "Why don't you go back to picking out china and reading to kindergarteners or whatever primitive things the First Lady does?"

She made it to the door when Evelyn came in.

"It's like you can read my mind," Liam said to her, as he rocked a sleepy Ethan.

"Mr. President," She shook Colemen's hand with a smile.

"It's nice to see you, Evelyn."

Meeting my eyes, she took Ethan into her arms and I kissed his forehead as the little guy rubbed his sleepy eyes. Colemen raised his eyebrow at me as though he was shocked that I could be a mother.

"Come on, peanut." She nodded at him as they left.

Great. Now we can get to business.

"Where can we listen to Avian speak?" I asked him.

Nodding to the door, we followed him out and into a separate office. There, Ivan spoke as Avian Doers, head of the F.B.I. Those who were already sitting around the table stood for the President as he entered, and I could clearly see how much Colemen enjoyed it. Money was not the root of all evil, it was just a vehicle that got you to power.

"Ladies and gentlemen, may we have the room?" he asked them. And without question, they all took their leave.

I focused on the words coming out of Avian's mouth partially amazed at how a snake like him could fit so well with the rest of us. "Good afternoon, ladies and gentlemen of the press. I will not be answering any questions today. Many of you are aware of the tragic and unfortunate events that have occurred with a few select former agents of the Federal Bureau of Investigation, and I would like to inform you that there is currently an in-house investigation underway. More cannot be said about the individual agents at this time, as many of the operations being handled were classified—"

"How is a federal agent murdering a hooker in a hotel room with hundreds of thousands of dollars and drugs classified information?" a man yelled, cutting him off.

"Does President Colemen have any comments on the matter?"

"What of the agent that was found hanging from the bridge?"

"Can you confirm that an agent was kidnapped from the Embassy?"

Avian stiffened, as his face remained hard and flat. I would have even dared to say that he was starting to feel stressed.

"Don't you just love the press?" Liam whispered to me.

"When we're controlling them, yes. Yes, I do," I replied.

"As I said," Avian spoke out once again. "I cannot answer any more questions at this time. However, I will say that I plan to do everything in my power to make sure a thorough investigation is completed. When we have solid information to share, we will do so."

"When you said I would take a hit, you never said it was going to be like this," the President whined as he watched the press conference being held by no other than the resident pain in my ass, Avian.

"What else does taking a hit mean?" Liam asked him as he leaned against his desk.

"The FBI are the police of the United States! I am the head of the United States. By attacking him like this, you're undermining me. I won't be reelected if people cannot trust—"

"Why do we have to keep repeating things to these people?" He turned to me as I looked through the email Declan sent me on my phone.

"For some reason, they keep underestimating our intelligence even though we continuously prove that we're not idiots." I said in return.

"I understand that you both have your grand master plan, but you need to give me something to work with. I have a staff of people all trying to do damage control, while I'm sitting on my hands. I cannot just take this. FBI agents are failing everywhere," Colemen snapped.

"Tell them that you are being updated on the situation and your prayer goes out to all of the people and their families who have lost their lives in service to their country. Then remind them that what makes America great is checks and balances. The FBI is not your personal army, and tell them that you are speaking with the director to see what can be done," Liam directed him.

"Without being too obvious on the matter, find a way to make it clear that the man running things is the director," I added as well. We were setting fire to Avian's own personal world.

Reaching for the intercom, he called in his Chief of Staff, and his former political strategist, Mina. As she stepped in, she looked over to us and sighed.

"So I'm guessing we're not putting out a statement?" she asked.

"No, you are. Mr. President, please fill her in," I said, already heading towards the door.

LIAM

"You're on speaker, Declan," I said as Monte drove us into town. I wasn't a fan of Washington; it had nothing on Chicago, and I found myself missing the smog, the wind, the buildings that touched the sky, and everything else that made Chicago great.

"You had us kidnap a federal agent, but not kill her. With all due respect, what the bloody fuck, Liam?"

Rolling my eyes, I rested into the leather seat.

"Where's the trust, brother?"

"Chained to the wall in the basement of an old steel mill," he replied.

"Has she said anything?" Mel questioned him.

"No, but I wasn't aware that she knew anything of importance."

"There's no harm in asking."

I gave her a look.

"Well, there is a harm, but not to us and that's all that matters. She's FBI not CIA, which unfortunately for her means that she isn't trained to endure the same type of torture," she clarified.

But I did want Intel. "I want her to give us a layout of the Federal building, all the ins and outs, and every secret

entrance she can think of. In fact, hold on, Declan…" I said
to him as I pressed hold. "Monte. Kain."

Nodding, they placed their earplugs in.

"What are you thinking?" Mel eyed me carefully as a
plan formed clearly in my mind.

"When you came home, you said there are only two wars
that Americans care about: the war on drugs—"

"And the war on terror. What's your point?"

"If you stop interrupting me I can tell you." I glared at
her and she crossed her arms. "What if we gave them terror? It won't be anything major, we'll just have our agent say
that she has been kidnapped by what appears to be a homegrown terrorist. The media will go crazy, Avian will have no
choice but to spend every moment either dealing with the
press, or trying to save her."

Her mind was turning as she reached over to take Declan
off hold. "Declan, has she seen your face?"

"No, but she must have seen Coraline's and Fedel's
when they took her."

"Hold on," Mel replied, putting him on hold again.
"We're going to have to kill her, and if we kill her, they will
not stop until they find who is responsible. Terrorism, even
mock terrorism, can—"

"It can be done, Mel. It can. We said we were taking off
the kid gloves, and this is the way to do it. No one will see
this coming. There are homegrown terrorists all over this
country, between you and Declan's hacking, I'm sure we
could find a scapegoat. We're actually doing the country a
service, and Colemen will look so good, he'll want to take
part in this." I could see it now and what made it great is the
fact that it crossed the line, it wasn't something that Avian
would ever think we'd do.

"Well, if there's anyone who can pull something like this off, it's me," she said.

Her ego sometimes.

"We're doing it," I replied, knowing that she was already working out the logistics in her mind.

Once again, she reached over and took Declan off hold.

"Declan, have Coraline slap her around a little bit, but nothing heavy. You and I are going fishing tonight. Be on standby." And with that, she cut the phone off before she looked to me. "Before we actually do it, I want our scapegoat already in place."

"Fine," I nodded.

"We're here, sir," Monte said somewhat loudly due to the earplugs. It was easy to tell that we were no longer in the prestigious parts of D.C., and that we were somewhere southwest of the capitol.

What was supposed to be a small photo-op at a newly built youth center, was actually the same place we'd be able to see our customers.

Southwest was one of our biggest consumers. Of course they didn't know it was us directly, but it didn't hurt to check in on the trade here.

Twenty-Three

"Someday you're gonna look back on this moment of your life as such a sweet time of grieving. You'll see that you were in mourning and your heart was broken, but your life was changing..."

—*Elizabeth Gilbert*

NEAL

I splashed the water on my face, and took a deep breath before I dared to look at myself in the bathroom mirror. Without turning, I watched as she walked in. Her blue eyes focused on me as she pressed herself against the door.

"Can I help you?" I asked her, as I took some paper towels from the dispenser. I scanned the bathroom to make sure that we were the only occupants.

"Neal, please don't be this way."

"What way?" I hollered at her. "What '*way*' am I being, Olivia? Tell me, seeing as how you know so fucking much."

Her head dropped and I strode determinedly to her, and grabbed her by the arm as I pulled her to me, and forced her to look me in the eyes.

"You've *disgraced* me," I sneered only inches away from her face. "You made me a fool. Of all people in this world, you should have known me. You should have known what I wanted and that was to not destroy my family. Family is *everything*. It comes before all else, and you didn't even think how I would feel if Avian killed my brothers, my father, my mother."

"I did it for us! You and I both know your family will never accept you!" she cried.

"You did it for yourself! Jesus fucking Christ, you don't give a shit about anyone but yourself. Now you stand in front of me, trying to seem innocent as if you didn't go against the code. As if you didn't spit on everything my family has spent decades building. Do you know what the Irish do to people who do what you have done? I'm being this way, avoiding you, smiling for the cameras, because it is the only thing that's stopping me from snapping your fucking neck and dumping you in acid." Letting her go, I walked past her and opened the door. "If you have ever cared about me, Olivia, play your part because we're done. Now, let's go."

She swallowed as she wiped her tears and fixed her dress. Turning to me she took my extended arm. With a smile, we walked towards the lunch table where my father sat waiting. Olivia went and kissed his cheek before she sat down, and I shook his hand in greeting. He gazed at me with the same tired look I had grown up seeing, and I wanted to tell him that I understood.

"So, Olivia, have you chosen a spot at the family burial plot yet?" he casually asked her while he poured himself some tea.

Her mouth dropped open.

"It's quite nice, we have photos engraved into the black marble," he added, as he took a sip.

It seemed as though everyone in the family had taken to torturing her in some way. But she'd made her bed and now she would lie in it, alone. There was no escape for her. Even though she was out in the open like this, Melody had made sure her orders were clear, if Olivia tried to run, we were to aim for her legs.

DECLAN

I watched her as she punched as hard as she could into his neck. He grabbed on to her arm, and pulled her up and over, until her body slammed onto the canvas of Liam's boxing ring. Crawling onto her side, she pushed herself up before she wiped the blood from her nose and regained her stance.

Fedel stared at her for a moment before he lifted his arms and took a couple of steps back. They circled each other, their eyes never wavering. Finally, she leaped forward, and he grabbed her waist, trying to stop her. However, she twisted herself, and wrapped her legs around his neck before she flipped him. They wrestled on the ground until I couldn't handle seeing him touch her any longer.

"Enough. Get the fuck off my wife," I said as calmly as I could while I walked towards the ring. They both looked at me, confused for a moment, but what pissed me off was the amused look that graced Fedel's face.

Without another word, he got up while Coraline remained on the ground, taking deep breaths.

"Thank you, Fedel," she said to him.

I watched as he nodded to us, and I followed his every move as he stepped out of the ring.

"Get ready, we're going to pay our guest a visit," I stated.

"I'll get right on it," he answered as he walked off.

Turning back to my wife, I saw that she still hadn't moved.

"You're being jealous for no reason, Declan."

"I'm not jealous, I just don't like watching my wife get beat on by any man."

She turned her head to me and gave me a small grin. "I had a fighting chance."

"He was holding back, believe me."

She looked so disheartened, that I want to kick myself. "Not that you weren't doing well, because you were. But Fedel has been doing this for decades. There were times you surprised us both, that leg thing you did was…"

Sexy.

"You do know that Fedel's gay, right?" she asked.

I was completely floored. My mouth opened as I tried to process the words she'd just said. "Did he tell you that?"

"No, but he doesn't need to. Seriously, you've never noticed?"

"Noticed what?" I'd noticed nothing!

"Declan, he's never once had a girlfriend since we've know him—"

"Who has time for a girlfriend? He's busy, I barely have time to have a wife with all the shit Mel and Liam have me doing."

She laughed as she rose from the floor before she came over to me. "He's never once talked about woman either. All the other men try to sleep with the maids or their eyes wander when we're in public. But Fedel…if a woman approaches him, he always says the same thing. 'Sorry, I'm not interested—'"

"He's dedicated to his work; the family doesn't pay to flirt on the job."

"Speaking of family events, we need to organize a get-together. We haven't seen them in a few months, I'll ask Mel and Evelyn." She snapped her fingers as she remembered.

"I can't believe he's gay," I whispered, still stuck on the first part of her statement.

She rolled her eyes. "Not all gay men run around with rainbows and sprinkles shooting out of their asses."

"I know, but come on, he would have at the very least tried to hit on me. He can't be gay."

She froze as she looked me over. Then without warning, she broke out into a fit of laughter. She laughed so hard that her eyes were watering.

"It's not that funny."

"No, it isn't. Your head is just so damn big, I'm going crazy from the lack of oxygen."

"Don't make me pin you down."

"Don't make me mess up your face, *pretty boy*. What's the Italian word for narcissist?"

Her smile still made me smile, even when she got on my fucking nerves. It reminded me of when we first met…she called me a narcissist then too.

"Hit the showers so we can go; you got pissed at me the last time I went to visit her without you."

She moved to get out of the ring but I stopped her and kissed her hard. Pulling her to me, I wrapped my arms around her waist as she leaned in and deepened our kiss. As I let go of her, she stumbled forward.

"Seriously, what man or woman in their right mind wouldn't want a piece of *this*," I whispered to her.

Shaking her head at me, she walked off and left me standing there.

"You're not that hot!" she yelled.

I grinned. "You're a bad liar, baby!"

CORALINE

I wanted to crawl into a bath of ice and never come out. All of my muscles were on fire, and yet Fedel looked perfectly fine. He sat in his chair, wearing a slim-fitted, black leather zipper jacket, with dark Ralph Lauren jeans, and black military boots.

"Do you need anything, boss?" he asked without opening his eyes.

"No. And you and I both know you don't think of me as your boss. You don't have to call me that, Fedel."

His eyes opened and his eyebrow rose. "We aren't friends, Mrs. Callahan. I work for your brother-in-law and your sister-in-law, and by extension, you. I call you 'boss' because they made you so while they're away. Noted that calling you as such is disrespectful to them. *Not* calling you boss means that I do not agree with their decision, which means I am questioning their choice. Thoughts like that are dangerous, especially in times like these. And only a fool would question or disrespect them. I've made it this long by not being a fool."

Loyal to the bone.

"If you work for me, then why are you here resting your eyes while Declan is in there?"

"You're mistaken, ma'am, I was simply listening to our surroundings. Take for example the rat right by the window above us trying to eat a stale piece of bread…"

Glancing up at the dirty, yellow, tinted windows of the factory, I saw the rat that he was referring to, eating what appeared to be some sort of pastry or bread.

"Also, there's a flag outside flapping in the wind," he stated, looking to the large red steel doors that stood about twenty feet from us. But they were sealed shut, how could he have heard that?

"There's also a blue Chevy driving this way, but it's just passing through."

Now I was just incredulous. I turned to face him. "How in the hell can you know that?"

He pointed to his ear. "We have men standing post and they're filling me in."

Crossing my arms, I pouted. "No one likes a smartass."

"Yes, ma'am. Now may I go back to resting my eyes?" he smiled and I nodded in acquiesce.

Resting against the chair, he closed his eyes once more as I walked around, and inspected the old rusted machines of the abandoned factory. Everything was so cold, damp, and dark. It made me wonder if Mel and Liam chose places like this to seem badass. Declan was down in the basement dealing with our "guest." I wanted to join him, but he was still using the training wheels when it came to me. At least he allowed me to carry a gun now, and even though I wasn't the best shot, I was good enough. I had two knives in my boots that I was able to wield more efficiently, and he'd bought me the same gloves that Mel used, apparently they were made from some fabric that didn't leave any DNA or fingerprint residue.

"Fedel, how many men do we have?" I asked him, as I jumped up onto the old conveyor belt.

"Within the state, or the country?"

I never knew there was a difference.

"The state?"

"Two hundred and forty-seven."

"Jesus, really? We pay all of those people?"

"If you want any more information, you're going to have to ask the boss." He shifted in his seat.

I frowned, as I stood up and walked slowly along the belt with my arms out to the side as though I was having trouble balancing.

"Fedel, what's the Italian word for narcissist?"

"Narcisista."

Well, that was easier than I thought.

"How many people have you—?"

"I've lost count," he cut me off before I could finish what I was going to say.

"I was going to ask you how many people you've dated."

"Are you ordering me to talk about my personal life?"

I didn't want to *order* him. "No, but—"

"Then I prefer to not answer your question, ma'am," he responded, and luckily for the both of us, Declan returned from the basement.

"We're done here, are they still standing guard?"

Fedel nodded, already on his feet. "Just like you asked, three at night, three in the morning. Also there is a new shipment of snow coming in."

Why didn't anyone tell me? Pricks!

"Good. Right on time. I'll let Mel and Liam know, they've been expecting it." Declan came upbeside me, and extended his arm to help me down. Accepting it, I jumped down as gracefully as possible.

"Did the permits come in for the new marijuana farm?" he questioned.

Fedel shook his head. "Apparently Chicago's not as liberal as we would've liked to believe."

"Well, it looks as though the bosses are going to have to buddy up to more people in Washington before they come home. They really want a home-based farm, right?" I asked, reminding them both that this was no longer a boys only club.

"What's happening to our guest?" I added.

They both gave each other a look...I knew that look. It was the same one that Liam wore when he first introduced Mel to the family. It was the look he had in his eye before he was arrested. It was a look that said, "the shit is about to hit the fan."

I sighed. "Do I have to start making 'Free Declan Callahan' buttons?"

TWENTY-FOUR

"The main reason he's in the business is to eliminate his enemies."
—Lorenzo Carcaterra

MELODY

"Have they noticed you?" I asked him as I searched through the lines of the green code on the screen.

"No, I don't think so. They're horrifyingly anal, but they aren't expecting anyone to be checking on them. Give me a second and maybe I can get us a live feed to make sure this isn't just some M.I.T. dropout living in his mother's basement," Declan replied on speakerphone.

"Already done." He'd apparently forgotten that I'd been doing this a long time.

Clicking on the web camera, I pulled up the live feed for both of us to see. Part of me did expect to see some loser dropout sitting in his dirty underwear and eating chips, just like the last three organizations we'd looked into.

Kain was coming in handy. It was best not to go to Colemen for this after getting the FBI list from him. So while in the Southeast, Kain greased a few palms and kept an open ear for any rumors of terrorist activity. The problem with law enforcement was that nine times out of ten, they assumed that people were stupid, and to their credit, nine times out of ten it was true. However, the difference was that they didn't bother to inquire. It'd been a week since Liam first came up with this idea, and now everything was beginning to fall into place. We'd paid visits to bars frequented by anyone who was relevant in the government, and we'd gotten a few names from our venture. None of them seem worth the trouble though, which was why they'd been written off.

"Are you seeing this?" Declan gasped in shock before he chuckled. "We've crossed over into a whole other world."

Pulling off my headphones, I turned to Liam who was lying in bed reading his comic book. I wanted to take the damn thing and chuck it across the room. Instead, I smacked him on the chest.

"What?" he snapped at me as I held up the laptop for him to see. His eyes widened as he sat up. "Holy shit."

Taking the device from me, he sat rigidly, as his comic book fell to the floor.

"Are those AR-15s?"

"No, those are 1975 Russian APS assault rifles. However, these," I said as I motioned to the guns on the far side of the wall, "are AR-15s. And those over there are original M1 Garand. My father gave me his on my fifteenth birthday. He had a Bushmaster M17S', a Colt LE901 and a SOPMOD, which I am certain is strictly for military issue. Liam, this equates to my dream kitchen."

Was it wrong that I was smiling? The room was an arsenal of weapons that had the potential to make me jealous. On the walls were maps of the different states that lined the East Coast.

"Who are they?" Liam asked me.

"They call themselves *Rsamas*; the Republic Soldiers Against More American Savagism. They're a brand new terror cell growing out of—"

"Let me guess, Mississippi?" he cut me off.

"Close—Alabama. Right now, they boast thirteen members that Declan and I can dig up. They are very active on private underground blogs and chat rooms. Most of their action seems to be cyber based— hacking and the sort, but nothing on a grand scale."

He looked to me. "They look as if they're preparing for war."

"Then it's a good thing we're here to provide the war for them."

"Can you be any more excited?" he chuckled as he brushed a strand of my hair behind my ear.

I held the screen for him to see again. "My dream kitchen, Liam. My dream kitchen."

"Well, it looks as if we've found our sacrificial lamb."

I leaned in as I zoomed over the guns at the bottom of the screen.

"No, Mel," he said as though I were Ethan.

"*Excuse* you?"

"I'm sorry, you didn't hear me? Let me repeat myself. *No, Mel*, you're not ordering anyone down south for a few guns. I'm sure you can get them off the black market anyway." He handed me back the phone, and took the computer from me.

"Not that one, it's a FN Herstal semi-automatic—"

"Love, I adore you, but can you be passionate about something else right now. Like, I don't know, setting these guys up?" The comic book nerd smiled.

I never said shit when he spent ten grand on his cartoon books.

"Pussy," I muttered as I picked up the phone. "Declan?"

"So, I'm guessing this means were doing this?" he sighed into the phone.

"Do you have a problem?"

"No, I'll get to work. When do you want this to happen?"

I looked to Liam, who had bent over to grab his comic. Angrily, I kicked him in the chest and off the bed. I was doing all the goddamn work while he was just on mother-fucking vacation. Just because I knew how to hack, didn't mean he got to slack off.

"What the fuck!?" he yelled at me.

Smiling, I focused. "Do the tape, then send it to me, we'll broadcast it tomorrow. Avian's been doing a pretty good job controlling the fallout from the FBI. I want to strike again before he comes after us."

"He's already tightening up the DEA busts around our supplies. It's as if he knows where all our imports are coming from."

I'd known that. But hearing it from his mouth annoyed me. Liam stood up and grabbed my legs. Instinctively, I tried to kick him away.

"Just get it done."

"I'll get right on it. And Mel?"

"*What,* Declan?" I gritted through my teeth as Liam grabbed my free arm and placed it behind my back.

"Did you know Fedel's gay?"

I was aware of that, but I was more shocked that he knew. Fedel was very good at keeping his personal life as private as possible.

"Get it done, Declan." I hung up and threw the phone onto the bed as I tried to wiggle free from Liam's grasp.

"You know, you're very abusive," he whispered into my ear.

"It's not my fault you're a *pussy,*" I replied, as I kicked my leg into his balls.

"BITCH!" he hissed out in pain as he involuntarily let me go.

I hadn't even kicked him that hard.

Grabbing his shirt, I pulled him onto the bed and sat on top of him.

"And you better not forget it, sweetheart." I moved to get off of him, but he didn't let me go.

"Liam—"

"Stop talking. Just sit on top of me until it feels better."

I tried not laugh. "And how is this helping?"

"Mentally it makes me feel better."

I roll my eyes as I sat on top of him for a moment longer before I got up. "We have a lot to do today, you've been through worse, so man up."

"Women underestimate how fucking painful this is," he grumbled as someone knocked.

"Maybe that's because we are comparing it to the fact that once a month Mother Nature punches us in the uterus for a week," I snapped.

He opened his mouth, but then closed it, obviously unsure how to respond as I opened the door.

Sedric gave me an odd stare and I could only assume that he'd heard the last part of our conversation.

"Yes?" I asked.

Shaking his head, he handed me a folder and I immediately wanted to smack him over the head! I'd specifically instructed him not to key Liam into this. Now he was going to ask me what the fuck was in it.

"Sedric—"

"Before you start, Liam came to me a week ago and asked me to do the same thing you wanted. There's no point in me doing it twice. This is everything for all of us, with the exception of Olivia, of course."

Liam came up beside me, and took the file. "You asked for new identities and didn't tell me?"

"I'll take my leave now," Sedric snickered, as he turned around. He paused for a moment before he turned to face us again. "Ethan and I are going to a hurling match tomorrow."

"Starting a little young, don't you think?" I grinned. Part of me didn't like the idea of Ethan, who's just a giant pillow of sweet baby, getting exposed to such a bloody sport. But then again, he was still young, he likely wouldn't remember it.

He shrugged, and smiled. "Liam always walked away when I tried to teach him. So, I'm going to teach Ethan before he can walk. He'll grow into it."

Liam rolled his eyes, and leaned against the doorframe. "Try all you want, old man, but Ethan is just going to cry and annoy everyone around you."

"You underestimate how much Ethan loves his grandpa," he replied, and waved us off as he left.

Taking the folder from Liam, I pulled out the passports, and checked through them quickly.

"Latvia." I frowned. "If we didn't have any other reason to kill Avian, then not going to Latvia would be it."

"Luckily, we have more than a dozen reasons," Liam replied from inside his closet.

Following him, I watched as he grabbed a new shirt and lifted two ties, one burgundy and the other navy blue, for me to pick. I pointed to the navy blue one, and he of course picked the burgundy one. He and I did this every day. I picked one and he chose the other. He had to have known that by now I always picked the tie I disliked, but I didn't think he cared...and neither did I.

"The plan?" he asked as he took out a pair of dress socks.

"While you are kissing up to the fat cats on Capitol Hill in regards to the marijuana grant back home, I'm going to start creating rap sheets for our scapegoats. Because of what we're planning, I want people to definitely believe that they were capable of everything when they finally get caught."

He nodded. "Phone records?"

"When Coraline took the agent, she was using a burner phone to speak with Declan. It was paid for in cash, of course, but that can be changed to leave a paper trail."

"It's takes twelve and half hours to get from the capitol to Alabama."

How the hell did he know things like that off the top of head?

"That's why there are tickets bought in their names at the perfect time. They aren't real, but I doubt that anyone will be diligent enough to check."

Standing in the doorframe, he came up to me, and brushed my hair back as he cupped my cheek. "You sure you don't want me to stay?"

"So you can read more comics? No. I think you need to get some work done. Now go make us richer."

Rolling his eyes, he kissed my forehead before he headed to the door. "I'll be back at five, have dinner ready for me."

Clenching my teeth together, I took a deep breath, as I gazed at him. "Sure sweetheart. There's no guarantee you'll survive it though."

He snickered as he closed the door behind him. Hearing a small whimper, I turned to Ethan, who was slowly waking up in his basket by our bed. He rested so quietly sometimes, I found myself needing to check his breathing just to make sure he was okay. Reaching into his basket, I pulled him into my arms and kissed his head.

"Mommy is going to frame a terrorist, do you want to see?" He whined and waved his arms before he started to cry.

"Food, then terrorists. Okay," I muttered, as I headed to the kitchen.

Evelyn was there, stirring a pot of beef something, and the second she spotted Ethan, she abandoned the pot.

"Do you need me to get him?"

She reached for him, but I held on.

"No, I got it."

She gave me a look as I reach into the fridge for his bottle.

"What?" I asked her, as I took the top off with one hand before I placed it into the bottle warmer.

She shrugs with a smile. "Nothing."

"I do not like being dismissed, Evelyn."

"Oh please, you're not scary with that little cutie on your hip." She made a face at him, but he wasn't having it. Just like Liam, he tended to get grumpy when he was hungry. "Anyway, I thought you were busy, changing the course of history, and leveling government institutions and all that."

"I'm a working mother, what can I say?" I muttered, as I reached for his bottle. She watched me with a giant grin as I tried to test the temperature of the milk on the inside of my wrist, but I couldn't with Ethan on my hip.

I felt as if she were challenging me, and just waiting for me to hand him over. But instead, I lifted my head and allowed a few drops to fall onto my tongue. Ethan hit my face as if to berate me, but I had to check. Placing the bottle into his mouth, I smiled as he relaxed and settled back.

"And to think, you once told me you didn't know how to be a mother," Evelyn said with a grin as she returned to stirring her magical pot of meat like a witch over a cauldron.

"I still don't. I'm just taking a page out of Liam's book and making up the rules as I go."

"Really, what rules?"

"Personal Mel rule number one: always feed Ethan when he's hungry or pay the ear-curdling consequences," I replied, as I leaned against the sink.

"Good rule." She laughed. "You've grown so much, Mel, you're basically a different person."

"That doesn't sound good. I liked who I was."

Pausing, she turned to me, her wooden spoon still in hand.

"You liked the loneliness? The bitter ang—"

"Watch it, Evelyn, I haven't changed that much, and baby or no, I can still do damage."

"Good to know. Now prove it and kill Olivia," she said bluntly, with unfamiliar severity.

Shifting Ethan's weight, I stood up straighter. "Evelyn, I don't answer to you. I don't need to explain why I do things, or why I don't. Liam and I run this family."

"I understand that, and truthfully, I've more than enjoyed having my husband back to normal. We've gotten to do everything I've always wanted to, but couldn't before."

There was that word again, *normal*. When would people learn that there was no such thing as normal?

"But with that being said," her jaw tightened. "There is an unwritten law, a code, we all live by. It has kept this family as strong as it is because we never make exceptions. *When you stand against us, you will be removed. When you betray us and endanger our lives, you die.* I want her dead, not in the basement getting Neiman Marcus dresses for events. I want my son free of any attachment to her, and I sure as hell do not want her filthy body buried in our family plot. She didn't want to be a part of this family, so let her rot in a fucking alleyway for all I care."

I seemed that Mama Callahan was out and ready to attack, wooden spoon and all.

"Anything else?" I asked since it seemed like I was taking fucking orders now.

"Yes. Are Liam and Neal going to be back soon? I'm making their favorite—Irish Lamb Stew and Soda bread. I can teach you if you like," she said, as she once more turned back to her pot.

I looked to Ethan who was happily sucking away on the teat of his bottle, and then back to her. This was all too much for me. Without answering her, I walked away from the kitchen.

If Avian could only see me now...he would weep.

LIAM

Five more minutes of this fuckery...just five more minutes.
Forcing a smile, I turned to the men behind me. "Well gentlemen?"

"How much would one of these sell for?" Senator Jeffrey Boxer, of North Carolina, asked as he touched the marijuana plant in our small D.C. shop. Mel and I didn't have time to set up here, however, we'd put just a *bit* of pressure on the owners and bought it. And after a few visits from Kain and Monte, they were more than willing to sell...it was nice of them.

"Ounces run from $350 to close to $600," I answered.

He, along with his colleagues, stared in shock. "Each?"

"Yes." I nodded as I moved to touch the green plants. "But almost no one buys in full ounces. The common choice is an eighth of an ounce, which runs from $50 to $80. With business moving as it is, that's over forty million dollars generated in yearly taxes. Taxes that can be turned over to each state to build schools and anything else your state needs."

"I've got to say...this is a pretty well-oiled machine," Senator Andrew Kelly, of Texas stated.

"Yes, which is why I'm surprised Washington isn't acting in favor of this, or are you? I'm ready to go state by state.

Those I'm already working with have been flawless for the last year."

"It's a very delicate matter, Mr. Callahan—"

"Making money always is, and so is who I spend it on." They tensed. "But I understand your point. I just hope you take the future into consideration. Not only my state, but yours as well."

I moved to the backdoor and held it open for them. After all, they were still politicians and they didn't want to run the risk of being seen at such an establishment. I shook their hands as they all went back to their cars.

"You scratch my back and I'll scratch yours, Mr. Callahan," Senator Boxer whispered before nodding to me.

"I never scratch first, but thank you for coming," I replied, as I let go of him.

I watched as they drove away before I stepped back inside and turned to face Neal who was waiting with a mask. Taking it, we walked through the maze of marijuana plants before making it to the back. There was a hidden trapdoor that led to the lower level. He pulled it up for me as I placed my mask on, and together, we headed down.

There were two conveyor belts, one for cocaine and the other for crystal. It had only taken us a few days to set up this factory of sorts, and the truth of the matter was that there was no better place to hide an illegal business than under a legal one.

The room was filled with six of our men, all of whom were sorting and placing the product into bags. Inspecting the crystal with forceps, I looked them over.

"They aren't as clear as the last batch," I said to Neal.

"Saoirse's daughter got hurt, I suspect she may have rushed through this batch," Neal replied, as he sifted through the glass-like meth on the belt.

"What happened to her daughter?"

"Her boyfriend decided to use her as a punching bag."

I sighed. Saoirse was our chemist. We rarely spoke and we all preferred it that way. She had her own fully staffed lab based out of Chicago that we never went near...well, Mel and I never did, but we had a few people check in on her from time to time. She made the crystal, we sold it, and she spent the money on funding new drugs for her lab.

"Declan, Coraline, and Fedel are all working on something else. Who do you think can go *help*?" After all, that was a part of the deal when you worked with us— wealth and protection for you and your family.

"Oisin and Tierney," Neal recommended. They were street muscle who weren't particularly close to us.

"Fine. Have it done, but make sure that Saoirse knows that if she produces anything like this again, we'll have to part ways," I replied, as I headed towards the coke.

Already on his phone, he nodded. Cutting into the coke, I dropped in the liquid and watched it turn purple. It was as good enough for now.

"I want it on the street by tonight."

Kain and Monte stood at the vault. Moving to it, I keyed in the passcode, which automatically changed every hour. It looked empty of course, but I walked to the center and peeled back a panel and stepped into the second hidden vault opening. We couldn't put all of our money into the bank when we got it, which was why we kept some money with other clan members for a short period of time before we could move it. Grabbing a few stacks, I placed them into two different bags for Kain and Monte. They'd know what to do with it.

Locking both vaults behind me, I headed upstairs.

MELODY

B iting into an apple, I stared at her while she slept. She was curled into a fetal position on the bed, her face stained with dried tears. As I kicked her thigh, I took another bite from my apple, and without waiting for her response, I dragged a chair over to the bed and planted it front of her.

"Wakey wakey, Olivia," I said to her as I took a seat.

She couldn't even pick herself up, and as she opened her eyes to look at me, she began to sob uncontrollably. Rolling my eyes, I waited for her to calm down.

"Olivia."

"Please, just —"

"Are you about to give me an order?" I asked before I took another bite.

She didn't reply.

"Evelyn asked me to kill you. She was quite cold about it actually. Note to self; never betray family…though you'd think that goes without saying."

Again, she sobbed, and her entire body shook.

"We're almost done, Olivia. It's almost over and you will be gone. So weep, pray, do whatever you need to do." It was to be her punishment and his test.

I headed back up the stars just in time to find Sedric, with Ethan in his arms, talking with Liam and Neal.

Noticing me, Liam broke away and I already knew what he wanted.

"It's ready and Avian is having a press conference in the morning. We'll stream it then. Get ready for an earthquake," I said to him.

He pulled me closer to him. "We better hold steady."

"Who's ready for dinner?" Evelyn called from the dining room.

"Irish Lamb Stew and Soda bread? You spoil me," Sedric said with a grin as he walked into the room while bouncing Ethan in his arms.

Both Liam and Neal perked up.

The Irish.

Heading to the dining table, we all sat around as Evelyn served us dinner. She seemed quite peppy.

"Evelyn, are you on something?" I asked her.

"Can't I make food for my boys?" She glared at me.

"Of course," Neal, Sedric, and Liam all said at once.

Jesus fuck, it was like she'd hijacked their brains. It almost made me want to cook...*almost*, but not really.

I reached over to take a piece of the bread, but Liam stopped me and looked at his mother oddly.

"It's the first Monday in June."

"So?" I asked.

"It's Lá Saoire i mí Mheitheamh." Neal grinned.

What? In all my studies of Irish history I'd barely heard about it. It was a traditional holiday known as Pentecost Monday or the June Bank. But it wasn't that big of a deal... was it?

Evelyn smiled. "I remember when your father and I took you to Ireland to celebrate. With all this foolishness going on, it only seemed fitting that we celebrate it. I've sent Coraline the recipe so that she and Declan can have it as well. We're family and people who go against that—well, let's keep things pleasant," Evelyn said and Sedric kissed her cheek.

This felt oddly *normal*. As I looked over to Ethan who sat in his highchair, I wondered if I'd be like Evelyn one day...the thought made me shiver. I really hoped that I was beyond Evelyn. This mothering thing was like a double-edged sword. I felt the need to be soft near Ethan, but feeling this soft made me feel...on edge.

Would I ever figure out this whole balancing thing? Would I figure out how to be Bloody Melody while still being able to make dinner for Ethan and his future wife or girlfriend? But I was getting way over my head. I needed to not only ensure that Avian was gone forever, but that this situation would never happen again.

As if he could read my mind, Liam placed his hand on my thigh. Leaning over to me, he whispered, "Just for a moment, stop thinking about Avian. He will get his."

Didn't he know by now that I'd never stop thinking? With a smile, I focused on Sedric as he spoke about 'the good ole days'...and he wasn't even that damn old! But the way he spoke, you would have thought he lived in a black and white gangster movie.

"Plus your mother couldn't look away from me!" Sedric spoke between bites.

"It was your fedora. You can't ignore a man in a fedora." She laughed as she rolled her eyes at him. Grinning at Ethan, she leaned over her food and asked, "For Father's Day, you should buy one for your daddy."

Was I supposed to help him with that?

"And hide this good head of hair? Blasphemy," Liam snickered. "Plus I fuc—"

"Liam," Evelyn and I both said at the same time.

"Dada. Dada. Da." Ethan laughed as he flapped his arms.

Liam and I froze.

"Did you all hear that?" Neal grinned.

"Say it again, I think your Mommy and Daddy are in shock." Sedric gave his fingers to Ethan to play with.

Ethan smiled, clearly enjoying the attention. "Dada. Dada!"

All of us, even myself, to my own surprise, cheered. Liam stood and picked him up before kissing his chubby cheek.

"Dadaaaaaa!" Ethan said again.

"Best gift I've ever gotten," Liam said, as he sat back down with Ethan in his arms.

Why did I feel a sudden desperation for him to say 'Mama?'

TWENTY-FIVE

"You only live twice: Once when you're born and once when you look death in the face."

—*Ian Fleming*

LIAM

This was my plan and I wanted it to be perfect. I could feel the coolness of the brandy snifter as it sat nestled in my hand. I stared out the window of our study, and from our position, I could see the capitol, the city on the hill, everything that was good about America was filled with nothing but snakes and rats.

"He's speaking," Mel said, as she leaned into the chair behind the desk.

Turning around, she increased the volume. Avian's image filled the screen, as he stood in front of the podium with his head held high and proud.

Not for long, bastard.

"Ladies and gentlemen, thank you for coming. As I said at the last press conference, an internal investigation is still being conducted. But I do want the nation to be assured that the FBI is removing anyone from our employment who does not hold to the standards of our office. Over the last few weeks we've had numerous arrests, including those of notorious drug rings and small time bosses."

Our motherfucking drugs.

"Agent Rebecca Pierce is not missing as was previously rumored, but is currently on leave due to an injury she sustained, and unfortunately, she will not be open for questioning for another few weeks—"

"Now." Mel said with a grin.

"*Breaking news,*" a news anchor reported, as the screen away from Avian. "*During the hour we've received video footage from a group called Rsamas; the Republic Soldiers Against More American Savagism, with missing FBI agent, Rebecca Pierce. We warn our viewers, the video contains material not suitable for children.*"

The feed switched to our little home video, and I allowed a grin to spread across my face. Rebecca Pierce sat up on her knees in front of the red Rsamas flag; her dark hair was matted together, and she was dressed in nothing but old rags. As the camera focused on her face, we could see that it was streaked with dirt and tears. Suddenly a pair of hands held up a recent newspaper up to the lens. Two men, whose feet were the only visible evidence to their presence, were seen holding AR-15's to her head.

"My name...is Rebecca Pierce, I was born in Quantico, Virginia...and have spent...the last ten years working...with the Federal Bureau of Investigation's cyber-crime unit. A few weeks ago...I was taken by terrorists—"

The moment she said the word, one of the men hit her with the butt of his rifle. She let out a small cry as she fell forward, and the other man reached down with a gloved arm and pulled her back to her knees.

"I was taken...by the revolutionary group; Rsamas...They are tired...of the hypocritical nature of our...government in this country. They are tired of the lies...and the cover-ups. They've tried to...get in contact with Dir...ector...Avian Doers and other agents, but their legiti...mate requests have all been... ignored, mocked, and pushed aside...They know now that they cannot fight evil with good, but only with more evil, …and they will not stop until not only the director…of the FBI stands…down, but the President as well," she stammered.

I looked to Mel at that, but she just grinned in reply. I was not aware that we wanted the President gone, especially after we'd spent millions to get him into office.

An altered voice recording spoke out. "It's time for the people to step up. It's time for the people to fight back. It's time for the people to become Republic Soldiers Against More American Savagism. If not, we will do as our forefathers have done and declare war. If you hear a rumble close by, or see a smoke cloud over the horizon, take that as proof of our intent. We're requesting that you, Mr. President and Mr. Director, step down, or the blood of many innocent victims will be on your hands." And with that, the video feed was cut, and Avian's broadcast was once more being shown as the reporter commented

He stood at the podium with a stony expression on his face as his agents filled him in on the latest developments. As they stepped back, he turned and glared into the camera with such intensity that it would have made even me flinch if I were a weaker man. Then he left without answering any of the questions that the reporters were hurling at him.

"I think he's angry," Mel smirked, as her phone rang. Pulling it out, she paused as she turned and showed me the caller ID.

"Mr. Director, I'd like to think that there are more pressing situations for you to be handling at this moment than calling to have a chat with your dear, old granddaughter," Mel mocked as she placed him on speaker.

"Do you know what you've just done?" he snapped.

My grin widened. We'd struck a nerve. "Why don't you inform us, Avian?"

"I've protected your imprudent, truculent, ungrateful, dirty family for decades. I know where all the bodies are buried. I know all the motherfucking codes to your bank accounts, any and everything you have is because I have allowed it. I am the hand of God, and you have bitten me. If you believe, even for a moment, that I was concerned with you or the insufficiency that is your family, then you were mistaken. But now, you have my full attention…and trust me, it's something you never wanted to have."

"Are you threatening us?" I hissed, as I took the phone into my hand. "You and I both know that you cannot expose us without exposing your-fucking-self. Self-preservation is in our blood. Come at us and I will drag you to hell with me, *grandfather-in-law*. We will expose secrets that will destroy all faith in the government that you care so deeply about. We will bring down your entire world. Our reign of terror will pale in comparison to what will happen here. So, I'm not buying what you're fucking selling. You're threatening the wrong motherfucking person."

"This day will haunt you for the rest of your pathetic life, Callahan. When I strike, I plan on destroying you, all of you…sooner than you think. I can guarantee that," he sneered before hanging up.

"I'd say he's pretty fucking angry," Mel muttered, as she leaned against the desk.

I handed her the phone as it once more began to ring. With a sigh, she answered. "Mr. President."

"Did you do this?!"

"Do what, exactly?" she asked him before sitting in the chair.

"These terrorists? Rsamas? You've crossed the fucking line, Callahan. You've all lost your minds. I have congressmen, governors, the FBI, CIA, and Interpol turning to me for a plan! I have to give a response in the next five minutes. You have no idea what you've done. You're dealing with things that are greater than you. I want this to end, now."

"Puppet—"

"Don't you dare! I am the President of the goddamn United States, and I will not allow you to fuck with people like this! I—"

Mel hung up, waved the phone in the air for a moment and even checked her nails before hitting redial.

"Did you hang up on me?" Colemen yelled so loudly that I was sure he'd popped something vital.

"Yes, I did, you were speaking nonsense again. So to spare you our rage, we thought we would start this conversation again. Are you ready to act like a grown up? Or should I call back later?" Mel asked calmly.

Silence.

"I'll take that as a yes," she stated. "You will not answer a fucking question from the press. You will not fire Avian Doers, you will send him to Ukraine, Turkey, Greece, wherever fucking suits your fancy. In his place, you will set up a special team to find Rsamas. Don't worry, the dream team list is with Mina. Remember, President Colemen, the United States does not negotiate with a terrorist.

"And finally, you will stand before the seal, with that shiny American flag pinned to your suit, and you will look strong. You will lead your people, and all of America will love you for it. If you in any way try to undercut us—I shouldn't even need to threaten you because you know what the end result will be. We promised you eight years, we never said they

would be easy, but we promised there would be eight. So
do as we say. Your five minutes are up and we're watching."

She hung up and turned on the television, waiting for
him to speak. I smiled at her back. She had a way with words
that was beyond me. She could disarm and cut people down
with them alone. It was a talent of hers. She had no need for
guns, she just liked them.

"I can feel you staring a hole into my head," she said,
without looking at me.

"Get over it." I smiled.

I heard her chuckle as the President came on the
screen. He looked both calm and collected, and even from
a distance I could see the American flag pin on his suit
jacket, just as Mel directed. But I couldn't pay attention to
his words because my phone beeped and as I looked down,
I saw a photo message from Avian.

My breath caught in my throat as the image registered
in my mind.

"What is it?" Mel asked me.

Adrenaline rushed through my veins, and I was up and
out the door as my fingers frantically dialed.

For the love of God, pick up.

SEDRIC

"I've never been a fan of this sport," Evelyn said with a laugh as Ethan rested in her arms.

We'd just left the Arena and we were outside with both Monte and Kain. Mel and Liam were beginning to get paranoid, or at the very least, they seemed to have forgotten who I was. But that tended to happen to people who got old and retired. People started to treat you as if you've somehow forgotten things that you'd been doing for decades.

"Sedric? Sedric?" Evelyn snapped her fingers in front of my face.

"What? Sorry." Shaking my head clear, I turned to find her smiling at me.

"Just like old times," she replied. "I swear, you're always worrying. I think it was after a game when you first found out that you were taking over the family. I couldn't get you to speak to save your life."

"I've gotten better." I laughed as I kissed her temple and then signaled to Kain who went off to get the car. "You know I've always lived inside of my head."

"Yeah, yeah, but with all this free time you have, you'd think you can still buy a lady a pretzel!" She nodded to the food stand in the corner, and I frowned at the thought of it. "Hey, princess, don't knock food carts, there was a time well before all this when we lived off of instant noodles."

I remembered that time well. My father had cut me off the year before my brother died and I had to take over. Too say it was hard was an understatement. Evelyn had taken care of most of our bills that year.

"Evelyn, I've come to expect a certain lifestyle," I said with as much faux dignity as I could muster.

She laughed outright and Ethan stirred in her arms. "Well, *I* haven't, princess. So hurry up before the car comes around." She pouted. And for a few moments it felt as if we were teenagers again.

I kissed her and walked over to the stands, where I found find a young girl and her father working it together.

"What would you like?" the girl asked with a large smile on her face.

"One pretzel, please."

"Are you sure you don't want two? They're really tasty." She was playing up on her cuteness factor. I looked to her father who I had to give props to. He sure knew what he was doing.

"Two it is then," I said, as I reached into my pocket for my wallet, but instead my phone rang.

At that same moment, I saw a glint reflecting off a nearby building out of my peripheral. The hairs on the back of my neck and arms stood up as my mind immediately identified it for what it was. I looked over at Evelyn, who was standing in the corner with Monte, oblivious to anything out of the ordinary.

As she kissed Ethan's head and fixed his hat, time itself slowed down as I dropped everything in my hands and ran towards my family. My throat burned. I must have been yelling, but I couldn't hear anything. My mind was focused on them, and only them. What felt like a lifetime passed before my hands landed on her, and I pushed her to he ground as hard as I could...

BANG.

LIAM

I was on fire. My skin, my nose, my eyes, everything. It felt as if my heart was pumping lava when Mel and I reached the hospital. The entire place was chaotic as we searched through the crowd, pushing and fighting our way to find our son.

"Boss!" Kain called to us from the corner.

"Thank God!" Mel gasped out, as she rushed up to Ethan who was in my mother's arms.

She held on to him tightly and refused to let go even though he was crying.

"Mom." She didn't respond. "Mom, it's Liam." Silence. "Can I hold Ethan?"

She still didn't respond, but she slowly released Ethan and Mel took him into her arms. I looked him over carefully, and only found a few scrapes on his arm. Forcing myself beside her, I took her hands and softly rubbed them, just like I used to when I was younger. She looked dazed, and she was covered in blood...

"Mom, whose blood is that?" I whispered, staring at her dress before looking back to Ethan.

He was alive. He was fine. So whose blood was that?

"Mom, where's Dad?" I whispered slowly.

She rocked back and forth over and over again. Her face contorted, and as her lips parted, a wail burst forth. A keen, painful wail that brought tears to my eyes.

"Mother, where is Dad?" I held onto her arms, trying my best to control the painful stirring in my chest, and the urge to shake her.

She shook her head as she continued crying and sobbing, until she fell out of her chair and into my arms. I held her, as I tried my best to push away the reality that was forcing the facts to the forefront of my mind. I started to quiver as the lump that had formed in my throat seemed to expand to encompass my lungs, forcing out all the breath from within my body.

This can't...I can't...

"I tried," she gasped out. "I didn't see it. He saw it. I didn't see it. He was just screaming and screaming for me to run, and I didn't understand, all I felt was the ground when he pushed us. I didn't see it! And he wouldn't get up...he refused to get up. I don't know, I don't...there was so much blood, all over the ground. I—I..."

No.

Peeling her off of me, I stared into her eyes as I shook my head again. "No. Where is the doctor? Who is the doctor here?" I got up to look around, only to find Mel whispering to Kain.

"What the fuck are you doing? Get me the motherfucking doctor!"

Kain had his head down, but he didn't move.

"Are you daft? Get. Me. A. Doctor. You. Fool."

"Liam." Mel took a deep breath and looked me in the eye. "He has no doctor. He was pronounced dead at the scene."

She had hurt me a lot in the past, but nothing compared to that moment. She was just trying to hurt me again, I knew it. This was just a game; she'd hurt me, I'd chase her and… and at the end of the day, we'd laugh about it, everything would be fine. I knew it. It had to be.

This was just a stupid game.

Looking down, I saw my crumbled mother on the floor, and the overpowering realization was once again forcing its way forward.

"No," I snapped, as I reached down to pick up my mother before I placed her back onto the chair, but she only cried harder. "I'm going to find the doctor, okay? Mom. Ma, stop, alright? I'm sure he's going to be fine."

"Liam." Mel reached out to me, but I slapped her hands away.

"NO!" I screamed into her face. "You do not *know* my father. He does not die. He does not die on the street like a fucking dog. He is a Callahan. He is not fucking dead, so shut the hell up and watch my mother. I'll find him myself."

He wasn't dead.

She took a step back and nodded before I stumbled through the crowd.

He wasn't dead.

I couldn't imagine a world where my father wasn't in it. I couldn't understand.

He wasn't dead.

MELODY

He was gone. Just like that. One moment he was here and the next he wasn't. It wasn't like Orlando—I'd known that he was dying. I was prepared, and even though it hurt, it was different. But this, I didn't understand it. My chest hurt and my lungs burned. There hadn't been many times in my life when I'd felt like this. I could feel my eyes clouding over with tears, but I couldn't let my emotions overpower me, not with Ethan here.

Neal had just arrived and they moved us to a private waiting room, but this was for Monte. He had taken three bullets protecting Evelyn and Ethan and was now in surgery. I handed Ethan to Neal, who looked up at me. His eyes were red and puffy, and the tears didn't stop falling, he had no control over them.

He wrapped his arms around Ethan, making sure that he was secure enough when he sat up straighter. Evelyn was curled up beside him asleep. I had given her some sedatives to help her rest.

"I'm going to find Liam. I'll be back," I whispered.

Kain nodded, already standing guard.

Walking down the hall, I waited until I was out of both sight and hearing range. Then, I ducked into an empty room, pausing only for a moment to ensure that I was completely alone before I released everything; I screamed. I screamed and punched the wall over and over again until my knuckles were numb, bloody, and exposed. Avian had sent us an image of Ethan and Evelyn with a message saying, "Goodbye."

And now...now Sedric was gone.

Just like that. Not only had he killed him—but ten other bullets were found, three were in Monte, one in Sedric, the others were bystanders and a driver who ended up driving into a building. And now Sedric's body was here in the morgue and I couldn't...

Fuck, this hurt.

Taking a deep breath, I followed the blue arrows and rode the elevator down. It smelled like actual death as I walked down the quiet hall. And there I found him, stiffly standing over the table. Moving inside the room, I sighed in relief at the fact that he had not unzipped the bag by himself. His hand, which seemed paler than I remembered, was hovering over the top of the bag. He was afraid, but I knew that he wouldn't believe it until he saw Sedric's body with his own two eyes.

Stepping up, I pulled the zipper down slowly and Liam took his hand away. I didn't want him to see this, not if he didn't want to, so I allowed my body to block his view.

"I'm ready."

No you aren't.

None of us were, no matter what we said. Moving back, I allowed him to see the single bullet wound in the center of his father's head. Liam's body hunched forward as his legs went weak, but I held on to him and caught him as the sobs erupted from his body; not just from his mouth, his entire body was wracked with painful sobs that caused my throat to tighten and my eyes to sting. He cried openly in my arms before finally moving over to face his father. He kissed his cheek and hugged him tightly.

"I'm sorry. I'm so sorry, Dad. I'm so sorry." He wept.

I didn't care what he said; we were going home.

He was going to take his father back home to Chicago where he belonged. We would have our revenge, but he needed this, and truthfully, so did I. We all did.

Someone still had to tell Declan and Coraline...and I knew that that someone would've been me.

Holding onto my husband, a burning need traveled through me. Something akin to adrenaline, but darker, much more vengeful, pumped through my veins and I made a silent promise: *Never again!*

Twenty-Six

"Hearts can break. Yes, hearts can break. Sometimes I think it would be better if we died when they did, but we don't."

—*Stephen King*

CORALINE

Wiping my face over and over again didn't help. Nothing seemed to dull the pain, or stop the tears. I sat on the edge of our bed waiting for my husband. He was going to be here at any moment, and I needed to be strong for him, but the damned tears wouldn't stop falling. When the door jiggled, I sat up quickly with my hands at my sides.

"Did you see the news? Mel and Liam are insane. I'm famous babe...well, my gun and my altered voice was. Who knew it would be so easy to—" he paused as he took off his shoes and looked me over. "What's wrong?"

I said nothing, choosing instead to move towards him I before gripped the sides of his face and kissed him deeply. He pulled me to him, and wrapped his arms around my body before he pulled back and smiled.

"What did I do to deserve that? Let me know so I can do it again!"

I didn't want to do this. I couldn't do this to him. He had lost the man who took him in and treated him like his own son all his life—he had lost his real father. The tears returned as I bit my tongue. Mel had said on the phone to just spit it out, that it was going to hurt no matter how I delivered the news, but I didn't want to see him in pain.

"Coraline, talk to me please," he whispered, as he placed his hand on my face. "Did I do something? I know I've been overprotective, but I can't help it, I just worry about you—"

I placed my finger on his lips and took a deep breath. "Mel and Liam are coming back tomorrow morning."

"What? Why?"

"Baby, I'm so sorry. Sedric's gone," I allowed the words to rush out.

His eyes widened as he took a step away from me.

Everything I'd been told spilled from my mouth. "Avian tried to have Evelyn and Ethan killed, but Sedric pushed them out of the way and...and took a bullet...he never got back up. Mel—"

"Stop!" Declan screamed at me.

I tried to reach for him but he pushed me away while shaking his head. "What are you saying? What? I don't...I don't understand. I spoke to him and Evelyn a few hours ago. Why are you saying this?"

"Declan."

"No, this is crazy. You're wrong." He snapped at me as I moved to him once more, this time I pulled him into my arms. He stood stiffly. "You're wrong."

His body began to shake as he held onto me. "You're wrong. I can't lose two fathers, Cora."

But he had and I wished I were wrong. I really did, because all I could see were dark days before us.

How did this happen?

NEAL

I needed to see her. It had been only a couple of hours without him and it still felt as if I'd just been told. It burned to think about reality. My throat felt as if it were closing, like my heart crawled through it, just wanting to be expelled. My eyes ached, and I wanted to rip them out if only to alleviate the constant stinging. Mel had taken Mom and Ethan home, leaving me with Liam and Kain. None of us spoke. We simply sat in our private waiting room in silence before I couldn't take it anymore. I had to see her.

We refused to leave without our father. We refused to let him stay there without us in a cold box as if he were no one. It wasn't right. I had planned to stay at the hospital all night when Olivia called for the ninth time. I'm not even sure why they bothered to leave her a phone, but I was sure it had to do with Avian—the fucking bastard. I was going to pull his lungs out of his ass.

The longer I thought about him, the more I thought of her. I had to see her, I had to know if she knew about this... if this had been a part of her plan all along.

Liam didn't even seem to notice as I took my leave, he just sat there with Kain, who stood at his side like a fucking rock. It didn't even seem as if he were breathing. I didn't want to leave him, but I needed to know.

"Evelyn, stop, please!" I heard her strangled scream as I walked towards the basement. There, on the bed, was Olivia trying fight off my mother who was on top of her. She continuously punched her, and her fists were covered in blood as they slammed into Olivia's face.

"You bitch! I welcomed you into my home, my family, and this is what you do? This is all your fault! I'm going to kill you! I'm going to fucking kill you! How dare you! You filthy cunt! Die! Just DIE!" She pulled her arm back and punched her one last time, until finally, I lifted her off of Olivia. Still enraged, she struggled out of my grip and smacked me hard across the face. With tears in her eyes, she glared at me.

"This is your fault!" she screamed at me, before pointing to Olivia, who now had a busted lip, a broken nose, and cut forehead. "You brought this trash, this snake, this evil whore, into our lives, our family. She wanted all of us dead and now she's getting her wish. For once in your goddamn life, Neal Callahan, stop being a disappointment! I've always been on your side, I've always wanted what was best for you, and this is how you repay me? By destroying me? I can't even look at you. How could you do this to me?!" She spat at my feet.

"Evelyn, come on," Mel whispered, but she refused to move. With a sigh, Mel pulled out a needle and stuck it in her neck. I went to help, but Mel shook her head before she wrapped my mother's arm over her shoulder and moved towards the door.

"I don't understand. What's wrong with her? What's going on? I haven't seen anyone in days. Not that I want to see anyone in this stupid fucking family. No one has anyone given me anything to eat—"

Something inside of me snapped. My hands were around her neck before my mind even made a conscious decision to move. I gripped her neck as tightly as I could.

"My father is dead and you're upset because someone didn't give you snack?" I asked her, feeling surprisingly calm as she struggled against me. Her nails scratched my arms as tears flooded her bloodshot eyes. Instead of the absolute dread I envisioned feeling when this day came, an unnatural calm took over my entire being. I felt nothing but an urge to rid the earth of this disgusting virus I'd blindly inflicted upon my family.

"Neal...this...not...like...you..." she choked out.

"You don't know me," I said, surprising myself once again with how unaffected I felt. Pushing as hard as I could onto her neck, I felt something snap, not within me as I was used to when dealing her, but I literally felt and heard the harsh and sickening snap as her windpipe finally collapsed under the pressure of my grip and she stopped fighting. Her body went limp and I stared into her cold, empty eyes. There was hardly a difference now than there was last week.

That was it.

She was gone.

Just like that, nothing fancy, not by Liam's or Mel's hands, but by my own. And I didn't regret it. I felt absolutely no remorse as I looked at her already cooling carcass.

"I'll handle this, Neal, now go to your mother," Mel said from behind me. "She'll awaken at any moment, and right now she needs one of her sons."

I gave Olivia one more look before getting up.

Mel grabbed my arm before I could leave the room. "We will have our revenge, I swear it, Neal."

I'm wasn't sure how to reply as my heart tried to escape by way of my throat once more. Heading to my parents' room, I walked up the stairs and it was as if someone was physically trying to pull me back. Perhaps it was Olivia's demented soul. Or maybe I was just damned.

Walking into the room, I stared at my mother as she gripped onto what I guessed was my father's pillow. It seemed as though she was trying soak up whatever essence he'd left behind. Taking a seat at the side of the bed, I didn't even try to stop the flow tears.

What happens now?

Twenty-Seven

"I will not say, do not weep, for not all tears are an evil."
—*J.R.R. Tolkien*

LIAM

Past

He punched me so hard that I spun around once before hitting the ground. Dazed, I lay there for a moment before I manage to get up and pull off my boxing helmet.

"You cheated!"

"Nope, you just suck," my father said with a laugh, as he threw me a water bottle.

I pulled off my gloves as fast as I could, desperate for something to quench my thirst. "My teacher said not use the word, 'suck,' because she knows I'm more educated than that."

"She said you're more educated, not me, kid." He rolled his eyes before pouring his own bottled water over his head. Standing up, I followed his lead and poured the ice cold liquid onto my body. I shivered as the water dripped from my face and onto the boxing ring canvas.

"Well, you're more educated than I am," I replied, as I shook the water from my hair. "At least you should be, right? You're old."

He frowned at me before he threw a glove at my head. Ducking out of the way, I grinned.

"Rule twenty: Your father is never old and it would be wise not to claim that he is. Also, remember, Rule twenty-three; just because one is old does not make them wise."

"You can't make up rules as you go!" I yelled at him. "You said they were given to you by your father and his father before him. You said it was a tradition."

"Liam, you're thirteen, don't hold me to everything I say, it's annoying. You're supposed to forget that stuff," he replied as he helped me out of the ring.

"Why would I forget it? You get annoyed when you have to repeat things." I frowned.

He sighed as he ruffled my hair. "You're too goddamn serious, Liam. Life is short; rebel a little. You're healthy, so enjoy life. Read a comic, binge eat, it's okay every once in a while," he told me as he pushed the button for the elevator.

"Grandpa says—"

"Grandpa is a hard ass, and no one can make him happy. Be who you are. I heard there's some dance at school coming up? Who are you taking?"

"No one." I frowned, as I leaned against the elevator wall.

"No one?"

"Yes, because I'm not going. I still hate school. I'm only going for you."

"Why, thank you," he snickered. "And you're going to the dance."

"Why?" I groaned and smacked my forehead. "I hate them."

"Because it makes you uncomfortable and you need to get used to doing things that make you uncomfortable."

I muttered an oath under my breath and he looked to me, daring me to defy him.

"Fine, I'll go. But I'm going to be miserable."

"You can thank me later."

Present

"Liam, you need to eat something," Mel whispered to me after we boarded the jet. I couldn't really remember the events that had led to me being here. I looked around the cabin, trying to piece together how long I'd been out of it, when I noticed some sort of soup and slices of bread in front of me.

"I'm not hungry."

"Fine. Then can you feed Ethan while I check on your mother?" she asked as she held both the bottle and Ethan in her arms.

I didn't want to deal with this right now.

"Mel, no I can't—"

She placed him into my arms and gave me the bottle despite my protests. Ethan looked up to me, waiting, and all I could do was stare into his green eyes...ones that reflected my own, and I froze.

"Dada," he called to me and I took a deep breath before I adjusted him for his meal.

He sucked happily and I watched him. He looked peaceful, happy. Relaxing into my chair, I held him close to my heart. Taking the bread up with my free hand, I ate along with him. Moment later, Mel came back from the jet's private room and quietly sat in front of me.

"How is she?" I asked her, as I took another bite of bread. We hadn't really spoken, and because I was a coward, I dreaded having to face her.

"Sleeping."

With a nod, I looked out the window at the sea of clouds. Part of me wanted to believe that he was taking this flight with us, relaxing on one of the wings...but to do that, it meant that I would've had to accept the fact that he was gone and that was something that I refused to do.

Past

I sat in the back of the car with my dad as we drove through the dark streets of Chicago. I looked to him and he seemed calm as he finished up his crossword puzzle. Every edge of his suit was crisp and sharp. His watch glinted in the mediocre light, and his dark hair was slicked back.

"Relax," he said to me.

With a frown, I leaned back into my seat. "I am relaxed."

"You seem nervous."

"I'm not nervous. You're the one butchering the crossword puzzle," I replied.

He glanced at me, eyebrow raised. "Well excuse me, Mr. Know-It-All, why don't you fix it then?" He handed it to me.

Taking the pen and the newspaper, I shook my head at some of his answers. "A fourteen letter word for a silent killer is *Carbon Monoxide.* Hundred and eight stories belong to what eleven-letter word— the answer is *Willis Tower.* The answer to four down is *Buckingham Fountain,* not Palaces, that is why you couldn't fill the space—"

"Show off," he grumbled, as he snatched the paper from me just as we came to a stop. "Move it, we're here."

Jumping out, I brushed my hair back, in an effort to keep it out of my eyes. He put his hat on, and handed his briefcase to the driver. His face became serious again as he glared down at me.

"I promised you for your fourteenth birthday that I would show you what I do. You are not to look away. You will stand there and make me proud, or I will not waste anymore time with you, are we clear?"

"Yeah," I said. Then, as his eyes narrowed at me, "I mean, yes, sir."

With a nod, he walked forward into a bar with flashing neon green lights above the entrance. The place went silent and everyone moved out of his way as he strode forward. Some even got up out of their seats and moved away from the bar and into the corner as we made our way to the back, while others nodded out of respect. I always knew my father was respected, and I had come to understand that the things he did weren't always good. But that was the nature of the family business. If I proved myself, he said I would do great things and I wanted that. I wanted people to respect me, to fear me, to stand when I walked into a room.

We went into basement, and there I saw a man, dripping with sweat and blood, and tied to a chair in the center of the room. The men around him took a step back when they saw my father. He took off his hat and handed it one of the men before doing the same with his jacket. He spent a long time rolling up his sleeves and I knew that he was enjoying this.

"So you're a cop, O'Neil?" he finally asked. "Usually we'd rough you up before putting a bullet in your brain. I really hate wasting my time on filth. But today is my son's birthday and before we go hunting tomorrow, I'd like to give him some practice."

One of his men handed him a bow and an a few arrows, which my father tested with the tip of his fingers before he walked to the other side of the basement. O'Neil was pulled to the other end where a glass of beer was balanced on his head.

"Liam, stand in front of him."

What?

My mouth fell open but I didn't argue, I simply obeyed and took a step in front of him.

"Turn and face him," he directed and I did as I was told. The moment I stood still, an arrow went past my ear and into the man's shoulder. I heard it slice through air before it hit him. I stayed as still as possible as Dad shot another, and another, and another, and each time he'd hit a different point on the man's body. The bottle of beer now shattered on the ground

"The last one is yours, son," he said to me, and I turned to find him handing me the bow.

I took it slowly as I looked back up to him.

"I'm all out of arrows, so you're going to have to pull them out of him, just like you do when we go deer hunting."

I didn't want to go anywhere near the bleeding man, but I refused to let my dad down. Moving towards O'Neil, I grabbed the arrow in his arm and pushed it through completely. The man cried and screamed, but what bothered me more was the fact that he was moving.

"Move if you want to, but it's only going to hurt more," I said to him before I began to remove the others. Then I went to stand in my father's place at the end of the room.

"Elbow down," he said to me as I positioned myself. "Pull back gently and just let it fly."

And I did. The first one hit him in the thigh, the next in the arm, and the other in his stomach.

"Stop," Dad said, as he took the bow and arrow out of my hands. "I'm growing tired of this, but at least you've hit him."

With that, he took the last three arrows and shot them into both of O'Neil's eyes, and the last into his heart before he looked back at me.

"You still need practice," he stated, before he turned to speak with his men.

I watched as they pulled the man out of his chair and lay him on the ground. The blood that flowed from him slowly crept across the floor as it made its way towards me.

"Liam."

"Yes, Father?"

He washed his hands and undid his sleeves before he put his jacket and hat back on. "We're heading home."

"What happens to the cop now?"

With his lips pursed he looked me over. "What do you mean 'what happens to him?'"

"What do you do with his body, you can't just dump it in the lake…can you?"

"That depends." He and his men snickered as he placed his hand on my shoulder and led me back to the bar.

I waited until we were both seated before I turned to him. "Depends on what?"

"On what the clean-up crew decides to do with his body. One thing you will always need is a good clean-up crew. Monetary expenses shouldn't be a problem, inspect them personally. Make sure anyone close to you does not get involved with the product we provide. Do you understand?"

I nodded as I leaned back. Then I remembered something important. "Are we really going camping tomorrow?"

"Yep. Maybe we can get your mother to not drown you in bug repellent again," he snickered.

"I wouldn't bet on it."

Present

"Liam? Liam?" Mel whispered.

I open my eyes to find her right above me, smiling. I loved waking up to her voice. I reached up and brushed the side of her face. "Hey, you."

She gave me a sad smile and touched my cheek. "We've landed. We have to go."

I paused as everything came back. I'd had a moment of reprieve, a moment where I'd thought it was just a nightmare, but it was real...and it hurt even more.

"I know," Mel whispered as if she could read my mind. "I know, but we need to get off the plane, Liam."

Nodding, I got up and grabbed my jacket and bag. I noticed that Jinx was holding Ethan, and for some reason, it bothered me. Taking my son out of his arms, I turned and exited the jet without another word.

I walked out to see Declan and Coraline hugging my mother, who for the very first time in all my life, was wearing sweatpants and a hoodie. She looked broken. And just the sight of her made my heart ache and my blood boil.

Coraline helped mom into her car before she entered, leaving Declan, Neal and I alone. Ethan tapped my face as if to remind me of his presence, before Mel came and took him from me. Part of me didn't want to let him go, but I knew that it would be better for my brothers and me to have this conversation alone.

Declan and I both drew in a deep breath as Fedel, Kain, and Jinx removed our father from the cargo hold of the jet. My father was now cargo. I wasn't sure how Mel had pulled it off, or whom she had bribed or threatened, but his body had been taken out of the morgue, cleaned, dressed and placed on our jet without issue.

Declan shook his head, his jaw tensed. "This is shit."

"Declan—" Neal started.

"Don't. This is your fucking wife's fault. How the fuck do know that she wasn't the one who tipped him off?! We've been telling you for years she was fucking trash and you were too blinded by her goddamn pussy—"

"Fuck you! You don't know shit! You no good—"

"Enough." I snapped. "There is only one man responsible for this and we will have our retribution. Until then, don't cock up dad's last moments before we bury him by acting like five year olds because I won't have it. I will kill the both of you before I allow you to fuck this up," I said before walking to the car where my mother was seated. I would've gone with Mel, but I needed a moment alone with my mother. When I got in, she was curled up and asleep again. Coraline stepped out and I took her place.

MELODY

I turned my attention to Fedel, and filled him in while he held the door open for me. As I sat down, I placed Ethan into his car seat before I put a blanket over him. Fedel sat up front while Jinx took the passenger's seat.

"I'm getting updates on Monte's status. He's alive, but they had to amputate his left leg," I told Fedel and he nodded. "I need you here and focused, Fedel."

"Of course, ma'am. What do you need?" he asked.

"Has the family been notified?"

"Yes, the news has spread and families are already leaving gifts and flowers outside the gates," he answered while searching through the photos on his phone.

"What about the press?"

"They're all focused on the new terrorists, Rsamas. They are actually saying the group is behind the sniper shooting," Jinx answered and I stared at the back of his head.

"How many people *know* about Rsamas?" The only way that this would work was if fewer people knew about what's really going on.

"The family, the agent, Kain, Monte, Jinx, and myself," Fedel replied, as he stopped at the red light.

Olivia was dead, and I'd taken care of her body with the aid of a vat of acid. The agent would be dead soon enough. The family was behind us, which only left the four of them.

"Let's keep it that way. Make sure to cover it up if any one starts to speculate. Am I clear?"

"Yes, ma'am," they both answered.

"I asked for details about the funeral, where are they?"

Jinx handed me the tablet, allowing me to sift through as fast as possible.

"No red roses. Evelyn likes the white ones. If she likes it, it means that Sedric liked them as well. The memorial won't be held at the manor. We'll have it near the Illinois River, I believe it's called *LaRue Pine*. We can have it on the cliffs, which will remind them of the ones in Ireland. It's the best we can do.

"Have tables, chairs, and a bar set up for at least two hundred people. I want heavy-duty protection in the trees and down below. Where did you find this caterer?"

"I, and a few of the men, including the Irish, have gone to their place. She's good, ma'am, trust me," Fedel replied.

"Fine, it will do, but have them send me a sample tonight. If it tastes like shit, it will be on your head."

"Yes, ma'am."

I inhaled deeply before I leaned back. I watched as Ethan spoke gibberish, and laughed as he tried to hit the window.

"Boss?"

"Jinx?"

"Should we worry about Olivia?" he asked, and I was reminded of the fact that no else knew what had happened.

"She's no longer an issue."

LIAM

Past

"Dad, I don't want to marry her," I told him as I entered his office.

"That's unfortunate, because you will one day," he said, not bothering to glance up at me from his desk.

Muttering under my breath, I moved to his couch and threw myself on it.

"Feet down, I'm not going to be yelled at by your mother again for ruining her furniture."

I groaned. "Dad, that's what I'm talking about, you're so whipped."

"Whipped? Were you listening outside our door again last night?"

"Ugh, Dad!" I gagged as he sat there laughing at me. "That mental picture is going to be stuck in my head forever. You're scaring me here!"

"You brought it up. When are you heading back to school?" he said as he laughed at me while stapling documents together.

"Are you trying to get rid of me?" I stretched to look at him.

"Yes, so I can get back to being *whipped.*"

406

"Stop it. The joke is dead! Can we focus on me for a moment here?"

"You're eighteen. I thought that meant I could stop focusing on you!"

I glared as I sat up and waited.

"Silence, finally. I thought I would never rest with you all back in the house." He smirked.

"I'm not marrying her. I don't need a babysitter once you kick the bucket—"

"Who said anything about a fucking bucket?" he snapped at me.

He hated it when I teased him about getting old. Once, I pointed out some of his gray hairs, and in response to my wily observation, he threw a vase at my head.

He froze before giving me his attention. "Are you planning on having me killed, son?"

Rolling my eyes, I rose. "Yeah, sure, old man, that's what I'm planning. Seeing as you eat like...well, me. I wouldn't be surprised if you collapsed tomorrow. Wasn't mom yelling about your heart the other day?"

"I'm fine, I made a deal," he replied.

"With whom, God or the Devil?" I grinned, as I trailed towards his brandy.

"Don't you dare. Your mother almost killed me when she found out that I let you drink."

"She's out shopping with Neal's new girlfriend, Olivia Colemen," I told him.

I paused as he thought about it for a moment before nodding. I poured him a drink as well.

"What do you think of her?" he asked me.

"She's...pretty. In a manufactured sort of way."

He rolled his eyes. "Go deeper than that, Liam, what do you *really* think of her?"

We'd only had a few dinners with her, but I wasn't sure.

"She talks a lot, and she likes the camera. I think she has the potential to be a stage five clinger. She's not stupid, but she not very bright either. All in all, I can't trust her until I get to know her better. Why? Don't you like her?"

"She's...she's not the type of woman I wanted for Neal." He paused to think. "He needs a woman that can keep him grounded and bring out the best in him."

"Wait, so you've thought all about the type of woman that Neal needs, and me you're just throwing to the Italians?"

"You sound jealous, Liam," he said with a snicker. "I don't have any favorites."

"Liar," I muttered. "If he likes Olivia, whatever. She looks like she makes him happy, but then again, couldn't a puppy do that?"

"Hey." He frowned at me.

"What?"

"He's your older brother, respect him."

"Easier said than done."

"Fine. If you don't want to marry Melody Giovanni, then you can marry Ms. Colemen."

"That's like asking if I'd like to be run over by a train now or later! I don't want to get married until after I take over. It shouldn't be a clause for me to become the Ceann Na Conairte." He had all these damn rules. He forced me to learn everything under the goddamn sun, yet he still treated me like a child.

"Giovanni or Colemen?" he asked as though he were bored.

"I—"

"I won't ask you again. Giovanni or Colemen?"

"Fine, Giovanni. I'll wait for the train. Maybe I can think of a way out of this contract. I don't know how you can trust them with the amount of shit that the Italians have put us through. Now I'm supposed to lie next to one. "

"At least you'll have good food," he replied.

"We have chefs for that—what are you looking at?" I moved over and saw a map on his desk. It was new trade routes for our supplies.

"Oh, well look at that, you *can* hold the girl talk for a moment," my father said.

Asshole.

Present

I stood out on the balcony staring up at the moon with a bottle of brandy in my hand. Drinking straight from the bottle, I shivered as Mel's warm arms wrapped themselves around me. Without saying a word, I stood and enjoyed the warmth of her presence. I'd been feeling cold and nothing could warm me up like she could. Drinking didn't help, tears burned, but she and Ethan were it.

"I know I have to be stronger, I have to be a leader," I whispered to her, "but I—I…"

"I get it, Liam. Everything will be taken care of tomorrow, you just have to show up."

No.

Shaking my head once more, I turned around to face her.

"I need you to give me the speech."

"The speech?" she questioned, confused.

Looking down, I swallowed and tried to form the words. "Tomorrow, I need to not only be the head of this family, but the leader of the entire Irish clan. Plus, your people will be there on top of that. I can't weep; I can't be anything except strong because all eyes will be on me, but right now, I can't even breathe. So I need you to do what you've always done and tell me the truth. You tear into people and lay everything on the table. I need that. I need to know how you functioned after Orlando died. You cried for one night and the next you were using him as bait. And I know you, you loved him, you are not as cold as you want people to believe. You were in pain. I need you to speak to me, because apparently I can't speak for myself. "

"My father and I had relationship that was much different than—"

"Mel...wife...please."

She wiped the corner of my eyes and took a deep breath before she stepped away from me.

"You have tonight," she said stoically. "That's it, one night. You can cry, you can scream, you can curse God. But when the sun comes up, you need to get your shit together, Liam, because that is the price of being the boss. We don't get to grieve with them. We do not get to lie in bed all day, we do not get to worry about the ifs, ands, and buts.

"Sedric is dead. He's not coming back, and neither you nor I have the power to change that. You will wake up, and for a moment you will forget that he is gone, and just when you're about to smile, it will hit you. A song will play, or you will eat his favorite food, drink his favorite brandy, go to his favorite place, and the pain will rip through you, but you will have to deal with it. We have to; we are going to hold this family together because without us, everything falls apart.

Everything he worked for and gave his life for will be meaningless, and if that happens, then Sedric would've died for nothing. That bullet was his last gift to you, and you have no fucking right to waste it. We bend, but we not break, and when we snap back, someone always suffers. Tomorrow, we will make sure that the message is clear: we can never be broken."

When she finished, I pulled her to me, and allowed the bottle to fall and shatter. Kissing her, I picked her up by her thighs, intent on showing her just how much I loved her. I had already wept in the morgue and cursed every deity known. Right now, I just wanted to make her scream my name and lose myself in her.

Past

I held her hand, trying to rush her into my room as she giggled. We were both a little tipsy, but who cared? Besides, it was my last real night of freedom. Just as we made it to my room, I saw him turn the corner into the hall. He looked up at us both from the book in his hand.

"Busted," Natasha giggled.

"Go in," I winked at her, and she smiled before she did as she'd been told.

Turning back to my father, I watched as he continued his path until he stopped at my side.

"How much do you care about her?" His monotone voice reached me as he flipped through his book.

"Dad—"

He glared, cutting me off.

"Look, it's my last night before I meet Melody. I'd like to have some fun, if you don't mind. It isn't serious. I swear, the moment we sign the contract, my loyalty will be to her and this family."

"The family should already have your full loyalty," he countered.

"You know what I mean." Or at least I hoped that he did. I knew what was likely going through his head.

"She'd better not get pregnant or I will kill her myself. I'm doing this for your future...one day you will thank me, son," was all he said before he continued on down the hall.

Thank him? Yeah right.

MELODY

Wrapped in his arms, I listened to him breathe as he played with my hair and stroked my hand. The sun was slowly beginning to peek into our room, but we laid still, fighting the evidence of a new day. Sadly, there was no stopping our alarm. Taking a deep breath, he sat up and ran his hands through his hair before he stretched. Then he turned to me.

"Olivia?" he asked.

"Dead. Neal killed her. I took care of the rest. Pity, because I'd planned to bury her alive."

"No," he mused. "It was better that Neal did it. She didn't deserve any more of our time. She was nothing and died as nothing. Her name will never be spoken of again. What of my father's funeral?"

"It's at eleven a.m. and the memorial is going to be near the Illinois River at LaRue Pine. Everything's already been taken care of."

"I want to wear a—"

"Fedora?"

He looks at me oddly, but nodded. "Yeah."

Sitting up, I got out of bed and walked over to his closet. "I had Fedel go out and get some, along with a few suits choices."

There were five different outfits I had put together for him, and all of them had a matching fedora.

I felt him come up behind me, wrapped his arms around me, and pulled me to his chest.

"Pick whichever one you like, I also had some brought in for Neal and Declan. I have dresses for Evelyn as well. Breakfast is at—"

"You did all of this?" he whispered, as he kissed my shoulder.

I smiled as I turned back to him. "Coraline helped."

"You're perfect." He tried to smile. And it was only when he did that I realized how much I missed seeing him happy.

"I'm going to get dressed." I grinned but he held onto my waist.

"Thank you, wife," he said as he kissed my forehead.

"You don't need to thank me. This is what families do, right?"

His grin turned into a soft snicker. "Yeah, this is what families do."

TWENTY-EIGHT

"To live in hearts we leave behind is not to die."

—Thomas Campbell

MELODY

This was not about me, nor Orlando. However, a small part of me felt guilty that I had not done anything like this for him. Never had I seen so many Irish people in one place, outside of Ireland. Even a few of my people were here. It had only been two days, but some had flown in just in time, while others drove for hours just to make it to Chicago to attend the memorial overlooking the river. It was beautiful with nothing but green all around us, and a dark blue river below.

Sitting at the table nearest to the edge of the cliff, I stared at the large photo of Sedric that stood beside the podium. It was the perfect summer day for this. The sun hid behind the clouds, but it was still warm, and even the wind had calmed, as if it too wanted to be respectful.

"Sedric raised me, and since he brought me into his home I saw him not as my uncle, but as my father, who I loved…love dearly. Cheers," Declan finished taking his shot before he stepped back to Coraline.

She hugged and kissed him before she went up. It was the first time I had not seen her bother to wear heels. "Hello," she said into the microphone. "Many of you know me as Coraline Callahan, wife of Declan. Sedric and I weren't very close. But he was kind to me. He made me laugh…he made everyone laugh without even trying. He had a dual nature to him; one moment he had this ability to freeze over the whole room, and the next, you forgot who he was. He had so much life in him, so much so that you almost forgot that he could die. People like him should live forever. Should live to see more grandchildren, more fights, more love. I'd like to think that he will, that he's here watching us all right now talking about him with a bowl of kettle corn in his lap because he's still afraid that Evelyn will find out that he got popcorn with extra butter and salt."

I hear a soft cry coming from the end of our table and I looked over to find Evelyn in Neal's arms, laughing and crying at the same time.

"Sedric Callahan was one of a kind, and the world is a darker place with him gone. We will never forget him. Cheers." She wiped her eyes and downed the liquid before she moved back to the table.

Neal stood up walking to where Coraline had just stood with a bottle in his hands. I felt Liam tense beside me as though he wasn't sure what to think of his brother speaking. Placing my hand on his thigh, he placed his hands over mine.

"I'm still at a loss for words," Neal began. "To some of you, that might not be surprising. I've never known what to say or where to be or what to do. I just followed my father's lead and hoped, and prayed that I was making him proud. There is no denying the fact that my father and I had issues, I dare you to find any father and son who don't, but I knew he cared about me. Many men in his position don't have time to take care of their sons, but he did. He always made sure to check up on me when he could.

"He thought that I didn't know. Early every morning, before the sun was even up, he would check up on me.

From the time I was eight until I turned eighteen...yes eighteen and I was not a tiny eighteen, he would come into my room and just talk to me about his day, about the stupid shit I had done. I looked forward to those brief moments when the door would open, and I was heartbroken when they stopped."

He dropped his head and nodded as though he was being told what to say, but I knew that he was just trying to force himself to stay strong.

"When I was fourteen, he was seriously injured and he'd lost a friend. When he was feeling better, and after he'd come back from his friend's funeral, he once again came into my room, leaned at the edge for the door and said, 'I don't plan on dying anytime soon, son, but if for some reason I do, you all better feast like Vikings and send me off like a fucking king. Oh, and you can let your mother know that I did trick her into dating me, and that I did kill her fish....but make sure I'm really dead before you tell her that."

With a grin on my face, I rolled my eyes. Beside me, Liam snickered. Of course Sedric would've said something like that.

"I knew it," Evelyn muttered shaking her head as even more tears fell. I wondered if they would ever stop.

"For him. Cheers." Neal lifted the bottle up and took a long swig that would've made any Viking or Irishman proud. Everyone drank in response, even Liam.

Liam stood and moved towards his brother and they hugged for a moment before he stood up to the microphone himself. He regarded us all before he began his speech.

"Deartháireacha, deirfiúracha, máithreacha, teaghlaigh. (Brothers, sisters, mothers, family.)" He spoke in Irish, and then, much to my surprise he switched to Italian and said, "famiglia allargata (extended family), thank you all for coming. I have always known that my father meant a great deal to so many people, however, seeing it now is humbling. Many of you have dropped everything just be here out of respect, love, and let's be honest, a little fear."

There were a few snickers that spread throughout the crowd.

"But great men ought to be feared, and my father was a great man. Even his flaws were great. He is gone and I find myself staring at shoes so large that they could've only belonged to a giant. We are here because somehow he figured out how to unite us all. Irish, Italian, it did not matter. There is nothing I can say about my father that you didn't already know. I have stories going back almost three decades, from the first moment he dropped me as a child to when he was twisting my arm around my back to marry an Italian...the feistiest one of them all at that."

I wanted to take a shovel to his head, but that would've only proven his point. Evelyn leaned to me, took my hand and squeezed it.

"He told me that everything I did as the leader of family was not just for me, or my immediate family, it was to make sure that we all remain strong. He wanted me to be someone who not only cared about our heritage but also reminded the people that no matter where they are, if they need help they can come to us. I owe all of my strength to him, and I will use all of it to make sure that the man responsible for his death burns."

Their cheers felt like thunder as they started to sing, holding up their drinks for Sedric. It wasn't sad, but beautiful, arm in arm, as loud as they could, they sang up to the sky to him.

LIAM

We all sat in silence in the study of our house, drinking shots from two bottles of ninety-year-old brandy that Neal had brought up from the cellar.

"What did he name his first car?" Declan asked.

"Hennessy," I muttered as I reached for my shot, but Declan blocked me.

"Wrong. It was Fiona. Where the hell did you get Hennessy?"

I looked to Neal, waiting for him to back me up.

"You said his *first* car, which was the Hennessy truck grandfather gave him when he was sixteen, not the first car he got after married." Neal snickered taking two shots.

"Hand me my prize," I grinned as I took the shot.

"Did he ever give you the '*be a man*' speech? Or was that just a Neal special?" Neal asked.

Declan groaned, leaning back in a seat. "That speech, I didn't even get in half as much trouble as you two did—"

"Bullshit!" I yelled at him. "You just never got caught, you sneaky bastard. Compared to some of the shit you did, Neal and I were saints. He almost killed you when you had Coraline sit with us at church only after a week."

Neal snorted. "At least he married her. Did you ever sneak two girls into your room only to be caught mid-go by Dad?"

"No," Declan and I said at the same time, but he just nodded.

"What did he do?" Declan asked.

"How old were you?" That's what I wanted to know.

"I was seventeen, and it was the night after mom had the Christmas Ball. There were these two hot girls all over me. Logically, I was super excited, and everything was going great till dad walked in. His face dropped; he gave me that emotionless stare and then just left. I, being the idiot that I was, finished up and had them leave. The moment he came in, I forgot what I was trying to say, but to sum it up, I was telling him that I had *needs*. He told me I was fool, that I was spilling my seed in women who only wanted our family's money. That being a man wasn't about fulfilling my needs but making sure the needs of everyone else around me were satisfied, and that if I didn't understand that by now, I was a fool that would end up paying child support for the rest of my life. He ended it by saying 'take a shower, you reek of desperation.'"

"Yep, that was the speech I got," Declan said with a laugh.

"Nope, I never had that problem," I lied as I leaned back in my chair.

"Yeah, sure. You do know we knew you before Melody, right? You slept with anything that had legs. I'm surprised dad didn't cut—"

"Urgh! Shut up," I cringed, but then nodded. "I don't want to think about the women before Melody, mostly because I think she has ears all over this room and will kick my ass later. It was like Dad knew how it was going to be between us. I'm grateful he kept pushing even when I fought him on it."

"You fought him on marrying Melody?" Neal asked me shocked. "I always thought you were the good little solider and did whatever he asked."

"No, I was actually pissed that you got to marry a woman you cared about, while I was stuck with some Italian chick I didn't even know. Then Declan here had to fall in love with Coraline in like ten minutes, making me feel worse. We fought about it often, and I finally accepted it, which led to me sleeping around. I think he only tolerated it because I wasn't bitching at him anymore."

"It wasn't ten minutes," Declan muttered drinking. Neal and I gave him a look. He was a goner from the get-go with her. I had no idea why he was even trying to pretend otherwise.

Neal shook his head and frowned as he knocked back another drink. "He told me not to marry Olivia. He said that she wasn't the woman I needed. And I got so pissed off, I told him to back the fuck out of it, that I was happy.

"We had this major fight, and I demanded that he tell me if he really gave a shit about me or if he wanted me to be alone and bitter all of my life…he shook his head and turned around. Here I am years later, wishing that I'd just shut my damned mouth and listened to him. Now his death hangs around my neck."

"Your neck?" *He was blaming himself for this?*

"You did kill Olivia," Declan whispered as he poured us all another drink.

"True, but I was also the one who brought her into this family. What's worse was the fact that I was blindsided by her. I never thought that it would get this fucked up. If I hadn't married her, she wouldn't have helped that motherfucking bastard, and dad might have still been here."

"I wish I could put it on your shoulders brother," I whispered as I took a deep breath and shook my head. "And as true as your statement on Olivia is, it was not your fault. It was mine. I take responsibility for it. It hangs around my neck, and my neck alone. Avian called me not even an hour before father was killed. I was the one who'd set a match under his ass, and it was my fault that he erupted."

I paused as I took a final drink before standing. "If he thinks this is over, or that I'm down and out of this fight, he is fucking mistaken. I'm coming back with a vengeance, and I won't stop until he dies in the worst type of way."

There was silence before I took the one glass that hadn't been emptied and poured it over the floor, spilling the drink in his honor.

Placing my hands on both of their shoulders, I leaned in. "Get some rest, brothers, because we start again tomorrow."

Before I headed back to my room I stopped at my mother's. I expected her to be in bed, but instead, she was sitting on the ground surrounded by photos, baby clothes, hats, and toys. They were everywhere as she slowly looked them all over.

Hearing me, she looked up, smiled, and reached out for me. Tip-toeing over everything, I made my way to the end of her bed and took a seat on the floor beside her. The very first thing she gave me was a picture of myself as a very tiny infant.

"He was so afraid that he would crush you." She giggled. "But after you looked up at him, he never wanted to let you go."

Swallowing, I looked to another picture of Neal and me. I was in Dad's arms and he carried me with this look of wonder that was spread all over his face.

"You don't know this, but I'm sort of a hoarder…a neat hoarder, but a hoarder nonetheless." She lifted up the outfit I was wearing in the photo before looking around her room. "I kept a lot of these things because your father told me to. Every New Year's he said he'd cheated death and one day he knew it would catch up to him."

"He told me he didn't believe in death. That he had a plan." I logically knew that that couldn't be true, but I didn't realize how much the mere idea of his argument had comforted me up until now.

She snorted and rolled her eyes. "Horseshit. He thought about it often and he worried you all wouldn't be old enough, should he die. He'd had a lot of close calls, but he said he just had to make it long enough for you to take over. Not because he'd die, but because you were ready to step up. He was thrown into this, but he wanted you to *choose* it."

"It didn't feel like a choice." I'd never known anything but this life. He had sculpted me and trained me for this life.

"If you truly didn't want to do this, he would have taken over again. He would have focused on Neal or Declan. All you had to do was let him know, but he knew you were different. He had a lot of faith in you. He came in sometimes saying that he'd felt like he was holding you over a giant cliff and watching as men bowed at your feet."

That certainly explained why we watched the *Lion King* as much as we did when I was a child. She pulled a small music box from under her bed. Opening it, I saw that it contained a small pile of letters. She selected a single one and handed it to me.

"Every year your father wrote you all a new letter just in case. I asked him to keep the old ones but he would burn those. His feelings and thoughts changed each year, and he wanted you to have the last, and best, version. He wrote this one a few weeks ago when Mel asked for him to create the new lives for us all," she said, as I took the letter from her hands.

"Did he write you one?"

"Yes. But I'm not ready to read it yet." She smiled sadly before grabbing another batch of photos.

"Will you read this one with me?"

She shook her head and kissed my cheek. "Go read it with your wife and son, Liam."

"Mom, can you promise me that you won't—"

"Kill myself?" She raised an eyebrow at me and frowned. "I couldn't, even if I wanted to. Your father made me promise that I would never do it no matter how bad I felt...what an asshole."

The tears built in her eyes again. "He will probably say that again in his letter and with my luck, I'm going to make it until I'm hundred and two."

Kissing her temple, I pulled her into a one-armed hug. "Ethan's going to need his grandmother. He has no other grandparents left...no pressure."

She laughed and squeezed me back before letting me go. "Okay, go. I don't want to break down again right now."

She wiped her tears and went back to looking at her photos.

"I love you so much, Mom," I told her when I stood up.

"I know. I love you too," she replied as I moved to the front door.

Stepping out, I closed the door and came across two maids.

"Have someone listen in on her every hour until the lights are off or you no longer hear anything, then check on her," I directed.

I trusted my mother, just not in this state, and I wasn't burying her too. She could be pissed off at me if she wanted, but I would rather be safe than sorry.

Heading to my room, I entered in time to watch Mel feeding Ethan his applesauce while she listened to the news. She had changed into one of my shirts and looked absolutely beautiful.

"Hey." She smiled at me as Ethan stretched to take a bite of the applesauce. Moving to them, I took a seat beside her.

"Can you read this while I finish feeding him?"

She nodded as we exchanged; the applesauce for the letter.

"What is it?" she asked while opening it.

"A letter from my father," I said, smiling at Ethan.

She said nothing else as she pulled the folded sheet of paper out of its envelope.

"Liam, if you've killed me I'm going to haunt for the rest of your life."

I laughed. Of course he would start off like that. "Ass."

"And don't call me an ass, that's disrespectful."

I froze as I looked over her shoulder, and sure enough there it was. Even in death, he knew my next move. I wasn't sure if I should've been pissed or in awe.

"Everyone else's letters have always come easy to me with the exception of you and your mother. Maybe it's because I can put myself in both of your shoes. I understand the pressure that you feel is now on your shoulders, how heavy you think every step is, and I understand how it feels to not have

a father to turn to. I've made it my life to be there for you,
and to give you the tools you need to make it without me.

"One of those tools was in fact Melody…and yes I am
calling her a tool, a weapon, your leg to stand on when you
need help. I knew who she was, I knew that she was the
one running her family, I knew that Orlando was dying. It
was one of the reasons why I pushed so hard for you two to
marry. As nice as it would have been to have peace with the
Italians, I cared more about having you both matched up
equally. That really is the secret to making it; having someone at your side to willing fight for you, die for you, kill for
you…so I'm not sorry I lied to you both. I've watched the
both of you in sheer awe and wonder. Never have I seen a
pair so matched, so loved, and so insane. This is the best letter I have ever written because I know now, without a doubt,
that you no longer need me."

That wasn't true.

"I take comfort in knowing that I leave this world with
no regrets. I've seen my son grow from a boy to a man, and
have a son of his very own. I know it hurts, or at least it better hurt you a little, you brat, because it hurts me too. I'm
proud of you. I love you dearly, and I want you to check
up on your mother. I want you to stop and breathe, have a
moment for yourself every day, God knows you will need it. I
want you to remember to laugh, remember that it's okay to
be happy without me.

"Remember your wife and son, and the lives that you
want them to have. But all of that happens after you take
care of Avian. Wipe that motherfucker off the face of the
Earth and then make sure that nothing like this ever happens again. I'm sorry that this letter isn't longer. But your
letters were never long. I never want you to dwell on me.

Goodbye, son. Stand firm and know that there is nothing you can't do. I hope these will help you if you ever need my advice in the future. Love you always, your father."

I looked over to see what else there was and laughed. He had, for the first time ever, written out his rules for me.

She folded the letter and I stared at Ethan as he licked his lips. As I brushed his hair back, and he grabbed onto my hands. The pain was still there, but the rage eclipsed it.

"Tomorrow we start again," I told her.

"Tomorrow," she agreed.

TWENTY-NINE

"Heroes don't exist. And if they did, I wouldn't be one of them."
—*Brodi Ashton*

PRESIDENT COLEMEN

I wanted to hate them, but how could I when I'd sold my soul? Every time I entered my office, the office of all offices, I saw their faces, I heard their voices.

Puppet. They'd called me, and it was true. For months, I had almost forgotten how I'd gotten here. It was simple enough with one of them locked away in jail and the other God only knew where. Now that they were back, my life's purpose seemed to require me to honor them and smile for them. What was worse was the fact that people truly believed in them. They were the like the Kennedys, the Vanderbilts, or the Rockefellers.

The Constitution stated that "no title of nobility shall be granted by the United States," and yet the Callahans were a family like no other. They were a dynasty, and while historians will tell you that that doesn't last, they are wrong. Dynasties had a way of fading into the darkness, making you believe they aren't there until they came back with a vengeance.

I had always believed the Callahans were like roaches. Their money was stained with blood and drugs...but it was money all the same. And when my Olivia met Neal, I just knew that there would be a price to pay. But I also knew that she, and our family, would be taken care of. I hated the

Callahans, but I hated the fact that I needed them more. Being "the most powerful man in the world" came at a price, and it when this ended, I would be able to relax again.

"Mr. President," Mina said as she strutted in as usual, smartphone in hand.

"No more press conferences." I groaned as I leaned back into my chair.

"Actually, the Director of the FBI is here. He wishes to have a word with you," she answered.

I knew the Callahans had some kind of vendetta against the man, but I had no idea why. The poor schmuck was probably clueless as to why the whole world was spiraling out of control and was now worried about his job.

"I thought I told him to go to Turkey?" I questioned.

She nodded. "I'll send him in."

Sighing, I stood up behind my desk and straightened my tie as he came in with his hands in his pockets. His head was held high, and he seemed to command an air of importance.

"Mr. Doers, I thought you would have been on a plane by now." I extended my hand towards him, but he did not take it. Instead, he looked around the Oval Office as if he were picking out something he wanted to take with him.

He ran his hand over the blue vase and then checked for dust. "How are you liking your office, Mr. President?" he asked as he moved to the couches and took a seat. Undoing his jacket button, he crossed his legs and faced me.

"It's growing on me."

He nodded before he got back up. "Well, it was nice speaking with you."

"Wait, you came all this way to ask me how I'm liking the Oval Office?" Of all the things we should have been discussing right about now, that had to have been the lowest on the list.

He paused. "No. I simply wanted to see the monkey dressed in a suit who thought he could give me orders."

"Excuse me?" He had crossed the line. "It's time you fell in line—"

"Or what? You'll call your sugar-daddies on me?" he snickered. "This house, hell this damn country, may be under the impression that you run things, but we both know that you are not even capable of thinking for yourself. You aren't going to fire me, and not because you do not want to give into *terrorists* but because you've been ordered not to. You are a monkey in suit who does not deserve this office and the trust of the people who serve you. I have dedicated *my life* to ensuring that the filth remains on the street and out of this house, out of this government, yet here you are, swimming in it and stinking up the place. I'm going to destroy your people, and then you're going to fade away as the worst president in history. I only came here today to get the mental *before-picture.*"

Enough. I'd had enough of these goddamn people talking to me as though I were a fucking child.

"I am the President of the goddamn country and you work for me, Director Doers. Whatever war you started with the Callahans needs to end. Kiss the damn ring and move on. People are dying—"

"I do not give a damn about the people," he said emotionlessly. "I care about order, about balance, about the damn republic. Melody and Liam Callahan are not gods. They are men, men who should not be able to have the world turning at their feet. Somehow these young, reckless, hubris children have gone from selling crack off the streets to having the President of the United States in their back pocket. You think I started a war? A war was going to come no matter what. The Callahans won't stop; they do not understand their place in the world, and the stronger they become, the more they forget that they too can bleed. A lesson I have just now started to impart on you."

It clicked in my mind so quickly that my face dropped in shock.

"*You* killed Sedric Callahan."

Again, he looked unfazed. It was as though the man had no emotion within him at all. I was staring at a shell of a man...at a dark figure...at death.

"I'm restoring order, and I shall not stop until they are gone...down to that little half-cast child of theirs." Moving over to the vase again, he picked it up and allowed it shatter against the floor.

"By the way, you might want to ask them about what happened to your daughter," he said as he wiped his hands and turned to leave. He opened the door and there stood Mina. She glanced up at him and immediately backed up out of his way.

"Get me in touch with Olivia, now," I snapped at her.

She nodded already dialing.

It rang.

And rang.

And fucking rang.

It was all I could hear in the background of my mind as I tried to remember the last time I had spoken to her.

THIRTY

"I'm a fighter. I believe in the eye-for-an-eye business. I'm no cheek turner. I got no respect for a man who won't hit back. You kill my dog, you better hide your cat."

—*Muhammad Ali*

MELODY

"*BREAKING NEWS: It is with great sadness that we report to you that the kidnapped FBI Agent, Rebecca Pierce, has been killed. Her dismembered head was discovered at the feet of the Lincoln Memorial statue by two passersby who immediately alerted the authorities. The rest of her body has yet been to be found. The FBI is now attempting to go through surveillance footage for any possible leads, however it seems that all cameras in and around the area had been disabled at the time of the event. How could this possibly happen? Now with our senior analysis...*"

I stared at the television not really listening to the gibberish and fake sympathy that poured from the reporter's lips. Turning away from it, I watched as Liam walked into my closet and flipped over the rack of my clothes to get to my secret stash of guns. He placed two of them at his back and slipped a knife into his shoe. I wasn't one hundred percent on board with his plan. However, I was going to have to give him this.

We'd arrived back in D.C. this morning, with Neal and Declan. Fedel and Kain had stayed behind in Chicago with Coraline, Evelyn, and Ethan.

Evelyn had spent most of her days in bed, or organizing things. She had been the hardest one to convince to move into the safe house. I had them all underground, and none of them were coming out until this was over. Liam had Fedel replicate Evelyn's room in the safe house.

Our house in Washington had become a command center. All the furniture had been pushed aside to make room for computers and guns. Declan, Neal, and Liam were all itching for blood. And ironically, I was the only one reining them in from basically setting the East Coast on fire.

Placing the brass knuckles in his pocket, Liam put his hat on his head as he stepped forward.

Pulling me to him, he kissed me hard with his hands on my waist and cheek. I wrapped my arms around him and kissed him back before I pulled away. He did this now, every time we were splitting up for a few hours; he would kiss me as though it were the last time we would ever see each other. I hated it and loved it, all at the same time.

"Have fun at lunch," I said to him as he moved around me and out the door.

"I plan on it," he replied.

Shaking my head, I grabbed a pair of pearls and black pumps. Stepping out into the living room where Declan had set up four computers, I looked over the screens. All of them contained lines and lines of coding. He had been there for the last five hours, and though he was dressed well, the bags under his eyes proved how he was dealing with things.

I understood how they felt, but I was starting to grow tired of mothering them. Heading to the kitchen, I grabbed an apple, a pre-made sandwich, and a bottle of water before I walked over and handed it to Declan. As he looked up at me, my phone beeped, notifying me that my car was here.

"I'm not hungry."

"I don't give a fuck. I'm not burying another one of you, nor do I want you to fuck up my plan. Let's go."

Rolling his eyes, he grabbed the sandwich and followed me out the front door. "I have the list and the photos. When do you want to release this?"

"Let's wait until Liam and Neal return," I replied.

I glared at the driver as Declan sat up front beside him. I disliked switching people even though they were in-house. *Note to self: visit Monte.*

The streets passed by in a blur of colors, and as I leaned back, I thought about how I had spent the last few days hacking and rerouting IP address across three different continents, just so I could go through FBI files and find every undercover cop and informant across the country. All of their photos, old and new, had been compiled into a three part video that Rsamas would be releasing tonight. And by tomorrow morning, there would be blood flowing through the streets.

"I'll have the message sent out in as many languages as possible," Declan said as he typed on his laptop, and I joined him by pulling out my tablet and reading through the chat rooms.

"Apparently they've gained a few thousand followers. Who would've guessed?" You could always count on people's hatred to propel bad news. On top of that, the actual Rsamas had already taken credit for our actions within these chat rooms. We needed to keep tabs on them; if I could've found them in less than an hour, the FBI could of as well. Declan and I had spent half the night making sure they weren't tracked...yet. There was a time and place for these idiots to be caught, and now was not that time.

"We're here, ma'am," the driver said as he pulled up to the gate. Parking the car, he came around and opened the door for me as Declan handed me my sunglasses. There were only a few photographers outside with flashing lights, and I smiled and waved to them as Declan and I walked through security. Outside the gate, the guards checked through bags and scanned our clothing. Usually we could walk right through as family.

They wanded us both, and when I showed them my ID, the guard shook his head.

"I'm sorry, ma'am, but you haven't been cleared," the fat guard stated as he handed me back my purse.

"I'm sorry?" I said slowly as I stared at him.

"No one gets into the White House without being cleared." He pointed to the checklist.

"May I ask who forgot to place the President's family on the list?" I asked him again fighting to keep my smile in place.

He frowned and shrugged. "Ma'am, I don't make the rules. The FBI gave me the rules. I'm sure it was a mistake."

My jaw tightened as I glared at him, trying my best not to bash his head in with my phone.

"They've been cleared," Mina stated as she walked up to us.

"I have to get a call—"

Mina dialed and he answered his phone inside his small white booth.

"The Callahans have been cleared," she said into the phone and the man nodded.

Moving forward, I shook my head. Walking into the White House was like walking into a newsroom. Members of the White House press corps were moving all over the place.

They were reading, recording, and trying to get any information they could out of anyone who would talk to them. However, no official seemed to pay any of them a second mind.

"As you can see, our house is on fire," Mina frowned as she continued walking through.

"It's only temporary," Declan reminded her coldly.

She faced him, eyebrow raised, but didn't say a word. Then she tuned to face me. "Just so you know, Avian came by earlier."

"Let me guess, he wasn't going down without a fight?" I asked as we headed to the Oval Office.

"You knew he wouldn't?"

"I was counting on it."

I smiled at the President's secretary who nodded for us to head in from behind her phone. She looked stressed out as she fielded calls.

"We have a press conference in two hours; please don't tear into him too badly today," Mina said with a sigh as she pushed open the door.

I looked her over for the first time; she was the only one who didn't seem stressed or worried. It was like she was going through the motions. In fact, she looked *pretty*.

"You and I are due for a chat," I told her, and fought back a smirk when I saw fear flash through her eyes.

"Mr. President, First Lady," Declan stated as we walked in.

They both stood near the desk.

"Where is Olivia?" the First Lady yelled as she rushed to me and grabbed onto my arm with her long, painted nails. "What did you do to our daughter? I know you did something! Oh my God, I knew something was wrong."

My very first instinct was to break her bloody hand, but for now I needed them on our goddamn side.

I shook my head at her and whispered in a shaky voice, "She...she's dead."

"Oh...oh...oh my God," she gasped as her body went weak.

I grabbed onto her as she broke down in sobs. I glared at Declan who looked more bored than sorry, until he finally gave in and took her out of my arms. Then I turned to face Colemen.

He was a statue with tears building in his eyes; they must have burned as he glared at me in pure hatred.

"You did this, you killed her."

I frowned. I wished I had killed her. "No. No, I promise you that I didn't."

"You're lying!" he screamed at me.

Walking over to him, I took his hands and stared into his eyes. "I swear to you, I did not kill her. And in all of the time that we've known each other, have I ever lied to you? I've always told you the truth even when you did not want to hear it. Olivia was family, and even though she betrayed us, we would never kill family."

"What do you mean *betrayed you?*" the Jackie Kennedy wannabe called from behind me as she sat on the couch.

Declan simply stood at her side. *So much for comforting her.*

Sighing, I faced her as well. "She was working with Avian, he hates this family, and when we found out, we used her to get Intel on him. But when he found out, he killed her... the things he did to her. He sent us a message regarding her fate the same time he sent us one about Sedric. We only just found out, that's why we came here. He came to visit you, right? He told you?"

Fake tears built in my eyes as I stared at him.

He nodded. "He asked me if I had spoken to her."

"He was messing with you. He wants to break you. He's sick, he wants to be the strongest guy in the room, and your daughter, my sister-in-law, got in his way."

"You got us into this! You dragged us into this war, this is your fault!" his wife screamed, and I fought the building urge to kill her now.

"Avian will pay for this, I swear to God he will pay for trying to destroying your family—*our* family. We just need your help." I looked into Colemen's eyes. "She was your only child, and he did not even give us enough to bury her."

"Get out," he snapped at me. The tears fell from his eyes as he went to hold his wife.

"I'm so sorry. I've already handled all the details, and when you're ready to talk, please call me...I know you need time. We all need time. But time is not on our side," I whispered to them, as I turned back to the door where Declan stood.

Closing the door behind us he shook his head in mock disgust. "How do you fake your emotions without making yourself sick?"

"By remembering that there is a bigger plan. We need them, and they need an enemy. Avian did what I thought he was going to do. A man like him would never just leave, and he would damn sure make that clear." I wiped the leftover tears from my eyes with ease.

"How did you know that Avian knew about Olivia?" he asked as we walked down the hall once again.

"Olivia hasn't spoken to him in days, and she wasn't in any of the paparazzi photos at the funeral. He would've put the two and two together, and knowing him, he couldn't

wait to use that to hurt Colemen for trying to push him out."
He thought that no one would be able to track him, but
surprise, bitch, I was a people hunter. He thought like me,
or I thought like him, maybe it was just in our blood. Either
way, I was going to do everything in my power to keep the
upper hand.

LIAM

There had to be at least fifty people within the restaurant, all of whom were talking, laughing, and going about their business as though nothing could interrupt their special day. However, I was deaf to it all. I could see their mouths, filled with food, in some cases laughing outright. I knew they were there, but they didn't matter to me. Each step across the beige marbled floor led me closer and closer to *him*. I could feel my pulse quicken and my hands twitched with the need to strangle him. I wanted to rip his intestines out of his ass and shove them back down his throat.

His guards stepped aside, allowing me to come forth. Unbuttoning my coat, I kept my gloves on even as I sat in the last booth, right across from the scum who had killed my father.

Do not let your emotions take over, Liam. Mel's voice rang out loudly in my head.

"Mr. Callahan." He fought back surprise as he washed down a mouthful of his lamb with a glass of orange juice. "What can I help you with?"

I grinned and relaxed. "Have you ever seen *The Princess Bride?*"

"My time is valuable. I try not to waste it on movies, *son.*" He grinned as he cut into his bloody lamb.

"Shame. It's a classic, and I would know, I'm a movie enthusiast. My favorite character has to be Inigo Montoya whose father was murdered. He swears that when he when he finds his father's killer, the very first thing he would say is: '*My name is Inigo Montoya. You killed my father. Prepare to die.*'"

"Really? And I assume that at the end of this fairytale, your hero murders his father's killer?"

"But of course. What good is a son that does not avenge his father?"

He snickered. "The son should have never gotten his father killed in the first place. Or better yet, the old fool shouldn't have retired. I've heard that it can be the death of some people."

My hand twitched.

"Callahan, I'm trying to enjoy my lunch here. So why don't you get to your point. Or better yet, get on your knees. We both know you have no cards to play here. This terrorist plot of yours was cute. But you've just started to scratch the surface on what it truly means to fight me. It could have easily been that mutt of a son of yours, or your mother, or that whoring granddaughter of mine. She reminds me a little too much of her father for my liking." He was fishing for my anger, and one more comment like that would get it.

Easy, Liam. Don't let him derail you from your plan. I heard Mel say in my mind.

Smiling politely in the face of stupidity and ignorance, I restrained myself from allowing him under my skin. It was only now that I truly understood how much effort it took to wait until the right moment.

Luckily, *this* was that moment.

"My name is Liam Callahan, you killed my father.... and, well, I think death is too good for you. Isn't that right, brother?!" I yelled the last part and at the snap of my fingers, Neal, along with seven of our men appeared. They were dressed in all black, with their faces covered, and their guns in hand.

Before anyone in the restaurant even had a moment to think, they opened fired. They shot every man and woman with precision, including the three agents assigned to cover Avian. Avian's eyes widened as he stared at the chaos unfolding all around him; the blood that splattered across the walls, the people who screamed for their lives as they ran to doors that would not open for them.

I reached over and took his orange juice and toasted to him. "What where you saying about scratching the surface? I may not be able to kill you just yet, but I will make you suffer a thousand deaths before I gut you like the pig you are."

Rising, I pulled out my burner phone and dialed 911.

"Help please...Rsamas..." I held it up so they could hear the gunshots.

"Sir! Sir! Where are you?"

"The Blue...Gard—"

I cut the call and kicked the phone over to one of the nearby bodies. It dragged through the pool of blood that covered the floor and came to rest inches away from the corpse.

"This is sloppy, you own this restaurant. Do you really think you can fucking get away with this?!"

"Actually, I don't own this restaurant. We figured you would come here under the belief that we wouldn't want to draw any attention to our business. Wait..." I paused dramatically. "Now that you mention it, you're right, it would seem odd that the Director made it out without a scratch." I pulled out the gun from behind my back and aimed downwards as I shot him in the kneecap. He dropped to the ground and bit down on his tongue to keep in the scream. Squatting, I looked down into his eyes. "Remember my fucking face. Remember as you sit with their rotting bodies, that you did this. You unleashed this and there is no going back. A man cannot live by two names. You shall suffer death by a thousand cuts. Consider these the first two."

Pointing the gun to the same kneecap I fired once again. "FUCK YOU!" he screamed as he gasped for air. "I will rain down hell on your motherfucking head, Callahan! If you think this means that you've bested me, then you're bloody fucking mistaken!"

"Save your energy, Director, you're going to have to give a speech soon. Rsamas has just claimed responsibility for this. You're going to be on the four o'clock news...after they fix you up, of course," I said as I stepped over him.

"Until next time," Neal muttered to him behind his mask. We walked out of there, knowing that there was not a soul besides Avian who was going to make it out alive, and I knew he wouldn't talk. Not now at least. Mel was sure he had something, some last *fuck you* to give us if we killed him out right. I was willing to take the risk. She and Declan could back-hack whatever it was, couldn't they? Apparently she wasn't of the same mind. She was right though...our futures depended on whether or not he had another shoe to drop on our heads.

MELODY

She entered my car, took off her sunglasses, and placed them on her head. Crossing her legs, she shifted to look at me.

"What can I do for the almighty Melody Callahan now?" She tried to joke, but I knew she was uncomfortable.

"Do you think you're better than me?" I asked her as I flipped through my phone.

"No—"

"Would you ever wish to replace me?"

"I don't understand."

"Answer the question, Mina," I replied emotionlessly.

"Replace you? No. Why would I want to do that?"

"You have a two year-old girl, right?" I asked her.

She froze before she swallowed. "If I've offended you—"

"You're wasting words."

"Yes, I have a daughter. Her name is Sayuri."

"Her father?"

She shifted. "He never wanted to be in either of our lives."

"Good, because I want you to get close to Neal Callahan," I told her as her mouth dropped open.

"Excuse me? Get close to?"

451

"Fuck him," I said more clearly. "Declan has his wife. Liam has me, and Neal needs someone. He's running on pure anger and adrenaline, but once that runs out, I don't want him going outside the family for comfort."

"I'm sorry, are you trying to pimp me out to *Neal Callahan?*"

"Pimp? Sure we can call it that, but that would make me doubt your intelligence because all you have to do is think of the prospects of being in this family...you'll no longer be the *help.* You've done well for yourself, but at the end of the day, you are still the help. You've already seen us at our darkest and yet you're still here. You know what we do, and best of all, you fear me. Which means that what happened to Neal's last wife will not repeat itself."

It was like watching a fish, the way her mouth opened and closed.

"I thought Avian killed her."

"We lied. Neal killed her for betraying us. But you're tough, aren't you? You have a black belt in taekwondo *and* jiu jitsu."

She didn't speak as the wheels turned slowly in her head...too slow for my liking.

"Right now, this family is in chaos. My job is to make sure that everything is balanced and that our family skeletons stay in our closet. You are intelligent, beautiful, and a fighter. Neal will come to worship you. He's the type of man that justifies his existence by those around him, and therefore tries his best to please. With a kid, and being the President's right hand, we both know that men shy away from you. You intimidate them. You have no family other than your daughter, and you cling to both her and your job for dear life. I'm offering you a seat at the round table, Mina, the Callahan table, and we both know how powerful that seat is."

"The public still doesn't know about Olivia," she whispered as she brushed her hair back, and I could see her coming over to my side, she just needed a final push.

"Tonight, I will be releasing a list of undercover FBI agents. Olivia's name will be one of them. She will have died in service to her country. It will not take any stretch of the imagination to understand how you and Neal had a friendship that blossomed into something more. In two or three years, you will be able to go public with your relationship." I hated the fact that I was going to have to elevate Olivia to being a damn martyr, but again, I was more focused on the big picture. This way, the President would look good and remain on our side. I would just have to take satisfaction in knowing how she truly came to an end.

"What could Olivia have possibly been doing as an undercover FBI agent within one of America's elite families?"

It was a good question.

"White collar criminals," I answered. "Million dollar art scams and all that. It fits perfectly. It's set up; all I need is your agreement."

"I'm not Neal's type."

"Are you female?"

"Of course!"

"Then you're his type," I replied, waiting.

She nodded. "Fine. Please just promise me that my daughter will be safe no matter what."

"She's now Ethan's older cousin. I promise you that no harm will ever come to her. Now get out of my car."

When she stepped out, Declan and the driver both stepped into their spots in the front.

"What was that about?" Declan shifted to look back at me.

I didn't answer, I just kept checking the news reports on my phone, until I finally saw the breaking news that I was waiting for.

The Blue Garden Massacre.

"Liam and Neal are done with their lunch." I told him.

THIRTY-ONE

"In a time of deceit telling the truth is a revolutionary act."
—*George Orwell*

MELODY

"Go to bed, love."

Liam's voice startled me. I jolted upright and drew my gun on him before he could come any closer.

He looked down at it, then at me. "Seriously?"

"Sorry," I muttered. And as I pinched the bridge of my nose, I placed the gun down beside my mouse pad. I stretched, and all my bones cracked as if I had aged overnight.

Pulling a chair beside my desk, he sat beside me. "It's 3:00 a.m., love, you need your rest, you can finish this later."

"I want to finish it now," I told him as I shifted in my seat again.

Glancing at Liam, I noticed that he was watching me intensely. I tried not to focus on the fact that he was wearing nothing but his pajama bottoms.

"What?"

He shook his head and kept on staring. "I've just been thinking a lot lately."

"About our plan? Because it's—"

"No. About you," he stated as he leaned forward. His face was serious and he looked like he was trying to read to me.

"Okay…" I wasn't sure where this was going. He usually gave me more to go on, but he seemed to be thinking it through as well.

"And how my father wanted me to marry you," he added. "I keep thinking about how much I fought him on it. How much I didn't want be with you. And yet, fast forward a few years and here I am, unable to imagine a world where you're not in it. Knowing you was the best gift he ever gave me."

I wasn't sure what to say to him, I wasn't good with words. Instead, I took his hands and kissed his knuckles.

"I'll get us some coffee since you won't come to bed." He smiled as he rose from his chair.

I didn't want him to think that I didn't care. Standing up, I followed behind him and wrapped my arms around his back as he entered the dark kitchen. As I kissed his spine, he tilted his head back.

"I love you," I whispered.

Breaking out of my hands, he turned around and lifted me up.

"I know you do," he muttered as he kissed my lips softly.

It would have been amazing had my bloody stomach not growled loudly.

He smiled into our kiss.

"Well, that's not sexy," I muttered.

"No, it's cute. Come on," he replied as he lowered me back onto my tip-toes and led me further into the kitchen.

He pulled out a frying pan and grabbed a few eggs out of the fridge.

"What are you doing?" I watched him as I leaned against the sink.

"Seeing that you're the worst cook on the planet, I thought I'd make us a grilled egg and cheese," he said matter-of-factly, as he grabbed the bread from the pantry.

"I can cook a grilled egg and cheese, Liam." I crossed my arms glared at his back and he looked to me, amused.

"Really?"

I didn't like the surprise in his eyes. Stomping from the sink to the stove, I took the eggs and tried to crack them over the skillet. Sadly, the first one broke in my hand.

"Don't you dare!" I snapped as he held back a snicker and handed me a paper towel. I cleaned off my hands.

"Try again," he replied handing me another egg.

I didn't take it. "You should just do it—"

"Oh no you don't, wife. You got yourself into this, and I'm not letting you out of it." He stepped into my path.

"I could so take you." I sized him up.

"And then you still wouldn't have your grilled egg and cheese." He smiled as he held up the stupid egg. "Come on, I'll help you."

Rolling my eyes at him, I turned around as he came up behind me. He placed the egg in the clear bowl with the rest of them and handed me a knife. Without thinking, the very first thing I did was flip it around in my hand to size up the weight before adjusting my grip.

He grabbed my wrist. "Wife, you're not using it as a weapon right now. We're just going to use it to get some butter."

He placed the butter in front of me.

"Why do I need a knife for that?" I asked him as I lifted the whole bar up with my fingers and dropped it into the pan.

"Mel!" He groaned and snickered at the same time as he placed his head against mine.

"What? You use the butter to grease the pan so the stuff won't stick, right? So I put the butter in the pan!"

"Yes, a *small* piece of it, not the whole damn thing!" he muttered as we watched the butter melt in the searing hot pan.

"Well, now we have extra." I hated cooking.

"Now, we'll die of diabetes," he said, and I could feel him shaking his head behind me.

Reaching up into cabinet, he grabbed a bowl and poured out some of the melted butter before lowering the heat.

"I like to grill the bread and the cheese first before doing the egg." He instructed as he waited for me to grab the bread. Grabbing two slices I lowered them into the pan as he placed the cheese on top.

"How long do we wait?"

"Until it starts to get golden and the cheese melts over it. If it burns we're screwed...we don't have any bread left," he replied.

I leaned over and watched it closely causing him to snicker once again. I just ignored him.

"Now take the egg and crack it over the bread," he whispered behind me. He was so close that I could feel his hot breath on my neck.

Taking the egg, his hand carefully covered mine as he helped me to hit the egg on the side of the pan, and with one hand, we poured it over the cheese.

"Perfect."

I shivered and didn't answer. Who knew cooking could be so sexual? His hands went to my hips as he showed me how to flip over the bread and allow the eggs to cook over easy.

"Good."

Damn him.

For some reason, neither of us spoke anymore. He helped me finish the sandwiches, and we grabbed two glasses of milk before we moved over to the kitchen island. He sat on the stool while I sat on the island.

"My father once tried to teach me how to cook," I confessed to him as I took a small bite out of my sandwich.

"But you didn't let him?" He hissed as the egg burned his tongue.

"I told him to stop treating me like a *girl*. I thought he wanted me to learn so I wouldn't focus on guns. So while he tried to teach me, I kept juggling knives. God, I drove him crazy sometimes. Looking back on it, it probably wasn't all that wise of a choice." I laughed.

"I think it was. I like you depending on me no matter the reason. My mother actually taught me how to cook. She told me that women loved a man who could cook. I guess she was right."

"I suppose it's nice. Though I would prefer my man to have different skill sets." I winked as I drank my milk.

"Your man? Someone has become possessive," he replied as he took another bite.

"Damn straight."

"Declan tells me you had a private conversation with Mina." He changed the subject.

"Way to kill the mood." I frowned.

"I'm your man, and I have to the skill set to bring the mood back anytime you'd like." This time, he winked at me as he grabbed his drink.

"Well, excuse me, Casanova." I grinned.

"Damn straight."

"To answer your question, I asked Mina to get romantically involved with Neal," I said, biting into my sandwich once more.

He froze mid-bite and looked to me. "What?"

"Now before you get pissed at me for not telling you what I was going to do, remember how you were yesterday morning. You had one thing on your mind; I want to get Avian as much as you do. But I also want to make sure that we'll still be walking on stable ground when this is all over."

"Mel—"

"Neal needs someone, Liam. Just think about it. You sometimes have sex with me to help yourself calm down and relax. I don't mind. I enjoy the fact that taking me makes you feel better. But Neal doesn't have anyone right now, and I would prefer that the next woman he brings into this family not be stupid enough to cross me."

"Mel—"

"And you might think that he isn't ready. I mean, he did care about Olivia, but the quickest way to get over someone is to get under someone else. She—"

He was up and on his feet before I could blink. His lips crashed into mine as he tightly gripped my hair.

"Will you please stop motherfucking interrupting me so I tell you that I agree with your plan?" he said only inches from my lips. I knew that look in his eyes. They were glazed over and full of lust.

"We aren't going to finish eating, are we?" I asked him as I dropped my sandwich onto the plate without breaking eye contact.

"Having someone to love makes me feel better, Melody. It isn't just your body. When I'm inside you, when you're moaning out my name, I'm happy because I'm as close to you as possible."

Rriiiipppp

My poor shirt was torn off of me, and with no bra on, my nipples grew hard. His mouth was on my neck; his hands cupped my ass as he lifted me up, and moved us from the kitchen into the living room. I knew that it was going to be rough, just the way I liked it, but in that moment, I mentally wished that I'd had the time to stretch first.

LIAM

The moment I laid her on to the couch, her legs wrapped around me like a snake and she flipped us over onto the ground. Taking my hands, she placed them over my head.

"If you move then I'm going to have to hurt you, husband," she whispered at me, and I grinned as I moved my hands onto her breasts. She stared at them for a moment before slapping me across the face.

"Fuck," I hissed, as I felt the burn spread across my cheek, but she didn't stop there. Leaning back, she grabbed hold of me, causing me to jump in her hands.

"Hands up," she snapped. And this time I listened. Shimmying down to my pajama pants, she pulled the string until it came loose and she then used it to tie my hands together.

"Mel—"

"No talking," she snapped at me once more.

She kissed me hard before moving to my neck. Then she rubbed herself on me as her feverish kisses became bites. I hissed in both pleasure and pain. She slowly worked her way downwards, trailing light kisses across my chest. I knew where she was going with this—she was hell bent on driving me insane with her tongue. I bucked forward when she took me in her hands again and kissed my navel.

"I wonder how long you can hold out."

"Mel, don't—"

But there was no stopping her as she licked from the base of my shaft to the tip over and over again. Biting my lip, I breathed in deeply through my nose.

"Fuck," I hissed when she finally took me into her warm mouth. I crunched forward and watched her as she took all of me in. She was enjoying the way I shivered at her every touch, and at the way my teeth clenched together.

She sucked harder as her teeth lightly grazed my shaft, but I refused to give her the satisfaction. Stopping, she wiggled out of her shorts and underwear before she ground herself against me.

"God fucking damn, Mel, take these things off of me," I snapped as I lift my wrists to touch her, but she smacked them away with a smile.

"Ahh…" I moaned as she slowly eased her way onto me.

Twisting the bounds at my wrists, I brought them down to my teeth and pulled with all my might until they finally broke. Once freed, I grabbed her waist and held her tightly as I flipped her over onto her back.

"Took you long enough—"

Her legs wrapped around my waist as I kissed her hard, but I held on to her thighs.

Pulling out of her slowly, her back arched upwards off the floor.

Slam.

"Fuck," she moaned.

Taking one of her nipples into my mouth, I bit down while I used my other hand to pull on her other one.

Slam.

"Liam, please just fuck me," she begged.

Again, I pulled out slowly and she bit back.

"Damn it—"

Slam.

She glared at me in frustration and all I could do was smile. Forcing herself to rock against me, I gave in to her needs. Gripping her thighs, I pounded into her hard and fast.

"Yes. Oh fuck, I—I..." Her breasts jiggled so much that she was forced to hold onto them.

"That's right baby, come," I whispered to her. "Come for me."

"Liam!" she answered my call.

But if she thought I was done, she was kidding herself.

"Get on your knees." I commanded.

Without question, she did as told, allowing me a perfect view of her ass. Rubbing myself against her she moaned.

SMACK.

"Fuck!" I screamed, as her ass jiggled and my hand imprinted itself unto her ass.

SMACK.

She was dripping for me and I licked it all up as she shivered.

SMACK.

One of her knees went weak.

SMACK.

"Ah!" She came for me, and I once more relished in the taste of her.

"You shouldn't tempt me like this, wife. I enjoy watching you shiver and moan far too much," I whispered.

SMACK.

Her ass was so red, my cock throbbed from the sight of it. I needed her now. Grabbing hold of her I slammed right into her.

"Jesus, fuck...!"

"Not Jesus, just me." I grinned as I grabbed a fistful of her hair and fucked her.

"So close," I hissed as the sweat from my forehead dripped onto her back. "Mel!"

I came so hard that my body shook. Without any strength left, I fell beside her.

"Fuck." I inhaled deeply as I tried to catch my breath.

"Fuck," she replied as she curled up beside me.

Wrapping my arms around her, I pulled her even closer to me, and we both rested in the dark without saying another word. The only sound that could be heard was the sound of our labored breathing until...

BEEP.

BEEP.

"What's that?" I asked as she sat up quickly.

BEEP.

At the third one, she jumped up and ran back into the office. With a groan, I followed her to the computer screens. Everything looked the same, there were files upon files of useless information.

"Holy shit," she whispered, clicking away.

"What is it?" I asked, unable to look at her face because I was beyond captivated with the rest of her.

"I knew it," she muttered with her hand on her lip.

That got my attention, and as I moved closer, I saw pictures, taxes, files, companies...and all of them were about us.

"What is this?"

"I set up a sniffer in Avian's computers. I've been sifting through data trying to find anything and everything he has on us. This is it, a timeline of everything we've ever done, and evidence he's buried for the Valero, along with us. It's all here."

"Can you delete it? Are there copies somewhere else?" If we had this now, we could kill the son of a bitch.

She didn't speak, and all of a sudden a timer popped up for the next twenty-four hours.

"Mel, what's going on? Why did we just find this now?" I had to snap my fingers in front of her face to grab her attention.

"This is the only copy."

"Good, so delete it."

She shook her head. "I don't have the ability to hack it, I need to delete it directly from one of his computers. I just need to know which one it is. It will take me days to delete this."

"Okay, so then we wait—"

Again she shook her head and pointed to the ticking clock. "He plans on releasing all of this information in the next twenty-four hours."

"That's suicide!"

As we stared at each other not knowing what to say, there was a ring at our gate, and as Mel switched over to the security feed, I saw him standing outside with a cigar in one hand, and a cane in the other. He had on his very best suit.

"Avian," I said over the intercom.

"Good, you're awake," he said looking up into the camera. "Open up the door so we can all die together."

It was then that it hit me. Here we were pretending to be terrorists, knowing full well that we would never blow ourselves up to get to Avian. However, he'd gone and done the exact opposite of that. He knew couldn't beat us, so he was taking us all down with him. He was going to expose us all.

He was the suicide bomber.

THIRTY-TWO

*"If you don't hunt it down and kill it, it
will hunt you down and kill you."*
—*Flannery O'Connor*

LIAM

"So let me get this straight, he just walked in here and said he wanted to die?" Neal asked as Mel and I stared at a strapped down Avian from behind a one-way mirror.

The room he was in was smaller than the rooms we had back home. However, our Washington home hadn't been designed with the same functions. It was a plain gray room with no outlets for natural lighting. There was just a single door and the glass panel that allowed us to look in. This make-shift jail was the only security we had invested in in this home. But it would get the job done.

He wasn't struggling. He sat as comfortably as someone who was strapped, almost naked, to a chair could sit. All he had on was his underwear, and a tight bandage around his kneecap. The blood was already starting to bleed though it. Obviously, he hadn't bothered with a doctor…however he didn't look to be in pain. Which was odd seeing as how both Declan and Neal had beaten the living shit out of him before they dragged his ass in here. His lip was busted, his eye was bruised, and he had a few cuts all over his arms, neck and face.

"Does anyone else think this is insane?" Neal went on. "This cannot be this guy's last move. He wouldn't just destroy everything he's spent a lifetime building."

"I agree. This is fucked up, even for him. But I'm going through all of this and it's all-real. It's our real bank accounts, even the offshore ones, our trade partners, factory sights; he wanted us to see he knew it all. And we have twenty-two hours left before this goes to every lead broadcasting outlet in the world," Declan snapped typing away on his computer screen. "He even has the names and emails of all the journalists he wants these files to go to lined up and ready to go."

Proving that he even wanted to control his own downfall.

I glanced to Mel and found her staring intensely at Avian. I couldn't help but wonder if she was thinking what I was thinking. How fast could we outrun this? *Could* we even out run this? We would have to run not only from our lives but we'd also have to change our faces. We would be on the top of the list for the FBI, CIA, and every other damn abbreviation in the book. We would be the most wanted people in the world. How could we run with Ethan? His face would be all over the media just like ours. They'd freeze all of our assets and tear down our operations both legal and illegal. The more I thought about running, the less and less likely it seemed to be an option. Which left us with two choices: stay and win, or stay and die—because they weren't going to be able to take us alive.

"You should talk to him," I said to her. Because if I did I might've actually skipped the talking part and immediately start beating his face.

She turned to Neal. "Bring Monte here as fast as you can, he's at the rehab center."

He nodded and hurried out of the room.

"I'll be right back," Mel said to the both of us as she walked out.

What the fuck? We didn't have time for this!

"Am I the only one aware of the doomsday clock that's ticking away right now?!" Declan asked as he slammed his hands on the table. "We aren't going to be able to hack this. Should I get Fedel and have the family meet us? We have to go now and get a head start on all this."

"We aren't running," I said to him as Mel returned with a bottle of whiskey, a first aid kit, and small duffle bag.

She said nothing to either of us before she headed inside the room and closed the door with her foot.

"Liam—"

"Declan, I will not fucking tell you again. We are not running. Shut up. Sit down, and wait. He wants to throw us off again, and you're letting him fuck with your head. Now focus!" I yelled at him, when in all honesty, I was speaking to myself.

Focusing on her, I watched as she undid his bandage, and exposed his knee's flesh, bone, blood, and skin. She took the whiskey and poured it on his wound, his leg twitched, but he didn't scream or even flinch for that matter. Noticing that, she shot me a quick look before she took the new bandage and wrapped it around his knee. If he didn't respond to this, then torturing the information out of him wasn't going to be possible. In fact, he would want us to waste even more of our time on him while the clock continued to tick.

When she was done, she grabbed a bottle of ibuprofen from her kit, tilted his head back and pinched under his jaw to force his mouth open. Dropping the pills in, she flushed it down with the whiskey.

"At least he's human," I muttered to myself as he coughed and sputtered.

We all had the ability to control pain, but some things were just human nature, like coughing up a liquid that had been forced down our throats.

Slowly, she packed up everything.

"You're wasting time," he spoke for the first time since getting here.

"I have all the time in the world," she replied.

"You're lying," he snickered. "I can see the fear in your eyes. You're thinking about how far you could make it if you run."

"You surprised me, Avian, I have to give you that. I never thought you would give up so easily."

He laughed. He laughed like a madman, and I wondered if this was where Aviela had gotten her insanity from.

"I haven't given up, Melody. I've won." He grinned, "Your husband made me see that with his little massacre yesterday. My name is already tarnished is the public's eye. And for some reason it didn't bother me as much as I thought it would. Thank you all for that wonderful revelation, it feels as though a burden has been lifted off my shoulders. You took away the only thing that I *thought* mattered to me. The only thing left that can satisfy me now is knowing that I destroyed you.

"Your world is over. I did that, and never again will any person rise to the same status as this family. You will spend the rest of your lives running like dogs until someone puts you down. You thought you were ruthless. You thought you were untouchable. You were wrong. There is only one. There is only me. So tell me, how does it feel to know that you've been under my foot this entire time?"

"Don't bleed out when this is over. I'm sure Liam would like to properly repay you for his father," she replied as she stepped out.

"Tick-tock!" he yelled before his manic laughter broke out once more. Mel made no reply as she shut the door behind her.

"If I ever lose my mind, you have permission to put me down," she said to me as she dropped the bag onto the table.

"Noted," I replied as she handed two watches to Declan and I, before she placed one around her own wrist.

"We're going to break into Avian's office, and I'm going to hack into his computer," she said.

"How do you know that's the right computer this program is from?" Declan asked her.

She shook her head. "I don't. You and Monte will be hacking all of these reporters. Just like when you were trying to hide my mother from me. Even when the timer goes off, I want to make sure that they aren't able to access any of this information."

"Why don't you attach a virus to it? That way if they open any of the files, it will destroy their hard drive," I suggested and they both froze.

"And this is why you're the fucking boss!" Declan clapped.

Mel moved beside him and looked over his screen.

"We don't have time to build one from scratch, do you already have one in your system?" she asked.

"As a matter of fact, I do—" He grinned. However, as he clicked on a folder, his whole system shut down.

"What the fuck just happened?!" I yelled at him, I could feel my heart in my throat, as Mel pushed him out of the way and reset everything only to have the clock pop back up. It spun out of control, until finally, it stopped.

"Damn-it!" Mel screamed as she grabbed the first aid kit and flung it at the one-way mirror.

I couldn't even speak. What was once twenty-two hours, was now down to eleven. Eleven motherfucking hours.

"Did you try to attach something to my program? Tsk-tsk. Didn't I tell you that that would cut your time in half? That was a little surprise your mother added for me when she set up the program. At least she was good for something." Avian laughed.

I couldn't stop myself from grabbing my brass knuckles. I stormed into the room, all but kicking down the door. As I grabbed onto his collar, I smashed into his face.

"You stupid son of a bitch!"

I punched him and his cheekbone cracked under the force of my blow.

"If you think I'm going to go down like this, you're mistaken!"

I punched into his nose, enjoying the way it felt as it broke in two places.

"Liam," Mel called behind me.

Gripping onto his throat while my other fist hung in the air, I said, "You better pray, old man."

He smiled and the blood in his mouth poured out like a waterfall along with a few of his teeth. "I don't fear death. I don't fear exposure. You have no control here. Tick-tock."

"Liam," Mel called again.

Letting go of him, I kicked into his chest with so much force that he and the chair fell backward.

Stepping out again I pulled the brass from my knuckles.

"What the bloody fuck happened?" Neal yelled as he entered the room and his eyes zeroed in on the clock.

He wheeled in Monte who was dressed in a pair of shorts and T-shirt. His left leg was gone and he had a cast on his right one. Thank God he still had his hands.

"Did he fill you in?" I asked him.

"I thought we had twenty or so hours left?" he asked.

"If you try to corrupt or change the program, it cuts the time in half. So if we can't kill it from this end, then start hacking into the journalist's computers. Set up the virus from their end and killing all incoming mail, along with anywhere else he planned on sending it," Mel said to him as we ran past him and up the stairs.

Neither of us spoke. We went straight for her guns in her closet.

"Liam, call Coraline," Mel said, and I froze as I was placing the magazine in.

"No," I told her. I knew what that meant, and I was not going to accept it.

"Fine, then I will," she said as she pulled out her phone.

"Mel, we're going to get through this—"

"Do you know that for sure?" she snapped at me as she rose. "Because I don't. This isn't the way this was supposed to go down! We planned for every motherfucking bullshit asshole move he could have made! Everything but this! We have eleven hours, Liam—"

"Don't you think I know that? I saw the fucking clock, Melody. I was there, but there has to be a way we get out of this. I will not accept that he is smarter than us! We will fight, or we will die. I thought that was the code we lived by!"

"It was, until we had a son!" she screamed at me as her face turned red and her whole body shook. "I know how hard it was growing up with one parent. You had them both, but Ethan will have nothing and no one. He will have to spend the rest of his life in hiding, and in shame. Excuse me for one moment while I deal with my goddamn human emotions that you were so hell bent on making me feel. Excuse me while I try to think if going out to fight is worth giving up the chance to run away with you and our son! Give me a goddamn moment, Liam!"

She pushed me out of the way already dialing.

"Coraline—Coraline shut up and listen to me damn it." She wiped a tear from her eye. "I want you, Evelyn, and Ethan all packed and ready to go in the next hour. Jinx will be there soon—No, just bring enough for a long flight, but not enough to weigh you guys down. You're running. I don't have enough time to explain, just get it done and make sure that no one stops you. Can I hear him for a moment?"

My head hung as I heard her voice crack when he must have gotten on the phone. Squatting down, I lowered the glock as she spoke.

"We're really going to have to teach you how to say 'Mama,'" she muttered into the phone.

He must have said 'Dada' again, and I couldn't help but feel proud of him for that. Each time I heard it, I was surprised and ecstatic all over again. What if I never heard that again?

Run. We still have time to run. We would be ghosts by the time this hit the news.

"Dada."

Mel placed the phone at my ear. I glanced up at her, but she didn't look at me.

"Be safe, Ethan. We'll be with you soon, I promise," I said to him.

"Daddddaaaaa." He giggled not understanding me.

Saying her goodbyes, she hung up before she came over to me and began loading the guns in her hand while she placed two spare magazines at her back.

"Do you want to run?" I asked her seriously. "Because if you do, I will. I'll walk away right now and spend the rest of my life with you and our son in some cave, if that's what you want."

She put her head on mine and we were silent for a single moment because that was all we had left to spare.

"He doesn't get to win like this. We aren't going to prison," she whispered.

So it was decided. We were going to fight. And if we didn't stop this, we were going to die; either by the police when they came, or by our own hands.

Thirty-Three

"This is your life and it's ending one moment at a time."
—*Chuck Palahniuk*

MELODY

I took a deep breath as I stepped out of our car and headed towards the federal building. It seemed as if everything and everyone was working against us. Was this really how our lives were going to end? Was this karma? Were we being tortured for all of our sins before we died?

With each step across the white gravel and towards the building, my heart hammered against my ribs as the warm summer wind cut into my face like the dull blade of a butter knife. I could feel the beads of sweat that crawled down my face, neck, and breasts and the story that was our lives played out in my mind—the first time I met Liam; the first time I shot him; the first time we fucked followed by the first time we actually made love; our first kill together; our first miscarriage; and our first child.

The sun felt like a giant interrogation light on my skin and I moaned softly to myself in disgust. Never had I hated the sun as much as I did in that very damned moment. I felt so exposed, you didn't do this type of shit in the day—everyone was awake, alert, moving around.

"We have nine hours left, Mel," Liam's voice sounded via the earpiece I'd donned. I knew that we have nine fucking hours; I'd watched the time fly by as we were stuck in rush hour traffic. It was a different type of hell being powerless in a car as time flew by. A whole motherfucking hour, if I didn't know better, I would have thought that Avian had planned that as well.

"Your purse and ID, ma'am," the security guard said at the entrance.

I gave him both, and as I stepped through the metal detector, another woman patted down the sides of my dress.

"State the nature of your visit."

"I have a meeting with Director Doers," I lied.

He nodded as he handed me my bag and ID. "Sorry for all the extra security, Mrs. Callahan. With the ongoing threats, we have to be thorough. Just head to the front desk and they'll let you through."

"Of course, I completely understand." I smiled, as I tucked the bag under my arm and walked to the black counter that sat before the elevator bank. When we'd first returned to Washington, we'd planned to break into the J. Edgar Hoover Building. I'd known that I needed to have a look at Avian's computer, considering that I couldn't hack it from the outside. However, our plan relied on only the night staff being here, not every goddamn agent.

I had walked across enemy lines and into their territory.

"Welcome to the J. Edgar Hoover Building, Mrs. Callahan. I wasn't sure if you were going to make it. Your husband is already upstairs."

"I came straight from the spa. I'd completely forgotten about this meeting," I giggled.

"That's alright. Ms. Mina Sung has already cleared you both on behalf of the President. However, as I told your husband, Director Doers has not yet arrived," the woman said from behind the counter.

I didn't *want* to have to use the President or Mina for this—it was messy; however, there was no way we could break in without drawing unnecessary attention.

"That's alright." I leaned against the counter. "He told us we could just wait in his office. Is my husband there now?"

She frowned. "I'm sorry, ma'am, that's against protocol."

Who gave a shit?

"Sarah," I read her nametag. "Does he need to call you or something?"

She sat up straighter. "I'm sorry, ma'am. Even if he were to call me and grant permission, I wouldn't be allowed to do so simply because it's against protocol and I could lose my job. The best I can do is give you a pass to go up and wait with your husband."

"Thank you." I took the pass from her and walked slowly towards the elevators. When her gaze moved to someone else, I shifted, and moved towards the sterile looking hallway that led towards the bathroom.

Checking under all of the stalls to make sure I was alone, I pulled off my pearls and quickly slid each jewel into the air vent.

Dear God, let this work. It had to work. It was our only chance.

I walked back to the elevator bank as calmly as I could and I saw, much to my relief, that her attention was already focused on a new arrival. The elevator doors opened and I got on.

"Hold the ele—" someone yelled as the doors began to slide shut, but I didn't bother.

"Is it done?" Liam asked in my ear.

"Yes. I'm here," I whispered.

When the doors opened, I saw him sitting in the front hall, as agents continued to work behind a separate glass door. Behind it, rows of grey cubicles occupied the space.

"How long do you think we'll have?" I whispered, as I took a seat beside him.

"For them to clear the whole building? A few hours if we're lucky. Do it now."

Pulling out my phone, I dialed 411.

"Mr. and Mrs. Callahan, can we get you anything?" a man with files tucked under his arm stopped and asked.

"No, we're fine, thank you. You all look busy enough as it is," Liam replied.

I didn't pay attention to his chatter. Instead, I stared at my watch.

"It's starting," Liam whispered and I followed his gaze to the air vents. The white smoke started to spread like the plague. It was slow at first. Then it began to pour in through every vent. It wasn't deadly, but they didn't know that.

"Sound the fucking alarm already," I hissed under my breath.

I didn't have to wait long before it went off.

"CODE BLACK! Everyone move to the stairs!" a man yelled as the smoke now rushed in.

Visibility was almost non-existent, and Liam and I were forced to trail our way along the walls. He and I didn't speak, choosing instead to focus on the shadows of room as we moved through the offices. Avian's office was locked with a keypad; however, we knew most of the codes already. Entering the code, Liam held the door open for me.

Liam moved over to the desk and stood on it in order to close off the air vents within the office. Then he lifted the window open.

Sitting at his desk, I noticed all the awards and photos of him with people of prominence; presidents, world leaders, the Queen of motherfucking England, even the goddamn Pope. He was willing to throw all of this away…that was how much he hated us, how much he wanted to destroy us… insanity must really run in my family.

Self-righteous son of a bitch.

"Declan is on." Liam came up behind me as I began the monumental task of attempting to hack into the computer.

"How's it going, Declan?" I asked as I logged into Avian's mainframe.

"Slow. There are too many names and not enough fucking time for us to go through all of them and stop it individually. Please for the love of God tell me that you've got the right computer."

My heart began to race as I found the program. Could it really be this easy?

"I think so—"

The moment I opened it, the timer once more spun out of control. What had once been a little under nine hours, reset itself to a little over four hours. It was like being slapped in the face and having my heart ripped from my chest.

"Goddamn it!" Liam hissed beside me.

"You guys need to get out of there now, that isn't the right computer, and all of Washington is about to descend on that building," Declan said.

I didn't want to touch it. I couldn't. But where could we run to if we didn't finish this? We had known this coming here, and yet we'd backed ourselves into this corner.

"Try again," Liam said to me.

My hands were on the keyboard, and the lines of code streamed past the screen. It was a maze of traps, some I could see, others were hidden, waiting for me to fuck up so the damned clock would divide itself once more.

"Mel, try again," he said.

With an almost silent click, the timer spun out. Two hours, two minutes. It was as if it knew my every move before I did. Like Avian was taunting me through the screen.

"We aren't going to win this one, Liam," the words came from my mouth and never in all of my life had I felt like such a failure.

There was a silence between us as the sirens blared outside.

"I know," Liam finally said, "but we don't give up, we fight this until we can't. Declan, can you still hear us?"

"Yes, Neal is here listening in as well."

"Did Ethan catch the flight?" I kept my voice tight.

Stop being a coward, Melody.

"They're all airborne as we speak," Neal answered. And with that, the fear was gone. I'd accepted the situation and I refused to break.

"Good, you should have an hour or two after this becomes public. Pack up and leave," I told them.

"What about Avian?" Neal shot back.

Screw him!

"Leave him there, this is what he wanted. When the police come looking, they will find him as well."

There was a short silence before Declan spoke up.

"What about you?"

Liam pulled out his gun, and emptied the magazine until only one bullet was left. "Don't worry about us brother."

"Liam, we still have two hours. We can still do this!" Neal yelled as he registered what we planned to do.

Liam looked to me and nodded.

There comes a time when you have to accept your defeat and understand that you were not untouchable. That there would be someone even more ruthless than you were. That somehow, someway, some fucked up miserable way, the world had to reset. We'd had a good...a great run. We would be forever remembered. Chicago, hell the whole damned country, would never forget us.

"Mel, what the fuck are you doing?" Declan yelled as I clicked into the next trap.

"I'm ending the torture," I told him, as I clicked on the bomb. Two hours became twenty-three seconds.

"Have you both lost your fucking minds?" Neal screamed.

"Goodbye, my brothers," Liam told them before he cut the line.

Taking my earpiece out, I pull out my gun, as Liam had done and I took out all but one bullet as I stood up to face him. We looked each other dead in the eye, his green eyes seemed to pierce right through me.

Twelve.

"I'm not a fan of the fedora," I said as I held the gun to his head.

Eleven.

"Brown isn't your color," he confessed, his gun only inches from my face.

Ten.

"When I first met you, I hated the fact that I was going to have to kill you because I thought you were attractive."

Nine.

He grinned; I loved that grin. "I just really wanted to fuck you."

Eight.

"I knew that already."

Seven.

"I know you knew, I just had to state that out loud. By the way, you were the best shag I've ever had."

Six.

"You fucking bastard," I said even though I couldn't help but snicker.

Five.

My heart sped up as the grip on my gun tightened.

"Did you ever want more kids?" he asked, swallowing slowly.

Four.

"I hadn't really thought about it. I wanted to be a better mother to Ethan first. He was finally starting to accept me," I whispered.

Three.

Stupid goddamn tears.

It took all my effort to fight the onslaught of tears as my resolve crumbled. He reached up and wiped them away with his thumb.

Two.

"I'm not the fucking emotional one in this relationship." I smiled at him.

One.

"I love you, Melody Nicci Giovanni-Callahan."

And we pulled the trigger.

THIRTY-FOUR

"Death ends a life, not a relationship."

—*Mitch Albom*

LIAM

It took a cold son of a bitch to look the love of their life in the eyes and then put a bullet into their skull. I knew from the very moment we spoke about this that I wasn't going to be able to do it. However, I was shocked that she also seemed unable to do it as well. She stared at me, her gun still raised and hot from the bullet she'd fired into the wall behind me, while my bullet remained lodged in the picture frame behind her.

Dropping my forehead to hers, we stood there for a moment as we breathed in each other's scent. Were we weak for not killing each other, or did that make us strong? I couldn't tell anymore. I felt dead inside, but I still had her and that was all that mattered.

"You didn't give me a chance to say, *'I love you too, Liam Callahan,'*" she whispered.

I wanted to smile, but I couldn't. This was the end. Pulling away from me, she turned to the computer. The numbers on the timer were all set to zero.

"We should go," I said to her just as all the data started to scramble, and all the files on the drive were sent off to the various journalists.

"What the hell?" Mel muttered before sitting down.

"Mel, we need to—"

"The files are deleting themselves," she whispered,
My heart took a thumping beat. "What?"

She tried to type, but the system immediately locked her
out and the pages, the pictures, accounts, everything that
he had on us, erased itself. It was like watching the end of
a solitaire game where all the cards were spread out before
they disappeared completely.

"Did you do this?" I asked her.

"No. There was nothing I could do. The program was
beyond me—"

She stopped when a video screen popped up and all of
sudden, there was Aviela with a large grin on her face and a
glass of white wine in her hand.

"Having trouble there, Father?" she snickered. "I wish I
could see your face right now. Oh my, you must be ready to
explode with rage. You probably want to beat the hell out of
me. Stab me a few more times, lock me up in a hole until
I behaved accordingly. It's a shame; you have most likely
killed me by now. Physically killed me at least. But I don't
care, I've been dead for a long time and I've taken your shit
for even longer. I may not be strong enough to destroy you,
but I damn well will not make it easy for you to obliterate
my daughter.

"That's right—if it came down to her or you I will
always choose her. You thought you could somehow
change that? And I let you believe that I didn't care, I shot
her, almost killed her family members, just so I could have
this one moment. This one victory. Everything you've
ever made me collect on her is here. My life's work—
the only scrapbook I have of her—and I'm erasing it.
There are no copies to be made, I've code stamped them
all to delete when this went off. Do your own fucking

dirty work, you sick, stupid son of a motherfucking bitch. Checkmate, Daddy."

My mouth dropped open as she raised her glass to him—to us.

"I'll see you in hell," she said as she drank the entire glass. "Oh, and one more thing, if you're in your office, you really should leave, I've got a few explosives ready to go off in that goddamned place. If you make it, tell my baby I said hi…and that I'm sorry I had to hurt her."

With that, she was gone, and I wasn't sure how to react. Melody sat back in shock, as her eyes roamed the computer screen while the files kept on deleting themselves and everything was wiped clean. She went to click on the video again, but a sudden and violent explosion went off, causing the windows and the walls around us to crack.

"Mel, we need to go!" I yelled as the ground shook violently beneath us. The foundation of the building was no doubt giving way.

"Give me a second," she said, as she took her phone and hooked it up to the processor.

What the fuck could she possibly be doing now?

Rushing to look outside, I saw the authorities below already clearing the block.

Another loud explosion echoed throughout the building, causing whatever hadn't yet fallen, to crumble to the ground.

"Mel—"

"Let's go," she said as she took off her heels and moved to the door.

The moment she opened it, thick, heavy, grey smoke encompassed us. Electrical wiring hung from the ceiling, as parts of the walls collapsed.

She ran through the aisle when the floor underneath her suddenly gave way.

"Mel!" I jumped forward, and grabbed onto her arm. "I didn't let you live for you to go and get yourself killed!"

"I didn't ask to be saved, you ass! Let me go. We can get out this way."

Rolling my eyes, I did as she asked and let go without giving her any warning. She fell hard against the desk below her.

"Goddamn it, Liam!"

"Sorry. I was too busy being an ass," I snickered as she rolled off the desk and I jumped down.

I got to my feet only to be punched in the jaw.

"Bitch!" I snapped as I wiped the blood from the corner of my mouth.

"Stop your whining, we need to get to the stairs."

Grabbing her arm, I pulled her into me and kissed her. My fingers wound their way into her hair as she gripped onto my neck.

"This isn't over," I told, her as I took her hand and ran. I placed my arm over my mouth, trying to keep as much of the ash-like smoke out of my lungs as I could.

We made it into the stairwell and down one flight when the ceiling caved in behind us.

"Is anyone there? Help me, please!" a man called from a level down. His leg was broken; snapped at an odd angle and bleeding.

Mel looked to me, annoyed.

We can just leave him.

"Someone help!" the man begged.

"We can use him to escape," I whispered. After all, we were still surrounded by almost every law enforcement agency. They'd be wondering why we hadn't left the building during the initial evacuation.

Mel moved to him, and pressed her thumb against his neck until he blacked out.

"He doesn't have to see us to help us," she said.

Good point.

Placing his arm around our shoulders, we made our way down the stairs. His legs dragged with every step we took, but there was a price for being saved, right?

"Three more!" a fireman yelled, as he rushed to us. We both kept our heads down, and stared at the gravel as they came to us.

"Sir, ma'am—"

"We're fine, but he's hurt badly," Mel said as they wrapped blankets around us.

"Is there anyone else in there?" a police officer yelled over the loud sirens and growing crowd that had gathered to watch the building burn behind us.

"We couldn't see anything. We got lost and trapped, and we found him as we were trying to get out," I yelled.

They nodded just as another explosion erupted inside, shattering all the windows on the top level.

"Move it. Move it! Clear the way!" the officer yelled, as he led us to the ambulance.

"We're fine, I just want to go home," Mel told them.

"Ma'am, we need to get you check—"

"I'm going home. This damn city is trying to kill me! Massacres, bombings! I feel like I'm in a fucking war!" she snapped as another bomb went off. The back part of the building began to collapse, sending a thick plume of smoke towards us.

It wasn't ideal, but it gave us the cover we needed to escape.

"Liam!" Mel yelled with a smile on her face as we moved away from the scene.

"What?"

"Did we just win?"

"Almost."

After all, we still had Avian to deal with.

MELODY

irt and dust coated every inch of me. My hair was heavy
with it, and I noticed that even the ends were burnt.
Liam looked just as bad, and from the smug look on our
faces, it'd be hard to imagine what we'd just escaped. We
walked into the basement, not expecting to find anyone but
Avian.

However, Monte, who sat at the computer, pulled his
gun on us as we walked in.

"Really?" Liam said, raising an eyebrow at him.

"Boss! What happened? Everything's gone. How'd you
do it?" he asked, as he wheeled his chair around to face us.

"What the fuck?" Liam grumbled as he noticed both
Neal and Declan beating the crap out of Avian. "I thought I
told them to leave!"

"Neal said he had nothing left, Declan called Coraline
and then they both went in there before I could talk to
them," Monte responded.

"Really? Before you could talk to them?" Even with one
leg he could have said something.

"Alright, maybe I wanted the bastard who took my leg to
get what was coming to him." He fought back a grin.

Shaking my head at him, I walked over and grabbed the
handlebars then wheeled him over to the window.

"Then here's a front row seat," I told him. I patted him on the shoulder just as Liam entered the room.

"Enough! I want him alive so I can kill him slowly," Liam said to his brothers.

They froze, their faces covered in blood splatter, no doubt shocked to see him.

"Liam, what in the hell are you doing—?"

"Get out," I said to them as I entered.

Dropping the brass knuckles, they cleared the room, but not before spitting on Avian.

Avian's head dropped, and blood dripped from the tip of his nose. He took a few deep shallow breaths before he spat up blood. With what little strength he had left, he pushed himself back in the chair. One of his eyes was swollen shut, and bruised. I had to give it to him, he was a tough old man.

"From your brothers' reactions, I'm assuming it's done?" he asked Liam as his good eye looked us over. "You all have more gall than I thought. I was sure you were going to kill yourselves. It's in your nature."

"Was it worth it, Avian?" I asked him. "I was in your office, I saw all your hard work and you threw it all away. I don't understand that."

"You can't win if you aren't willing to lose it all. I fear nothing. I lose nothing. I grieve for no one, and in return, I can spend my life torturing you as you did to me. The fear rolling off you made it worth it. Besides, if I truly wanted to, I could've made a deal with the DOJ, and spent the rest of my life under house arrest…"

"You thought you could get out of this?" Liam asked him. "Why not go straight to the DOJ and make the deal? Why did you allow us to do this to you?"

"I'm not afraid of pain. I welcome it. It makes us strong. Bones, bruises, cuts, they all heal. My mind is something you can never touch."

"The Department of Justice wouldn't touch you with a ten-foot pole," I said to him.

He snickered as he spat out more blood. "I didn't get to where I am without collecting dirt. Before Olivia, I paid off your maids, I went through your trash, and I hacked into satellites just to triangulate your jet. I have dirt on them all. They would sooner drop me off on a deserted island than let me spill their secrets. I'm the ultimate hunter, I know how to protect my back."

"You mean my mother was," I corrected.

He shook his head. "Your mother couldn't move without me, let alone think. She did as she was told. She wasn't a hunter, she was bait, a pawn."

"She was smarter than we all gave her credit for." I pulled out my phone and played the video.

"Having trouble there, Father?"

I watched as his eyes widened and his mouth dropped open in shock.

"No," he whispered, before he started to scream. "No! You stupid cunt! NO!"

"Well, Mr. Hunter, it seems like the fox tricked you," Liam said as Avian struggled against his seat. He walked around him, stood at his back and placed a hand on his shoulder, he leaned down to his ear and whispered, "But it's okay, you don't fear pain, right?"

"I'll ask my question again." I smiled as I put the phone away. "Was it worth it?"

Liam began to take off his shirt.

"Wife, I may not make it to dinner," he said to me softly, and I knew what he wanted. *Revenge.* Blood by his own hands for his father, and I would let him have it. Taking his shirt from him, I nodded.

"Take all the time you need," I said before turning to Avian. "Goodbye, grandfather. It was never a pleasure."

"This will be a very barbaric," Liam whispered to him as I made my way out the door.

LIAM

I whistled as I wheeled him into the crematorium. He screamed against the duct tape, but it was music to my ears. Slamming on the button, the steel gates opened up as the heat from the pre-warmed oven escaped. The fire roared, exciting me even further. He was incapable of moving anything more than his neck after my little chair episode.

"Have you ever read *A Thousand Horrible Ways to Die?*" I asked him knowing that he couldn't answer. "It's a great read—crucifixion, pit of snakes, impalement. I was going to just pick a random number, but the wife said we needed to go deal with Rsamas now. I've spent too much of *our life* on you already."

He didn't fight against the straps as he was already weak from blood loss. I patted him on his chest and I knew it burned.

"Stay alive for a few more moments. In the end, I need to see you burn. You'll die by fire, while we were reborn through the flames Aviela unleashed at your office. It's all quite poetic, don't you think? We can't all be the phoenix, some of us have to be the ashes."

Pressing the button, I watched with joy as the flames took him before the doors closed.

"Just think of it as returning to hell," I said, as his instincts kicked in and he began to struggle.

His loud muffled screams could've woke the dead.

"Checkmate," I said, turning as the gate snapped shut.

MELODY

As Liam made it onto the plane, I looked over the seats and waved to him.

"Finally," Declan muttered from the first class seat behind us.

"Greedy bastard couldn't even allow us to watch," Neal snickered.

I turned to them both and they immediately placed their headphones on, and relaxed into their seats.

"Sorry I'm late," he said as he placed his bag in the overhead compartment.

"Had fun?" I questioned, knowing full well he had.

H smiled and winked in reply. "Jinx knows where to meet us?" he asked a few seconds later and I nodded.

I'd sent Coraline a message telling them to stop in England. They hadn't been in the air for that long anyway. We all needed a break from the chaos; even if it was just for a day or two.

A sudden movement caught my attention, and I looked towards the front to see Mina, with a little girl in her arms, speaking to the flight attendant. She passed our row and stood where Neal and Declan were seated. I watched as she looked at her tickets, which were no doubt the ones I had sent to her, before looking at Declan.

"I think you're in my seat," her soft but confident voice caused Liam to look to me in surprise.

"Oh, sorry," Declan said as he stood up and looked around in confusion. Then he shuffled off to his assigned seat. The little girl in Mina's arms reached over and smacked Neal, in an attempt to get his attention.

"Sorry about that," Mina said to him.

"No, it's no problem." He smiled.

I turned in my seat, and looked forward with a small smile on my face.

"Ladies and Gentlemen, please turn on your screens to view a message from the President of the United States," the pilot spoke over the intercom.

"Right on time," Liam whispered before he turned it on.

"*Good evening. Tonight, I am pleased to report to the American people and to the world that the United States has conducted an operation that has resulted in the disorganization and decimation of the terrorist group known as Rsamas.*

"*As you all know, they have been responsible for the murder of dozens of innocent men and women within the last month. Today, at my direction, special agents targeted an operation in the small town of Roster, Alabama. And after a firefight, the men responsible for The Blue Garden Massacre, the bombing of the J. Edgar Hoover Building, and the murder of federal agents across the country, including my daughter, as well as many of your sons and daughters, were brought to justice.*

"*Today, all those who seek to bring forth terror are reminded of the greatness and zero-tolerance of this country and the determination of the American people. We will not bend to terror. We will face it and say not today. Not Ever. As such, a memorial shall be built to commemorate the fallen. We must—and we shall—remain vigilant.*

Thank you. May God bless you, and may God bless the United States of America."

The passengers erupted into cheers as Liam kissed the back of my hand.

"We won. It's over," he whispered to me.

"This is can never happen again," I whispered back.

"I know."

I nodded, but I couldn't speak. Yes, we'd won this war and I was going to make damn sure that it would be the last one we ever fought. Things were going to have to change. But right now—right now all I cared about was having my son in my arms and my husband at my side.

Epilogue

"Clothes covered in red,
Eyelids sore and blue,
Never forget the ruthless
Because they won't ever forget you."

— *J.J. McAvoy*

MELODY

I sat patiently with my legs crossed and my hands folded. I was trying my best to keep calm as the teacher in front of me went on about what was possibly wrong with my son.

"...it's my personal belief that your son has a social anxiety disorder. He rarely plays or talks to the other children. In fact, in all of his time here, I've never seen him interested in anything other than his doodles. I understand that you are both incredibly—"

"I'm sorry, is my son failing your class?" I ask her through a smile.

"No, but—"

"Has he been disrespectful in anyway?"

"Again, no—"

"Are you a licensed psychiatrist?"

Her nostrils flared as she took a deep breath.

I smiled. "I'll take that as a no. You're a teacher, a very well paid teacher I might add. After all, this is the best private school in the state. Now, if you took the time to actually look at these *doodles*, you would see that he has a great talent and a very imaginative mind. I'm guessing the reason he isn't responsive in your class is because he's bored... those packets you give, he finishes in less than a few minutes while at home. So instead of blaming my son or trying to label him with a disorder, which we've already established is not in your job description, why don't you try a few other methods?"

Her mouth dropped open as if she hadn't been expecting me to say anything, as if I was supposed to just take my son and get his head checked.

"I think we're done here, Ms. Henderson, thank you for bring us in." Liam stood and fixed his suit and tie before he offered me his hand.

"Of course, Mr. Callahan. And Governor, I just want you to know that I'm an avid supporter of —"

"Goodbye, Ms. Henderson," I cut her off, and took Liam's hands as he led us out.

Fedel and Monte both stood, at the doors.

"Why do you look so glum, sugar plum?" I asked my son as he swung his legs back and forth on the bench in the hall.

"Am I in trouble?" he asked softly.

"No, your mom here yelled at your teacher," Liam snickered.

His dark brown messy head snapped up and his mouth dropped open. "Mommy!" he scolded.

"I did not yell. I just corrected her mistake is all," I said to him and he crossed his arms, and glared at me as though he didn't believe me.

"I don't want to be moved into another classroom again, I just started to like this one," he groaned, as he put his head in his hands.

Dropping to my knees in front of him, I brushed his hands away. But he still refused look at me.

"Wyatt, look at me, please."

He sighed and looked to me with his familiar, big, brown eyes, though his had specks of green in them.

"If you like the class, why don't you speak? Or talk to the other students? I know you aren't as shy as you act. You and Ethan can talk the ears off an elephant." I said with a smile as I tickled his stomach.

He tried to not smile, as he wiggled away from me. "I don't know. Can we go home now?" He looked to Liam who stood behind me.

"Fine," I said, as I held out my hand to him, but he ran between Liam and me, and grabbed both of our hands.

"Daddy, can we get burgers from Sal's?" he pleaded.

"Grandma is having a picnic this afternoon, you don't want to be too full, do you?" Liam asked.

Wyatt gave him a look. "Daddy, I'm seven now, my stomach is bigger. I can eat just like Uncle Neal."

God, I hope not! I thought as we stepped outside.

Our car, along with two others, one in the front, and the other in the back, pulled up. Kain stepped out and opened the door for us, and Wyatt hopped in, took off his backpack and threw it aside.

"Take us to Sal's please," he demanded before buckling himself in.

"Wyatt, I said no," Liam told him sternly as we entered the car to sit beside him.

"Can't we negotiate? I promise to get one for Ethan and Dona this time." He smiled, and I laughed outright.

"Do you want to negotiate or compromise?" I asked, as I ran my hand through his hair.

He shrugged. "Whichever one gets me a burger."

"Rule seven," Liam reminded him.

Wyatt pouted as he crossed his arms. "Never argue with the boss."

"That's right, so why are we still talking about this?" he asked him.

"Fine, let me starve. Dona will never speak to you again," he sighed, as he reached into his navy blue jacket pocket to pull out his mp4 player. Turning his music on, he shut us out and I fought with all my might to keep from laughing.

Liam groaned, as he pinched the bridge of his nose. "I can hear my father laughing at me. But honestly, I don't remember being this frustrating," Liam whispered.

I squeezed his thigh. "I'm sure you don't. Relax, he's just taking after Ethan," I said.

"You just had to get pregnant again so soon after Ethan. As if handling him wasn't more than enough."

"Excuse me? Whose idea was it to take a second honeymoon—?"

"We never had a first, so how could there be a second? Besides, you loved London, *Governor.*"

I wanted to kick him. Instead, I copied Wyatt and turned my back to him. I still couldn't believe that it had been eight years since we'd gotten rid of Avian. Eight years since I'd gotten pregnant again, with twins this time; Wyatt Sedric Callahan and Donatella Aviela Callahan. I loved them both, but sometimes I felt the same way when dealing with Donatella as Liam did with Wyatt. It must be due to the fact they were so much like us. Donatella had Liam wrapped around her fingers so tightly, it wasn't even funny.

It had been eight long years of controlled chaos, and because Liam and I never wanted the events that took place to ever repeat, changes needed to be made. We were now more removed from the drug trade. The trade was still overseen by us, but we no longer got our hands as dirty. Weed had taken off big time, and we had the largest hold on the market. There was still a demand for the usual though—cocaine, meth, and heroin, but they were no longer made in Illinois. After all, Liam's plan for the first female governor of Illinois was to clean up the streets and actually do it.

We'd taken a page from the Roman playbook—we basically allowed sellers to keep moving a product in exchange for less violence. It wasn't about the money, it was about the power; the control. Avian taught us that.

Drug dealers were strangely civil when you had a gun to their heads. Lesser gangs and cartels were a different story. They tended to get out of control and we were usually forced to send in a clean-up crew. It took a good dozen group deaths for the rest to get the bloody message. They had no idea who we were and that only served our purpose by scaring the shit out of them. With Chicago shining as it was, I was elected not only once, but for a second term. I had been in office for almost five years now.

At first, I thought that Liam should've been the one to run, but he'd pointed out the fact that he needed to keep up the *business* aspect of our lives...though I knew he secretly enjoyed having his Mad Hatter title. I had given this state almost five years, and now everyone was waiting on edge to see what my next move would be.

"Melody." Liam pulled me from my thoughts, as he showed me an alert on his phone. "Apparently someone in the FBI has been checking up on us."

It wasn't unusual. The FBI checked out every governor... mostly because they were usually corrupt. The only difference between them and us was the fact that we couldn't be caught. Once the J. Edgar Hoover Building was rebuilt, Liam and I donated one hundred million dollars towards the new technology labs. Unknown to them, Declan, Monte and I had set up an alert program. If anyone ever looked into our names, or our lives, we knew about it instantly and we decide how to handle it.

"What are they looking at?" I asked as he scrolled through.

"Tax returns." He shook his head before he placed his phone back into his pocket.

"Of course," I snickered as Wyatt relaxed into my arms.

"This picnic is going to drive me mad though." He groaned as we pulled up at the park. "Promise me you'll be nice."

"I'm always nice."

"You know, after all these years, I still don't believe you." He winked at me.

Ignoring him, I pulled out one of Wyatt's earbuds. "We're here and I think I see burgers."

He sat up and pressed his face against the window. "I can't see anything, all the cameras are in the way."

Bloody press. We couldn't leave the goddamn mansion without them following us around.

"We'll be out soon, and please be nice to your cousins," I told him.

"I'm always nice, Mommy," he said matter-of-factly.

"Like mother like son," Liam muttered behind me causing me to elbow him.

LIAM

D addy!" Donatella screamed the moment I stepped out of the car. She ran as fast as she could before she leaped into my arms.

"Now, who are you?" I asked, as I held her out in front of me. She was an almost carbon copy of her mother; dark brown hair, a dazzling smile...but she had my eyes...my green eyes.

"Daddy, you know who I am." She pouted at me.

"You look familiar? Have you ever stolen one of my ties?"

"I've borrowed some."

"Now, I remember you." I pulled her to my chest. "You eat all of my favorite cereal, borrow my ties, and play pranks on your brothers."

"Daddy!" She giggled, and wrapped her arms around my neck as we walked to the grassy park. She hid her face in the crook of my neck, annoyed by all the cameras just as much as I was.

"Mr. Callahan, does your wife have future plans to run for President?"

"Mr. Callahan, what are her plans for the rest of her second term?"

"Ladies and Gentlemen," I turned to them, as I shifted Donatella to my hip. "When my wife makes a decision, you will all know about it. Now if you'll excuse us, we have a family picnic—"

"And burgers!" Wyatt yelled from further up ahead. He wrapped his arms around his mother as if it would save him from me. Mel tried hard to hold in her laughter, I could see it as she patted his head.

Wyatt was her baby.

"We have a picnic and *burgers* to attend to," I said to them.

Donatella wiggled out of my arms and I found myself wanting to pout as she ran to Wyatt and grabbed his arm before they both took off towards Neal who stood around the fire pit.

"Food trumps father." Mel rubbed it in before taking my arm.

"You would think we never fed them," I muttered, as I scanned the area for any sign of Ethan.

He wasn't with Mina and Neal's kids. Neal had adopted Mina's daughter the year before she had given birth to their son, Sedric. Mina was good for him, and more importantly good for us, since she was now Melody's campaign manager. For Neal, I knew what attracted him to her the most was her blunt honesty...she was an open book. She had told him on their very first date that it was Mel who wanted them together. He was pissed at her for all of five seconds before deciding not look a gift horse in the mouth.

"Where's Ethan?" I frowned to myself still not seeing him.

He wasn't with Coraline and Declan, who were busy dancing to music while their two kids danced around them. After Coraline's recovery, she hadn't been able to carry any children herself. So instead, they'd adopted a baby girl,

Helen, and then, through a surrogate, they were able to have a boy, Darcy. Helen and Donatella had formed an alliance against all the boys in the family. Every water, snow, and dirt fight was their doing.

"There he is." Mel pointed to Ethan, who had donned his favorite hat while he sat perched on a tree branch with a book. "It looks as if he's trying to be mature again."

Since he was the eldest boy, he tried to act as though he was above his siblings and cousins. He wanted to be treated like a grownup.

"You got this, or should I?" Mel asked.

"I got it."

She nodded as she moved over to my mother who sat behind her easel trying to paint. It was the only thing that made her happy anymore, outside of the family of course. And she'd become really good at it. She'd even done a family portrait and managed to put my father it in, right where he should be.

"Ethan," I call up the tree.

"Hi, Dad," he said, not looking up from his book, which wasn't really a book but an Italian dictionary.

"Are you trying to learn Italian?" This was new.

He shrugged and looked down at me. "I wanted to know what mommy was yelling at you."

"She was not yelling—"

"She was. She was really mad, and mom only speaks Italian when you do something bad," he stated

These kids were going to kill me.

"Well, what have you gotten so far, smarty?"

He grinned as he lifted up his paper. "Are you fucking—"

"Okay, that's enough," I cut him off.

"Yeah, that's all I have anyway. She talks too fast."

"Well, can you join the family now?"

He looked around the park then shook his head. "They're all babies and you told me I had to start being a man."

"I meant that you had to stop ratting out your uncles and me when we have poker nights without your mom." He needed to stop taking everything so literally.

"Dad, I don't want mommy to yell at me in Italian. Rule sixteen: Never displease mother."

Now he was using our rules against us.

"Yes, but rule: Fifty one says always tell your mother the truth *unless* it goes against the wellbeing of your father."

His mouth dropped open, and he jumped out of the tree. I caught him, but he rushed out of my arms, making sure that no one saw.

"That is not a rule!" he said as he placed his hat back on his head.

"It is too." *Now.*

"It is not."

"Ethan, you can't argue with the maker of the rules."

"I want these rules in writing, like the bible or something." He huffed as I laughed...he would get them the same way I did.

"Ethan, it's family time, go have fun and act like a kid, that's an order."

He pouted but sighed. "Fine, but only because you told me I have to."

"Of course." He nodded and began walking off. Suddenly I remembered what I intended to ask him. "Ethan?"

"Yeah?" He stopped and looked back to me.

"Why doesn't your brother talk in class?"

He grinned. "It's a secret."

"Ethan."

He sighed. "He likes a girl and he made her cry before, so now he's scared to say anything when she's around. Don't tell him I told you, okay? And don't tell Mom!"

"Okay." I couldn't help but smile.

So Wyatt had a crush. I knew why he didn't want their mother to know.

"Mr. Callahan," Avery Barrow, my former cellmate from what seemed like a lifetime ago, walked up to me, escorted by Monte. He had grown into a highly revered political correspondent and reporter over the years.

"Avery, thank you for making it."

"Of course, Mr. Callahan, I'm assuming it's time for me to pay off my debt?" He smiled and I nodded before I turned away from the family.

"I'm going to need you to take care of something for me," I said to him as Monte handed him a photo.

His mouth dropped open.

"Is there a problem?" I asked him.

He shook his head, but opened his mouth anyway, a small smile lingered on his lips. "I always thought the bad guys lost in the end. That world had to balance itself out."

My eyebrow raised at him as I snickered. "You know why they invented superheroes? Why billions cling to fictional characters in movies and books?"

He shook his head.

"Because they know that here in real life, the villains run the world. Why else do the good die young?"

"I look forward to living a long life," he replied, reminding just how much he'd changed.

"Make her look good, Avery," I replied as I left him, and headed back to my wife.

She sat on a white blanket while Donatella ran back and forth every few seconds, and left a dandelion in her mother's hand with every trip.

"What's going on?" I asked, as I took off my shoes and sat down.

"She wants to make a crown of dandelions, but the wind keeps blowing them away," Mel answered as Donatella came back with a *single* dandelion and placed it in her hands.

"Sweetheart, you know you can pull more than one at a time, right?" I asked.

"I know," she said before she went back to get another one.

I look at Mel who just shrugged. Things were either done Donatella's way or no way at all.

"So Avery—"

"He's going to take care of it," I told her.

"Aren't you going to miss Chicago?" she whispered as she looked at the skyscrapers that stood in the distance of the park. She was already getting her ahead of herself...but then again we always got what we wanted.

"It's only for eight years."

I leaned in to kiss her when a dandelion was shoved into my face. I glanced at Donatella who grinned as I accepted it. Then without another word, she ran off again.

I tucked it behind Mel's hair before I said, "Melody Callahan, future President of the United States of America, I love you."

"Liam Callahan, future First Husband, I love you more." She kissed me.

This is my life. Our life. And I wouldn't have traded it for the goddamn world.

THE END

THE CALLAHAN FAMILY RULES

1. You kill for family. You die for family because you can't trust anyone else.
2. Take no prisoners and have no regrets about it.
3. Just because you sell drugs for a living isn't an excuse to not dress well.
4. No bloody divorce.
5. One family. One roof.
6. Sometimes in order to win you have to lose.
7. Never argue with the boss.
8. Money is money. If you can't make it, then take it.
9. A secret is only a secret if one person knows it.
10. You must marry before thirty. Choose wisely.
11. Don't shit where you eat, both figuratively and literally.
12. Never sell shit products. It's a disgrace to me and the family.
13. Make them remember you at any cost.
14. Be ruthless people to outsiders who know who we truly are. Be generous to those who don't. And be the heart, soul and mind to the family.
15. If family ever betrays family, show no mercy, no forgiveness, and put them in the earth.
16. Never displease your mother.
17. Heed your mother's warnings.

乙

18. Your mother is the only one who will ever speak honestly to you. Accept it without fault.
19. Never keep mother waiting.
20. Your father is never old and it would be unwise to claim that he is.
21. You father will one day die. Honor him and move on.
22. Surpass your father.
23. Just because one is old does not make them wise.
24. Just because one is young does not make them foolish.
25. Listen to all the voices on the streets.
26. Never forget where we came from and how much we sacrificed to get here.
27. Never forget our people. The clan must be cared for both here and aboard.
28. Remember that it is the clan that gives us our power.
29. Remember to give to them and we will get in return.
30. Never forget our native tongue. Pass it on to your children so that they may pass it down to theirs.
31. Never forget our history, both personal and public.
32. Indulge in what you have so you may never wish to lose it.
33. Never indulge to the point of stupidity or blindness.
34. You need people in order to rule.
35. Respect the help; they know more than they let on.
36. Make sure the help has just as much, or more, at stake than you do.
37. Be the thing men and women fear.
38. Always be ahead of the police.
39. Have at least one man on the inside.
40. Then have another man you trust more on the inside with him that he knows nothing thing about.
41. Weak links are never acceptable. We are a machine. If someone fails, make sure they never fail ever again.

42. Control the media at whatever cost.
43. Have an exit plan not just for yourself, but for the family.
44. Never turn off your phone.
45. Remember: Knowledge is power. But power is also strength, money, speed and skill.
46. Family is family even when you wished they weren't.
47. Points made in blood will always be remembered.
48. Love your wife above all else...after all, she is the one who can either keep you warm at night or make sure you never wake up.
49. Never cheat. Affairs destroy the family. No face or body is worth it.
50. We are Callahans, if anyone ever disrespects us, don't just end them, end everything they have ever cared about both past and present. Make them the example as to what happens when you fuck with the wrong family.

Also By J.J. McAvoy

Ruthless People Series
RUTHLESS PEOPLE
THE UNTOUCHABLES
AMERICAN SAVAGES
DECLAN + CORALINE (a novella)

Single Title New Adult Romance
BLACK RAINBOW (out May, 2015)

About the Author

J.J. McAvoy was born in Montreal, Canada, and currently studies humanities at Carleton University. As a child, she wrote poetry, where some of her works were published in local newsletters. J.J.'s life passion with literature has always been the role of tragic and anti-hero characters. In her series, *Ruthless People*, she aims to push the boundaries not only with her characters, but with also readers. She is currently working on a new adult contemporary romance entitled *Black Rainbow*, coming out in May, 2015.

http://iamjjmcavoy.com/

Made in United States
North Haven, CT
28 September 2022

24651236R00300